A HARRIET GORDON MYSTERY

A.M. STUART

TERROR IN TOPAZ

Terror in Topaz: A Harriet Gordon Mystery

1st edition Oportet Publishing 2023

ISBN (ebook) 9780645237894

Cover Design: Fiona Jayde Media

DEDICATION

This story is dedicated to my readers, without whose support and encouragement this book may not have been written. Thank you for believing in me. The series will continue!

ONE
SINGAPORE

MONDAY, 28 NOVEMBER 1910

From her comfortable chair on the verandah, Harriet Gordon watched the curtain of water fall from the glowering sky. The evening's torrential downpour reflected her mood.

Her ward, Will Lawson, sat on a stool nearby, engaged in what was now his nightly duty—oiling the absent Inspector Robert Curran's cricket bat. The sickly-sweet smell of linseed oil hung in the heavy air, adding nausea to her threatening headache.

"Will, enough! Put that stinking stuff away and get on with your homework," Harriet snapped and then, conscious of her harsh tone, added, "Please. I'm sure it doesn't need to be oiled every single night."

"But I promised the inspector," Will mumbled.

"I know you did, but what little I know about cricket bats, I do know they don't need to be oiled quite so regularly."

Will glared at her. "I will hate it if he comes back and thinks I didn't look after it properly."

Harriet summoned a smile. "I am certain he won't think that,

Will." She pointed at the door. "Homework."

Will picked up cloth, oil, and cricket bat and stomped inside. Oiling a cricket bat was infinitely preferable to schoolwork.

The side gate that led from St Thomas House to the school squeaked, and Harriet's brother, Julian, headmaster of St Thomas Church of England Preparatory School for English Boys, ran toward the house, the large umbrella he held doing very little to keep the rain at bay.

Reaching the verandah, he stopped, panting from his exertion, water streaming from his sodden hair down his face. He closed the useless umbrella and leaned it against the verandah rail.

Harriet rose to her feet, but he forestalled the question on her lips by holding up his hand.

"Let me get dry and changed and then we'll talk," he said. "Pour us both a whisky. I think we need it."

It seemed like an age before Julian reappeared, his still-damp hair sticking up where he had roughly toweled it. He patted it down, adjusted his glasses, and accepted the glass Harriet held out for him.

"That bad?" she asked, her voice high with tension.

"I haven't lost my job," Julian said.

Harriet let out a breath. That had been her greatest fear.

Two weeks earlier, she had lost her job, a contract to provide typing and shorthand services to the Detective Branch of the Straits Settlements Police. Inspector Robert Curran, who had employed her services, had himself been suspended and replaced by Inspector John Keogh, a self-righteous prig of a policeman brought in from the Federated Malay States Police Force.

On discovering Harriet's history with the suffragist cause in England the previous year that had landed her in Holloway prison for a brief time, Keogh had dismissed her. As if that wasn't enough, he had taken it upon himself to officially inform the Trustees of Julian's school that they were employing a woman with a criminal past. Though 'employing' was a word used lightly, as the school didn't pay her for her administrative duties. It was understood that board and lodging with the headmaster was sufficient recompense for her services.

The trustees had summoned Julian to a meeting to explain himself.

"They could hardly claim they didn't know," Harriet said.

"Indeed. Before I even suggested you come out to join me, I discussed it with the bishop, and he raised it with the others. They were prepared to turn a blind—some might say Christian—eye to your transgressions, but once it came to an official notification from the police, they had to be seen to do something."

Harriet sank into her chair. "And what is that something?"

"They officially reprimanded me and banned you from the school premises. You are not, however, banned from continuing your, and I quote, 'excellent services.' The school typewriter will be relocated here, and I will have to bring the work to you."

Harriet uttered an unladylike and blasphemous response.

Julian held up his hands. "I know, but in the circumstances, it is the best compromise we could arrive at."

Harriet looked down at the glass she cradled in her hands. "Oh, Ju, I am so sorry to get you into strife."

Julian shook his head and smiled. "I'm not. You know I'm proud of you, Harri."

She managed a watery smile. "I suppose I should be grateful that they are letting me go on typing school reports and demands for school fees."

Julian stood up and poured them both another whisky. "It's timely in a way. I received a letter from the acting headmaster of the Prince Alfred School in Kuala Lumpur only yesterday. They're looking for a new senior master in classics and wondered if I would be interested."

Kuala Lumpur, or KL as it was referred to by most people, was the capital of the Selangor State, one of the Federated Malay States. About two hundred miles north of Singapore, the state had grown around the incredible wealth from the tin mining industry. Such riches were not something the British could resist. Unlike the Straits Settlements, of which Singapore was one, which were under British rule, some thirty years earlier, the Sultan of Selangor had agreed to allow the British to administer the State under a British 'Resident Minister' or 'Resident', without relinquishing his own control. As other Malay States had joined the Federation, KL had become the administrative center for not just Selangor but all the Federated Malay States.

Harriet stared at him. "Kuala Lumpur? But Julian, you are the headmaster of your own school. It would be something of a backward move for you."

Julian swilled the whisky in the glass he held. "Truth be told, I've been feeling a bit restless. It would be a relief not to have the responsibility of being a school principal and to go back to teaching senior boys again." Julian sat down, leaning his forearms on his knees as he looked up at his sister, his face grave. "The position comes with a house but, best of all, Harri, it means Will could attend at a master's rate. The Prince Alfred School has an excellent reputation, and he'd get the best education we can provide for him."

And that, Harriet had to agree, was a good argument. They were struggling to find a suitable school for Will when he finished at St. Tom's next summer. A senior school that they could afford would be a godsend.

"I don't have to give Robertson an immediate answer," Julian said. "He's invited me—us—to visit and look over the school, meet the other staff, and see if we would like the move to Selangor State."

"Both of us? When?"

Julian hefted a sigh. "The sooner the better. How about this weekend? I am inclined to make a trip of it. I've checked the train timetables. There's a night train that leaves Singapore at 7.15 and gets into KL at 6.56 in the morning. If we go up on the Friday night train and back on the day train on Monday, you can play the tourist in Kuala Lumpur while I hobnob with the school. You've not really seen anything of the Malay Peninsula beyond Singapore. Seems like a splendid opportunity."

"I have to admit a change of scene would be most welcome," Harriet said.

Julian straightened and drained his glass. "So be it! If you can prevail on Louisa to take Will in for a few nights, I'll make the travel arrangements."

"Where shall we stay?"

"Didn't I mention? Henry Robertson has invited us to stay with him and his wife at the headmaster's house."

"That's very kind. I hope we won't be an imposition. Do you know Robertson?"

"I've met him a couple of times. Nice chap. I haven't met his wife. She's younger, I gather. They have a small child, and I'm sure she would be glad of some company." He paused. "You will find Kuala Lumpur is a little different from Singapore. It's less well established. A much smaller European population, so a new face is always welcome."

"As long as his wife is happy for some company. Does she have a name?"

"Enid..." Julian frowned. "No... Edith."

"I think this sounds like an excellent plan, Julian," she said.

Julian straightened and smiled. "I agree. Even if I don't take to Prince Alfred, at least we shall have a break from routine. A change is as good as a holiday."

Harriet finished her drink, and her mood lifted. After the despondency of the last few weeks, a weekend in Kuala Lumpur gave her something to look forward to, and her mind turned to her packing. As Julian had observed, since her arrival in Singapore the previous January, she had little opportunity to travel and her mind raced to the practicalities of travel and accommodation, and adventure.

TWO

KUALA LUMPUR, SELANGOR STATE

WEDNESDAY, 30 NOVEMBER, 1910

A suffocating early morning humidity hung over Selangor State and by the time Robert Curran—sometime Inspector with the Straits Settlements Police Force, but currently on suspension—had scrambled up the steep slope to the entrance to the Batu Caves a few miles outside of Kuala Lumpur, he was dripping. He removed his hat, a stylish fedora purchased at great expense from John Little & Co. the previous week, and mopped his face with a clean handkerchief.

Order restored, he paused a moment to take in the cathedral-like beauty of the caves. This first chamber soared above him, hung with heavy stalactites; the ancient stalagmites below, broken and stained by the frequent visitors to the cave system. A second chamber lay before him, open to the daylight, with vines and the roots of trees that had taken hold in the rocky cavities, creeping over the craggy walls as they reached for the sun.

Since leaving Singapore, Curran had been kicking his heels in a run-down plantation house while he waited for a proper briefing on his secret assignment. A brief meeting with the Resident of Selangor State, Henry Belfield and Henry Talbot, Commissioner of the Federated Malay States Police, an old acquaintance from his cricketing days, had provided him with very little useful information except that he had to wait until someone they trusted with a full brief contacted him.

The message had come at last. *Be at the Batu Caves at nine in the morning and ask for directions to the Dark Cave.*

A European man dressed, like Curran, in a linen suit with a high starched collar, stood framed in the entrance to the second cavern. He glanced over his shoulder and, without acknowledging Curran, stepped down into the cave, disappearing from view. Curran waited a few minutes before crossing the floor of the first cavern. He followed the other visitor into the open space beyond. Above him, troops of monkeys, chattering with indignation at the intrusion, scaled the walls to the fringe of trees that overlooked the space below.

"Good morning," the stranger said.

He sat on a rock, one ankle crossed over his knee as he pulled a pipe from his pocket, carefully packing it with tobacco from a leather pouch.

"Can you direct me to the Dark Cave?" Curran asked.

"It will be closed at this time of day." The man looked up. "Curran?"

Curran nodded his affirmation. "And you are...?"

"Stephens, Archibald Stephens."

"This is all a bit Rider Haggard," Curran said, referring to one of his favorite authors.

Stephens lit his pipe, inhaling and blowing out the smoke. "We don't know who to trust any more. When you suspect everyone from the Resident down, what else can you do? That's why you're here, isn't it?"

"Apparently." Curran caught the scent of the smoke rising from the pipe. "That's a nice twist."

Stephens removed the pipe and inspected the contents. "I

have it made especially by a little chap in Colombo. Costs me a fortune to bring in, but it's the simple pleasures in life, don't you agree?"

Curran brought his attention back to the reason for this clandestine meeting. "When it comes to trust, can I start with you? Who are you, and why should I trust you?"

Stephens nodded. "You must understand, Curran, our relationship with the Sultan and the Council of State is a delicate one. Here in KL, we not only have the administration for the State of Selangor, but also the overall establishment for all the Federated Malay States. We are cursed, my friend, with not only a Resident for Selangor, Henry Belfield, but also the Resident General for the Federated Malay States, Reginald Watson." Stephens paused. "Over-governed, Curran. That's when mistakes occur." He removed the pipe from his mouth and continued. "As to why you should trust me, that's an excellent question. You can check my *bona fides* with Belfield himself if you wish. I work in the office of the Accountant and Auditor. It is our task to see that we are, well, how to put it ... we are rendering unto Caesar all that is Caesar's. In the past two years, certain irregularities have been detected, most notably in the area of excise and duties being collected within Selangor State."

There had been no mention of excise and duties in Curran's short clandestine briefing on the case. Excise and duties were not part of Curran's regular duties, let alone any irregular investigations.

"In what way?" he asked, more out of politeness.

"The only dutiable goods imported into the Federated Malay States are opium and spirit liquor. We're not concerned about the liquor, but we are concerned about opium. There is more opium coming in than we are receiving in duty."

"The import of opium is not illegal," Curran pointed out.

He fought back the urge to point out that the question of the appropriate duty not being paid on opium seemed irrelevant when hundreds, if not thousands, were victims of the vile substance. In his opinion, opium should be banned, not used for profit. But wars had been fought on that subject. It was not for him to argue the point.

"No," Stephens agreed, "it's not. But avoidance of duty is. And we're not talking a few pounds here, Curran. We are talking about thousands of pounds. Money that should be going to the administration of the FMS and into the pockets of the Sultan. He is asking questions."

"Smuggling?"

Stephens nodded. "Yes. We think it is coming in via Penang."

Curran's curiosity sparked, and he knew the answer before posing the question. "Any suspects?"

Stephens nodded. "Khoo Zi Qiang. I believe you may already have crossed paths with him?" Stephens raised an eyebrow.

Curran's blood ran cold. Khoo Zi Qiang ... Li An's brother and the head of a powerful clan in Penang. His investigation into Khoo Zi Qiang's illegal activities in Penang and his involvement with the man's sister, Li An, had nearly killed him—nearly killed them both. The last encounter with Zi Qiang, as he thought of him, left both Li An and him with scars, both physical and intangible.

"I am quite familiar with Zi Qiang's activities," he said.

Stephens took a puff of his pipe and regarded Curran thoughtfully. "I know. I've seen your record and I was in Penang at the time. Do you mind me asking if you are still involved with his sister?"

Curran minded. That pain was still fresh, the scar of Li An's departure barely healed.

"No," he said. "She has returned to Penang." He returned to the subject in hand. "What makes you think Zi Qiang is involved in Selangor State?"

Stephens removed his pipe and pulled his pipe-cleaning tool from a leather pouch. He stared scraping out the bowl of the pipe as he said, "Until recently, his activities have been confined to Penang but as you probably know, the authorities there are making it increasingly difficult for him, so we suspect he is moving into more vulnerable states, such as Perak and Selangor."

"I still don't see why I have been sent up here?"

Stephens pocketed his pipe. "The problem with missing duty is only one symptom in what could be widespread corruption in the colonial administration. That's why you are here, Curran. I am told that the administration needs someone from outside of Kuala Lumpur to get to the center of the corruption, a certain establishment that has been a thorn in our side for the last two years."

"The Topaz Club?" Curran suggested.

Stephens' mustache twitched. "What do you know about the Topaz Club?"

Curran hesitated. He knew more than he could reveal. In recent weeks he had learned that his half-sister, Samrita, had been kidnapped from her home in Laxmangarh and taken to work in the Topaz Club, a mysterious and exclusive 'Gentleman's Club' offering beautiful women and other clandestine pleasures.

When his superior in the Straits Settlements Police, Inspector General Cuscaden, had proposed the assignment in Selangor State, Curran had jumped at the chance it offered to save his sister.

"In my initial briefing from Cuscaden, he suggested this might be the case and my brief includes any associations with the Topaz Club," Curran said.

Stephens nodded. "The Commissioner of the Federated Malay Police, Talbot, believes the Topaz Club is being used as a front not only for the illegal import issues but also other nefarious dealings." He looked up at the bright blue sky beyond the bowl of the fallen cave. "Whoever is behind the club is using it as the means to coerce favorable contracts and deals from the administration."

"By coerce do you mean blackmail?" Curran interposed.

"Quite."

"And is Khoo Zi Qiang connected to the Topaz Club?"

Stephens let out an audible sigh. "Maybe, but he is not an idiot. He uses various companies and other legal entities to cover their tracks. It would take more manpower than we have to trace every single suspect contract. And our other problem is that we don't know exactly who he has in his pocket. This is a small community, Curran, and we think the very mystique and exclusivity of the Club has made certain senior officials vulnerable."

"Who exactly?"

"Customs and excise, colonial civil servants, lawyers ... police. It may even go as high as the Resident's own office."

"You may be right," Curran said. "I have been indirectly looking at the trafficking of the girls who service the club."

Stephens raised an eyebrow. "Is that so? It's not your jurisdiction, so what is your interest?"

"Personal," Curran said. "A favor for a friend, but as you have said, once you start looking behind the Topaz Club, it gets very murky." He steadied himself before he gave too much away. "So, what is it you think I can do?"

"Your assignment is to find out who is behind the Topaz Club and to retrieve the evidence the Club is using as coercion. Everything is done through the man at the Club, Gopal Acharya. Acharya is a slippery customer. He's done nothing we can bring him in for, apart from running a brothel and gambling premises, none of which are illegal. It's not just girls and drinks at the Topaz Club ... there is easy access to opium and gambling. Put all of that together and it spells the end for many a promising career, does it not?"

"Have you visited this establishment?"

"No." Stephens stood up. "I am ambitious, Curran, and have no wish to stall my career in the colonial service through indiscretion. For all intents and purposes, I live the life of a monk. It can be a lonely existence."

"I admire your self-discipline, Stephens."

Stephens allowed himself a small smile. "You have the full support of the Resident, and of course our Police Commissioner Talbot, but, for obvious reasons, they are staying at arm's length. You are on your own, Curran."

Not quite.

In his meeting with Talbot, Curran had been given a name ... Detective Inspector Charles Wheeler. Curran had meet Wheeler on a couple of occasions.

"He's a teetotaling Methodist with eight children. Devoted to his wife by all accounts ... or too scared of her to step outside the front door. I doubt he's even heard of the Topaz Club. But keep him out of it if you can, Curran. With Keogh in Singapore, he's got enough to deal with," Talbot had said.

"Where do you suggest I start?" Curran said.

Stephens rose to his feet. "The Topaz Club. We want those files. That is our priority. Once we have those names, we can deal with the rest. To make it more complex, we had a contact at the club who said she had the files, but she has disappeared and with her, the files."

Curran thought of the girl who may have been his sister Samrita's friend, Lakshmi. If he was correct, disappeared meant dead.

"If the club no longer has the files, what is the problem?"

Stephens snorted. "The problem is, Curran, we don't know who has been compromised and just because our friends at the Club know the files are missing, doesn't mean our chaps do. They can go on being compromised. We need the files."

"But if the girl is dead?"

Stephens's eyes widened. "I never said she was dead."

"What do you know about the body of a girl pulled from the Klang River a few months ago?" Curran asked.

Stephens shook his head. "I vaguely remember something about that. What about her?"

Curran shook his head. "She may be your missing girl."

Stephens turned away. "Damn it! How do you know that?"

Curran shrugged. "I don't. Just a policeman's instinct, Stephens."

"That makes finding the files even more urgent," Stephens said.

Curran took a moment to digest the information.

"First things first," he said. "Where is the Topaz Club?"

The address Curran had followed up in his initial search for Samrita had yielded nothing except an empty house.

"It keeps moving. A few months ago, it moved out of town to what I can best describe as a fortified position, well concealed off the road to the Batu Caves. Not far from here, in fact. I defy anyone to get near it ... walls, dogs, and guards. No one gets in or out unless they have a reason to be there. Anything else?"

"Any idea how I get into the Topaz Club? I have this." Curran produced the card he had taken from the commodities broker, George Sewell, in his last case.

Stephens took the card and turned it over. As Curran knew it contained no information except a gold circle on a black background.

"It's a start, but from what I know, you will need a member to introduce you. I suggest the Selangor Club on the Padang is the best place to make the sort of contact that will give you an introduction."

Stephens fished in his pocket and produced an envelope.

"I've been told you are using the name Ronald Sutton as an alias?"

"Correct," Curran said and rasped his chin, which had reached the point of just looking disreputable. He needed longer before he could sport a decent beard.

"If there are any problems with gaining entry to the Selangor

Club, this is a letter of introduction from a respectable Gentlemen's club in London. I am sure the club will welcome you with open arms."

Curran took the envelope and tucked it into his own pocket. "How do I contact you?"

"Leave a message with the concierge at the Empire Hotel addressed to Mr. Giles. It needs to say nothing more than 'The Batu Caves are highly recommended' and I will find you."

Curran refrained from rolling his eyes. He was a plain policeman and had little time for these *Boys' Own* adventures.

He left Stephens gazing up at the vault of the sky above him and returned to the outside world and his newly acquired motor vehicle, a blue, 1908 Sheffield Simplex that he'd picked up for a song in Johor. He abhorred motor vehicles but recognized he needed the independence that having his own transport gave him, and he liked the Sheffield Simplex because it had only two gears: forward and reverse.

On the drive back into town, he passed through the rows of rubber trees and patches of jungle, but saw no building resembling Stephens's description. If the Topaz Club was tucked away off this road, it was indeed well hidden.

THREE

The privacy provided by the old plantation house a few miles outside Kuala Lumpur that Curran had rented, allowed him to prepare for his assignment and given him much needed time to develop a relationship with Jayant Kumar, his newfound younger half-brother.

In the hope his brother could be of some practical help, Curran had spent the last two weeks teaching Jayant some basic weapons handling and self-defense skills. While Jayant had already proved himself handy in a fight, when it came to handling Curran's service revolver, he had neither interest nor aptitude, preferring to pass his days with a nose in one of the many mildewed books that filled the bookcase of their temporary accommodation.

Despite his brother's protestations, Curran had yet to be convinced that Jayant was not a habitual opium user. Jayant had been working in a notorious opium den in Chinatown and Curran had walked in on his brother in an opium stupor. He had been a policeman long enough to recognize the signs, and over the last week, Jayant had become increasingly irritable and restless. He had made no attempt to find his own way into the town, so Curran held out some hope that Jayant was fighting the craving.

Curran made a brief stop at the Post Office in town and discovered a letter from Griff Maddocks, the journalist on the Straits Times, sent *poste restante*. The contents were brief but enough to galvanize Curran into action. He booked a hotel in KL and bought a ticket on the night train to Singapore before returning to the plantation house.

Curran looked in on Jayant and found him asleep. He ate a quick lunch of *nasi lemak*, a spicy and coconut rice neatly wrapped in a banana leaf. Having learned Jayant had a sweet tooth, he had also purchased some squares of *kuli seri muka*, a sweet treat of glutinous rice and a pandan custard. He left these on a table with a note and took himself off for a long walk through the abandoned nutmeg trees to the jungle behind.

These walks had become a daily practice and with each step, he put Li An a little further behind him – or at least he hoped he did. Li An had chosen to return to Penang to take on her mother's business interests. Interests that put her in direct opposition to her brother Khoo Zi Qiang, but she had a powerful ally by her side, her cousin Teoh Gum Loong. The woman who had walked out of his life had done so with confidence. Curran had no part to play in her future. He belonged to her past, the scar her brother had left on her face, a constant reminder of the price they had paid for their love.

But the past had a habit of returning, and now Zi Qiang was back in Curran's life. The memories of that night on Penang harbor when Zi Qiang had left them both for dead, still raw, a painful reminder of his own failure.

On his return, he found the food he had left for Jayant was still untouched and the door to his brother's bedroom remained closed. Curran rattled around the house, packing his bags and making enough noise to wake the dead before settling back with a bottle of beer in a dilapidated planter's chair, one of several on the verandah of the old house. A light breeze rustled the leaves of the neglected nutmeg trees and an annoying mosquito droned around his head. He flinched, swatting ineffectually as it flew just out of reach. As a sufferer of recurrent malaria, he loathed mosquitos, but there was no escaping them.

He took a swig of the beer and shook open the day's copy of the Malay Tribune. The door rattled and Jayant stepped out onto the verandah. He slapped at a mosquito as he collapsed into a chair beside Curran.

As Jayant did not drink alcohol, Curran did not offer him a beer.

"You were a long time," Jayant said, his voice thick from sleep.

Curran cast him a sidelong glance. Jayant's eyes looked heavy, his one good eye red rimmed and bloodshot, the damaged eye drooping, the faint scars around it more prominent.

"You sound like an old man of eighty," Curran said.

"I feel like one," Jayant said and held up a hand. "I woke with a headache, and it has been getting worse all day." He caught the suspicion in Curran's eyes and scowled. "No, it is not a hunger for opium. I have told you, I am not an addict."

Curran said nothing. He'd heard this story so many times, not only from Jayant but every opium addict he had met in the course of his profession.

"I left some *nasi lemak* for you," Curran said, returning to his paper.

"I am not hungry," Jayant said. "You haven't told me where you went this morning."

Curran set down the paper and took another swig of beer. He rested the bottle on the broad arm of his chair and decided the time had come to confide in his brother. He had hinted that his suspension from the Straits Settlements Police may have been a ruse to get him out of the way, but until he knew more about his assignment, there seemed to be no point in elaborating.

"I had a meeting with a contact. He gave me my orders."

"I see," Jayant responded, the uncertainty in his tone indicating the contrary. "What do you have to do?"

"There is something going on within the British administration that has raised the suspicion that senior colonial officials are opening themselves up to blackmail and coercion." Curran paused. "It may be connected with the Topaz Club."

Jayant visibly stiffened at the mention of the establishment he believed responsible for the disappearance of his—their—sister.

"But there are police in Kuala Lumpur. I don't understand why you are being sent to deal with this matter."

"Senior police officers may be compromised."

Jayant nodded. "Ah, now I see. They want someone who is above reproach to get to the heart of the matter. Are you above reproach, Robert?"

"I'm not a saint, Jayant," Curran replied. "I have been openly living with the sister of a known head of exactly one such organization for the past two years."

"That is an excellent point." Jayant shook his head. "But putting the heart to one side. Miss Khoo Li An is no longer in your life, and if I were to put my trust in anyone in the colonial administration, it is you."

Curran smiled. "I appreciate your faith in me, Jay."

"I see our father when you smile," Jayant said.

The mention of Edward Curran brought a now familiar stab of pain and, yes, resentment to Curran's heart. Jayant had had something Curran had never known: a relationship with the man whose blood they shared.

Jayant ran a hand over his eyes. "What do we do now?"

Something in his gesture set Curran's instincts on edge. "Jayant? Are you all right?"

"I told you, I woke with a headache this morning, and my joints ache."

Curran stood up and crossed to his brother. Close up, Jayant looked terrible, his face the color of damp clay. Curran swept a hand across his brother's forehead and swore. "You are burning up, Jay."

Jayant looked up, his one good eye dark and wide. "I promise you it is not opium. It's just a fever. I will be fine in the morning."

Headache, aching limbs... it could be opium withdrawal, but they were also symptoms of something all too familiar to Curran.

"I need to get you to a doctor. It could be malaria."

"But Samrita..."

"You're not going anywhere. If it is malaria, you are going to be out of action for days."

"Robert, I—"

"Enough. I'll pack our bags. It's time to leave."

By the time Curran had organized their luggage, Jayant had admitted defeat and sat huddled in the chair on the verandah, his teeth chattering with the fever.

Curran had to half carry him to the vehicle, where Jayant hunched in the passenger seat, his head in his hands. Curran lit the lamps and cranked the handle before turning the vehicle out onto the narrow country lanes that led to their hideaway.

It was only a few miles to the town of Kuala Lumpur and the hospital, but every bump and pothole provoked a groan from Jayant and the drive took longer than Curran would have liked.

An Englishman knocking on the door of the hospital provoked an immediate response and wardsmen hurried out with a stretcher. Curran paced the corridor while Jayant was seen to. It seemed like an age before a doctor came out.

"It looks like your friend has dengue," the man said.

Curran let out a breath. Dengue, like malaria, was a mosquito-borne disease and just as bad. In a moment of utter selfishness, Curran hoped he hadn't contracted the infection as well. Dengue on top of his recurrent malaria could well be fatal, but for the moment, he felt fine.

"What's to be done?"

The doctor shook his head. "The fever must run its course. Is there anyone at home to care for him?"

"Damn it," Curran assumed the persona of Ronald Sutton, a gentleman writing a travel guide to the Malay Peninsula. "This is dashed inconvenient. Mr. Kumar is my assistant. We're just passing through."

The doctor nodded. "of course, but it is going to be some time before he is well enough to travel. He is probably best here where we can keep an eye on him for the next few days. You can leave your details with the ward clerk. Where are you staying?"

Curran made a show of consulting a notebook. "The Empire Hotel."

"Very nice," the doctor said. "You'll be quite comfortable there."

"Can I see Mr. Kumar?"

The doctor stood aside and gestured at the door to the ward. "Very well, but the fever is high. Not sure he'll make much sense."

It was visiting hours and the ward buzzed with chatter. They had placed Jayant in a general ward. Had it been Curran requiring hospitalization, he would have had the comfort of a smaller, more comfortable ward set aside for Europeans.

The nurse stopped by a bed at the end of the ward, partitioned off by a screen. "A few minutes, that's all," she whispered.

Curran leaned over his brother. "Jay?"

Jayant's eyes flickered open. "Robert ... so sorry ..."

"Not your fault. You are going to stay here."

"But I won't be able to help you." Jayant grasped his sleeve. "Samrita?"

"You have my promise I will find her."

"Do you believe she is still alive?"

Curran met his brother's fevered gaze. "Do you?"

"I like to think that I would know... here." Jayant placed a hand over his heart. "I will believe she is alive until I have proof to the contrary."

Curran laid a hand on his brother's shoulder. "I think that the search for Samrita and the mystery of the Topaz Club are linked. The answer to one will lead to the other. Leave it with me, Jayant. You need to rest and recover. You've done enough."

He straightened and checked his watch. He still had time to make the night train to Singapore and a meeting with Griff Maddocks.

FOUR

SINGAPORE

THURSDAY, 1 DECEMBER 1910

L ouisa Mackenzie accepted the cup of tea Harriet offered and reclined in her chair with a grace that came of long practice. Grace was not one of the virtues ever ascribed to Harriet.

"Of course, Will can come and stay this weekend," Louisa said. "What's behind this sudden desire to go to KL?"

Harriet told her friend about the invitation to visit the Prince Alfred School.

"A very good school, from what I hear." Louisa set down her cup. "When the time comes, Euan is insisting we send Roddy to Glenalmond College in Perthshire, where he went to school." She shuddered. "Poor Roddy. He'll never survive the Scottish winters, let alone the horrors of public-school life. Keep Will close, Harriet."

"We have little choice," Harriet said. "There is no money from Will's father's estate and no family in England prepared to support him. A place with reduced fees is very tempting. You've lived in KL, Louisa, what do you know about Henry Robertson, the current head of Prince Alfred?"

Louisa shrugged. "We were only there for a few months before Euan transferred to Penang. I thought Henry Robertson was a bit of an odd fish. Not public school, but a good sort. He directed the church choir and volunteered for the fire brigade. I don't know his wife—they married after we left KL—but I knew her mother, Mary Chapman. A bit of a dragon. She and her husband have lived in KL for years and rather viewed themselves as the king and queen of the English community. As for living in KL ... Harriet, it is a cesspit of gossip. Too small a community, and you know how the mems live for transgressions, however minor. I couldn't wait to get out of the place." Louisa's mouth drooped. "Don't leave Singapore, Harriet. I will miss you dreadfully."

Harriet managed a laugh. "This is all hypothetical, Louisa. I'm not going anywhere. However, I do need work. The money I earned from the police was more than useful."

Louisa leaned forward. "On the subject of the police, have you heard from Curran?"

"Not a word," Harriet said, adding with a forced smile, "Not that I expected to."

"Euan said he's gone to ground somewhere up north with that brother of his. If you ask me, there is something a bit odd about Curran's suspension, don't you agree?"

"Not really. He assaulted a prisoner," Harriet said.

Whatever her own thoughts on Curran's suspension might have been, she felt compelled to keep the official story consistent and Curran had indeed broken the nose of Lionel Ellis. Since Ellis had provoked Curran and was universally disliked by everyone, no one blamed him. However, it was not appropriate for senior police officers to assault prisoners, however unpleasant, and standards had to be maintained and an example set.

Louisa shrugged. "An act that earned him the applause of the entire community. Hardly grounds for suspension, but there was the drinking after Li An left ... Do you think she will come back?"

The mention of Curran's former lover, Khoo Li An, brought an unexpected knot to Harriet's throat. Li An had returned to her dying mother in Penang, and to a future that did not involve Curran. Her departure had left Curran bereft.

"And not a word from her, either?" Louisa continued.

"She didn't strike me as the letter-writing type," Harriet replied, rather more sharply than she intended. She had hoped that she and Li An had developed a genuine friendship that transcended geographic separation.

Louisa cast her a curious glance. "Harriet? Is there something you're not telling me?"

Harriet schooled her face. "I've no idea what you mean, Louisa."

Louisa straightened. "You have visitors."

Grateful for the interruption, Harriet stood up as Simon Hume's familiar green Maxwell Tourer came to a halt with a grind of brakes. The driver pushed back his goggles, revealing Griff Maddocks. Simon Hume sat in the passenger seat, gripping the side of the car with white knuckles.

Maddocks dismounted the vehicle and bowed extravagantly to the two women.

"My two favorite ladies," he said. He glanced at the vehicle. "Hume has been teaching me to drive. I am buying the old girl from him."

Simon came around the vehicle and clapped Maddocks on the shoulder. "He needs a bit of practice." He smiled up at Harriet. "Harriet, Louisa, lovely to see you both."

"We were just taking tea. Care to join us?" Harriet said.

Harriet and Julian's housekeeper, Huo Jin, brought out extra cups and a fresh pot of tea. They chatted about the weather as Harriet poured for the gentlemen.

As she handed the cup to Simon, their eyes met. "When do you sail?" she asked.

"Tonight," Simon said. "I hoped to see you again before I left."

Simon and Harriet had been keeping company since August, a growing relationship that was about to be cut short by a summons from Simon's editor at the Melbourne Argus to return to Melbourne.

"Harriet's off to KL for a couple of days." Louisa broke the sudden awkward silence.

Maddocks cocked an enquiring eyebrow. "Business or pleasure?"

"A bit of both, I hope. Julian is doing a reconnaissance for a possible change of employment," Harriet said.

"Surely not! What could be better than St. Tom's?" Maddocks said.

"He's restless and the Prince Alfred School has an excellent reputation," Harriet said. "And if he accepts, it would mean a place for Will."

Maddocks nodded. "I can see the attraction, but don't rush into a decision. KL is not Singapore."

"So, everyone says." Harriet cast a sharp glance at Louisa. "I have all the more reason to go and form my own opinion.

Maddocks set down his cup and glanced at his watch. "Thank you for the tea. Sorry, I can't stay. I'm meeting someone. Can I offer you a lift home, Louisa?"

Louisa glanced from Maddocks to Hume. "Is he safe?"

Hume smiled. "Perfectly. He has had an excellent teacher."

Louisa stood, prompting both men to stand. "Then I shall accept the offer of a ride in your automobile, Griff." She turned to Hume and kissed him lightly on the cheek. "This is goodbye then, Mr Hume?"

Hume smiled. "For the moment. My regards to your husband."

Louisa cocked her head and gestured at the vehicle. "Are you coming with us?"

"No," Simon said. "I, um, you know..."

They all did. He wanted a few minutes alone with Harriet to say goodbye.

"I'll join you shortly, Maddocks," Hume said.

Maddocks waved from the driving seat. "Have a good sojourn in our northern neighbor, Harriet. It is the world's most boring town. Nothing ever happens there."

Harriet and Simon stood on the step, waving as the motor vehicle coughed and spluttered down the driveway and onto the lane.

Alone, Simon took Harriet's hands, turning her to face him.

"Harriet," he began. "This is difficult."

He dropped his hands and turned away, pacing the verandah.

"Simon, please stop that pacing and just tell me what the problem is."

His face creased. "I've not been entirely honest with you. I know the reason I've been summoned back to Melbourne. They are offering me the post in London."

"That's a terrific honor."

"It comes with conditions. Harriet, I'm engaged to be married."

The floorboards beneath Harriet's feet tilted. "Engaged?"

"I'm a complete and utter cad. I should have told you the first time we met, but I didn't, and I really liked you and enjoyed your company."

"Stop babbling," she snapped. "Who are you engaged to?"

"Her name is Elizabeth Truscott, and she's the daughter of the Argus's editor-in-chief. I'm going home to marry her in the new year before we both sail for London."

Harriet stared at him. She didn't know how she was supposed to react. Should she slap him? Burst into tears?

Instead, she felt nothing ... completely numb.

"I'm sorry I led you on. I didn't intend to. I was quite prepared to throw Lizzie over for you—"

"But? Did the job in London come with the condition you go as a married man?"

He nodded. "It wasn't put quite that way but, effectively, yes. Truscott as good as told me we'd waited long enough, and the church was booked for the new year."

"Do you love her?"

He screwed up his eyes. "I've known her for so long. I'm not sure that what we have is love, but we rub along together all right."

Harriet turned away. "That's a great basis for a marriage."

"I don't feel for her as I do for you."

Harriet took a moment to compose herself before facing him again. "Enough, Simon. You've said your piece. I assure you I won't die of a broken heart. I am just disappointed in your lack of honesty with me."

"We had some fun," Simon said with a hopeful note in his voice.

They had indeed had some fun and Simon had reminded Harriet what it was to enjoy the company of a man she liked. Liked ... but didn't love.

That didn't mean she intended to let Simon Hume—cad, bounder, and deceiver of women—off quite so lightly.

"It just remains for me to wish your new wife joy of you. If she can trust you," she said with a waspish bite to her tone.

Simon winced. "I deserved that."

"You did." She pointed at the gate. "I think you better leave now. Safe voyage Mr Hume."

He bent in to kiss her, and this time she slapped his face.

FIVE

Curran had arranged to meet Griff Maddocks in the bar of a less-than-reputable hotel near Clarke Quay. The journalist looked around the boatmen's drinking hole with a mixture of curiosity and distaste.

"Everyone is wondering where you are," Maddocks said. "Am I the only one who knows you've been in KL licking your wounds?"

Curran shrugged. It suited him for his friends to think he was nursing a grievance about his suspension from the Straits Settlements Police.

"Something like that."

"I like the beard." Maddocks gestured at Curran's face.

"I don't. It's damned uncomfortable."

"Then why have you grown it?"

Curran pulled a face. "I am hoping it makes me a little less recognizable." He rubbed the growth on his chin. "Still got a way to go before I can emulate our newly crowned King's style."

Maddocks circled his glass in his hands. "You're missed, Curran. Your replacement Keogh is an insufferable prig."

"And that's being complimentary," Curran agreed. He paused. "How's Harriet?"

"You heard Keogh dismissed her?"

"I did. Keogh is a piece of work."

"Not only that, but he also informed the trustees of Julian's school about her past, and now they're both in trouble."

Curran tightened his grip around his glass, imagining for one quick second it was Keogh's neck. Punish him, but not Harriet or Julian. Neither of them deserved that.

"Hopefully, all will be forgiven and you will be back soon enough," Maddocks said.

"If I want to come back," Curran said with a careless shrug. "I am rather enjoying being a gentleman of leisure. After all, I was born to it."

"Liar," Maddocks said. "You may have been brought up in a grand house, but you're no more a gentleman than me."

Curran took a draught of the beer and set his glass down. "I thought Hume was coming?"

Maddocks cleared his throat. "He'll be here. I left him saying goodbye to Harriet. He sails tonight."

"Of course," Curran said, imagining with an odd twinge he didn't recognize, a long, passionate farewell.

"It's not what you think." Maddocks read his mind.

"What do you mean?"

"Our friend Hume omitted to mention that he had left a fiancée in Melbourne. He's going home to get married. He's confessing all to Harriet."

A wave of indignation washed over Curran. Harriet Gordon did not deserve to be led on by a man with a fiancée waiting for him at home.

"I wondered about the weekly letters penned with a female hand, but I thought they must have been from his sister," Maddocks admitted. "He said nothing to me."

As if he had conjured the man, Simon Hume entered the

dingy bar. Red-faced and sweating, he pulled up a chair and looked from Maddocks to Curran as he mopped his face with a spotted handkerchief.

"What?"

"How did Harriet take the news about your forthcoming nuptials?" Curran said in a tone that dripped ice.

Hume glared at Maddocks. "You told him?"

"Of course, I did. Harriet is our friend. She deserves better than you," Maddocks said.

Hume's mouth tightened. "I never meant to lead her on and if you really want to know, she slapped me." He touched his cheek. "I deserved it. But we're not here to discuss my appalling behavior. You want to know if I had any luck with my contacts in KL."

In November, Simon Hume had spent some time in KL after stumbling on to the story involving the trafficking of girls to work in the Topaz Club. Hume had spoken with a woman by the name of Jameela, who had escaped the brothel and was now living in apparently happy domesticity.

Curran had no doubt Jameela had valuable information about the workings of the mysterious Topaz Club that would not only help him trace Samrita, but also assist with the official assignment.

"Short answer is, they want nothing more to do with me and they certainly won't talk to you," Hume said.

He fished in his pocket and handed over a letter. Curran scanned the contents of the unsigned missive.

Mr Hume, Our decision to talk to you was an error of judgment. We both feel strongly that we should put the club behind us and look to the future, not the past. We have nothing further to say to you and cannot assist your friend. Our contact with you has brought trouble enough. Do not try to speak to us again.

Curran set the note down and ran a hand through his hair. "For God's sake, Hume. Who are these people? I need to know."

Hume sat back and crossed his arms. "I'm sorry, Curran, I can't tell you. Believe it or not, we journalists do have some ethics and if this girl doesn't want to be contacted, then that is that."

"This from a man who spent the last few months omitting to tell the woman he was keeping company with that he was already engaged?"

Hume's eyes flashed. "That's a low blow, even for you, Curran."

Maddocks held up a hand. "Enough. Hume's right, Curran. He can't betray these people's confidence."

"Even for the sake of my sister and the other women who are being forced to work in this club?"

Hume stood up. "You are a policeman, Curran. There is nothing to stop you from looking for these people yourself. Now I have a few things I need to do before I leave tonight." He held out his hand. "It's been an honor to know you."

Curran faced the journalist and shook the proffered hand. "I wish you the best for whatever your future holds, Hume."

Hume nodded. "London calls me," he said. "I am sorry about Harriet. She's a grand girl and deserves better than me. Truth is I genuinely liked her. I may even have--" He glanced at Maddocks who hadn't moved. "Don't forget you're driving me to the ship."

"I won't. I'll see you at the bungalow, Hume."

Curran watched Hume leave the bar before sitting down again. He turned the empty beer glass around in his hand, thinking back to the first conversation he'd had with Hume about his contacts in KL. There had been something Hume had said ... something about the husband and where he worked.

He set the glass down with a bang.

"What did Hume say when he first told us about the girl? Her husband was something to do with a department store. There's not that many department stores in KL. He shouldn't be too hard to trace." Curran frowned. "Do you think he let that slip deliberately?"

Maddocks shook his head. "If that's what Hume said, then that's on him. You didn't hear it from me. Another beer?"

They drank in silence for a couple of minutes, each occupied with their own thoughts.

"What's your plan?" Maddocks asked at last.

"I'm returning to Kuala Lumpur tonight. Jayant is down with dengue and is in hospital there and I have things to do." Curran raised a finger in warning. "If, by any chance, you should have business in KL and come across me, my name is Ronald Sutton, a gentleman of leisure, writing a travel book on the delights of the Malayan Peninsula."

"You and half the world. I shall look forward to reading this tome," Maddocks said. "Would you like a review in the *Straits Times*?"

Curran glared at him.

Maddocks pushed his empty glass to one side and stood up. "Whatever you are up to, Curran, I wish you all the best. I hope you find the girl."

After Maddocks left, Curran glanced at his watch. He had time to pay a call on Harriet Gordon. He realized how much he missed sharing his thoughts with her, and her uncanny knack of knowing the right thing to say. As a friend, he needed to reassure himself that she would survive the loss of her job and Simon Hume's crushing revelation.

But what could he say to her? His own life was in too much of a mess to have anything to offer her beyond platitudes. Harriet was stronger than she gave herself credit and she would survive. For now, he had a job to do, and he had delayed long enough.

SIX

KUALA LUMPUR

FRIDAY, 2 DECEMBER

Curran arrived back in Kuala Lumpur in the early morning and collected his motor vehicle from the garage where he had left it. He took up the room he had booked at the Empire Hotel, a magnificent two-story mansion, which had, until recently, been a private home on the edge of the Padang. No expense had been spared converting it to a modern hotel with electric lighting and fans and private bathrooms with running water.

It also had the convenience of being across the road from the famed Selangor Club.

As Ronald Sutton, he had assembled the wardrobe of an English gentleman—good quality linen suits and shirts, evening dress, and a new pith helmet. The wardrobe that a gentleman, newly arrived from England, would be expected to sport. He was grateful that these not-inconsiderable expenses were being covered by his employer.

His first visit was to the hospital. As it was outside visiting hours, he could not see his brother and was given the worrying news that Jayant's condition had worsened as the fever deepened. He walked away from the hospital, experiencing for the first time a real sense of concern. If this brother he had known for such a short time did not survive the dengue, his grief would be profound and real.

At the offices of the *Malay Tribune*, he scoured the back issues of the newspaper and in the edition of 15 October, he found the first account of an unidentified dead woman pulled from the Klang River. A subsequent article included an image of the birthmark and called for anyone knowing her identity to come forward, but the initial prurient interest had soon died away, and after only two days, other matters such as the falling price of tin had supplanted the death of an unknown Indian woman.

After lunch, Curran paid a visit to the first of the department stores in Kuala Lumpur. John Little's on New Embankment Road was familiar to him from its sister store in Singapore. He asked to meet the manager and when asked about the nature of his business, he gave his well-rehearsed story. He was writing a book on travel in Malaya and wished to include a section on the local businesses. This guaranteed a prompt and obsequious introduction to the manager, a man well into his forties, balding and bespectacled. A photographic image in a well-polished silver frame of a heavily corseted woman and four small children graced his desk.

Curran quickly concluded that this man did not match the description given by Simon Hume, but pretended to make notes as the self-important manager rattled off the history of John Little & Co and the services it provided to travelers and "Outstation" customers. Of course, the man Hume met could have been exaggerating his importance in the business and as he was leaving, Curran cast a quick glance around the male employees of the store. None of the men he saw seemed to match Hume's vague description of a 'successful Anglo Indian'.

The second department store, Whiteaway Laidlaw & Co, was

another familiar name from Singapore. Like Little's, it offered its services as a general outfitter and a specialty purveyor of drapery, furniture, china, glass, and travelling goods. Curran offered up the same story and, as with John Little, was shown directly to the manager.

A dark-haired man in his early thirties came out of an office with the name *A. Blake, Manager* emblazoned in gilt. The man introduced himself as Ashton Blake and showed Curran into his office. No images of wives or children adorned Blake's less than pristine desk, and the heavy fog of cigarette smoke mingled with the close humidity. The lazy circling of an electric fan did little, except stir the thick air.

"What brings you to Malaya, Mr. Sutton?" Blake asked as one of his staff entered, bearing a tray with lemon tea. A welcome refreshment.

Curran smiled. "A bit of adventure, Mr. Blake," he said. "I have procured a motor vehicle and I am enjoying the challenge of exploring the roads and the people of this fascinating country. There is a world beyond England, is there not?"

Blake shrugged. "My world is limited to Penang and Selangor State. If there is anything beyond that, I am yet to discover it."

"You were born out here?"

"My father settled in Penang," was Blake's brief reply. "I've never had the slightest desire to visit the 'home country' as he persisted in calling it."

Curran's policeman's instincts prickled. Blake was the right age and, with the background he had just described, could be Anglo Indian. He had found his man.

He had the pretense of the travel book to go through and he repeated the process he had used with the manager of John Little, making notes and asking pertinent questions. At the end of the interview, both men rose and shook hands. Curran made his way back to the relatively fresh air of Ampang Street and retired to a coffee shop across the road to watch and wait.

On the stroke of six, the doors to the emporium closed, the shop assistants and other staff drifting out. At six-thirty, Blake left the building, bidding a night watchman goodnight. The guard locked the door behind him, and Blake hailed a ricksha. Curran did likewise.

It was no trouble to follow Blake out of the central part of town to a wide, tree-lined street of conventional, European-style bungalows. Telling his ricksha wallah to wait out of sight around a corner, he followed on foot.

At one undistinguished house, Blake stopped, paid the ricksha wallah, and without looking to the right or left, opened the gate, and strode up the front path. The front door opened without him knocking and closed behind him.

Curran smiled. He had found the home of Mr Ashton Blake. If Jameela was a resident of the house, she would still be there tomorrow. He had to choose his time if he stood any chance of convincing them to help him.

SEVEN

That evening, Curran presented at the Selangor Club. In local circles, it was known as the "Spotted Dog" in mock tribute to the wife of a former Resident who had always brought her Dalmatian dogs to the club.

The mock Tudor building, which had been recently refurbished, still carried a lingering smell of cut wood, paint, and polish. The majordomo allowed Curran to enter the club after verifying 'Ronald Sutton's' credentials.

"I say, a new face!"

In the main bar, a man of much his own age with hair greying at the temples and a sun-darkened face straightened and held out his hand. "Charles Hughes. Social secretary of the Spotted Dog."

"Ronald Sutton," Curran replied, shaking the proffered hand.

"What brings you to KL?"

"I'm writing a travel guide to the Malay Peninsula. There is a great deal of interest back home." Curran smiled. "Big game hunting, picturesque beaches, good railways, exotic temples..."

I've been in the company of journalists for too long, Curran thought. Such purple prose came too easily.

"Visiting is all very well. Living here is another matter. Can I get you a drink?" A well-muscled, balding man with a London accent straightened, raising a whisky glass to his mouth. Not his first, Curran thought. A miasma of alcohol hung over the man.

"Very kind," Curran said. "A beer? And you are...?"

"Walter Stewart," the man replied. "How long are you out here?"

"A couple of weeks. I've just come up from Singapore and I'll be moving on to Penang via the town of Ipoh."

"Train?" Hughes asked.

"No. I've a nice little motor vehicle. Gives me a better chance to really see the countryside."

"Pleasant town, Ipoh. Take some time to get up to the Kinta Valley and you'll see the extent of the mining operations," Stewart said.

Hughes shot his companion a sharp glance. "Not everyone finds tin mines fascinating." He turned back to Curran. "Stewart here is a mine manager."

"Was," Stewart said. "The mine I was managing, Salak South just out of KL, has gone *phut*."

"By which you mean?"

"The ore has dried up."

"Gone *phut*!" Hughes scoffed. "Truth is, the place was just pure bad luck. Put this in your book, Sutton. Salak South, the cursed mine... The first investor lost every penny he put into it and then last year it flooded, wiping out the equipment. Even Stewart here couldn't resurrect it. And then a few months ago, Stewart's assistant dropped dead. There are those who say it was situated on an old burial site and the local *bomoh* put a curse on it."

"Absolute rubbish," Stewart said. "Poor old Isaacson had a heart attack, nothing more sinister than that."

"There are some interesting temple caves at Ipoh—Chinese

and Hindu. There is a great deal of local interest in our Batu Caves, and we could see them become shrines," Hughes said.

"I have visited the Batu Caves," Curran said.

"The highlands are nice," Hughes continued his travelogue. "Almost a reasonable climate up on the Cameron highlands." He raised a finger. "You mark my words, in a few years people will be flocking to them... guest houses, golf courses. You won't be able to move for people seeking rest and recuperation in a more salubrious atmosphere."

"What business are you in?" Curran asked.

Hughes smiled and made a mock bow. "The esteemed legal fraternity, my friend."

Curran turned back to Stewart. "If your mine has closed, what do you do these days?"

"I'm working for a firm of consulting engineers, going around troubleshooting mine equipment failures. But I must admit, it is something of a relief to be away from the Salak South mine. And I quite enjoy travelling around. Gets me away from here."

"You mean it gets you away from your woman trouble, Stewart," Hughes said.

Stewart straightened. "What the hell do you mean by that?"

Hughes held up a placatory hand. "Just wise to stay clear of the married mems, Stewart."

Stewart's eyes blazed but just as quickly as it had flared up, the anger died, and he cast a glance around the room. "Do you play rugby, Sutton?"

"Not me. Cricket's my game," Curran replied.

"Pity. We're short for a game on Saturday."

Curran smiled. "I don't have the build for rugby, Stewart. Besides, I don't know how anyone can play rugby in this climate."

"Bowl or bat?" Hughes enquired, turning to cricket.

"Bit of slow bowling," Curran lied. He had a formidable reputation as an opening bat and had even played at county level in his youth, but just in case anyone thought to associate him with the dashing batsman from Cambridge, it paid to remove that nexus.

They fell to a discussion about cricket and the newspaper reports of the current tour of Australia by the South African team.

Curran was on his third beer when loud voices came from the front hall.

Stewart snorted. "It's that rabble from the Residency."

"Now, now. That's no way to talk about His Excellency," Hughes chided.

"His Excellency is all right. It's the bloody hangers-on."

"What's it to be chaps?" A voice, louder than the others, boomed as a party of five men entered the bar.

Curran froze, his beer halfway to his mouth.

He'd know that bellow anywhere.

Surely not? What perverse fate could have brought his cousin George to Kuala Lumpur?

He turned his back to the newcomers, but there were too few people in the bar and no escape without appearing obvious.

The Honorable George Bullock-Steele, the heir to the Earl of Alcester, approached the bar, ordering drinks in his loud, unmodulated voice.

"Good evening, Hughes. How goes life in the legal fraternity?" George boomed.

"Busy enough, thank you, sir," Hughes replied obsequiously.

"I see a new face ... How'd you do ... Good God ..." George stopped mid-sentence, his hand outstretched.

Curran moved fast, seizing his cousin's hand and shaking it vigorously as he said, "Ronald Sutton. I'm surprised you remember me, Bullock-Steele. It's been a while since Cambridge."

George continued to stare at him.

A large paunch strained against George's tropical evening clothes and perspiration sheened his forehead, dripping into a magnificent mustache. They hadn't met in the seventeen years since Curran had been sent down from Oxford for brawling ... with George. He had broken his cousin's nose when he had caught him cheating. Yet it was George who had stayed at Oxford while Curran had been banished by his uncle to an army commission and overseas postings.

Curran's hand tightened a warning before he released the pudgy flesh. "It's good to see you, old man," he said between gritted teeth. "Let's take a bit of fresh air and catch up."

To his surprise and relief, George picked up his beer and followed Curran out onto the terrace.

"I say, Curran, what the hell—" George blustered once they were out of earshot.

Curran held up his hand. "I'm no happier to see you than you are me, George, but for the love of God, please do not call me Curran. I'm working on an important case—a highly sensitive case—and I don't need the world to know my real name."

George raised an eyebrow. "Still policing?"

Curran flinched at the derision in his cousin's tone. Despite both men now being in their late thirties, George still managed to make him feel inadequate.

"Sutton. I told you to call me Sutton. And yes, I am. What are you doing in KL?" Curran asked.

"My wife's cousin is married to the Resident," George replied. "We've come out for a spot of hunting and to spend Christmas with the family. Are you going to tell me what your case is about?"

"No."

They stood in silence for the length of a few heartbeats, during which every injustice meted out to him during his miserable childhood, crashed through Curran's memory. Curran's mother, the daughter of the Earl of Alcester had eloped with the son of the head groom. She had died in childbirth and Curran's father, Edward, was given a commission in the South Sussex Regiment and sent away, leaving Robert Curran to be brought up with his cousins at Deerbourne Hall. His aunt and her offspring never let a chance to punish or humiliate the cuckoo in their nest go by.

They would be even more appalled if they knew Edward Curran had survived and fathered a second family with an Indian woman.

Curran cleared his throat. "How is your family?"

"Pa is gouty and wheezy, and Mama is still firmly in charge."

And from his tone, she could still cow George.

"And Elly?" Curran skipped the rest of his odious cousins to Eloise, the youngest of the Bullock-Steeles, and the one person who had made his time at Deerbourne Hall bearable. Now Lady Eloise Warby, she was a notorious suffragette.

George snorted. "That sister of mine! Total disgrace to the family. Banned from Deerbourne. Pa just about has apoplexy every time she turns up. Dragging our family name through the mud in the courts with her suffragette nonsense. Three times she's been in Holloway. *Three* times ... a Bullock-Steele!"

"To be fair, George, she hardly bears the family name. She's now a Warby."

"She might well be, but everyone knows she's one of us." George straightened, puffing out his chest in outrage. "And that bloody husband of hers encourages the nonsense."

Curran counted to five before he asked in a steady voice, "I meant, how is her health?"

When Curran had last had news of his favorite cousin, she had been close to death following a hunger strike in Holloway.

George deflated. For all the disgrace his sister was bringing on the family escutcheon, Elly was still his sister and, as the youngest, had always been a family favorite.

"She's not the best, to be honest, Curran. What can you expect if you're going to go on hunger strikes and such? I just wish she'd give the whole idea away and just concentrate on hearth and home."

"Not Elly. Never Elly," Curran said.

"Agreed," George said, and for a fleeting moment, Curran saw a shred of human decency in his cousin. Maybe the years had mellowed him?

"I think we've been out here long enough," Curran said. "Remember, my name is Sutton, and you and I were passing acquaintances at university. Nothing more."

"Sounds rather fun," George said. "Anything I can do to help? I've been here a month and I am dying of boredom up at the Residence." He leaned in and said in a low voice. "If you're after a bit of fun, there's a place just out of town. Gambling tables, stunning women, all the drink you want—"

"The Topaz Club?" Curran could hardly get the words out.

"That's it. Been there?"

"Not yet."

"I can get you in."

Curran would rather have had bamboo splinters inserted under his nails than involve George in his enterprise.

"No, thank you," Curran said. "Just stay out of my way, George."

EIGHT

KUALA LUMPUR

SATURDAY, 3 DECEMBER

As Julian had pointed out, Harriet had not left the island since her arrival in Singapore at the start of the year, and for the first time in weeks, her spirits lifted as they left the Singapore train and stepped aboard the ferry, which would bear them across the Straits of Johor, to pick up the Friday night train from Johor to Kuala Lumpur.

"What a shame we will be travelling by night," Harriet grumbled as they sat at their table in the dining carriage looking out into the dark. She could only imagine the sights she was missing.

Julian looked up from the guidebook he was perusing. It proclaimed itself as a *Pamphlet of Information for Travelers*, put out by the Federated Malay States Railways.

"We are only going to miss the beautiful views of the Rembau Valley," he said. "The rest is quite uninteresting."

"It's all interesting," Harriet said. "And you are as excited as I am. Tell me what your book says about Kuala Lumpur."

Julian picked up his guide again. "Largest town in the Federated Malay States and the center of the Federal Administration.

It is divided by the Klang River into Asiatic and European town..."

Harriet pulled a face. "Like Singapore?"

"Smaller than Singapore. There is a golf course, polo ground, rifle range, cricket and football ground ... a Padang, like Singapore. There are the Batu Caves, which are said to be very interesting and some hot springs."

Their meal arrived, and Julian set his book down. "I will be hosted at the school on Saturday," he said. "I hope you will find something of interest. Henry Robertson says his wife is very excited to meet you."

"It will be good to have someone local to show me around," Harriet said.

Julian set his fork down and studied his sister. "Harriet, we haven't really talked about Simon."

Harriet met his gaze. "Nothing to talk about, Ju. My pride is wounded, but my heart is perfectly intact."

"I had hoped ..." Julian turned back to his meal.

"Honestly, Julian, I will be fine. I'm quite content looking after you and Will and if that's our future, it's not so bad."

Julian smiled, but, knowing him so well, Harriet caught the sadness behind his eyes as he said, "I wonder sometimes how different things would be if Jane–"

Harriet laid her hand over his. Only a month before their wedding, the love of Julian's life, Jane Meacham, had contracted pneumonia and died. Her death had sent Julian into a dark place, and he had left the comfortable parish where he had been dearly loved and taken a teaching position at his old school. That, in turn, had led to his move to the Far East to take up a teaching post and subsequently the role of headmaster of St. Tom's.

"One day we have to stop running, Julian," Harriet said.

He patted her hand. "You are quite right, oh wise sister. This chicken is awfully good, and it is going cold—"

After their excellent dinner, Harriet retired to her cabin. She had the luxury of a well-appointed cabin to herself, while Julian had to share. She lay back on the crisp linen sheets and fell asleep to the gentle *click clack* and sway of the train carriage.

They served breakfast on the train early, well in time for the arrival at the Kuala Lumpur station on time at quarter to seven in the morning.

Julian leaned out of the window as the train drew into the station.

"Good heavens, there's Robertson. He's come to meet us," Julian said, waving as a bespectacled man of middle height and slight build, carrying his hat in his hand, pushed through the crowd to meet them at the door to the train carriage.

Introductions were made and the headmaster of the Prince Alfred School grasped Harriet's hand in both of his.

"So pleased you could come as well," he said. "Edith has a full day planned for you, so I hope you are not too fatigued from your journey."

"Not at all. I slept very well," Harriet said. "But I'd hate to inconvenience her—"

"She is thrilled to have a visitor. I have a carriage waiting. Let me take your bag."

Significant building works were going on and something that looked like a Moorish palace appeared to be rising from the ground. As they picked their way through the building debris, Robertson looked back at them. "Sorry about the mess. They are building a grand new station which is expected to open next year. Meanwhile, we must put up with the inconvenience of a building site. The school's not far. We could have walked, but I wasn't sure how much luggage you had. Here's the *gharry*. Let me help you up, Mrs Gordon."

They loaded bags and passengers into a waiting *gharry*, and set off, pushing their way through the chaos of the gathered crowd of train passengers and builders. Above them soared an edifice worthy of an Eastern potentate, complete with minarets.

Once completed, the new railway station would certainly make a statement.

Robertson leaned forward. "It will have a hotel and the latest conveniences," he said, "but let me tell you something amusing. Rumor has it that according to the specifications for the building of railway stations across the British Empire, the roof is rated for snow."

"I sincerely hope we never see that eventuality," Julian said.

"I hope you will enjoy your stay. We are all very excited to show you the school, Reverend Edwards." Robertson turned to Harriet. "Of course, I'm only the acting headmaster while Mr Buchanan is on extended home leave, but it allows us the use of his lovely bungalow—a great improvement on our previous bungalow on Brickfields Road, which we had to share. Edith loves having the entire house to herself."

The carriage ride from the train station to the school took barely ten minutes. They crossed a sizeable river—the Klang, Robertson said—and turned in through a pair of handsome gates onto a driveway that skirted a sports field. It led to a large bungalow at the rear of the school property, built beside a loop in the river and surrounded, like St Tom's House, by a high hedge.

A diminutive, fair-haired woman in a white muslin dress stood at the top of the flight of steps leading up to a wide, airy verandah. She waved as the carriage drew up, running down the steps to greet them.

She spared Julian only a cursory greeting, taking Harriet by the hands.

"You must be Mrs. Gordon. I'm so pleased to meet you."

Julian had said she was younger than her husband. Younger by nearly twenty years, Harriet thought.

Edith Robertson had the slender prettiness of youth, with fair hair and brown eyes. Only a slightly sulky cast to her mouth in repose detracted from her attractiveness. The hand that grasped

Harriet's was fine-boned, the pale skin almost translucent in the harsh tropical sun.

"We don't have many visitors," Edith continued, with a sideways glance at her husband. "If you are not too tired, I have ordered a carriage for ten and we will take a drive around town and have lunch at the club while the men talk school business."

She tucked her arm into Harriet's, escorting her up the stairs and across the wide verandah scattered with rugs, chairs and tables, and into the house itself. She showed Harriet into a bedroom furnished with heavy English mahogany that made a dark room even darker.

"Mrs. Buchanan has rather different taste to me," Edith said, surveying the room with a frown puckering her forehead. "I hope she doesn't come back. Then I can completely refurnish this gloomy house."

"It looks very comfortable," Harriet said, though she eyed the sagging mattress with doubt.

"You probably wish to freshen up. There is a bathroom through that door. Have a rest and when you are ready, we will take tea on the verandah while the men go up to the school. Henry has so much to discuss with your brother. They will be gone all day."

Harriet set her hat on the lace bedspread and let out a breath. In just a brief acquaintance, she already felt smothered by Edith Robertson's effusive welcome. It would be a long two days.

NINE

Washed and changed from her travelling clothes into a light blue muslin dress that she hardly ever wore, Harriet paused in the doorway to the verandah to take in the domestic tableau. Edith reclined on a cushioned chair, watching as a small girl of about three with a riot of fair curls played blocks on the oriental carpet with her Indian amah.

Every now and then, the little girl would look up at her mother. "Look Mummy," she'd say. Edith would smile and reply, "Very good, darling." But it seemed to Harriet there was little warmth in her smile. If this had been her child, Harriet would have been down on the carpet playing with the girl herself, not watching like a disinterested spectator at the cricket.

She chided herself for being too judgmental and stepped out onto the verandah. Edith straightened in her chair with a welcoming smile.

"Mrs. Gordon, you look quite refreshed. This is Dorothy," Edith said. "Say good morning to Mrs. Gordon, darling."

Dorothy stood up and, with her hands behind her back, intoned. "Good morning, Mithus Gordon."

"Good morning, Dorothy. You have lovely manners," Harriet replied.

Edith waved a hand. "Do sit down, Mrs. Gordon. Amah, you can remove Dottie now and tell the boy I would like coffee served."

"Yes, Mem," the *amah* responded, taking the little girl by the hand. "Come let us see what cook is making for lunch."

Edith let out a heavy sigh and laid a theatrical hand on her forehead.

"Do you have children, Mrs. Gordon?"

"I'm a widow, Mrs. Robertson. My husband and son died in India."

Edith straightened. "How simply dreadful. I'm so sorry. I do that, I say stupid things. I just blurt them out."

"You weren't to know." Harriet smiled. "How old is Dorothy?"

"She's almost three," Edith replied. "I had the most terrible time after she was born. I suffer from anemia and headaches. I am quite prostrated with my health."

Harriet had little time for what her mother called 'willowy women,' but she mustered suitable tutting and sympathy. The arrival of a male servant carrying a tray with a coffeepot and a plate of biscuits cut short any further conversation about Edith's health..

"I've just remembered," Edith said as she poured coffee for Harriet, "Henry said you were looking for a suitable school for your boy. I am confused. Is that Reverend Edwards's son?"

"Neither. Will Lawson is our ward."

Edith looked up. "Your ward? How did that come about?"

"He's an orphan," Harriet said in a flat tone that she hoped would curtail questions about their guardianship of Will.

Edith did not take the hint. "Is he a relation? How long has he been in your care?"

Will, a student at Julian's school, had come into their care after the death of his father. The events that had led to John Lawson's death at the hands of a murderous gang of gem smugglers still caused Harriet to wake in a cold sweat some nights.

"He is a student at St. Toms. His father died earlier this year, and Julian and I were granted guardianship. He has no one else." Harriet changed the subject. "What a delightful view."

The bungalow stood in a bow of the river, with a garden that ran down to the riverbank. In the other direction, beyond the hedge, was the long, low, white-washed walls of the school building crowned with a clock tower. If it was not for the oppressive humidity, it could have been a school in any corner of England, Harriet thought.

"Henry may have mentioned this is officially the headmaster's bungalow, but while Mr. and Mrs. Buchanan are in England, we are permitted to occupy it. I have added the carpets and the pot plants and cushions and cheered it up a bit."

Edith looked around the verandah and smiled. Harriet had to agree that the pot plants and pretty, embroidered cushions did indeed liven the drab furniture.

"How do you spend your days?" Harriet asked.

"I have a small job." A slight color rose to Edith's pale face.

That Edith 'worked' intrigued Harriet. It went against every precept of colonial society, which dictated the memsahibs did good works or reclined at home with embroidery and letter-writing. Working for money, as Harriet herself had done, put a woman outside the bounds of acceptable behavior, unless it was doing something worthy such as nursing or teaching, and even then, only if you were unmarried.

The very idea of a married woman working was even more unusual.

"What sort of work do you do?" she asked.

"I'm a teacher," Edith began, but added with a deprecatory

smile. "I help with the kindergarten classes at the Methodist Girls' School. Miss Marsh is the headmistress."

Harriet raised an eyebrow. If the recent interaction she had observed with Edith's own daughter was any indication of Edith's affection for working with very young children, she seemed an unusual choice for a role in a kindergarten.

"And your husband agreed to the arrangement?"

"Oh yes, Henry was more than happy. He understood I was bored being stuck at home all day. Besides, it is rather jolly earning my own money." She pulled a face. "Henry was always complaining about how much I spent at John Little's. Now if I see a hat I want, I can just buy it."

"You are fortunate. Not all husbands are quite so accommodating."

"I know. He is a sweetie and quite devoted to me." She paused and her face stilled. "There are times I think he deserves better."

Knowing she was expected to say something, Harriet responded, "I am sure that is not the case, Mrs. Robertson."

A silence fell between the two women as they sipped their coffee.

"May I call you Harriet?" Edith broke the silence. "You will find life here is just tea and gossip. There's church, of course—St Mary's. I sing in the choir." Her eyes brightened. "And I love amateur theatre. We've just done *Trial by Jury* and the newspaper made a special comment about my role as First Bridesmaid. Do you like Gilbert and Sullivan?"

Harriet suppressed a shudder. "I have rather gone off them in recent months," she said, her recent experiences with the Singapore Amateur Dramatic and Music Society still fresh in her mind.

"I would love a leading role, of course," Edith continued, oblivious to her guest's discomfort. She sighed theatrically, "Maybe next time".

She clapped her hands. "Now, if you are revived, the carriage will be here any moment, and I shall show you the sights of Kuala Lumpur. Be sure to wear stout walking shoes and bring a parasol. I am very keen to show you the Batu Caves, but it is a short walk from where we must leave the carriage and, I warn you, it is quite a climb."

TEN

Edith's chosen outfit for sightseeing was a blue and white striped cotton dress adorned with lace and blue bows with a matching hat. Beside her, Harriet in her simple dress and wide-brimmed straw hat felt positively dowdy. Both women opened their parasols against the midday sun. Edith's a white lace concoction that did little to ameliorate the sun, Harriet's a red and gold paper lacquer umbrella she had purchased in Chinatown.

Edith chattered brightly as they drove through the school in the hired, open topped carriage. She told Harriet that she had been born in Kuala Lumpur and her first trip outside Malaya had been to England on their honeymoon.

"And I was so awfully sick," she said. "I was pregnant with Dottie. It was no fun at all and so cold and dreary. I couldn't wait to get home."

"Do your parents still live here?" Harriet asked.

"Oh yes. They came here in the '80s and I don't think they will ever leave. We were all born here. I have a sister in Ceylon, but my brother and my two other sisters live nearby."

"How lovely to have all your family close by," Harriet said.

Something flickered behind Edith's eyes, and she didn't respond.

Having done a round of the *Padang*, the large open area that served as sports ground and military parade ground, and viewed the church of St Mary's, and the extraordinary colonial offices— like the new station, constructed in some sort of homage to Moorish architecture—Edith suggested they should take lunch at the nearby Selangor Club.

"Simply everyone who is anyone is a member of the Selangor Club, Harriet. It is the place to be seen," Edith said. "The locals call it the Spotted Dog. I think it is because its emblem is a leopard." She shrugged. "There are all sorts of stories."

Telling the carriage to wait, Edith led the way into the club, a mock Tudor-style building with two wings and a central pavilion overlooking the *Padang* to the Government offices beyond.

As Edith bent to sign the visitors' register, a woman's voice cut across the sepulchral silence.

"Edith!"

Edith straightened and spun on her heel, two spots of color darkening her cheeks.

"Mama. What a pleasant surprise."

An older woman, heavily corseted and wearing an outfit several seasons out of date, stood in a doorway through to what looked like a lounge area. Neither woman looked pleased to see the other.

"What are you doing here? Don't you have responsibilities?" Edith's mother demanded.

"We have important visitors from Singapore. I'm showing her around." Edith cast a quick glance at Harriet.

The woman's gaze flicked to Harriet, looking her up and down and, from the slight curl of her lip, finding her wanting.

"How rude of Edith not to introduce us," she said, holding out her hand. "Mrs. Chapman. I am Edith's mother."

"Mrs. Gordon," Harriet responded.

"I hope Edith is looking after you," Mrs. Chapman said with an acerbic glance at her daughter. "Please excuse me. We are playing mahjong in the ladies' card room." She turned away and looked back. "Of course, you are welcome to join us."

Edith responded, "Thank you, Mama, but we will take luncheon and then we are driving out to the Batu Caves."

With a flick of her skirt, Mrs. Chapman turned away, passing through a door that shut firmly behind her.

"Insufferable woman," Edith muttered more to herself than Harriet, as she ushered Harriet through to the shaded verandah area, choosing a table in full view of the main entrance. With one eye on the front door, it seemed to take Edith a few moments to arrange herself to her satisfaction.

"I must apologize for my mother. We are not close. She has always resented me and never resists any opportunity to make me feel her disappointment. Do you get along with your mother?"

Harriet smiled. "When we are not living in the same house."

"Then you can understand why I married Henry. My parents thought him quite unsuitable." A nasty little smile curled the corners of her lips. "All the more reason, in my view."

"How did you meet your husband?"

Edith gave a small shrug. "As you may have gleaned, this is a small community. Papa is very important in the Public Works Department, and he runs the fire brigade. When he first arrived, Henry joined the fire brigade, and I met him at a party at our house. Unfortunately, Henry dislikes shooting and hunting, which are my father's favorite pastimes, and he is, as my father put it, 'only a schoolmaster' so not good enough for a Chapman. Papa even contrived to be out of the country for my wedding. One of his friends had to give me away." The high color had returned to Edith's cheeks. "It was galling."

"Henry seems devoted to you," Harriet said, anxious to placate the other woman who had clearly worked herself up since her encounter with her mother.

"I couldn't ask for a sweeter husband," Edith said, but something in her flat tone belied her words.

As they ate their luncheon, several people passed them, but beyond a curious glance at Harriet, accorded Edith little more than a casual nod.

It would seem, Harriet concluded as they resumed their journey in the carriage, that Edith Robertson was not one of Kuala Lumpur's most popular residents and with such a tiny European population, that must be hard. She was young and possibly naïve, but Harriet was left wondering what Edith had done to earn such open enmity, even from her own mother.

ELEVEN

On Saturday morning, the hotel had, at Curran's request, organized a horse and a packed lunch to facilitate his declared intention to go birdwatching. For what he needed to do today, a horse would be considerably more useful than a motor vehicle and besides, he missed his faithful horse Leopold.

Curran appeared after breakfast, dressed like an English gentleman in immaculately cut jodhpurs, high polished boots, a waistcoat, and a dark linen shirt with a silk scarf tied loosely around his neck. All topped with his pith helmet. He'd been unable to find a suitable book on birds of the Malay Peninsula to wave around, but he carried a satchel with a notebook and drawing materials and completed the picture with a pair of binoculars.

His Webley revolver, wrapped in oilcloth, added to the weight of the satchel. Unfortunately, it was not of a convenient size to be carried inconspicuously on his person.

A bay gelding in immaculate condition, held by a syce, stood waiting at the front door of the hotel. Curran had inherited his love of horses from his paternal grandfather and spent some time looking into the animal's eyes, getting a feel for the temperament of the horse.

"What is his name?" he asked the syce.

"Berani," the man said.

Berani... Malay for *brave*.

"A good name," he said, and the man smiled and nodded.

"Where do you plan to ride, *tuan*?"

"The Batu Caves."

The syce smiled. "A good ride."

Curran swung into the saddle, accepting a water canteen from the hotel porter.

His intention was to locate the Topaz Club. Archibald Stephens's description of the premises being 'off the Batu Road' was not much of a direction, and it was close to eight miles from his hotel to the Batu Caves.

For the first part of the ride, Curran spurred Berani into a canter, enjoying the feeling of being back on horseback, at one with the animal. But as they left the bounds of the town and turned onto the road to the caves, fringed with palm trees, banana trees, and orderly rows of scraggly rubber trees, he slowed to a walk.

He thought the club would unlikely be on the side where the railway line ran up to the caves—far too public. Instead, he concentrated on the west side, turning down narrow lanes that wound through the rubber plantations.

He stopped to ask a group of coolies if they knew of a big house with high walls nearby.

The men looked at each other before one, braver than the others, spoke up.

"A little way, there is a track marked by a stand of banana trees. Beyond is such a house," he said.

Any further questioning elicited only shrugs and head shakes as the men turned back to their work.

He followed the loose directions. In a countryside where

banana trees predominated, it still took a few wrong turns before he found the track. From the road it was barely discernible but beyond the banana trees, he was in jungle and the track flattened out to a well-used byway.

He dismounted and led Barani into the trees, well away from the road. He tied the reins to a fallen log, allowing enough slack for the animal to graze on whatever he could find to eat, and picked his way back to within sight of the track.

He made slow progress through the undergrowth, not wanting to be caught on the track, a decision for which he was grateful as a small two-seater motor vehicle passed, heading toward the main road. Curran flattened himself to the ground and let the vehicle go by.

It had only one occupant, a male driver in goggles that rendered him unidentifiable, an almost inhuman creature, his gaze fixed on the rough track. In his anonymity, the driver of the vehicle seemed to epitomize everything about the Topaz Club.

An icy shiver ran down Curran's spine as he stood up, dusting leaves and mud from his breeches.

Curran finally stumbled on the house, nearly a mile into the jungle. A ten-foot wall encircled what appeared to be a two-storied house of modern design with wide verandahs on the upper story. A pointed tower rose from one corner—an odd confection, but probably no stranger than the Moorish architecture that characterized the colonial buildings in town.

A cleared area of some fifty feet circled the house. No one could approach those walls without someone's eyes on them. Curran kept to the tree line, grateful for the deliberate choice of the dark shirt.

He trained the binoculars on the front gate. The elegant wrought-iron gates had been faced on the inside with sheet metal, making it impossible to see inside the grounds. The track leading to the front gate forked off with a second track skirting the walls to the back of the house. Keeping to the undergrowth, Curran followed this track.

Unlike the front of the house, the back gate stood open. He assumed someone had opened it to allow the motor vehicle out. He crouched down, scanning the service yard with his binoculars, but the place seemed deserted until a man wearing a long, white tunic and an anachronistic red fez walked out of the house carrying a metal bowl. As he passed from view, the frantic barking of several large dogs turned Curran's blood cold.

As the dogs fell silent, the man returned, carrying the bowl by his side now, the contents no doubt provided to the animals. As he passed the gate, the man paused, looking out. His gaze passed over the place where Curran lay concealed and he set down the bowl, coming forward to shut the gates. Curran decided discretion was the better part of valor and retreated.

He retrieved the horse and, checking to see that there was no passing traffic to note his exit from the hidden track, turned toward the Batu Caves. There Curran hoped to climb the massif and get a view across the valley, but one look at the vertical walls put that thought away.

Leaving the horse with a syce, he had to content himself with joining the other visitors in the scramble up to the cave mouth. This allowed something of a view across the treetops of the remaining jungle and the orderly rows of rubber trees and palms to the town beyond.

With the aid of the binoculars, he could make out the red roof of the hidden building that was the Topaz Club. It was, as he suspected, surrounded by the jungle—a perfect hiding place, he thought, stowing the binoculars back in their case.

He returned to the place where he had left the horse. Several motor vehicles had pulled up in the shade and carriages, attended by uniformed servants or scruffy drivers, also waited on visitors. An open topped carriage had drawn up, and the driver was assisting two ladies to dismount. They were too far away to be clearly identifiable beneath wide hats and parasols, but something about the red and gold Chinese parasol one carried seemed familiar—very similar to one that he kept tripping over in the office of the Detective Branch of the Straits Settlements Police. Harriet never seemed to find a safe place to put it.

He dismissed the thought. It was a common accessory for the memsahibs. Harriet was playing in his mind, nothing more.

Back in town, he purchased *samosa* and fresh coconut from street vendors, and returned the horse. He washed and changed before heading to the hospital, just catching the end of visiting hours.

He found Jayant still feverish, and he had to confront the very real fear Jayant may not survive the fever. He managed a smile and Jayant pulled himself up on his pillows, eager to hear what Curran had learned about the Topaz Club.

Curran shared his news, including his suspicion that the department store manager, Ashton Blake, was married to Jameela; and that he'd located a building he believed to be the current location of the Topaz Club.

Jayant stared up at the ceiling. "It sounds impenetrable. Do you have an army battalion at your disposal, brother?"

Curran huffed a laugh. "I don't even have a policeman I can trust."

"Perhaps," Jayant began and frowned. "Perhaps, if your Inspector General is willing, at least one such policeman could be found. Your Sergeant Singh?"

Sergeant Gursharan Singh, Curran's sergeant in the Detective Branch, had been demoted to traffic duty by Curran's replacement, Inspector Keogh. Surely Cuscaden would agree to Singh being relieved of that duty and sent to Curran's aid?

"That is an excellent suggestion," Curran said. "I will see what can be done."

"And this Ashton Blake?" Jayant asked.

"I will go there tonight."

As he stood to leave, Jayant caught his arm. "Tread carefully, brother."

TWELVE

Once away from the oppressive atmosphere of the Selangor Club and on a road leading out of town, Edith had resumed her role as a tour guide.

"I have saved the best until last, Harriet. You cannot help but be impressed. Henry says the Batu Caves are ancient, hundreds of millions of years, and he knows all about these sorts of things."

The road followed the railway line to a small, neat station in the shadow of a massive limestone outcrop soaring high above them. As Julian's guidebook had suggested, the cave area was apparently a popular spot for visitors. A few Europeans, their red faces sheened in perspiration, sat waiting at the railway station. They spared the newcomers no more than a passing glance. Beside the station, motor vehicles and carriages vied for shade with horses and bicycles.

As the carriage driver helped her from the carriage, out of the corner of her eye, she caught a tall Englishman walking toward one of the horses. Something about his build and the confident stride snatched at her heart.

She would know Curran anywhere.

She gasped and almost stumbled. Edith caught her arm.

"Are you all right, Harriet?"

Harriet summoned a smile. "Just caught my heel. Lead on."

But when she looked back, the man and the horse had gone, and she told herself sternly that she had been imagining the resemblance.

"Hurry, Harriet!" Edith's voice cut across her thoughts, and she scurried to join the woman. Edith stood, parasol over her shoulder, looking up at the massif. "Isn't it wonderful? Come, the path is this way."

The walk was a little further than Harriet had expected, and she was grateful for the suggestion of wearing stout walking shoes. The path wound through rubber trees where teams of coolies, busy with tapping the trees and used to passing tourists, did not look up from their work.

At the end of the path, they came into an open area at the start of the climb. Here, bored vendors of fruit and coconuts pressed their wares on the two women, but Edith dismissed them in curt Malay, her attention on the winding path that led up to a gaping maw in the side of what looked to Harriet like a cliff face.

"We have to hike up there." Edith said, "It's become so popular that there is talk of putting in steps, but for now, we'll have to climb."

As Harriet toiled up the uneven path that wound between boulders, Edith bounded ahead of her, giving a lie to her claim of perpetual ill health.

Reaching the top, Harriet stopped to catch her breath, turning to look out over the fields of rubber trees and jungle to the distant town of Kuala Lumpur. The view alone was worth the effort.

"This way, Harriet," Edith urged, and Harriet turned to face a lofty hall carved from the rock by the forces of nature over millennia.

"Oh," was all she could say.

The limestone walls, marred in places by what was probably

centuries of graffiti, curved upwards to a ceiling from which stalactites still clung. Green and blue moss added color to the rocks. Huge pillars of stone rose from the floor of the cave, like a massive medieval cathedral crafted not by the hands of man but by some other fabulous being.

"There are stairs cut in the rock here. Watch your step. It is quite slippery."

Once again Edith went on ahead, leaving Harriet to pick her way down the rock-hewn steps into the chamber. Light flooded in from a second cavern, adding to the impression of a gothic cathedral, beckoning Harriet onwards.

Heedless now of Edith, Harriet picked her way across the boulder-strewn floor to the second gallery. There were places where her heels struck a hollow sound, and she wondered how far the cave system extended below the surface.

She stood poised on the threshold of what would once have been an even mightier chamber, except that here the roof had long since fallen in, leaving it exposed to the sky like a giant bowl of tumbled rocks and hardy plants. Above her, monkeys screeched their protests at the invaders, scrambling up the long ropes of tree roots belonging to the greenery that clung to the lip of the bowl.

Harriet sat down on a boulder, looking up, mesmerized by the contrast of blue sky with the white rock and the fringe of green around the collapsed roof. Other tourists wandered in small groups, murmuring in hushed voices as if they were in a truly holy place.

Unclasping her handbag, Harriet pulled out her handkerchief and mopped her face. The humidity seemed trapped in these caves, and perspiration dripped into her eyes. She looked around her, wishing she had thought to bring her sketching pad.

On the wall nearby, half concealed by an overhang, some long-forgotten hand had carved a small herd of elephants. The sharp edges of the carving were blurred by time, but the four elephants were still identifiable, each with its own personality—one raising its trunk, one with its ears flapping, and the third and fourth a mother with her small calf.

She stood up, intending to call Edith over to admire the little carving, but Edith had remained in the first chamber and was now engaged in conversation with a well-dressed European man. They had drawn into a shadowed gallery and stood close together in animated discussion. As Harriet watched, Edith shook her head, laying a hand on the man's chest. He took a step back and removed her hand, letting it fall.

Harriet waited for a heartbeat or two before turning away and calling Edith's name with a pretense that she had lost sight of her companion.

"Over here, Harriet," Edith returned her call and when Harriet turned to the place, she had seen the couple they had moved back into the main part of the cave and were standing well apart like casual acquaintances.

Edith gestured to her and as Harriet joined them, the man raised his pith helmet, revealing a high, domed, bald head with just a circlet of hair above his ears. She judged him to be in his late thirties, his face strong and probably best described by someone like her friend Louisa Mackenzie as 'ruggedly handsome' or a 'manly man', the sort that enjoyed an outdoor life of sport and other recreations.

Edith drew her lips into a sulky moue. She did not look best pleased by Harriet's intrusion into what had evidently been a private conversation—or maybe she had not been happy with the conversation itself.

As Edith did not seem inclined to affect an introduction, the man held out his hand.

"Mrs. Gordon? I'm Walter Stewart. A friend of the Robertsons," he added with a glance at Edith. "Is this your first visit to KL?"

Harriet smiled as she took his hand. He had a firm grip, and she felt her bones crunch. "It is. My brother has business with Edith's husband."

Edith tossed her head and Harriet cast her a curious glance.

"What do you think of our famous Batu Caves? Impressive, aren't they?" Stewart waved his hat in an arc that took in the curve of the roof above them. "This is one of my favorite local haunts. I find it very peaceful, almost spiritual."

"It certainly has the atmosphere of a cathedral," Harriet agreed. "I've seen nothing like it."

"The local Tamil population sees it as a place of veneration," Stewart said. "The entrance to the cave is said to resemble the tip of the spear carried by *Lord Murugan*, son of the warrior goddess *Korravai*. In one of the smaller caves, you will find a small temple for *Lord Murugan*."

"There are other caves?" Harriet asked.

"Oh yes, quite a complex. No one knows how far it stretches beneath our feet. Probably miles out into the land around. See that cave mouth up there?"

He indicated a dark shadow halfway along the path to the entrance. "That's the Dark Cave. Are you going to take your guest down there, Mrs. Robertson?"

"No. As you well know, it's full of bats and snakes and frogs and things and it smells vile. And I'm not paying for a guide." Edith glanced at her little wristwatch. "I think it is time for me and Mrs. Gordon to return home. Good afternoon, Mr. Stewart."

With a flick of her skirts, Edith strode off toward the steps to the cave mouth.

Harriet smiled at the man. "It was a pleasure meeting you, Mr. Stewart."

He inclined his head. "And you, Mrs. Gordon. I hope we meet again."

He tipped his hat and turned away, making his way to the second cavern.

Harriet scurried after Edith, catching her at the start of the descent to the plain below. This time Edith took her time, apparently deep in thought, her shoulders slumped, oblivious to Harriet's presence.

"Edith?" Harriet prompted the silent, thoughtful woman. "Is everything all right?"

Edith shook herself, bringing her gaze to meet Harriet's with a smile not echoed by her eyes.

"My apologies, I was thinking of ..." she paused as if searching around for an excuse. "I was thinking of Dottie. She is teething again, and so out of sorts." She looped her arm into Harriet's. "Goodness, sightseeing is tiring, particularly in this heat. It is time to return home for a nice cooling drink and a chance to put our feet up before supper. The men will probably wonder where we are."

"Did that man upset you in some way?" Harriet asked.

Edith's footsteps slowed. "Man? Oh, Walter Stewart ... no, not at all. He's a friend of Henry's. He's come to dinner a few times, but we are only acquaintances."

Harriet sat back against the threadbare squabs of the hired carriage and left Edith to her own thoughts. She was certain she had not been mistaken in thinking Walter Stewart was more than just 'a friend of Henry's.' There had been something in their proximity, the way Edith had touched him, that spoke of a much greater intimacy.

She sighed.

This was the colonies, and things were not always what they seemed.

THIRTEEN

On their return to the bungalow, Edith retired to her bedroom pleading a headache. The men had still not returned from the school and Harriet settled on the pleasant verandah overlooking the river. She scoured the bookcase and found a tome to interest her and reclined in a planter's chair with a cup of tea provided by the houseboy, a pleasant young man who gave his name as Sami.

The *amah* came out onto the verandah with Dottie. Seeing Harriet, the woman scooped up her small charge and turned to go back inside.

"Stay," Harriet said.

Amah cast a glance at the open doorway. "Mem does not like to be disturbed if she is sitting out here," she said.

"I am not Mem," Harriet responded. "Dottie can play out here. Fetch a book and I can read to her."

Harriet did not consider herself as especially good with small children, but Dottie came to her willingly enough, a copy of Beatrix Potter's *Tale of Tom Kitten* in hand. Harriet caught her breath—her son, Thomas, had been sent a new Beatrix Potter from his aunt Mary every year for his birthday. *Tom Kitten* had been the last one, arriving after the child's death with a cheerful *For our own Tom Kitten!* note. Holding the little book again brought a wave of pain, and Harriet was conscious of the *amah* looking at her with concern.

"Mem? You want I take her away?"

Harriet shook her head. "No, no ... Come up here, Dottie, and let's read all about naughty Tom Kitten."

She spent a pleasant sojourn with Dottie and her *amah* until the time came for the child to go in for her supper. In the torpid late afternoon heat, the journey and busy day caught up with her and she dozed in the comfortable chair to be woken by the men returning just after five.

She could see from the smile and the gleam in Julian's eye that the day had been a success and when he suggested a walk to the river before supper, she agreed.

"Well?" she asked when they were out of earshot.

"Harri, it's everything we could ask for as a place for Will. There is a mix of students from all races. The academic program is excellent and there is ample opportunity for cricket and rugby."

She squeezed his arm. "But what about you? Is it what you have been looking for?"

He shrugged. "It would be a reduction in status and salary," he said. "But on the other hand, I have missed teaching older boys and frankly, I'm worn out by the responsibility of being a headmaster."

But for all his words, Harriet sensed regret in her brother's tone. He would be giving up a great deal to take this position.

"How was your day?" Julian asked.

"Strange." Harriet glanced up at the house. "Edith Robertson is an odd little creature. I think Mother would describe her as flibbertigibbet."

Julian smiled. "She has her husband wound around her finger. I think he mentioned her in every second sentence."

Harriet shrugged. "We had lunch at the Selangor Club, and it was obvious that she had done something to set the mems against her, including her own mother, who was positively beastly to her. This is too small a community to afford that approbation." She paused. "I confess I am curious, Julian."

Julian raised a finger. "I can't afford your curiosity, Harriet," he said. "If we are going to make the move up here, we need to do so with a blank canvas. No preconceptions on either our part or the community."

Harriet laid a hand on his arm. "I know. We leave on Monday, and I promise I will be on my best behavior."

A bell rang from the house, and they turned back to find both host and hostess waiting beside a table set for four on the verandah. Edith had changed into yet another outfit, this time a daringly cut gown of blue silk. She bestowed a charming smile on her guests, all trace of her headache and her sour mood gone, and once again the consummate hostess.

A single electric light cast a warm glow over the scene and Harriet commented on the modern conveniences that must make life easier.

"Oh yes," Edith said. "Mrs. Buchanan insisted on the electric lights being installed. We are the only people we know with lighting."

Henry Robertson offered sherry. Harriet would have preferred a whisky or a gin and tonic, but she downed the warm sherry.

After she had dutifully admired Edith's pretty dress, Harriet apologized for not realizing that they would need to dress for dinner.

Edith waved a hand. "Oh, this? I find evening dress so much more conducive to the climate, nothing more."

Harriet remained unconvinced, particularly when Edith tilted her head and smiled at Julian, her fingers twirling a stray lock of hair, as she said, "Did you have a pleasant day, Reverend Edwards?"

Oblivious to the obvious flirtation, Julian nodded. "Excellent, thank you. And you, ladies?"

"Harriet and I had a lovely day," Edith said as they sat to eat. "We went up to the Batu Caves and Henry, you wouldn't believe who we met up there?"

"Probably not," her husband said, with an indulgent smile.

"Mr. Stewart. He sends his best regards."

The smile slipped from Robertson's face. "What on earth was he doing up there? I thought he was out of town."

Edith smiled. "He tells me it is one of his favorite places. Mine too. It is quite enchanting. Don't you agree, Harriet?"

Harriet had her mouth full and could only nod in agreement.

"It is certainly very interesting," Henry Robertson said, sparing Harriet from responding. "Millions of years in the making."

"You're not a creationist?" Julian asked.

Robertson's eyes widened. "No. My views tend to the agnostic, for which I apologize. I forgot you're a man of the cloth."

"I am not a believer in creation either. The work of Darwin and those who have followed him are more than enough evidence of a long period of evolution," Julian said.

"On that point, we are agreed," Robertson said and turned back to Harriet. "There is no doubt the Batu Caves are special."

"Quite magical," Harriet replied.

"There are similar rock formations throughout the peninsula. Many of them are used as places of worship and probably have been for centuries. At Ipoh, for example, both the Chinese and the Hindus have adopted the caves as temples. There is a small shrine in the Batu Caves and talk among the local Tamils about extending it." He shrugged. "Scientists think the cave system might extend well beyond the massif. So much to explore ... so much unknown. That is one of the things I love about this country—the flora, the fauna, and the geology. All fascinating."

They chatted about the sights and delights of Malaya before Edith asked, "What shall we do tomorrow, Henry?"

Henry Robertson sat back, dabbing the corners of his mouth with a table napkin. "Church," he said with a raised eyebrow at Julian. "We normally attend morning and evening service at St. Mary's."

"I thought you said you were agnostic," Julian said.

"I am also pragmatic. The Resident, Henry Belfield, is an ardent church attender and if you want to remain in his favor, it is politic to be seen as an active member of the congregation of St. Mary's. Besides which, I enjoy the music."

"I sing in the choir," Edith piped up, "and Henry is the choir director. Everyone attends Evensong because that is where you are seen, Harriet. Seen by the right people. The Resident keeps notes on who is absent. And standing in front of the choir is a good way to be seen, don't you agree?"

Robertson reached out and covered his wife's hand with his own. "She has the voice of an angel."

Edith colored but did not protest. Her husband addressed Julian. "Do you know the current vicar? He only arrived from Singapore a few months ago."

"Oh yes, Reverend Grahame, I know him well."

Robertson glanced away from the table into the darkened grounds. "Lunch at the Club and then a walk in the botanical gardens in the afternoon—"

"You forget, Henry," Edith cut across him, "We have an engagement at the shooting range tomorrow afternoon. It was hard enough to get a booking on a Sunday." She cast a smile at Harriet. "I am sure our guests can amuse themselves for a couple of hours. They don't need our company for a walk in the park."

"We'll be fine," Julian said. "A quiet afternoon on the verandah with a good book is all we need, isn't that so, Harriet?"

An afternoon at a shooting range seemed an odd pastime, particularly when there were house guests to amuse. Harriet forgot her promise to her brother to curb her curiosity and asked, "You shoot?"

"Henry has recently acquired a Webley revolver and needs the practice," Edith said.

"Do you mind me asking what brought you to acquire a revolver?" Julian asked.

Edith squeezed her husband's fingers. "We were plagued with a few burglaries in the old house on Brickfields Road and Henry thought it might be prudent to have some means of self-defense, so I bought him the Webley for his birthday."

Harriet started so suddenly that some of the wine in her glass spilled. She hastily mopped it up with her table napkin.

"A revolver is a novel birthday present," she said.

Henry smiled. "I wasn't all that keen on the idea, but Edith insisted. I suppose it helps if you are brought up, as Edith was, in a house full of guns of one sort or another."

"Papa is a very keen hunter and taught us all how to shoot," Edith continued. "My brother Noel was recently in all the papers. He and some of his friends brought down the biggest *seladang* anyone has ever recorded. Noel wounded it, and it took three days to track it down before they could kill it. Noel says it must have been at least eighty years old. Papa is having the head stuffed and mounted for the front hall of the house."

Harriet repressed a shudder. *Seladang* were a species of large, wild cattle. In India, they had been called *Gaur*. The thought of an eighty-year-old beast being stalked to its death for three days filled her with revulsion.

She had never understood the preoccupation with large game hunting. Her husband, James Gordon, had taken her to a shooting party in the Scottish Highlands during the early days of their marriage, where the sight of the beautiful deer being carried back after a day's stalking had nearly caused her to turn and run home to London.

"There is a very active women's rifle shooting club here,"

Robertson picked up the thread of his wife's conversation. He turned and smiled at her fondly. "Like all the Chapmans, Edith was a champion."

Edith sniffed. "Of course, since I married Henry, I gave all that away. I was weary of the company and besides, I don't think they liked me winning all the time."

"I've done some small arms shooting in Singapore, but not competitively," Harriet said, ignoring Julian's boot on her instep.

"Do you own a weapon, Harriet?" Edith asked.

"I have a .22 caliber Smith and Wesson. My husband purchased it when we lived in India—like you—for self-defense. I have since learned how to use it myself."

Robert Curran had spent several sessions teaching her the proper handling of her late husband's revolver. He had allowed her to practice shooting his Webley, but she preferred the smaller Smith & Wesson.

"Do you have it with you?" Edith asked in the same tone of voice that she would use to enquire if Harriet had brought her tennis racquet.

"No, I didn't bring it with me."

Why would she even have considered bringing the weapon on such a weekend?

"Would you care to join us tomorrow afternoon? I would love to see how well you shoot," Edith said.

Harriet's troublesome curiosity got the better of her. "If it's no bother? It's been a while since I've been out on the range, and it pays to keep up the practice."

"Edwards?" Robertson enquired.

Julian appeared oblivious to the man's hopeful tone. "You will have to excuse me. I am a man of peace. I barely tolerate Harriet's revolver in the house. No, you go ahead, I shall thoroughly enjoy a quiet afternoon, knowing I am not likely to be bothered by any school matters."

Edith clapped her hands. "Excellent. So, church in the morning, lunch, and then the shooting range. Time for a rest and then Evensong."

"And you are both most cordially invited for supper with Mr. Haycocks," Henry Robertson said to Harriet and Julian. "It was an invitation made before we knew you were coming. As you are taking the day train to Singapore on Monday, I do hope you will join us?"

"Mr Haycocks?" Harriet enquired of her brother.

Robertson replied, "Edward Haycocks. He's one of the senior masters. Your brother met him today. He shared our house up on Brickfields Road until we moved in here, and now he has the old place all to himself. Lucky devil."

"It sounds like a full day," Harriet said. "We will be quite ready for the train on Monday morning."

FOURTEEN

It had long gone dark when Curran knocked at the door of Ashton Blake's respectable little bungalow. A houseboy in a long white robe answered his knock. He looked Curran up and down and asked for his name and business.

Curran hesitated. "I would like to speak with Mr. Blake and his wife. My business is personal."

The door slammed in his face. Curran took a step back before knocking again. After a moment or two, the door reopened, and a man dressed in trousers with his shirt undone at the collar stood in the doorway, the light behind him so he appeared as a silhouette.

"I'm Ashton Blake. What is your business with me?"

Curran stepped forward and as the light from the house fell on his face, recognition sparked in Blake's eyes.

"Mr, Sutton isn't it? What can I do for you? Were you after more material for your book?"

"No. There is another matter I wish to speak with you about."

Blake frowned. "How did you know where I live?"

"I followed you."

Blake took a step back, and his voice shook as he said, "Did they send you?"

"No one sent me. I am looking for a girl. Her name is Samrita Kumar, and I believe your wife may be able to help me find her."

"No! We can't help. I've never heard of this girl."

"You have heard of the Topaz Club?"

Blake made to close the door, but Curran was faster, a well-placed booted foot preventing the door from closing.

"Please Blake, I'm not here to make trouble. A few months ago, you and your wife spoke with a man called Simon Hume, and we ... I believe you have information on the workings of the Topaz Club."

Blake's nostrils flared, and he lifted his chin as color flooded his face. His hands balled into fists by his side and Curran took a strategic step backwards.

"And you think it acceptable to lie your way into my office and now my home? We were foolish to have agreed to meet with him. Now leave."

"Please, just a few moments of your time and that of your wife. It is a matter of life and death."

Something flickered behind the man's eyes, and he paused, his hand still on the door.

"What's your interest in this woman?"

"Her brother, Jayant Kumar is looking for her."

"And where do you fit in?"

"I'm a friend."

Blake's jaw tightened as he hesitated before stepping back. "Very well ... a few minutes only."

Blake admitted Curran into a comfortable living room, illuminated by a single kerosene lamp sitting on a table beside an armchair.

There were feminine touches in the living room ... brightly colored cushions and a pretty glass vase containing two cut orchids, but no sign of the woman, Jameela, or any evidence of children. Hadn't Hume mentioned a couple of children?

The houseboy hovered in a far doorway, and Blake dismissed him with a wave of his hand.

"Your wife?" Curran asked.

"She's not here. She's gone to visit my sister in Ipoh," Blake said.

"Has she taken the children with her?"

Genuine confusion crossed Blake's features. "Children?"

"She told Hume you have children."

Blake ran a hand through his hair. "I don't believe my family is any concern of yours, Mr. Sutton. What do you think Jameela can tell you?"

"I hoped she could tell me if Samrita—Lily, they called her at the club—is alive or dead?"

"And what good will that information do?"

"If she is dead, it will allow her family peace. If she is still alive ..."

Blake turned away to a cabinet, and without asking, poured two glasses of whisky. He handed one to Curran.

Blake turned away to look out of the window into the dark, damp night. "She's dead."

The news came like a physical blow. Curran sank into the nearest chair. "Dead? How? When?"

Blake shook his head. "I don't know. I don't want to know. That place is evil."

"But you patronized it?"

Blake let out a heavy breath and turned back to Curran. "I fancied myself a man of the world, Mr. Sutton, but my grandmother was not European, so I was never one of *them*. However, once I had enough money to make it worthwhile, the English were happy to include me in their circle. A penchant for losing at gambling helps. That got me to the Topaz Club. There are high-stakes games played there. The girls are meant to dance with the gentlemen, keep their drinks topped up, and then provide them with a reward for their endeavors."

"And Jameela?"

Blake looked away. "I am not proud of my actions in going to that place, but I am proud of the fact that I saved the woman I loved."

"How did you save her?"

Blake took a heavy swig of the whisky. "They let her go because I paid them a great deal of money," he said.

"Who did you pay?"

Blake glanced back at Curran. "How much do you know about the Topaz Club?"

"I know a man calling himself Gopal Acharya runs it."

"That is who I paid. Jameela's freedom was brought on condition that we never spoke of the Club to anyone."

"But you spoke to Mr Hume."

Blake tossed his head. "That was an error of judgment. A well-meaning friend interfered in something he knew nothing about and brought that bloody journalist into our lives. We naively assumed that speaking to a journalist from a distant newspaper would not pose any risks. After Hume left, we realized it had been a terrible mistake and when he contacted us a few weeks ago, wanting permission to pass our details to a trusted friend, we declined. I take it you are the friend he mentioned?"

"That is correct. Hume didn't betray your trust," Curran said. "I traced you through my own means. Have you been threatened?"

Blake gave a hollow laugh. "Oh yes. I came home from work and found a dog dead on the doorstep with a note."

He crossed to a desk in the corner and pulled out a drawer. He thrust a crumpled scrap of paper at Curran. The few words were typed on a cheap paper.

Speak out of turn again and you know what will happen.

"What will happen?"

Blake looked down at the contents of his glass before replying. "Our agreement with the Club will end... probably in our deaths ... or there are fates worse than death. Jameela would prefer death over being returned to the Club. So now you know why I wish you anywhere else but here."

"Why don't you go to the police?" Curran asked.

Blake laughed. "The police? Who is there we would trust among the police? They are themselves caught in the snare of the Topaz Club. They gamble and they lose, they dance with the girls ... The death of one girl is of no interest to them."

"What are the names of these officers?" Curran forced the words out between gritted teeth.

Blake shook his head. "Even if I could tell you, why would you want to know? What can you do, Mr. Sutton?" His eyes narrowed. "Why are you really here?"

"I am writing a travel guide ... and looking for the missing girl."

Blake set his empty glass on the table. "I don't believe you."

Curran shrugged. "You told Hume that Jameela recognized the description of the girl pulled from the Klang back in October. I believe her name was Lakshmi. Why was she killed?"

"I don't know, and before you ask, neither do I know who killed her."

"But her death is connected with the Topaz Club?" Curran persisted.

"All I know is that she is dead, your friend's sister is dead, and so will I be if they know I have talked to you. Now please leave my home, Mr. Sutton? You bring trouble with you, and my wife and I do not wish to attract such attention."

Blake gestured at the front door, his face set in stone.

Curran set his glass on a side table. Blake knew more than he was saying, and Curran hesitated on the brink of revealing his true identity, but knowing Curran was a policeman would probably make the situation worse.

"Thank you for the drink, Blake. You can trust me. I am not without some influence, and I wish to put an end to the Topaz Club, but I can only do so with your help, and that of your wife."

Blake shook his head and opened the front door. "We can't help you. Good evening, Mr. Sutton."

As the door closed behind Curran, somewhere in the house a baby wailed. The thin, high cry of a very young baby.

Curran stiffened and turned back, but the door had shut.

FIFTEEN

Feeling in need of a drink and company after his interview with Blake, Curran sought out the Selangor Club to find it nearly deserted.

"Quiet tonight," he remarked to Walter Stewart who was nursing a whisky at the bar.

Stewart raised his gaze from his glass and gave Curran a bleary-eyed stare. "What day is it?"

"Saturday."

"Saturday ... that's the night the bloody Topaz Club puts on a show."

Curran's breath hitched, but he kept his voice calm as he remarked, "The Topaz Club? I've heard of it. A chap I ran into in Colombo told me about it. He gave me a card."

He produced the card and waved it under Stewart's nose.

Stewart snorted. "You need more than that to get in. Personal invitation only, Sutton."

"Can you get me in?"

Stewart shook his head. "No. I have nothing to do with the place. I don't think it's the sort of place you'd want to put in your travel guide."

Curran returned the card to his wallet.

"Now I'm curious. What is the attraction?"

"Girls, gambling ... drugs. If that's your thing." Stewart returned to a contemplation of his whisky glass." He straightened and looked around the nearly empty room. "But if you are keen for a taste of what it offers, you need to get in with that crowd from the Residency. That's why they're not here tonight. That big fellow you said you knew ... the Honorable George Bullock-Steele? See if he can wangle you an invitation."

George had been weighing heavily on Curran's mind and he had concluded that for all their lifetime of enmity, George could prove quite useful.

He bought a round of drinks and sat down with Stewart.

"Nowhere better to be tonight?" he asked Stewart.

The man shook his head. "I should be at home, but I've got things to do this weekend, so I'm staying in town."

"Where's home?"

"I stayed on in the mine manager's house at the Salak South mine. Owners are happy for me to keep paying rent."

"Married?"

Stewart shook his head. "No, but I do have a rather sweet local woman who keeps house for me. She may not be socially accept-able, but she seems to like me and she's a damn sight less demanding than any memsahib. You?"

"No." Then he remembered he was a visiting Englishman with a cover story. "But I have a girl back home. Hope to tie the knot when I get back to England. Just had to get the travel done before I settled down. Can't see her taking to life in the colonies."

"Not the life for a girl out here," Stewart agreed. "This town is full of neglected wives and lonely bachelors. Sometimes the two collide."

"Are you speaking from experience?"

Stewart took a swallow of his whisky. "Trying to disentangle a clingy female is worse than having a python wrapped around your neck." He set his empty glass on the bar. "That's enough."

Curran watched the man go and ordered another whisky. The scent of frangipani drifted in through the open window and he tried to push back the memories of the woman who had waited for him on so many long, lonely nights, who had always been there, seated in her favorite chair on the verandah reading a book by the light of the kerosene lamp.

He had always thought if Li An left him, he would fall apart. Yet she *had* left him, and he was still in one piece. He swilled the whisky in the glass, the light catching on the amber eddies. It didn't matter how many whiskies he drank; nothing would change that. His heart and his pride hurt, but there had been no irreparable damage. They had begun drifting apart long before she had walked away, and he had been too blind to see it.

He left his second drink sitting on the bar and returned to his room in the hotel where he lay, fully clothed, his hands behind his head, staring at the electric fan as he formulated a plan to infiltrate the Topaz Club.

Sixteen

Sunday, 4 December

It occurred to Harriet, as she stood for the closing hymn, that Sunday service at St. Mary's could have been Sunday service in any church in any village in England. The same well-dressed English men, women and children with the same prim and proper faces, indistinguishable from the same crowd that would gather at St. Andrews or indeed the Wimbledon parish church of her childhood, St. Matthew. Without even glancing at the books in their hands, they recited the familiar words of the Book of Common Prayer and sang loudly from Hymns Ancient and Modern.

On one hand, it was reassuring and comforting to know that wherever she went in the world, the familiarity of the Church of England service would wrap around her like a warm, comforting blanket. On the other hand, she was conscious that just a stone's throw away, a mullah in the grand new mosque called his faithful to prayer, while in the Chinese and Indian temples scattered through the city, incense burned, and priests intoned their own calls to a deity. The God of the European community was an interloper. He did not belong here.

Beside her, Julian, wearing the 'dog' collar that marked him as a priest in his own right, must have sensed his sister's disquiet, casting her a quick, reassuring smile, his voice rising in his fine tenor.

They sat alone, as the Robertsons' place was in the choir stalls. Henry Robertson sat across from his wife, his gaze never leaving her. Edith, wearing a pink voile dress with black polka dots and a matching hat, seemed unconscious of her husband's adoring scrutiny. Every now and then she looked around or adjusted her hair, but never did she glance her husband's way unless he was conducting the choir.

After the service concluded, the congregation gathered outside. Julian lingered in conversation with the Reverend Grahame. Edith and Henry Robertson were busy stowing kneelers and prayer books, and Harriet found herself temporarily unattended. This provided an ideal opportunity to study the Kuala Lumpur locals. The men and women clustered in small groups, cast her curious glances, while the children in their Sunday best chased each other around the adults' legs.

"Excuse me, are you Mrs. Gordon?"

Harriet started at the sound. She turned to find herself face to face with a woman of much the same age as herself, a few silver streaks in her otherwise thick dark hair coiled in a fashionable style beneath a wide-brimmed straw hat. The woman smiled, her eyes crinkling as she held out her hand.

"Sorry, I didn't mean to startle you. How do you do? Edith Robertson tells me you are Mrs. Gordon, up from Singapore. Allow me to introduce myself. I'm Esme Prynne. I am a teacher at the Methodist Girls School. Your name is familiar to me. I believe we have a mutual friend in Lavinia Pemberthey-Smythe?"

If this woman was a friend of Lavinia Pemberthey-Smythe, then Harriet was certain she shared Lavinia's suffragist sympathies. She cast a surreptitious glance at the woman's left hand and saw no wedding band.

"A pleasure to meet you, Miss Prynne."

"Do you mind me asking, but are you close friends of the Robertsons?" Esme Prynne asked.

"Not at all," Harriet said. "We are their guests for the weekend, but this is the first time we have met. Our visit is purely professional. My brother is the headmaster of St. Thomas in Singapore."

The woman's shoulders relaxed, and a delighted smile lit up her face. "Your brother is the Reverend Julian Edwards?"

"He is."

Esme looked around. "I would love to meet him. I am a huge admirer of his work on Virgil."

"Someone has actually read it?" Harriet's surprise was quite genuine. Julian had spent long hours working on a translation and interpretation of Virgil's *Ecologues* which a highly academic publisher in Cambridge had turned into print. But the print run had been small, and Harriet had doubted anyone beyond his family and friends had ever bought a copy, let alone read it.

"I do. I am a keen student of the classics, and the Reverend brings a fresh interpretation to the ancient words that really appeals to me."

"You're in luck. Here he comes."

Julian strode across to where the two women stood, his hat in his hand and a bright, excited gleam in his eye.

"Grahame has asked me to preach the sermon at Evensong tonight," he said.

Harriet smiled. "That's very kind of him. There goes your afternoon of quiet reading."

Conscious of Esme standing beside her, she made the introduction.

"This is a terrific honor to meet you, Reverend Edwards,"

Esme said as they shook hands. "I am a classicist at heart, and I have all your translations and commentaries on the Greeks."

An unfamiliar flush rose to Julian's cheeks. "Thank you," he said. "I'm working on Virgil's *Aeneid*—"

"Miss Prynne!"

An older woman stood by the gate, beckoning Esme.

Esme started and glanced at a little wristwatch. "Oh goodness, look at the time. That's the headmistress, Miss Marsh. We need to get back to school for the boarders' lunch."

She held out her hand to Julian. "I do hope we meet again, Reverend. I would love to talk to you about Virgil and your approach to translation."

For once, Julian seemed entirely bereft of speech. "Jolly good," was all he could stammer out.

Harriet watched the woman mounting a carriage where the older woman waited, parasol raised. As she settled into her seat, Esme Prynne raised her hand in a gesture of farewell. Julian stared after the departing carriage and Harriet gave him a gentle shove.

"She seems nice," she said, giving her brother the benefit of a wide, innocent smile.

Julian coughed. "There are the Robertsons. I think we better be going. I have, as you have pointed out, a sermon to write this afternoon."

SEVENTEEN

Curran hated hospitals. He loathed the particular smell of carbolic, boiled cabbage, and linoleum polish. After the incident in Penang that had nearly taken his life, he'd spent weeks in hospital and privately considered that his stay there had greatly increased his recuperation time.

His boots echoed off the polished linoleum as he walked the length of the half-empty ward to find Jayant sitting up in bed, poking a spoon at a bowl of clear broth.

He pushed the tray away as Curran approached, his face breaking into a grin.

"Robert, how long do I have to stay here?"

Curran consulted the chart at the end of the bed. He knew enough about hospital procedures to know that Jayant was still running a fever and was days, if not weeks, away from full recovery.

"A few days yet," he said.

Jayant pulled a face and glanced at the window. "I should be out there helping you, not lying here counting the hours."

Much as he disliked hospitals, Curran found himself saying, "You are in the best place. The worst thing about these sorts of diseases is they can give you the illusion of recovery, only to knock you down again."

"You've had dengue?"

"No, but I suffer recurrent malaria. Similar."

Jayant shook his head. "Neither to be taken lightly."

"Correct."

"Do you have any news?"

Curran walked over to the window and stood looking out over the wide verandah beyond which an afternoon rainstorm lashed the trees. "I paid a visit to the Ashton Blake residence last night."

He heard his brother's sharp intake of breath. "Well?"

"The girl's not there." Curran turned back to face Jayant. "Or at least that is what Blake says. I don't believe him. It is possible that whoever controls the Topaz Club business received word of their chat with Hume and issued threats. He–they–won't talk to me."

"Did he say anything about Samrita?"

Curran took a breath. This bit was not so easy. "I'm sorry, Jayant. Blake says she is dead."

Jayant straightened his shoulders and shook his head. "No!"

Curran laid a hand on Jayant's shoulder. He intended the gesture as comforting, but when Jayant stiffened, he realized it could also be interpreted as patronizing. He withdrew his hand and stuffed it into his pocket.

Jayant buried his face in his hands. "How? Where is she?"

"I don't know. He didn't tell me."

Jayant looked up, his face creased in grief. "You must find out. I must know. These people... the murdering swine must be brought to justice."

"I'm doing my best. I will get to the truth," Curran responded, a sense of his own inadequacy washing over him.

A bell rang, and a loud female voice declared visiting hours were over.

As he turned to leave, Curran looked back at his brother. "Oh, I took your advice and sent a telegram to Cuscaden this morning."

A smile twitched at the corners of Jayant's lips. "That is good. See you tomorrow, Robert?"

Curran's smile echoed his brother's. "Tomorrow."

As he walked away, he thought back to his visit to Ashton Blake and the cry of the baby. It could just as easily have been a child of one of the servants, but it had come from inside the house, not the servants' quarters. Would Jameela have left a very young baby to go visit relatives?

He doubted it.

EIGHTEEN

After lunch, Harriet left Julian sitting at the table on the verandah, deep in contemplation of the gospel of the prodigal son for his sermon. It was a subject he had preached on many times, so she suspected he would spend his afternoon dozing on one of the well-cushioned planter's chairs.

Edith appeared, dressed in a dark green skirt with matching waistcoat over a light muslin blouse, topped with a straw hat trimmed with a green ribbon. The woman, Harriet decided, had an unlimited wardrobe.

She, herself, had dressed in her workaday dark blue skirt and white cotton blouse with a plain straw hat.

Edith set the wooden box she carried on the table. Julian looked up and obligingly moved his papers. With two hands, Edith undid the catches and lifted the lid.

"It's a Webley Mark 4," Edith said.

It was a similar weapon to that on issue to the Straits Settlements Police, but Curran carried an earlier model, with a longer muzzle he had kept from his army service.

Henry Robertson put his hands on his hips and grimaced as

he looked down at the revolver in its velvet-lined box. "I told Edith it wasn't necessary. I don't like guns of any sort."

"And I told you, Henry, it's about familiarity," Edith said. "The more confident you are in handling it, the better you will feel about it. Imagine if you had been out with Noel and you came across that giant *selandang*. What would you have done?"

Henry Robertson's eyes didn't move from the weapon in the box as he said, "I think the chances of my ever being out in the bush with your brother, let alone encountering giant *selandang* is extremely unlikely, my dear, but if you insist."

A carriage arrived at two and, leaving Julian to the contemplation of the prodigal son, they traveled the short distance to a shooting range, a little way out of town.

The shooting range comprised a long range for rifle shooting and a shorter range for handguns, and every stand was busy with both men and women. The English and their guns, Harriet thought as she followed Edith, all efficiency and business, and far from the flibbertigibbet of the previous day to the lane allocated to them.

Edith set the box on the table and took out the revolver. With practiced efficiency, she put six bullets into the star-shaped loader, flicked the weapon open, and dropped the rounds into the chambers.

Curran would be impressed, Harriet thought.

"So easy to load," Edith said. "That's what I like about a Webley."

She handed the weapon to her husband. "Now remember what I told you, double-handed grip ... That's it. Now ... steady."

The Webley fired both single and automatic action and it was clear Henry Robertson was not comfortable with either. He jerked the weapon up and fired with his eyes closed. His wife quickly lost patience with him.

"Really, Henry, it's not hard. Watch me."

Edith, on the other hand, had a steady hand and a clear eye

and her shots hit the target with unerring accuracy. For a diminutive creature with an eye for clothes and hats, Edith Robertson certainly knew her way around weapons.

Harriet took her turn and while moderately more confident than Henry Robertson, she didn't have Edith's practiced hand.

An hour and a half in the heat was enough and Robertson called an end to the excursion, as the first drops of a tropical downpour threatened. They had kept the carriage waiting for them to finish, but it was past four before they returned to the bungalow all wet to the bone.

Julian met them on the verandah. "I was getting concerned," he said.

"No need," Robertson said.

"How did the practice go?" Julian asked.

Robertson pulled a face. "I think if I am ever confronted by an intruder, I will be lucky to give him a bad scare. Probably more likely to hit him if I threw the weapon at him!"

"Nonsense, Henry. A little more practice is all you need," Edith said. "I am drenched, and my hands are filthy. Just look at the time. We must hurry to wash and change before Evensong."

As she bustled inside, Edith set the box containing the Webley on the bookshelf on the verandah. Her husband followed her into the house, leaving Julian and Harriet.

"How was it?" Julian asked.

"Another strange afternoon," Harriet said in a low voice. "I'll tell you about it later."

She inspected her hands, black with the powder from the weapon. "Right now, I need to clean up and change for church."

NINETEEN

Evensong was a repeat of the morning service with the same faces in the same pews, the same familiar hymns and words. Edith, in her pink spotted dress and hat, once again joined the choir with her husband directing. In her frills and bows, it was almost impossible to believe this was the same woman who had handled a revolver with such practiced efficiency only a few hours earlier.

With Julian participating in the service, Harriet sat alone until Esme Prynne slipped into the pew beside her.

"Sir Reginald takes notes of who is absent," she whispered to Harriet.

Unlike the morning service, the Resident for Selangor State, Henry Belfield, and the Resident General, Sir Reginald Watson attended Evensong without fail. Together with their respective entourages, they took up several of the front pews.

An enthusiastic and off-key bellowing of hymns drew Harriet's attention to a large man in the Watson party.

"Who is that man?" Harriet whispered to Esme.

"He and his wife are visiting from England. I believe she is a cousin of Lady Watson." Esme frowned. "The Honorable George Bullock-Steele. Heir to the Earl of Alcester."

Harriet dropped her prayer book. Curran's *bête noir*, his cousin George, was here in Kuala Lumpur.

At the conclusion of the service, Esme had to hurry away and Harriet busied herself helping Edith collect the prayer books and hymnals while Julian chatted to the Reverend Grahame.

"Excellent sermon," she overheard Grahame saying. "It even kept Sir Henry awake. Mine just seem to send him to sleep."

Edith asked Harriet for the time. Harriet glanced at the little watch she wore pinned to her blouse. "It is getting on for six," she said.

"Are you ready to leave?" Henry Robertson approached them. "I thought we might have time for a quick drink at the Club as we're not due at Haycocks's until seven thirty."

They strolled across the Padang to the Selangor Club. Robertson was met with a warm reception, while his wife was accorded the barest of polite greetings.

As they passed the door to the gentlemen's only bar, Harriet glanced inside. A tall, bearded man stood at the bar, watching the comings and goings. For a moment, his gaze met hers and her heart gave a leap.

She leaned into her brother. "Julian, the man at the bar—with the beard. It's Curran."

Julian frowned. "I don't see anyone. Which man?"

"There ... Oh ..." The bearded man had gone. "I would swear it was Curran."

The corners of his eyes crinkled. "Maybe you just see what you want to see, Harri."

"Don't patronize me, Ju. I tell you it was Curran."

But as they took their seats, she wondered if Julian may have been correct, and she was conjuring Curran. He'd been on her mind as she fired the Webley that afternoon, that was all.

The party ordered drinks and, as she had the previous day, Edith's gaze kept straying to the entrance.

"Oh, look, Henry," she said, her face lighting up. "It's Mr Stewart. Fancy seeing him here on a Sunday night."

Walter Stewart greeted Robertson with a hearty handshake, renewed the acquaintance with Harriet, and was introduced to Julian. He acknowledged Edith with a quick nod of the head.

"Unusual to see you here on a Sunday, Stewart," Robertson said.

"I'm having dinner with friends at the Empire," Stewart replied. "It won't be a late night. I'm due to head up country to check out a tin mine in Perak tomorrow." He turned to Julian. "What brings you to KL?"

"An invitation from Robertson," Julian replied. "I'm head-master of St Thomas in Singapore—professional colleagues and all that."

"Reverend Edwards is a keen cricketer," Robertson said. "We watched the lads playing the Chinese school yesterday."

Stewart pulled a face. "Not my game. I prefer rugby."

Indeed, he looks like a rugby player with his solid frame, Harriet thought.

"Mrs. Gordon?"

Harriet excused herself from Julian to turn to Edith Robertson's mother, Mary Chapman, accompanied by two younger women.

"I saw you in church this evening. Your brother gave an excellent sermon. Have you enjoyed your stay?" Mrs. Chapman enquired.

"It's been a lovely break from Singapore. I have had little opportunity to travel since I arrived in Singapore back in January."

Mary Chapman looked around the room. "You will find us a much closer society than Singapore. Personally, I find Ceylon a more congenial place, but my husband's heart is here so here we stay. Let me introduce you to my daughters."

Not my other daughters, Harriet noted, as she greeted Mrs. Hickey and Mrs. Bird. Both women were older than Edith by a few years and did not appear to bear much resemblance to their fey, fair-haired sister.

"I do hope Edith is looking after you," Mrs. Hickey said.

"She has been an excellent hostess," Harriet said with a smile. Faced with Mrs. Chapman's open hostility to her youngest daughter, she felt curiously protective of Edith.

Mrs. Hickey's gaze drifted to Edith sitting by herself, staring into the last of her gin and tonic. "Don't tell me that is another new hat!"

Mary Chapman rolled her eyes. "Edith spends so much time in the millinery department of John Little's, some believe that she works there. Small wonder poor Henry agreed to her taking the job at the Methodist Girls' School. A Chapman woman working ... whoever heard such a thing."

The two younger women tittered in agreement.

As if conscious her mother was talking of her, Edith set her glass down and rose to join them. She greeted her mother and sisters, who acknowledged her with the politeness reserved for mere acquaintances. Harriet thought of the effusive hugs and kisses she would have shared with her sister, Mary.

"When do you return to Singapore?" Mrs. Chapman asked.

"Tomorrow. We are taking the day train so we can see something of the scenery."

"Such a tedious journey. It has been a pleasure to meet you again, Mrs. Gordon. Safe journey. Come girls," Mary Chapman said and turned away.

"I've just ordered us another gin and tonic," Edith said, and they resumed their seats at the table.

Harriet had settled with her drink when one of the bar staff approached her.

"I beg your pardon, Mem," he said and handed her a folded slip of paper.

She took it, recognizing at once the scrawl on the outside: *Mrs. Gordon,* written in Robert Curran's appalling handwriting. Her heart jumped as she opened the folded paper.

I'm outside at the far end of the terrace, the note read.

"Who is sending you notes?" Edith demanded.

Harriet cast around. "Your mother wishes to have another word," she lied.

Edith pulled a face. "Probably wants to know what I am up to. Honestly, I swear she spies on me. Say only nice things, Harriet."

Harriet smiled and assured Edith of her complicity as she rose and made a dignified exit.

A man stood in the shadows at the far end of the terrace, looking out at the Padang, a cigarette in one hand and the other in his jacket pocket.

Harriet slowed her step until she was almost upon him.

"Curran?" He half turned and for a moment her breath caught. "I thought it was you I saw in the bar."

"Good evening, Harriet."

"It's good to see you."

"And you."

"I don't like the beard," she said.

He rubbed his chin. "Neither do I, but needs must."

"Were you also at the Batu Caves yesterday afternoon?"

His eyes widened slightly. "You saw me there?"

"I wasn't certain. I'm glad to see you, Curran." The words came out in a rush.

They stood in awkward silence for a long moment.

"Did you know your cousin George is in KL? I saw him in church tonight," Harriet said.

"Yes. There is apparently no escaping anyone in this town. I have spoken to him. I don't trust him to tie his own shoelaces, but hopefully, he will keep quiet." He ground out his cigarette on the low wall that separated the verandah from the Padang. "What brings you and your brother up here?"

"Julian has been invited to consider a position at the Prince Alfred School," Harriet said. "We are staying with the headmaster and his wife but don't worry about us. We leave tomorrow."

Curran nodded. "No offence, Harriet, but that's a relief. When I saw you this evening, I thought I better let you in on my current alias. Just in case."

"An alias? How mysterious. Who are you?"

"Mr. Ronald Sutton, gentleman and adventurer, writing a travel guide."

"I see. Is Jayant with you?"

"He's in the hospital. Dengue."

"Oh no, will he be all right?" Harriet said with genuine alarm. Dengue could be a killer.

"I'm hopeful. He seemed better today."

"And are you any closer to finding your sister?"

Curran paused. "Yes, and no. I tracked her to the ... establishment where she had been, but I think we are going to have to face the fact that she may well be dead. Everything is pointing that way."

"I'm sorry."

He sighed. "So am I."

She frowned, knowing Curran too well. He was not telling her everything. "But it's not just about your sister. The disguise, the alias ... there's more, isn't there, Curran?"

He stuffed his hands in his pockets. "Confidentially, Harriet, I'm doing a job for the Federated Malay Police."

She had to resist an urge to crow. "I knew there had to be something. It was all too convenient just letting you go on suspension."

He held up a warning finger. "Not a word to anyone, not even Julian."

"I am offended you would think that of me. What is the job?"

"I can't tell you, but it is tied to the Topaz Club."

Harriet nodded, suppressing a thousand questions that bubbled up inside her. "Very well, I understand."

He smiled, that achingly familiar smile that crinkled his eyes at the corners. "I trust you implicitly, Mrs. Gordon. How are things in Singapore?"

"Keogh disbanded the department. Singh is back on traffic duty, Musa has been sent back to Changi, and as for me—"

"I know, Harriet. Keogh is a bastard, but I'll see it righted when I get back."

"And when do you get back?"

He shrugged. "When this assignment is finished." He gestured at the door where the light spilled out onto the terrace. "You better get back to your friends before you're missed."

"Curran—" She cut herself off. "Be careful."

"You know me, Harriet."

"I do. That's why I'm asking you to be careful." She laid a hand on his chest. "It's good to see you. I ... we've all been concerned."

He looked down at her hand, and she snatched it away.

"It's good to know I have friends," he said, lightly reaching out and touching the sleeve of her dress.

"You do. Come home safely."

As she turned to leave, she glanced back. "Where are you staying?"

"The Empire Hotel. Room 15 if you need me."

Julian met her at the door. "There you are! I was getting worried. Who were you talking to... it didn't look like Edith's mother—"

Harriet dropped her voice. "Curran. It was Curran. Say nothing, Julian. He wasn't here, we haven't seen him and if we do encounter him again, we're strangers."

"But—"

"I'll explain later."

Harriet apologized to the Robertsons for her absence. No one expressed any curiosity as to where she'd been, but she was conscious of Julian watching her.

On returning to the bungalow, Harriet retired to her room to dress for dinner. Through the walls came the muffled sound of an argument coming from the Robertsons' bedroom and on emerging onto the verandah, a red-faced Henry Robertson summoned a humorless smile.

"Edith is feeling unwell," he said. "She would prefer to stay here and write letters. I hope you don't mind being the only female in our party, Mrs. Gordon."

"Not at all. I hardly need a chaperone, Mr. Robertson."

His slender shoulders rose and fell and this time the smile was not forced. "Thank you for understanding."

"I'll just look in on your wife," Harriet said.

Edith lay in the darkened room, lit only by a kerosene lamp turned down low. She had changed into a loose peignoir of ruffles and lace and reclined on the bed, a dampened flannel over her eyes.

"Is there anything I can get you?" Harriet asked.

"No, no... I'll be fine shortly, but I think I need to stay at home. Dottie can't be left with just the cook. Amah and the boy have the night off. Do have fun."

Harriet bid her goodnight and joined the men outside. A hired carriage arrived, and Julian helped her in. As they drove away from the bungalow, Harriet glanced back at the silent house and an icy chill ran down her spine.

TWENTY

Curran stood in the shadows on the verandah of the Selangor Club watching Harriet return to the brightly lit rooms. He lit another cigarette and watched the smoke curl away.

He supposed that it was inevitable that he would run into someone who would recognize him. George's appearance had shaken him to the core, but Harriet and Julian's presence in KL was somehow reassuring.

He took a drag on the cigarette and reflected that it had lightened something in him to see Harriet. She could always be relied on for sensible insight into his cases and ... well ... just for being Harriet Gordon.

He finished his cigarette and stepped back inside the Club, relieved to see Harriet and Julian and their hosts had left.

"Sutton!"

Curran winced as he turned to be confronted by George Bullock-Steele.

"Saw you when I came in. Thought you'd left for the night."

Curran forced a smile. "Good evening. Drink?"

"The usual," George said, as if he assumed Curran would recall what his 'usual' had been. Curran ordered two beers.

George downed half without taking a breath. "One of the downsides of staying with the Resident is he is a stickler for attending Evensong," his cousin groused. "As if that wasn't bad enough, they had some visiting cleric from Singapore give a long-winded sermon. I thought he'd never finish. In my opinion, no sermon should be longer than ten minutes."

"Reverend Edwards?" Curran ventured.

"That's the chap. Do you know him?"

"Yes. He plays cricket for the Singapore club," Curran said.

"Don't tell me you still throw the bat around? Getting a bit long in the tooth, aren't you?"

Curran refrained from commenting that his cousin, who was much the same age, could probably do with some regular exercise himself.

He looked around. Satisfied no one was within hearing distance, Curran dropped his voice.

"George, I have a favor to ask you."

George snorted. "Me? I don't think I owe you any favors."

"Hear me out," Curran said between gritted teeth.

"Very well. What is it?"

"You mentioned you are a member of the Topaz Club. Are you able to introduce me?"

"I've lost enough money up there for them to welcome me with open arms," George smirked. "You up for some sport?" he added in a low voice, dripping with innuendo.

"That's not what I asked, George. I just need an introduction. I have this." He produced the card he'd learned only got him halfway to the door of the Club.

"Where'd you get that?" George asked.

"Doesn't matter."

"Is this police business?"

Curran hesitated. "Yes," he said.

George's eyes widened. "I say, some excitement at last. Anything to help the law." He frowned. "It will have to be Tuesday. We've got to attend some frightful reception up at the big house tomorrow evening."

"Can you collect me from the Empire Hotel?"

George nodded.

"Dress code?"

"Tropical evening dress and, Cur ... Sutton. No weapons. They will search you." George glanced at his watch. "Better get going. Sunday night supper and bridge."

"Sounds fun," Curran said with a smile.

George scowled. "I'm useless at bridge. Frankly, can't wait to get on the boat back home. I'm missing the hunting season." He brightened. "Although I am promised a trip up to the Highlands after Christmas. Might bag myself a tiger. That would look good in the hall back home."

Curran shook his head and let his cousin go with a wave of his hand.

TWENTY-ONE

It was a short drive to Edward Haycocks's bungalow on Brickfields Road, about a mile and a half from the school.

"This was Edith's and my home before the Buchanans went on long leave," Robertson said as the carriage turned into the driveway of the neat bungalow. "Haycocks is a good sort, and he lodged with us for some six months before we moved."

"What will happen when the Buchanans return?" Harriet asked.

Robertson shrugged. "I suppose we will have to move back. That won't please Edith. She has rather enjoyed having the head-master's house to herself."

Edward Haycocks came down the front steps to greet them. A younger man, probably more Harriet's age than Julian's, he had a shock of fair hair and a broad, cheerful countenance.

"No Mrs. R. this evening?" He addressed Robertson.

"Edith sends her apologies. It's been a long day, and she's feeling somewhat under the weather," Robertson said.

Robertson introduced Harriet and Haycocks waved them up the steps to the verandah. "Welcome, welcome," he said. "We'll be dining on the verandah, although I suspect we are in for some rain this evening. I can hear the thunder."

As the headmaster went ahead, Haycocks escorted Harriet up the stairs. "Mrs. R is always under the weather," he muttered. "Perfectly amiable woman most of the time, but she can be a veritable shrew when the mood takes her."

Harriet cast the man a sharp glance. "I suspect you are speaking out of turn, Mr. Haycocks."

He had the grace to color. "I am. Unforgivable."

The rain that had lingered all afternoon and evening began afresh about nine o'clock, but it was dry on the verandah and rather pleasant listening to the splash of the raindrops on the tin roof. As the only woman in the party, Harriet set herself to endure an evening of discussion of rugby, cricket, and hunting or, given the occupations of the three men, education. She let the conversation on such mundane matters as the teaching of Latin and Ancient Greek drift over her.

The pleasant back and forth of conversation came to an abrupt halt as an Indian man in a white dhoti came running up the drive. He stopped, panting heavily, at the foot of the steps.

"Good God, it's my cook," Robertson said, rising to greet the intruder. "What is it, man?"

The man rolled his eyes, gesticulating wildly, "*Mem panggil lekas, lekas.*"

Harriet's Malay was rudimentary whereas Julian, who had lived in Singapore for over two years and had a natural ear for language, spoke it fluently.

"What's he saying?" Harriet whispered to Julian.

"The Mem says to come quickly," Julian interpreted.

"What's happened?" Robertson asked the man in English.

"Dead ... the *tuan* is dead," the cook's voice grew higher and higher in his agitation.

"What do you mean the *tuan* is dead?" Haycocks said.

But there was no more sense to be got from the cook, who

hunkered down on his haunches, his arms wrapped around himself, wailing.

Robertson summoned the carriage and gave orders to return at speed to the school with Robertson, Haycock, Harriet, and Julian. Harriet had to hold Julian's arm as the carriage driver whipped the poor horse into a canter.

As they turned in through the school gate, the feeling of impending doom that had haunted Harriet all evening intensified.

The previous evening, Edith had proudly pointed out the single electrical light that illuminated the cozy living area on the verandah. Now, darkness had engulfed the house.

As they neared the entry into the headmaster's house, a wraith appeared out of the darkness and the rain. The horse stopped abruptly, going down on its haunches and jolting everyone in the carriage as a woman in a pale dress, her hair disordered and hanging loose in long, damp tendrils, staggered toward them, holding out her hands as if in supplication.

"*Hantu!*" the driver yelped.

Harriet knew that word—ghost!

"Edith!" Henry Robertson jumped from the carriage, almost before it had come to a halt.

"Blood ... blood ..." Edith said before collapsing into her husband's arms. "Oh, Henry, I've shot a man."

Henry Robertson gathered his wife in his arms as Edward Haycocks jumped down and collected the lamp from the carriage. With Haycocks leading the way, they all walked toward the house.

They did not have to go far before the full horror confronted them. In the furthest reaches of Haycocks's light, a large form—a man, made anonymous in the rain and the dark, lay half on the carriageway and half on the grass lawn.

Even Harriet, who was not unfamiliar with dead bodies, gasped.

"Stay here," Julian ordered. "Come with me, Haycocks."

The two men ran across to the prone man. Julian hunched down beside him and reached out, feeling for a pulse in the man's neck. He looked across to where Harriet waited with Robertson, an arm around his wife, and shook his head.

"Who is it?" Robertson asked, his voice high and tight.

"It's Mr. Stewart," Edith replied, her voice muffled against her husband's chest. "I shot Mr. Stewart."

Over the top of his wife's head, Robertson's eyes widened, and his Adam's apple bobbed and his voice shook as he said, "Good God! What was Walter Stewart doing here?" He turned his wife to face him, grasping her by the forearms. "Edith, just tell me what happened."

"I don't remember!" Edith wailed. "It's all a blank. Henry, you must believe me!" She buried her face into her husband's shirt again, sobbing as he stroked her hair.

"It's all right, Kitty Kat," he said. "It will be all right."

No, it won't, Harriet thought, unable to avert her gaze from the fallen man. Haycocks stood behind Julian, who still knelt by the body—in prayer, she supposed.

Robertson disengaged from his wife. "Mrs. Gordon will look after you. I will take the carriage and fetch the police."

Edith looked up at him, her eyes wide. "The police?"

"Sweetheart, you shot a man. The police have to know, but I am sure there is a good reason and they'll understand."

Edith turned to Harriet, and Harriet put an arm around the woman's shoulder. "You are soaked through, Edith. Come up to the verandah and I'll find a shawl for you."

Edith sagged against her, and Harriet signaled for Julian or Haycocks to assist her. Julian didn't move, so it was Haycocks who came to her assistance, supporting the half-fainting woman up to the verandah.

Harriet fumbled for the light cord and the single electric bulb flashed to life, illuminating what looked like the scene of a struggle. The wicker table stacked with books had been overturned, scattering the books across the carpet. An unmistakable trail of blood drops led from the front door to the steps.

"Tea ... we need tea," Harriet said as Haycocks settled Edith into a chair.

But there was no one to make tea. They had left the cook in the care of the servants at the house on Brickfields Road.

Leaving Haycocks to watch over Edith, Harriet checked firstly on the child, who was still asleep, before going to Edith's bed chamber. Discarded dresses littered the floor and it took some time to locate a Kashmir shawl. This she carried out to the verandah, wrapping it around the woman's shoulders.

Edith clutched at the wrap with fingers that were blackened with the powder used in the shells of the Webley. They left ugly, black smears on the pale lamb's wool. In the light, Harriet could now see dark smears on Edith's face and splashed across the sodden skirt of a once pretty, white evening gown decorated with sprigs of green flowers. A lovely dress with a low-cut neckline ... not the dress Edith had been wearing when the rest of the party left for dinner at Haycocks's home.

Blood.

Harriet shuddered.

"I must wash," Edith said. "I need to wash—"

She made to rise, but Harriet gently restrained her.

"You rest, Edith. The police will be here soon, and it's important that you don't wash away any evidence."

Edith blinked. "Evidence?"

She looked at her hands in a manner that reminded Harriet of Lady Macbeth. She almost expected Edith to quote: *Out, damned spot! Out, I say! What, will these hands ne'er be clean? Here's the smell of the blood still: all the perfumes of Arabia will not sweeten this little hand.*

"I'll pour us some brandy," Haycocks said. "I know where it's kept."

"Try not to touch anything and don't step in the—!" Harriet

indicated the trail of blood spots. Conscious she sounded harsh, she added, "I used to work for the Straits Settlements Police. I know the police will want the scene as undisturbed as possible."

"The scene ..." Haycocks murmured, looking around and blinking rapidly behind his glasses.

"Just brandy or whisky and a couple of glasses," Harriet added.

She nodded to Julian, who had come up to the verandah, shaking water from his hair before turning back to the weeping woman.

"Mrs. Robertson, what happened after we left for dinner?" Julian asked in what Harriet called his 'best vicar's voice', pulling up a chair beside the woman.

Edith took a deep, shuddering breath. "My headache improved, so I rose and changed, took a little supper and I was writing letters when Walter Stewart arrived. I told him Henry was not at home. I said if it was important, he would find Henry at Mr Haycocks' home. He said it could wait. We talked about this and that." Her gaze went to the river. "We discussed the river rising and the possibility of the house flooding. I asked why he never went to church. He said he was agnostic, and I said, so is Henry. Then I got up to find a book of Henry's. That was when he ... he grabbed me around the waist with one arm. He ... started to pull up my skirt. Harriet, I told him to stop, but he wouldn't. He pushed me toward the door to the living room where there's a daybed. He made it quite clear that his intentions were not ... were not honorable. As I struggled, I put my hand on the revolver." Her lower lip quivered, and her blue eyes filled with tears. "I fired at him. He released me and turned away and I ..."

Haycocks appeared at Harriet's elbow with a decanter of whisky and a stack of glassware. Harriet nodded, and he poured them each a glass.

"Did you hurt him with that shot?" Harriet asked.

Edith wrapped both hands around the glass Haycocks handed her and took a sip.

"I think so, he staggered and clutched his side ... he ..." She looked from Harriet to Haycocks. "I can't remember what happened next."

"Where's the revolver now, Edith?" Julian asked

"I don't know. I threw it away," Edith said. The tears were flowing now, making tracks in the drying blood on her cheeks. "I want Henry. I want it all to go away. Papa will be so cross with me."

"How far away is the police station?" Harriet heard Julian ask Haycocks in a low voice.

"Not far. I can hear them coming now," Haycocks replied.

Harriet had been involved in such situations before and although she knew what to expect, amidst police, doctors, mortuary wagons, lights, and noise, it all felt as surreal as if she were a player in a stage production.

Haycocks and Julian went out into the night to talk to the arrivals, and Harriet tried not to look as the lights of torches and lanterns circled the body and the shadows of men moved like carrion crows around the mortal remains of Walter Stewart.

One man detached himself from the crowd and strode across to the house. A sturdy man in a khaki uniform with three pips on his shoulders mounted the steps. Harriet wanted the man to be Curran, but this man was a stranger.

He gave his name as Detective Inspector Wheeler and asked for her identity.

"Mrs. Gordon. My brother and I are houseguests of the Robertsons," she replied.

Wheeler turned to Edith Robertson, fixing her with an unblinking gaze. "And this is Mrs. Robertson?"

"It is," Harriet said, although she suspected Wheeler would have known Edith Robertson. The English community was too small. They all knew each other.

"Mrs. Robertson, I need to speak with you. You can leave us, Mrs. Gordon, gentlemen."

Edith grasped Harriet's hand. "Stay with me, Harriet."

"This woman is clearly in shock, Inspector. We would prefer to stay," Julian said.

Wheeler's hard gaze took in the three witnesses. "Very well. Her husband will be here shortly. I left him making a preliminary report at the police station."

In contrast to Curran, Wheeler had a square jaw and a ginger mustache, and his shoulders strained the material of his khaki jacket. Where Curran would have adopted a gentle manner with a witness such as Edith, Wheeler appeared to prefer a more formal approach compounded as he put his hands behind his back, the formality of the 'at ease' position adding to the discomfort of the situation.

"Mr. Stewart is dead," Wheeler said. "I've examined the body and there appear to be multiple gunshot wounds, but as to the official cause of death, that's up to the doctor to determine. Your husband says you have confessed to shooting the man. Is that blood on your cheek?"

Edith obligingly turned her face to the light. "And my dress," she added.

"What happened here, Mrs. Robertson?"

Edith launched into the same story.

"And where is the revolver?" Wheeler asked when she had finished.

"I ... I threw it away." Edith gestured to the side of the house. "Somewhere out there."

Wheeler nodded to his constable. "Search the grounds." He turned back to Edith. "Hold up your hands, Mrs. Robertson."

Edith held up her slender, fine-boned hands. Wheeler clasped her by the right wrist with no gentleness and turned it over.

"Gunpowder residue," he said.

Edith straightened. "I am not denying I fired the weapon," she said, "but it was in self-defense. The man attacked me. He would have ... would have molested me. There was no one here to come to my aid."

"And you just happened to have a loaded revolver handy?" Wheeler could hardly disguise his skepticism.

"As Mrs. Gordon can tell you, my husband and I had been practicing on the range this afternoon. Neither of us had time to check its state when we returned home. I just placed it on the bookshelf and went to church." She turned large, blue eyes welling with tears on Harriet. "Mrs. Gordon? You were there, you can back me up?"

Wheeler turned to Harriet, who gave a curt nod of her head. "It's true," she said, the uncomfortable feeling that she was being used to create an alibi intensifying.

Her answer seemed to satisfy Wheeler. He turned back to Edith.

"I have to get the doctor to examine you," he said.

Edith gave a small cry. "Why?"

"To check if there is any evidence of," he cleared his throat, "molestation or attempted assault of that description."

"He didn't ... I ..." Edith had turned chalk white.

"Nevertheless, it should be done. And I'll need that dress as evidence. Perhaps you could adjourn to your bedroom. The doctor will be with you presently."

Julian cleared his throat. "Inspector, my sister and I have a booking to return to Singapore tomorrow morning."

Wheeler shook his head. "I'm sorry, Reverend, but I must insist you remain in Kuala Lumpur for the time being. There are statements to be taken and your presence will be required at the hearing of the charges. Hopefully, that will be as early as tomorrow morning, but you will need to delay your return." He looked up and down the verandah. "I believe you've been staying with the Robertsons? I would advise you to seek alternative accommodation tonight. Under the circumstances, it would be inappropriate for you to remain here."

Harriet and Julian exchanged a quick glance. Staying in a house where a murder had just occurred did indeed seem highly inappropriate.

"Of course, Inspector. Anything we can do to assist," Julian said.

Wheeler turned to Harriet. "I've been trying to place the name. Are you by any chance the Mrs. Gordon who is employed by the Straits Settlements Police?"

"I was," Harriet said. "Your Inspector Keogh no longer required my services."

Something flickered in Wheeler's eyes, but if Keogh's name provoked any strong reaction, he kept it well hidden.

"I can assume, therefore, you have some basic knowledge of police processes?" Wheeler said.

Harriet nodded.

"Then could I prevail on you to assist Mrs. Robertson?"

He left unspoken the words... And make sure no evidence is destroyed.

"Of course, Inspector."

She turned to Edith. "Come, Edith, let's get you to your bedroom. The doctor will be in to see you shortly."

Edith leaned heavily on Harriet as she assisted the woman into her bedroom.

"He loved this dress," Edith murmured as Harriet undid the hooks and the skirt fell to the floor.

As she folded the damp clothing, an uncomfortable thought crossed Harriet's mind.

Was Edith referring to her husband, Henry Robertson—or to Walter Stewart, the man she had just shot?

Edith ran the light material of the sleeves through her fingers as she unfastened the bodice. "I love wearing this dress in the evening. It's so much cooler than any of my day dresses," she said.

"So pretty ... Ruined now. I suppose they won't give it back to me."

Beneath the dress, Edith wore only a thin chemise, stockings and garters, black patent evening shoes with silver buckles — and nothing else except an expensive perfume. Harriet caught the unmistakable scent of Lily of the Valley in the warm air.

The nagging feeling that something did not ring true prickled at the back of Harriet's neck.

A pretty, low-cut evening dress, perfume, fancy shoes ... yet no corset and, most significantly, no drawers? Apart from being an odd choice of clothing for an evening alone, even in the tropical heat, a lady would not dress in such an unseemly manner unless ... unless she had an assignation with someone. Her lover?

Harriet suggested Edith lie down on the bed to wait for the doctor. She pulled a sheet over the woman. With her fair, still damp hair falling like a cloud around her head and her hands neatly folded over the top of the sheet, Edith looked for all the world like a carved marble image on a tomb. Only the smear of blood on her cheek and her blackened fingers told a different story.

"Don't leave me, Harriet," Edith clutched at Harriet's arm.

"I'll stay for a little while, but the police have ordered Julian and I to leave the house," Harriet said, conscious it hadn't been much of an order, more of a polite suggestion.

As Harriet bent over her, brushing the hair away from Edith's face, in the dim electric light, she made out something else, a faint mark on the woman's neck and darkening bruises on her forearms as if someone had held her with considerably more force than Henry Robertson had exerted.

Harriet dismissed her earlier suspicions and chided herself for them. She, as a woman, should not assume the worst. Here was clear evidence of some sort of altercation. What if Edith was telling the truth?

TWENTY-TWO

On seeing the doctor, who was known to her, Edith burst into tears and the doctor requested Harriet remain for the examination.

Despite the sobs and hiccups, he remained professional and thorough, and when Harriet pointed out the bruises on Edith's arms and neck, he nodded and jotted in his notebook. But he found no other signs of what he tactfully referred to as 'interference' or bruising on her legs that would fully substantiate Edith's story of assault.

By the time he had finished, Edith was hysterical. Screaming and crying out for her husband.

The doctor administered a strong sedative and, with a quirk of his eyebrow, left Harriet to deal with the agitated woman.

Fortunately, Edith lapsed into a drugged sleep within minutes and Harriet could leave the room with a profound sense of relief.

She found the police inspector on the verandah, sitting with Julian and Robertson. Haycocks had returned home.

She handed Wheeler the bundle of Edith's clothes and slumped into the nearest chair, drained and longing for the oblivion of sleep.

"The doctor has given her a sedative. She's asleep," she said, addressing Henry Robertson.

The poor man looked as if he had aged ten years, his face grooved by deep channels of distress and strain.

In the damp world beyond the light of the verandah, shadowy figures still roamed the grounds. She watched as Stewart's body was loaded onto the mortuary cart. In life, he had been a big man, and his booted feet protruded from the end of the cart. It seemed an undignified last journey.

Wheeler nodded. "Thank you for your assistance, Mrs. Gordon. In normal circumstances, I would have taken her into custody, but there seems little point. I will leave a couple of constables on duty for the night."

"Why?" Robertson asked. "I can look after her."

Wheeler gave him a withering look. "To ensure her safety, Mr. Robertson." He looked at Julian. "If you and your sister would care to fetch your bags, Reverend, I can give you both a ride to the Empire Hotel. Hopefully, they will have rooms available."

It was nearly midnight before Harriet climbed gratefully into her bed at the hotel. Despite her exhaustion, her restless mind kept going over the events of the weekend. She tossed and turned for an hour or more, conscious that she needed to talk through her muddled thoughts with someone who understood ... someone who was in room 15 of this very hotel.

She pulled a skirt and blouse on over her nightdress and tied her hair back. Barefoot, she crept through the silent corridors of the hotel, down two flights of stairs to the grander rooms on the first floor.

Outside the door, with the number 15 displayed in gleaming brass, she paused. What did she think she was doing, creeping around like a thief in the night—or worse, like a woman on a secret assignation? What if she was seen? She glanced up and down the gloomy corridor. Someone a few doors down coughed, and she started.

Now or never.

She tapped lightly, hoping Curran was not a heavy sleeper. When he didn't come to the door, she tapped again a little louder. This time she heard movement. The light did not come on, but the heavy tread of footsteps approached the door.

It opened a crack.

"Who is it?"

"Me ... Harriet."

The door swung open, and Curran grabbed her arm, pulling her inside, as he shut the door. "Did anyone see you?"

"No."

She saw with a jolt that he held his Webley in his right hand. He laid it on the table and ran a hand through his tousled hair. He was barefooted and wore crumpled trousers and a shirt only half tucked in, and she felt a pang of guilt for having disturbed his sleep.

He peered at her with bleary eyes. "What in God's name are you doing here, Harriet?"

"There was a shooting tonight. Edith Robertson shot Walter Stewart at the headmaster's bungalow at the school."

He stared at her. "Walter Stewart?"

"Do you know him?"

"I met him a couple of times at the Club. How? Why?"

"I don't know ..." Tears sprang to Harriet's eyes, and she sat down heavily on the nearest chair, covering her face in her hands.

Curran hunkered down in front of her and took her hands in his. "Tell me everything that happened. Spare nothing."

She'd been through this before—several times now. But this time it felt personal. If her friend Doctor Euan Mackenzie had been present, he would probably have suggested she was suffering from a delayed shock.

Her words tripped and raced as she tried to put together the events that had led to that ghostly, blood-spattered figure stepping out in front of the carriage, painted in a watery golden light of the rain and the carriage lamp.

Through her recitation, Curran held her hands, and her breathing slowed in his calm presence.

"And now we're stuck here," she said. "There is some sort of court hearing we have to attend tomorrow and then ...?"

Curran released her hands, pulled a second chair over, and sat down. Tomorrow, they will bring formal charges against her. Then there will be a committal hearing and then, if there is sufficient evidence, she will be sent to trial. Frankly, being caught with the gun in your hand and saying 'I did it' might well be enough to do just that."

"Don't be flippant, Curran."

He smiled. "I'm not ... gallows humor. If her defense is strong, then she should have nothing to worry about." He paused, and she recognized the gleam in his eyes. The policeman pulling the threads of a puzzle together. "Do you think there was some sort of relationship between the two of them, beyond friendship?"

"I didn't say that."

"No, you didn't, but in my last conversation with Stewart, he hinted he was trying to extricate himself from a relationship with a married woman. Harriet, you know I trust your judgment in these matters. You're rarely wrong."

Harriet nodded. "When I saw them together in the Batu Caves, I thought that there might have been something more than just casual acquaintances."

"Stewart intimated he had a new woman, a local girl."

"Edith would have hated that. Do you think she set up the meeting tonight in an attempt to win him back?"

Curran shrugged. "Maybe. But did she intend to kill him? Could it have been self-defense? Or something else?"

Harriet's blood ran cold as she remembered the careless placement of the box containing the revolver on the bookcase on the verandah. Would Edith have had the time to open the box and extract the revolver while fending off the amorous attentions of a big man like Walter Stewart?

Harriet swallowed. "She said her hand found the revolver, but she could only have done that if it was out of the box and in a convenient place."

"And loaded," Curran added. "Was the weapon empty when you left the range?"

Harriet nodded. "I was the last to fire, and I checked it myself before I gave it back to Edith. She put it straight back in the box."

"*Heav'n has no Rage, like Love to Hatred turn'd, Nor Hell a Fury, like a Woman scorn'd,*" Curran quoted.

Harriet nodded. "I suppose all of this will come out in the trial," she said. "Her poor husband."

Curran stood up and held out his hand. "It's late, Harriet. You need to get back to bed."

She summoned a smile, and her fingers closed on his. She stood up and continued to hold his hand for a few moments longer than propriety demanded before he extricated his fingers, and she made a show of smoothing down her crumpled skirt.

"Now I have to get back to my room with no one seeing me." At the door, she turned to Curran. "Thank you for hearing me out. I wish you had carriage of this case instead of Wheeler."

"Wheeler is a solid investigator. He'll do a fair job but, in all honesty, Harriet, it doesn't look good for your girl."

"She's not my girl," Harriet said. "I've only just met her, but I do feel sorry for her. She seems to be an outsider, and I don't really understand why."

"She's also neither your responsibility nor your problem, Harriet," Curran said. "Remember that. Say what needs to be said and move on. You can't let yourself get emotionally involved."

"Is that the policeman talking?"

"It is the wisdom of long experience."

"And what about you, Curran? You know you can trust me."

"I know, but for now you have enough to worry about

without concerning yourself about me." Curran reached out, tucking a lock of her hair behind her ear. "That's better. You look a little less wild." He smiled. "Goodnight, Harriet."

The door closed and Harriet stood alone in the silent, musty corridor.

TWENTY-THREE

MONDAY, 5 DECEMBER

Harriet slept badly over what remained of the night. She rose at first light, her eyes heavy and dry from lack of sleep. She pulled a chair across to the window and sat watching the daylight break over the Padang and the town come to life.

She surveyed her limited wardrobe and selected her conservative everyday skirt and a clean blouse. As her imminent return to Singapore now looked to be uncertain, she put out a pile of laundry for the dhobi.

Julian had already taken a table for breakfast when she joined him. She looked around the dining room but saw no sign of Curran.

Her brother set down the letter he had been reading.

"I've had a note from Robertson," he said. "He's asked that we return to the bungalow this morning and help with preparing Edith for the hearing at eleven. And don't look like that," he added as Harriet grimaced. "Whatever our personal feelings, we need to put them to one side. Robertson is in need of our help, and we must provide it."

There were times when being related to a man of the cloth could be quite tedious, Harriet thought as she buttered her cold, dry toast while keeping an eye on the entrance to the breakfast room in the hope Curran would appear, but he didn't.

At the bungalow, they found Robertson waiting on the verandah, dressed but unshaven. As Harriet mounted the steps in the daylight, she shuddered at the sight of the dark splotches of dried blood on the verandah boards and the top steps where the rain had not reached.

Robertson greeted them warmly and subsided in the rattan chair, rubbing his eyes. "She's asleep at last," he said. "Even with the sleeping powder, she spent the night in floods of tears and self-recrimination. She will be hardly fit for court, I fear."

Harriet straightened her back. "I shall organize some tea," she said.

Robertson nodded. "Thank you. That would be a kindness."

In the kitchen behind the house, the cook was just stoking the oven into life. He, too, looked like a man who had not slept.

"Please, could we have some tea brought to the verandah?" Harriet asked in her halting Malay.

The man nodded and replied in English. "Tea. Yes, Mem."

But after setting the kettle to boil, the man slumped on a stool, his head in his hands. "Terrible, terrible," he said.

"It must have been a great shock to you," Harriet replied. Her Malay was still rudimentary, so she had no choice but to resort to English.

"I was resting," the man waved vaguely toward his sleeping quarters, "when I hear bang and then bang, bang, bang. I ran outside and the Mem was standing there and the man ..." He shuddered. "*Tuan* Stewart comes often to the house. Very nice man."

"Often?" This seemed to contradict the Robertsons' assertion that he was no more than a nodding acquaintance.

The cook looked up at Harriet, and his eyes narrowed. "When the *tuan* was from home—"

The arrival of the *amah* interrupted whatever else he had been going to say. She addressed the cook in rapid Malay, giving him what appeared to Harriet to be a sound telling off.

The man did not respond. He rose from his seat and removed the boiling kettle from the stove.

The woman turned to Harriet. "I will bring your tea, Mem. Do not concern yourself with the loose tongues of people who should know better."

Harriet managed a smile. She had been dismissed.

She returned to the verandah, and soon the *amah* set the tray with teacups and a teapot on the table. Harriet poured them all tea, which they drank in silence, three pairs of eyes fixed on the spot where Walter Stewart had died. Even if the rain had washed away the rest of the blood, the scuffed gravel and trampled grass told its own story.

"Is the hotel comfortable?" Robertson spoke at last.

"Very," Harriet said.

"I'm sorry to have to put you to such inconvenience, but the police seemed quite emphatic you don't return to Singapore today." Robertson set his cup down and leaned forward, his head in his hands. "I don't understand why Walt Stewart would have come here last night?"

"Is it possible your wife invited him?" Harriet said and regretted her blunt words as he looked up at her, his face stricken.

"Mrs. Gordon, I am aware that Edith has welcomed him into our home on occasions when I have been away. Believe me, I more than anyone understand the loneliness of being a bachelor in this colony. I considered myself the luckiest man alive when Edith agreed to be my wife." He straightened. "Besides, Stewart has a woman."

"A woman?" Julian asked.

Robertson shrugged. "A Chinese girl. I believe she moved into his quarters recently. It's common enough."

Harriet did not look at Julian, but she was conscious his gaze had flicked to her. Robertson evidently did not understand that what he had just said contradicted his wife's possible defense. Why would a man with a live-in lover make improper advances to the married wife of a friend?

"Do you go away often?" Harriet asked.

Now Robertson's eyes were guarded. "I am, of course, tied to the school during the term, but during the holidays I have undertaken important trips out of Malaya on school business. I have a business interest in a school in Hong Kong and I try to get over there a couple of times a year."

Julian shot his sister a warning glance, but Harriet pushed a little further. "And does Edith accompany you?"

"No. She has her commitments to the Methodist Girls School and our daughter to care for. She couldn't come with me." A humorless half-smile touched his lips. "She is a terrible traveler."

As if on cue, a child's wail echoed through the house and Robertson flinched. "How am I going to explain any of this to poor little Dorothy?"

"She is too young to understand and if her mother has to go away for a length of time, it will not be easy," Harriet said.

The color drained from Robertson's face. "You think it will come to that?"

Harriet shook her head. "If it was self-defense, I am sure a court will view the situation with compassion."

"But you can't be sure," Robertson's voice was flat. "Emptying an entire chamber into a prone man won't be to her credit."

"No," Harriet agreed.

Whichever way she looked at it, Edith's defense was, at best, shaky.

"What are you all doing out here? Why didn't you wake me, Henry?"

Edith Robertson stood in the doorway, wearing nothing but a nightdress, her hair unbound and unbrushed.

Everyone stood up.

"Edith, sweet girl, you should be asleep," Robertson said.

"Dottie woke me," she replied. "I'm rather hungry. Can I have some breakfast?"

"Why don't you go back to bed for a little longer and I'll wake you when breakfast is ready?"

Seemingly oblivious to the guests, Edith wandered out onto the verandah and leaned her hands on the rail, looking out over the carriageway, to the place where Walter Stewart had fallen.

"I'm not a bit tired." She turned to look at her husband. "What's going to happen today, Henry?"

Robertson swallowed. "Sweetheart, you have to go to the court."

"Why? I told that policeman it wasn't my fault."

"It's not that simple, Edith. You killed a man. There is a process to be gone through."

For the first time, realization seemed to dawn on her, and her eyes widened. "You mean I have to appear in a public court for everyone to see?"

Robertson nodded.

"Does Papa know?"

"I sent him a note first thing this morning. He'll be at the court. Please go back to bed for a little longer or at least make yourself presentable. We have visitors."

Edith's gaze flicked to Julian and Harriet. "How rude of me. I hope you both slept well last night. Are you still returning to Singapore today?"

Harriet and Julian were spared from reply by the arrival of a motor vehicle carrying two men. Everyone stood up as the driver drew up in front of the house and Edith gave a sharp cry, drawing back against her husband as the older of the two men pulled off goggles and helmet. Robertson's arm went around his wife.

"What the hell do you mean by sending me a note telling me my useless daughter has killed someone?" the man barked.

Edith's father took the steps to the veranda two at a time, ignoring Harriet and Julian and rounding on the Robertsons. Edith whimpered and buried her face in her husband's shirt. Robertson's arms circled her, drawing her in closer.

"Well? Explain yourself, girl?" her father roared.

"Now, now, Chapman ... calm down." The younger man, a good-looking man in his thirties, had followed Edith's father up the steps. "Excuse our precipitous entrance," he addressed Harriet and Julian, holding out his hand. "Charles Hughes, barrister at law. I don't believe we've met."

Julian hurriedly introduced himself and Harriet.

"And this is Joseph Chapman." Hughes indicated his companion.

Chapman took a step back and turned to Harriet and Julian. "My apologies. It's the shock of waking up to a note telling you that your daughter has shot a man in cold blood." He looked at Charles Hughes. "Fortunately, Hughes here was available to come with me and help get this unfortunate misunderstanding sorted out."

"Hardly a misunderstanding," Hughes said. "I was able to have a quick conversation on the telephone with Inspector Wheeler, so I am appraised of the basic facts. What we need to do is sit down and discuss what can best be done for Mrs. Robertson in a calm and rational manner."

Everyone gave Hughes a watery smile of gratitude for his calm assessment of the situation and the defusing of Joseph Chapman's fury.

"Edith," Harriet said. "Why don't you come with me and get dressed? I will see that some more tea and refreshment is organized."

Robertson cast Harriet a grateful look and relinquished his hold on his still-trembling wife and Harriet put an arm around Edith's shoulders and led her back into the house.

"I knew Papa would be cross," Edith said as she sat down on her bed. She buried her face in her hands. "Why did this have to happen?"

Why indeed, Harriet thought.

She left Edith to wash while she went to speak to the cook about more tea and breakfast. When she returned, she found Edith exactly where she had left her.

It took some encouragement to get Edith respectable. Harriet selected one of the few outfits in Edith's wardrobe that would do service in court, a navy-blue outfit with a matching hat trimmed with blue and white ribbon, and a veil that covered her face. Edith regarded her reflection in the long mirror and hefted a heavy sigh.

"I suppose it is like wearing a costume in a play," she said. "I must play the part."

Yes, Harriet thought, you must play a part.

TWENTY-FOUR

The story had already broken in the morning's newspapers, and a sizeable crowd gathered at the door to the Magistrate's Court. Inside the stuffy courtroom, the public gallery was filled with curious onlookers drawn from all corners of KL society. Despite an electric fan that circled slowly above the room, the stifling heat, and the presence of so many bodies pressed together, was almost unbearable.

As they were not required to give testimony, Julian and Harriet were permitted to enter the court, and room was made for them on a hard bench at the front of the gallery. Harriet fanned herself with the little Chinese paper fan she carried in her hand-bag, but all it accomplished was to stir the air.

Haycocks slid onto the bench beside Harriet and Julian.

"Mr. Daly is presiding," he said in a low voice. "That's good. He's a fair man."

Harriet could only see Edith's back. She sat beside Hughes, who wore heavy legal robes and a barrister's wig. Her husband sat in the row behind her, leaning forward, his elbows on his knees and his right foot tapping. He looked around and, seeing Julian, Harriet, and Haycocks, relief flooded his face, and he managed a faint smile. He had no reason to be happy to see them, Harriet reflected. Any evidence the three of them had to give would not help his wife's cause.

The police inspector, Wheeler, occupied the other table.

"Just a formality," he had told Julian and Harriet when they had encountered him before the hearing.

The court rose as the magistrate, a man of middle years with a luxuriant mustache and a heavy thatch of greying hair, entered the court. As a magistrate, he was not required to wear the heavy robes and incongruous wig of the lawyer who appeared before him.

The magistrate banged his gavel and the court fell silent.

"Mr. Hughes, you are representing the defendant?"

The sweating barrister rose to his feet. "I am, Your Worship."

"Very well. I am pleased to see she has able counsel assisting her. Mrs. Robertson, please stand," the magistrate said.

Edith, her face concealed behind the heavy net, appeared to cast her husband a quick glance as she rose to her feet, her gloved hands clutching a neat navy leather handbag in front of her.

The magistrate studied her from over the top of a pair of glasses before saying, "Mrs. Robertson, this is the first of many distressing procedures you will be subject to over the next weeks and months. The purpose of your appearance today is to formally lay the charges against you. Please remain standing. Mr Wheeler?"

Detective Inspector Wheeler rose to his feet. "We wish it recorded that Mrs. Edith Louise Robertson be charged with the murder of Walter Frederick Stewart on or about nine-thirty on the evening of Sunday, 4th of December 1910."

Edith gasped, one hand going to her mouth and Mr. Daly turned to her, fixing her with a hard, unblinking gaze.

"You are not required to plead to the charge today, Mrs. Robertson, and Mr. Wheeler will not be leading evidence. However, it is customary in cases of such gravity for the defendant to be taken into custody pending the formal hearing of the evidence."

"Oh no, not jail. I couldn't bear it," Edith's voice broke, and she swayed on her feet.

Charles Hughes stood up. "Your Worship, in view of the nature of this case and the sensitivity of the lady's feelings, would you be prepared to release her into the custody of her husband on payment of a surety, pending the formal committal which we believe will be heard early next week?"

"Inspector? What do you have to say on this motion?" The magistrate turned to Wheeler.

The magistrate turned a hard, unblinking gaze on the policeman and Harriet doubted that Mr. Daly felt inclined to spare Edith's sensitive feelings.

The policeman shot Edith a quick look and cleared his throat. "In the circumstances, I have no objection."

The magistrate turned back to Edith and her lawyer. "Very well, I shall take the unusual step of releasing the defendant on the payment of the sum of one thousand dollars as surety pending the committal hearing. Is there anyone prepared to stand surety for her?"

Robertson's shoulders sagged. One thousand dollars would be well beyond his capacity.

Joseph Chapman rose to his feet. "I will."

"For the record, your name?" the magistrate said.

"Joseph Chapman. I am Mrs. Robertson's father."

"Thank you, Mr. Chapman. Please see the clerk of the court at the conclusion of the proceedings. Mr. Wheeler, in consideration of the proximity of this matter to Christmas, how much time do you require to prepare the case for the preliminary hearing?"

"The facts are straightforward, Your Worship. As I previously indicated, a week?"

"Very well, I fix next Monday, 12th December for the preliminary hearing into the charge on which Mrs. Robertson now stands accused." He brought down his gavel with a thump that made everyone in the court start. "Mrs. Robertson, please stand."

Edith rose to her feet again. She swayed forward and her barrister caught her arm to steady her.

"Mrs. Robertson, you understand that thanks to your father, you are free to leave this court today but come next Monday you will be taken into custody and a preliminary hearing into your guilt or innocence will be conducted. If the court decides you have a case to answer, then you will remain in custody pending your trial."

Edith glanced at her barrister, who nodded.

She mumbled inaudibly.

"Speak up, Mrs. Robertson."

Edith's voice quavered. "I understand," she said.

The magistrate banged his gavel again and everyone stood as he left the court. The whole proceeding had taken ten minutes.

Haycocks mopped his face with a large handkerchief. "I can't believe this is happening," he said. "I lived with the Robertsons. Edith is ... She is surely not capable of murder?"

"She claims it was self-defense," Julian said.

Haycocks shrugged. "Let's hope she can prove it."

Harriet heard the uncertainty in his voice and wondered if Haycocks knew something about Edith and her relationship with Stewart that he was not telling ... and probably would never tell.

Outside in the relatively fresh air and bright light of a clear day, Edith, sandwiched between her husband and her father, pushed through the crowd and into a waiting carriage.

Robertson turned back and hurried across to where Harriet and Julian stood with Haycocks. He looked even worse than he had at the bungalow earlier that morning, with dark circles around his red-rimmed eyes and a grey cast to his face.

"Mrs. Gordon," he said. "I have an enormous favor to ask of you. I know you are probably anxious to return home, but I wonder if you would consider remaining in Kuala Lumpur until the committal hearing? It would be the most enormous comfort to Edith and myself to know she has a friend."

It was on the tip of Harriet's tongue to point out that she was not necessarily a friend of Edith's and would, in fact, be giving evidence for the prosecution, but Julian nudged her, and she summoned a smile.

"Of course," she said.

Henry Robertson glanced at Julian. "I will, of course, cover the hotel expenses, or you are welcome to return to the bungalow."

"That's not necessary," Julian said.

Harriet glanced at him. The cost of a week in the Empire Hotel would be a hardship, but their father back in London was a lawyer and they both recognized distance needed to be maintained.

"I have responsibilities back in Singapore and I am hoping to return on the night train if the police permit me," Julian said, "But Harriet can remain, and I am sure she will do whatever she can to help your wife through this difficult time."

Robertson grasped Julian's hands between his and turned to Harriet, repeating the gesture. "Thank you, thank you."

The relief on Robertson's face was almost painful as he turned away and hurried back to the waiting carriage.

Haycocks huffed out a breath and mopped his face again. "This is a bad business," he said. "I suppose I should get back to school. We will meet again, but sadly not in the best of circumstances."

He straightened his shoulders and hurried away to hail a ricksha.

"What now?" Harriet said.

"Let's return to the hotel and have some lunch," Julian suggested.

Inspector Wheeler had been talking with Edith's barrister and seeing them, he raised a hand to detain them.

"Reverend, Mrs. Gordon, I know you are anxious to return to Singapore, but I will require your attendance as witnesses at the committal."

Julian frowned. "Inspector, I am the headmaster of a school in Singapore. I cannot sit here for a week twiddling my thumbs. I am needed."

"I understand. If you would both attend my office at two this afternoon, I will take your formal statements and you are free to leave on condition you return in time to give your evidence in person next Monday."

"I shall remain in Kuala Lumpur, Inspector. You will find me at the Empire Hotel," Harriet said.

The policeman frowned, distracted by something or someone. Harriet and Julian turned to see what had caught his attention. Excusing himself, the policeman strode over to a large tree under which a well-dressed, bearded European man with a fedora hat pulled low over his face stood in the shade.

"Curran," Harriet said under her breath.

"I do believe you are right," Julian said. "What's he up to?"

Harriet took her brother's arm and turned him aside. "Whatever it is, is none of our business, Ju. We haven't seen him. I think your suggestion about lunch is excellent. I fancy a curry tiffin."

It took all her self-control to walk away.

TWENTY-FIVE

Curran had taken his time over breakfast at the Empire Hotel. Over coffee and toast, he perused the article in the Malay Tribune titled Kuala Lumpur Tragedy: Former Mine Manager Shot Dead; A Distressing Story.

A distressing story indeed. After Harriet's midnight visit, the policeman's curiosity had been piqued and he glanced at his watch. The arraignment had been set for eleven and he had no other plans for the morning.

He had arrived late at the court, slipping into the back of the crowded courtroom. Over the heads of the crowd in the public gallery, he'd identified Harriet and Julian sitting with a fair-haired young man.

He'd recognized Detective Inspector Wheeler at once. They had met on a couple of occasions and, unlike Keogh, for whom Curran had no time, Wheeler had always struck him as a solid, if slightly unimaginative, policeman. Curran hoped his informant, Stephens, had been correct in his assertion that Wheeler could be trusted.

A rustle and murmur had run through the court as Edith Robertson had been called and rose to her feet. From his vantage point, he had gained the impression of a slight woman with fair hair pinned up beneath her hat and net. Only the trembling of her slender shoulders as the magistrate addressed her gave any indication of her emotional state.

After the court was dismissed, Curran turned and left the building before Harriet or Julian could see him. From his position in the shade of the trees, he observed Edith Robertson leaving the court with her father on one side and her husband's arm around her slight shoulders. She did not look like a cold-blooded killer who would empty the chamber of a Webley revolver into a man, but it didn't seem to be in dispute that was precisely what she had done.

The question was, why?

He bided his time in the shadows. Only when Wheeler had moved to talk to Harriet and Julian did he raise his hat, catching the man's attention. Harriet and Julian glanced his way but gave no sign of recognition as they turned and walked away to the line of rickshas.

"Cigarette?" Curran offered as Wheeler came to stand beside him.

"Thank you."

Curran produced his cigarette case and lighter and the two men stood together in companionable silence for a minute before Wheeler said, "What the hell are you doing here, Curran? I heard you are on suspension."

"I have a little business of my own here in KL," Curran said.

Wheeler cast him a disbelieving glance and a sudden light of understanding gleamed in his eye. "Ah! Is this to do with Talbot? He told me someone might contact me on a top-secret matter."

"How far did your briefing extend?"

Wheeler shook his head. "Just that. All very 'need to know' basis. So, what is it that I need to know, Curran?"

"To begin with, my name for the moment is Sutton. Beyond that, now is not the time."

"I see," Wheeler said, although from the confusion in his eyes, plainly he didn't. "I have little time for this sort of secrecy."

"You have enough to do with this case, without worrying about what I am up to, but I hope if I have need of you, you can be available?"

Wheeler shrugged. "If it is within my jurisdiction."

"Missing Keogh?" Curran asked, changing the subject.

Wheeler snorted. "I'm happy for him to stay down in Singapore as long as he damn well pleases."

Curran smiled. "I hope to be reinstated when this assignment is concluded, and you can have him back. There is one thing you can do for me, Wheeler."

"What is that?"

"I'd like to see the file on a dead woman pulled from the Klang a couple of months ago."

Wheeler ground out his cigarette. "We're always pulling bodies out of the Klang. Can you be more specific?"

"Around October 15th. A young Indian woman with a distinctive star-shaped birthmark on her upper arm. I don't believe the body was ever formally identified."

"Oh yes, I remember that case. One of Keogh's. Why do you want to see the file?"

"I suspect her death is related to my assignment. I might know who she is, and it would be good for her family's sake to put a name to her, don't you agree?"

"Fair enough. I'll see what I can do. I better go. As you pointed out, I have a big case to prepare and only a week to pull it together. Were you in there?" He jerked his head toward the courtroom.

"I was. Good of you to agree to let her out on a surety. Not sure I'd have been quite so magnanimous."

Wheeler shrugged. "She's not likely to take off and this is one case I must treat with kid gloves. An Englishwoman shooting her lover? It will shake the entire colony to its core."

"Was Stewart her lover?"

Wheeler nodded. "Oh yes, common knowledge around the town. My wife told me about a dinner party she threw while her husband was absent in Hong Kong. No one saw the hostess. She spent the whole evening in the back seat of Stewart's car. Don't be taken in by the wide-eyed innocent. She's a conniving little—" Wheeler straightened. "You didn't hear that from me. I never prejudge my cases. If I dig out this file you want, where do I find you?"

"I'm staying at the Empire Hotel under the name Ronald Sutton."

Wheeler's mustache twitched, and he repeated the name a couple of times. "I'll get on to it as soon as I get back to HQ. For my sake, I hope that is the last I hear from you."

"I hope so too. Thank you, Wheeler."

The two men parted, and Curran hailed a ricksha to take him to the Blakes' home.

No one answered his knock and an unnatural silence hung over the house. He knocked again and thought he heard some scuffling from inside. He walked around to the side of the house, but the shuttered windows were too far off the ground for him to look inside. The servants' quarters seemed deserted, and the back door locked.

Only recent washing flapping on the line showed that the occupants might still be around. A man's white ducks and shirts and, more telling, a woman's *kurta* and *pajamas* plus a large selection of square white cloths which he assumed were baby nappies along with tiny little smocks that would have fitted his cousin Ellie's favorite doll.

Whatever Blake might claim, a woman and a baby were living in the house.

TWENTY-SIX

After taking a quick lunch at the hotel and spending a hot and tedious couple of hours giving their statements at the police station, Harriet and Julian returned to the Robertsons' bungalow and found Edith and her husband taking tea on the verandah in the company of the lawyer, Charles Hughes.

Edith had changed into a white cotton dress trimmed with blue ribbon. She had wound a similar ribbon into her hair and she looked young, fresh, and innocent.

Henry Robertson's tea remained untouched and a slice of cake sat unregarded on his plate as his eyes repeatedly wandered towards the location where Walter Stewart's body had been found. By contrast, from the crumbs on her plate, Edith seemed to have eaten several slices of cake. As Julian and Harriet mounted the stairs, Hughes set down his cup and decorously dabbed his mouth on the table napkin before rising to greet the arrivals.

Edith threw herself into Harriet's arms with a cry of, "I'm so glad to see you!"

"I was just saying before your arrival," Hughes said,

addressing Harriet and Julian as they all resumed their seats, "our case will be that Edith acted in self-defense."

Edith's blue eyes widened. "The court must believe that the man assaulted me. He would have ..." Her lips trembled, and she hastily dabbed at her eyes with the table napkin. "I had no choice."

Harriet wondered who she was trying to convince ... the rest of them ... or herself?

Edith reached across the table and took Harriet's hand. "Wednesday is Mahjong at the club. Do you play, Harriet? We must go—"

"No," her husband said in a tone that must cause the boys at the school to quake. "Kitten, how many times must I say it? You cannot leave the house. Whatever my thoughts on the matter, and I do believe you, dearest, you cannot be seen in public. You are very fortunate the magistrate allowed you to come home at all. Anyone else would be in prison."

She blinked. "Prison? Oh no, Henry, I'm not going to prison. That's for bad people and I'm not bad." She turned to Harriet. "Have you seen the Pudu prison, Harriet? It's not for people like us."

Henry Robertson turned an appealing gaze on Harriet.

"Edith," Harriet said gently. "I used to work for the police. There is no difference between a white woman or a coolie when it comes to the law."

Edith turned back to her husband. "You mean I really could go to jail?"

Robertson frowned and bit his lip in an obvious effort to control his emotions.

Charles Hughes intervened. "As I've explained to you, Edith. Next Monday there will be a hearing at the Magistrate's Court. All the evidence will be presented and if the magistrate says you have to go to trial, then it doesn't matter what I or your husband and father say, you will have to go to jail ... to Pudu."

Edith's eyes filled with tears. "Oh no, I will die in a place like that!"

Harriet caught her brother's quick glance. If Edith was found guilty, there was a chance she would indeed die—hanged by the neck.

Edith pleated the table napkin beside her plate with restless fingers. "That horrid magistrate. I shall go mad if I may not leave the house. You must come and visit every day, Harriet," she said.

"Edith needs her friends," Henry Robertson put in.

Harriet thought of the women at the Selangor Club and wondered if any of them counted themselves as Edith's friend. She suspected Edith was indeed on her own.

"I'm not sure that I can," Harriet said, trying not to make the commitment. "If I have to give evidence at your trial, it could be very awkward."

Edith withdrew her hand and gazed wide-eyed at Harriet. "Don't you believe me, Harriet?"

"It's not a matter of what I believe, Edith. I will be questioned about what I saw."

"Quite right," Hughes put in.

Edith looked from one to the other. "Oh, I see," she said. She straightened in her chair and her chin jutted defiantly as she said, "Then I will just have to convince them I was defending myself," she said.

Charles Hughes coughed. "My dear Edith, if you are telling the truth, you will be believed."

She turned her blue eyes on him. "I shall tell the truth. I always tell the truth."

There was no answer to that.

Twenty-Seven

"She is either innocent or an excellent actress," Julian said later as he and Harriet sat over an early supper on the verandah of the Empire Hotel.

"I don't know what to think," Harriet said. "I just wish you didn't have to go back to Singapore."

Julian glanced around at the well-appointed comfort of the hotel. "I don't want to go, but we can't afford two rooms, Harriet. Besides, Will needs one of us at home."

Harriet sniffed. "I was going to make Christmas decorations with Will this week." She bit her lip. She didn't like to think how Will had spent his last Christmas or any Christmas since his mother had died. His wastrel of a father had probably been too obsessed with his dubious business dealing to spare a thought for the time of year.

"I really want to make Christmas something special for him," she said.

Julian chuckled. "And you will. It's still a couple of weeks away." He reached into his pocket and pulled out a small paper-wrapped object. "At least I have a little souvenir for him."

They had stopped at a market stall and purchased a bright red *gasing*, a spinning top, a popular toy with the local children.

Harriet picked up the object and smiled. "I hope he likes it."

"He will. I just worry about leaving you here by yourself."

Harriet huffed out a breath. "I am not good with silly women," she said. "Particularly silly women who think it acceptable to empty the contents of a Webley revolver into their former lovers."

"You are prejudging the case," Julian said in a warning tone.

"Is this chair taken?"

They both looked up. Harriet's heart lightened at the sight of Curran.

Before Julian could say something, Harriet waved at the spare seat.

"Mr. Sutton, please join us," she said, rather louder than their previous conversation. "Julian, have you met Mr. Sutton? He is writing a book on traveling on the Malay peninsula."

Julian half rose and made a show of shaking Curran's hand. "Pleasure to make your acquaintance. Tell me, what aspects have you found of the most interest so far?"

Curran's eyes creased at the corners. "I am particularly enamored of Singapore," he said and lowered his voice. "Less so of Kuala Lumpur. There are undercurrents here."

"You've noticed that?" Harriet said.

"I am glad to see you, Cur ... Sutton. You just caught me. I'm not needed until the committal hearing, so I am taking the evening train back to Singapore," Julian said. "The Robertsons are keen for Harriet to stay on and it will be a relief to know that there is someone to keep an eye on Harriet while I'm gone."

"I don't need anyone's eye on me," Harriet bridled. "Besides Mr. Sutton has his own concerns."

Julian gave Curran a thoughtful glance and asked in a low voice, "Still looking for Samrita?"

"Yes. Jayant is in hospital with dengue and likely to be there for a while." He glanced at Harriet. "Fact is, I could do with an extra pair of hands that I can trust."

Harriet brightened, all thoughts of a week spent babysitting Edith Robertson vanishing. "Is there something I can do?"

Curran narrowed his eyes. "Maybe. I am trying to talk to the woman that your friend Hume interviewed. I've spoken with her husband, and he claims she is in Ipoh, but I was around there this morning. No one answered the door, and the house seemed to be deserted, but I am certain that there is a woman and a baby in residence." He paused and looked directly at Harriet. "If the household has been ordered not to open the door to an Englishman, a woman may not alarm them so much."

"Harri..." Julian growled.

But Harriet ignored her brother's warning. "Of course. I can go tomorrow morning. What do you want me to ask her?"

"I will be in the hotel lounge this evening," Curran said. "When you've seen Julian off, I will give you the brief."

"Curran, please don't involve Harriet. She has more than enough with the Robertson woman," Julian remonstrated.

"It is entirely up to me," Harriet responded, giving her brother a hard stare. "I am going to need more to occupy me this week than visiting Edith Robertson." Julian shook his head, and she patted his hand. "Please don't worry about me, Ju."

He gave her a ragged smile. "I do."

Harriet smiled in response. "And I love you for it."

Curran rose to his feet and said loudly, "It's been a pleasure meeting you, Reverend Edwards, and you, Mrs. Gordon. Safe travels, Reverend."

Both Julian and Harriet murmured suitable responses and Curran turned on the heel of his well-polished boot and left them.

"Harriet. I don't like this," Julian said.

"He's only asked me to pay a call on the woman, Julian. It's nothing I haven't done before. I'll stay out of trouble. I promise."

TWENTY-EIGHT

On returning to his room, Curran found a large, sealed envelope pushed under his door. He sat at the table and pulled out the police file on the discovery of the woman in the Klang River.

An accompanying note directed him to return the envelope to the front desk for collection by Amir at six the following day.

The details were scant and the few accompanying photographs were far from pleasant. A local fisherman had found a woman's body had snagged in the mangroves, her face so badly beaten that identification had been impossible, even without allowing for immersion in water for several days.

Curran forced himself to look at the photographs. Jayant could have identified Lakshmi in life, but the doctor noted that post-mortem, someone had smashed her face with a blunt object, obliterating any identifying features. Curran grimaced, grateful his brother was not here to demand to see the images of the woman to whom he had once been betrothed.

He turned to the rest of the information. Two elements distinguished this body from the others that came to the surface of a river like the Klang. First, the young woman wore what looked to be the remnants of a pink satin, western-style evening dress trimmed with black lace, and second, despite the level of decomposition, she had a clearly identifiable star-shaped birthmark on her upper left arm. Whoever had destroyed her face had not considered this other feature.

Fortunately, the photographer had thought to take an image of the birthmark, and Curran took out his notebook and carefully copied it. That at least was something Jayant could identify.

He put the photographs to one side and turned to the rest of the scant paperwork.

Efforts to ascertain the woman's identity by the newspaper appeals had been unsuccessful and, in the absence of witnesses and identification, the unknown woman's remains had been cremated in a Hindu cemetery, and the case was no longer actively being pursued. Curran snorted at the name at the bottom of the report. Keogh. The lazy bastard. If the woman had been European, all hell would have broken out; but an anonymous Indian woman, even one as unusually dressed as this one, was of no further interest.

No statement had been taken from the man who had found the corpse, and the description of the location was vague. Half a mile down from Taman Kinrara meant nothing to him. Besides, it was highly likely she had gone into the river further upstream. Even if she had been killed on the banks of the river, identifying the site would be impossible.

Curran turned back to the photographic images. Bashed to death and dumped in the Klang, no doubt with the hope that the body would be carried out to sea. What had Lakshmi done to warrant her sad end?

He returned the papers to the file and secreted the envelope beneath the mattress on his bed, far enough in that the housemaid would not find it.

After taking a light supper, Curran retired to the hotel lounge with a copy of The Sharer, the latest book by Joseph Conrad, an author whose work he particularly enjoyed. He kept half an eye on the door and at quarter to nine, Harriet entered the room, dispatching the staff with a request for tea.

Curran set his book down and jumped to his feet. "Mrs. Gordon, will you join me? Can I offer you something stronger than tea?"

"No, tea is just what I need," Harriet said as she took the seat across from him and fanned herself with the much-thumbed and crumpled copy of the day's newspaper that had not yet been removed from the table.

The tea arrived, and Harriet poured herself a cup. "There is thunder in the air tonight." She sat back with a sigh. "This was supposed to be a pleasant break from Singapore."

Curran raised an eyebrow. "Really?"

"No, not really ... Prince Alfred School has offered Julian a job and it would mean that we have a good school for Will but..." she looked around the room. They were alone. "I don't really want to move here. Particularly not after what's happened."

With a finger, she traced the headline in the Malay Tribune —*Kuala Lumpur Tragedy: Former Mine Manager Shot Dead; A Distressing Story.*

"Will isn't going to school in England?"

"No. We can't afford to send him to the schools we would like and the thought of him being there ... alone." She shuddered. "No. We will find something closer to home, even if we have to look in India or Ceylon."

"Or Australia?" Curran ventured.

Harriet smiled. "I've rather gone off Australia. Simon has just announced his engagement to the daughter of his paper's chief editor. Apparently, the engagement was expected before his arrival in Singapore. He played me along for a fool."

"I heard. I'm sorry," Curran said.

"Don't be. I'm not heartbroken. There was always something

a little too good to be true about Simon Hume." She gave him a hard gaze. "And you...?"

"You mean ... Li An?" When she continued to hold his eyes, he looked away with a twitch of his shoulder. "I've heard nothing from her—or of her." He returned his gaze back to hers. "And neither do I expect to. It was over even before she left, Harriet. I just didn't want to admit it."

Harriet rested her elbow on the arm of her chair and cupped her chin in her hand, looking away. "To be honest, Curran, I don't quite know what to do. Keogh has seen to it that I will never work for the Straits Settlements Police again and I've had no enquiries from private clients. I'm not very good at sitting at home making cushion covers and now that my history is out there, no one will employ me."

Curran leaned forward. "When I return to Singapore, Harriet, I will move heaven and earth to have you back on my staff."

She smiled. "Would you?"

He would. But he had a job to do before he could even consider returning to Singapore. Two jobs to do.

Harriet straightened, and as if reading his mind, said, "Now, what do you want me to do about this woman? Jameela?"

"The man she lives with is Ashton Blake."

"Didn't she tell Simon she was married with children?"

"There is at least one child. As for their marital state ... it doesn't matter."

Curran gave her the address and Harriet asked to borrow the only image he had of Samrita: the family studio portrait of her and Jayant with their parents. Harriet studied it, a small frown creasing her forehead.

"I see a lot of your father in you, Curran," she said at last. "It's around the eyes and mouth."

Curran took back the photograph, but as always, failed to see what others saw. "I barely remember him," he said. "But I adored his father, my grandfather. I used to escape to the stables and spend time with him. He taught me everything I know about horses."

"You always paint your childhood as being utterly miserable," Harriet said. "Surely you must have some happy memories, like those of your time with your grandfather."

Her observation startled him. "I suppose when you are a child, you accept things for how they are, not what they could have been. My maternal grandfather taught me to play cricket and chess and gave me the run of the Deerbourne library and I had the company of my cousin, Eloise." He grinned. "We got into some scrapes and somehow I always got the blame for leading her astray when generally it was her idea."

Harriet smiled. "She does that."

"Of course, I forgot you know her. George says she is not in the best of health."

Harriet said nothing, but he sensed she was reliving her time in Holloway with Eloise. Unhappy memories. She roused herself and asked what George was doing in KL.

"Spending Christmas with the Resident General. His wife is some relation of the Resident's wife."

"I see," Harriet said, but her frown said she didn't see at all. "I don't think your disguise is proving very effective."

"No, it's not. I'm a plain policeman, Harriet. I'm not meant for this cloak and dagger stuff."

"What is your plan?"

He only hesitated for a moment. "Tomorrow night I am visiting the Topaz Club."

"What will you do if you find Samrita there?"

"I don't know. She's not the only reason I need to gain access."

"Are you going to tell me what this secret assignment is about?"

He shook his head. "No."

She frowned. "I worry about you."

"I'm glad someone does."

He caught the eye of the attentive waiter who hovered by the door. "I'm having a nightcap. Are you sure you don't want something stronger than tea?"

She hesitated. "Maybe a small whisky? I didn't sleep well last night."

Over glasses of an excellent Scotch whisky, they talked about their childhoods and trivial matters far removed from the corner of the British empire they now found themselves in ... and the dark deeds of men and women with darker hearts and souls.

TWENTY-NINE

TUESDAY, 6 DECEMBER

Harriet sat at breakfast, planning her day. She would pay a call on the Blake residence in the morning and then a visit to Edith Robertson, probably in the afternoon, leaving the evening free to amuse herself.

She looked around the dining room. The hotel seemed to be well patronized, with every table occupied. Some single men, probably planters down in town for a few days, young couples, and the occasional family. It struck her that she rarely saw elderly Europeans—hardly anyone over the age of fifty. People like the Chapmans, who seemed settled for life, were unusual. The custom was to retire back to the home country upon reaching a certain age and it made for an oddly unbalanced society.

"Harriet!"

The sound of a familiar voice caused her to start slopping tea into her saucer as her friend Griff Maddocks, reporter for the Straits Times, slipped unbidden into the spare seat at her table.

"Griff, what are you doing here?"

Maddocks removed his hat and summoned a waiter, sending him away with an order for a hearty breakfast and coffee.

"Train just got in," he said.

"Didn't they feed you on the train?"

He shrugged. "That was ages ago. The paper's paying so I might as well make the most of it."

The waiter soon returned with Maddocks's breakfast, which the reporter tucked into as if he hadn't eaten for a week.

"You didn't answer my question," Harriet said when her friend paused to draw breath.

"Oh yes. It should be obvious why I'm here ... the Robertson murder. The biggest piece of news for months. The paper's sent me up to cover it."

"Nothing more is going to happen until Monday," Harriet said.

Maddocks raised his hands. "If the paper wants me to spend a week sitting around a comfortable hotel, I'm not going to argue. There's always a background to ferret out." He smiled ingratiatingly. "Is it true you and Julian were guests of the Robertsons at the time of the murder?"

"Quite true, unfortunately," Harriet said.

"But I should know better than to try to get anything useful out of you?" Maddocks rolled his eyes.

"Exactly. As you know, we came up to KL for Julian to assess a possible position at the Prince Alfred School. I never met the Robertsons before last Saturday."

"Hang it all, Harriet, do you believe that the man attempted to ravish her? I hear she claims she shot him in self-defense."

"That is her defense," Harriet said carefully. "To be honest, Griff, I don't know. It is not for me to decide whether or not I believe her." She hesitated. "Both Julian and I are certain that the magistrate will send her to trial."

"Better for a jury to decide."

"They don't have a jury here. Her barrister, Charles Hughes, told me that because of the difficulty in finding 'twelve good men and true' from such a small English population, it will be a judge sitting alone with two advisors." She paused. "It would fascinate father."

Her father, a Crown Prosecutor in London, would be very interested and she would write to him this evening. George Edwards had been happy to indulge his daughter's curiosity about the workings of the law until she suggested she would like to study law and become a lawyer herself.

"Women lawyers? Preposterous!" Her father had declared to be echoed by his wife with her well-worn refrain.

"Education is wasted on girls, Harriet. You will be marrying and starting a family, and then what?"

Maddocks poured himself another coffee and sat back in his chair. "What are you planning to do today?" he asked.

"I have a call to make this morning," Harriet said. "And this afternoon I am expected for tea with Edith Robertson." She held up a hand. "And don't ask if you can come. Though I suspect Edith would love to meet you, I am sure her husband and lawyer will be less enamored of a visiting journalist."

"Ask her," Maddocks wheedled. "I have all week and I'm friendly."

"You also have a nose for sensationalism."

Maddocks shrugged. "It's a big story and an exclusive interview with Mrs. Robertson herself could well be syndicated around the world. This could be a huge career move for me."

"Griff!"

"At least dine with me tonight?"

Harriet pushed back from the table and smiled. "That I can do. Now please excuse me, Griff."

Having only planned on a visit for a couple of days, Harriet's wardrobe was limited. She wore the freshly laundered blue muslin dress she had worn on Saturday, but it quickly wilted in the heat.

She examined her reflection in the full-length mirror and decided it would have to do.

Outside the hotel, she hailed a ricksha and gave him the address Curran had shared with her. As the poor ricksha wallah toiled up the hill to the quiet backwater in the European quarter, a hot, unrelenting sun beat down, unrelieved by her parasol.

The Blakes lived in a small bungalow on a wide, tree-lined street. Like the other bungalows of similar design, it was set well back behind a hedge of bright bougainvillea. She alighted from the ricksha and told the man to wait. He squatted in the shade of a tree and produced a small pouch, popping something into his mouth. Betel nut, Harriet suspected.

Taking a breath to settle her nerves, she opened the gate and strode up to the front door. It stood open to let the breeze, such as it was, into the house. Beyond it, she could see into a large living area with a corridor running straight to the back door with rooms on either side. In one of these rooms, a woman was singing. She didn't recognize the song, but it had the cadence of a lullaby.

She knocked, and the singing stopped. A woman stepped into the corridor. She wore a *kurta* and *pajama* set of light material with a scarf artfully draped at her neck, her hair pulled back, probably in a plait, but her face was shadowed in the gloom.

"Who are you?" she asked in perfect but accented English.

"I am Mrs. Gordon, I am collecting for the next fête at St. Mary's," Harriet said.

"St. Mary's? We have nothing to do with St. Mary's."

"Your husband is Ashton Blake, is he not? Manager at Laidlaws? We were hoping for a generous donation."

"You must speak with my husband, but he is not at home. Please leave," the woman came forward into the living room ... and the light ... and Harriet's breath caught.

"Samrita," she said.

THIRTY

The young woman stared at her for a moment, her eyes wide, her hand going to her mouth.

"Jameela," the woman said, too quickly. "My name is Jameela. Who are you? Get out!"

Harriet crossed the threshold and opened her handbag, taking out the photograph Curran had given her. Without a word, she handed it to the woman, who took it and studied it.

"Where did you get this?" she asked in a low voice.

"Your brother gave it to me."

The woman looked up and her lips trembled. "My brother? Jayant is here?"

"Yes, Jayant is here, though he is currently in hospital with dengue. But I did not mean Jayant. I meant your other brother."

"I have no other brother."

"Robert Curran. Your father's eldest son—the one he left behind in England."

The fragile piece of card fell to the floor and Harriet stooped to pick it up as Samrita sank onto the nearest chair.

Harriet studied the image and looked up at the young woman. "You are Samrita Kumar?"

"I was ... once," Samrita said. "I left that girl behind in India. For a time, I was Lily. Now I am Jameela. Tell my brother ... tell my brother that I am dead, and he is to go home."

"I don't think you know either of your brothers very well," Harriet said. "Jayant has searched high and low for you since you vanished."

"And this ... this Robert Curran? Was it he who came here on Saturday and spoke with my husband?"

"Yes. He is a policeman in Singapore."

Samrita turned her face away, her hand to her mouth. "You don't understand, Mrs. Gordon, I have a life here, a life I have built with Ashton. He is good to me. I cannot go back. I cannot pretend I was the same girl who left Laxmangarh."

"No one is asking you to do that. If you are content with the life you have here, that is all they ask, but they know about the Topaz Club and your friend Lakshmi—"

Samrita jumped to her feet. "Lakshmi is dead, and that is why I will say nothing to anyone about that place. That too is in my past. I think you should leave, Mrs. Gordon. If you will not tell them I am dead, tell my brother—my brothers—that I am well and happy and that is an end to it."

From somewhere within the house came the wail of a young baby. Samrita started, and she tensed, her gaze going to the corridor leading to the other rooms.

"The baby needs me. Please, Mrs. Gordon, do not concern yourself in my business."

"But—"

Samrita rounded on her. "There is no 'but'. You must stay away. If they find out you have been here, you will have placed us all in the most terrible peril."

"Who are 'they'? Let us help you, Samrita—"

Samrita's lip curled. "I do not need help and there is no one to help those girls at the Topaz Club. No one."

She advanced on Harriet, forcing her to back toward the door. "Please leave."

As Harriet turned to leave, Samrita said, "No, wait. I have something you can give this Robert Curran."

Samrita rummaged through a drawer in the desk and took out a card, which she handed to Harriet.

It was a postcard of the Batu Caves, the same as many Harriet had seen on sale from the vendors at the caves. She turned it over.

There was no writing except a single L and a crudely drawn pictogram of what looked to be four elephants, one smaller than the other.

"I received this the week Lakshmi died. A boy came to my door and said a lady at the caves had given it to him and asked him to bring it to this address. She had given him a dollar for his trouble."

"Is it from Lakshmi?"

"I think so. The Letter L is written as she would write it with the loop."

"How did she get to the Batu Caves?"

Samrita shook her head. "I do not know, but within days, I saw the report in the paper about her death and knew this card was important. Now you must go, Mrs. Gordon. They are watching the house."

"Who are 'they' Samrita?" Harriet asked again.

But she shook her head and pointedly held the door open.

Harriet stepped back onto the verandah. As the door closed behind her, she said, "If you need me, my name is Harriet Gordon. I am staying in Room 3-17 at the Empire Hotel."

The street was quiet, and she saw no one except her own ricksha wallah. Nonetheless, a cold shiver ran down her spine as she walked away from the Blake house.

THIRTY-ONE

I have found Samrita!
The words kept pounding through Harriet's mind as the ricksha wallah trundled her back to the hotel.

She thought if she couldn't tell Curran right away, she would burst out of her skin, but Curran was not in his room or anywhere else at the hotel. She considered rushing over to the hospital to tell Jayant, but she did not know him well enough, nor whether his state of health would permit such a shocking revelation.

No, she would have to practice patience and wait for Curran.

In her room, she took the postcard from her handbag and studied the card again. She had seen the four elephants, or something like them, in the Batu Caves. Why was it so significant? Whatever the answer, it would have to wait. She secreted the card between the pages of the book she had been reading and went downstairs to lunch.

In the afternoon, as Curran had still not returned, she gathered her courage and took a ricksha to the Robertson bungalow.

She found Edith alone, playing with her daughter Dottie on the verandah. A picture of domestic bliss, Harriet thought. No one could possibly suspect the pretty, fair-haired young mother of being a cold-blooded murderer.

On seeing Harriet, Edith stood up, dusting off her linen skirt. Little Dottie ran to Harriet and flung her arms around her. Harriet picked up the little girl and hugged her tight.

Poor little thing... what would become of her if her mother were to hang?

"Amah!" Edith summoned the nurse. "Take Dottie away."

"Oh no, please don't send her away on my account," Harriet protested. The little girl's presence was a note of normality in this strange situation, but the amah had already scooped Dottie up.

"It is time for her afternoon nap," Edith said.

She sent for tea, and the two women sat on the verandah, looking out over the school.

"Henry went to work today." Edith pulled a face. "I couldn't stand his fussing anymore. I have another meeting with Charlie Hughes tonight, but he uses so many big words and is quite tedious. He says that what I did was self-defense, and I was protecting my person as I am entitled to do." She looked up at Harriet. "They will believe that, won't they?"

Harriet spread her hands. "Edith. I am the daughter of a lawyer and yours is the sort of case my father would prosecute. The prosecution has to prove beyond reasonable doubt that you had intended to kill Mr. Stewart. You have to show that you were acting in self-defense and that you did not exceed the authority that a self-defense claim affords you."

Even as she spoke, Harriet thought of the five additional rounds Edith had fired into the dying man on the ground, and knew her father would say that she had far exceeded her authority to defend herself. Stewart had been in retreat when Edith followed to finish what she had started.

"I have to tell them how he attacked me, Harriet. He put his hands up my skirt. He touched me!"

Harriet bit her tongue, ignoring the horror and outrage in

Edith's tone. Edith Robertson had worn no underwear beneath her filmy evening dress. A good prosecutor, such as her father, would have no trouble with that salacious piece of information. Edith's defense grew flimsier by the moment.

"How well did you know Mr Stewart?" Harriet asked.

Edith shrugged. "He was a friend ... no, more of a distant acquaintance. He lived alone out near that mine he used to manage, but he came into town quite often. I think he was lonely."

"But didn't he have a native woman living with him?"

Edith's eyes widened. "Who told you that?" She waved away Stewart's live-in companion. "Some Chinese woman kept house for him, but it meant nothing. Not a native."

Harriet flinched, remembering the passionate relationship between Li An and Curran. That had meant something far greater and deeper than Harriet had ever known. She had judged herself happily married to James, but even in the early days of their marriage, she would hardly have described it as passionate.

Edith looked down at her cup and bit her lip. "They won't send me to jail. After all, I am an Englishwoman. I don't belong in a place like Pudu. That is for the natives, not me."

Harriet took a breath. "They can and they will, Edith, and if that happens, all you can do is set yourself to endure it ... as I did."

Edith looked up, her eyes wide. "What do you know about being in jail?"

Harriet swallowed. "I was arrested at a suffragette rally in London and sentenced to six months' imprisonment. They sent me to Holloway."

"Oh, Harriet. How simply dreadful." Edith looked genuinely shocked, although Harriet was unsure if her shock was sympathy for Harriet's plight or surprise that a seemingly respectable woman had a criminal record.

She could have gone on to describe the torture she endured in the weeks she spent in incarceration, but changed the subject.

"You are fortunate to have a husband who cares so much for you. Why didn't your parents approve of him?"

Edith leaned forward. "Henry is not one of *us*. He didn't go to a good school or know the right people."

One thing Harriet had learned in her years in India and her time in Singapore was that the worst of the British were those who were reinventing themselves. Back in Manchester or Birmingham, they were ordinary people leading ordinary lives, mired in the British class system through which they could never hope to rise. In the colonies, the men became *nabob* or *tuan*, the women *memsahib*, putting themselves at the top of the ladder both within the expatriate society and the local community, and openly despising anyone they considered below them.

It didn't matter that Henry Robertson was an excellent teacher, administrator, sportsman, and the like; without the right connections, or pretense to the right connections, in a small community such as Kuala Lumpur, he remained an outsider.

"It doesn't help that he tells everyone he is an agnostic," Edith continued. Her lip trembled. "I was having this very conversation with Mr. Stewart ..." She glanced at the bookshelf and swallowed. "I was showing him one of William's books. That one ..." She pointed to a book, The Agnostics Apology. "When he grabbed me." Tears filled her eyes. "He said ... he said ... 'Never mind the book. You look bonny. I love you.'" She took a deep, shuddering breath. "How could a man with a Chinese woman say he loves me? What does he know about love when he goes home to *her*?"

The spite in Edith's voice piqued Harriet's interest in the mysterious Chinese woman. As for an answer to her question, she thought again of Curran and Li An and the times she had observed them together, oblivious to the outside world and the opinions of society. That had been love, true love.

"Shall we play cribbage?" she asked, suddenly anxious to turn her thoughts away from Curran.

There was no further conversation about the nature of love.

Edith fetched the cribbage board and a well-used pack of cards from the bookcase and after playing a few rounds of the game with Edith, Harriet took her leave with some relief.

On her arrival back at the hotel, she hurried straight up to Curran's room, heedless of who saw her, and knocked on the door. When he didn't answer, her heart sank, remembering he intended to visit the Topaz Club that night and he had probably gone to visit Jayant.

Back in her room, she penned him a note.

Visit surprising. J not who you think, but someone long sought after. Reception less than warm but I have some important information for you. H

She sealed the note in a hotel envelope and slid it under Curran's door.

THIRTY-TWO

C urran had spent the day in the stifling humidity of the jungle, watching the coming and goings at the Topaz Club. Despite changing his position between the front and the back of the house, he had seen very little movement. The gates remained shut blocking any view of the ground level. A couple of girls had appeared on the upstairs verandah in the early afternoon, cigarettes in hand. They could have been two girls from anywhere, laughing and chatting about who knew what.

He returned to the hotel about five and found a note from the hospital waiting for him at the front desk.

Mr. Kumar's condition worsening. Request your attendance.

Curran looked down at his filthy, sweat-soaked clothes. It had been a long, hot day, and it was going to be a busy night. He had hoped to get some rest before meeting up with George. Now he was needed elsewhere.

"See anything of interest?" The hotel clerk asked with a smile.

It took a moment for Curran to recall he was supposed to be

birdwatching. He knew very little about birds, so he fudged. "A few hornbills," he said.

The man nodded. "I saw a crested argus pheasant, last weekend," he said.

Just my luck to encounter a bird lover.

Curran whistled through his teeth in admiration, and the man grinned. "Pity I have no evidence. It is very rare—"

The man seemed set for an entire conversation, but Curran cut him short and retreated to his bedroom. He found another note, this one pushed under his door, his name written in Harriet's hand. He tossed it, unopened, onto the table, washed and changed, and hurried downstairs. He hailed a ricksha in the rain and arrived at the hospital damp and out of sorts

Despite it being outside visiting hours, the hospital admitted him and an English doctor intercepted him. From the grave look on his face, Curran feared he may be too late.

"Mr. Kumar...?" Curran began, his voice tight with concern.

The doctor held up his hand. "He's still holding his own," he said. "If we can get him through the night, I would be more hopeful."

Curran swallowed and took a breath, regaining his composure. "May I sit with him a while?"

The doctor nodded. "Of course."

They had drawn a screen around Jayant's bed and his brother lay tangled in the bedsheet. A nurse looked up from sponging his face.

"I'm a friend," Curran said. "The doctor has allowed me to sit with him."

"He's very poorly," the nurse said in a strong Lancashire accent, reminding him of Griff Maddocks's friend, Sister Doreen Wilson. The frown on the nurse's face told him everything her words didn't.

"I'll leave you alone," she said.

Curran pulled up the chair beside his brother's bed. He rarely felt quite so inadequate. What was he supposed to do?

"Jay?" he ventured.

Jayant's eyes flickered open.

"It's me, Robert," Curran said, his inadequacy increasing by the moment.

"Have ... you ... found ...her ...?" Jayant's words came in a hoarse whisper.

"Not yet. I am going to the Topaz Club tonight and..." he trailed off. He had no other news to impart.

"She's not dead. I would know it ... here ..." Jayant tapped his chest. "But I—"

Jayant's eyes closed, his breath coming in ragged gasps after the exertion of speech.

"You've come too far to give up now," Curran said. "Keep fighting, Jay."

Jayant's eyes closed and Curran found himself unable to move, fearful if he turned away, Jayant would slip from the world, leaving him alone again.

The nurse returned with a cup of tea, which he drank gratefully. "It's getting late," she said. "Nothing to be done here. You go home and we'll let you know if there's any change."

Curran stood up and patted his brother's arm. "I'll be back tomorrow," he said to the semi-conscious man. "Be here."

He returned to the hotel with barely enough time to dress for his rendezvous with George.

As he struggled with the bow tie, he cast a glance at his faithful Webley revolver before locking it away in a drawer. Even if he could have concealed it beneath the unforgiving evening dress, George had been clear. No weapons. It left him feeling curiously naked.

At the last minute, he picked up the envelope with Harriet's note and stuffed it in his trousers' pocket, to read when the opportunity presented.

George pulled up to the Empire on the dot of ten in a darkened carriage drawn by two horses.

"Hardly recognized you. You scrub up well," George commented as Curran seated himself across from his cousin.

He expected some snide rider to the comment to follow, such as for a stableboy. Heaven alone knew he had heard them all, but George said nothing more.

The coach lurched forward, and Curran reached for the strap. He hated to admit it, but he was growing accustomed to traveling in motor vehicles and found the carriage uncomfortable and tediously slow.

"Did you ever marry?" George asked at last.

"No"

"Lucky dog. I don't recommend it."

"Is that why you patronize the Topaz Club?"

"Don't take that tone, Curran."

"What tone?"

They were ten-year-olds squaring for a fight again. Curran took a breath. "I didn't mean it to sound like I was judging you, George."

"You haven't met my wife," George responded. "She's an American, the 'lie back and think of the Empire' type of woman. Her father owns railway lines—ghastly little man—but stinking rich. But she loves all things English and cannot wait to be a Countess. She's the savior of the Alcester estates. I go to the Topaz Club for the gambling tables since you ask."

"And the Topaz Club doesn't trouble your conscience at all?"

George was silent for a long moment before he said, "No. It's harmless fun. The only thing I've lost is a good deal of money on the gaming tables. That's how it is with our sort, Curran. You know that." He gave a snort of laughter. "Or maybe that is one thing you never learned?"

There it was: the snide remark.

"You can't help yourself, can you, George?" Curran

responded, conscious of the petulance in his own tone. He held up a hand. "Look, it's been a long time. We're not children anymore and, like it or not, we are blood, so let us at least retain a degree of civility."

"Absolutely," George said. "You must meet Sarah."

Curran glanced at the shuttered window of the carriage. "I will be pleased to make her acquaintance. Do you have children?"

"Two girls. We left them at home with Papa and Mama."

"That will be a fun Christmas for them," Curran remarked drily, memories of the many miserable Christmases at Deerbourne watching his cousins unwrap a cornucopia of fabulous toys and books surging to the front of his mind. One year he received a bible, and the following year, new stockings.

George leaned forward. "Come on, Curran. Tell me. What is it you are up to?"

Curran brought his gaze back to his cousin. "I can't tell you. Please, for the love of God, do not call me Curran tonight."

George tapped his nose. "Understood."

The carriage turned off the main road. Curran peered out into the dark night. Judging from the jolting that they had turned down the rutted and potholed lane that led to the Club. The carriage stopped and from beyond the coach, he heard the protest of heavy gates being opened, and then the carriage rolled forward onto a smoother gravel that crunched beneath the wheels.

THIRTY-THREE

Glad to be out of the stuffy, claustrophobic coach, Curran jumped down before the uniformed servant lowered the steps. He found himself in the elegant, well-lit *porte cochère* of the mansion. As he tugged at his jacket and straightened his tie, he looked around like any curious first-time visitor. Up close the house struck him as even more incongruous, a fantasy building in the middle of a jungle and rubber plantations.

At the door, they were met by an Indian man in evening dress, his dark hair well-oiled and combed back from a high forehead, his mustache neatly clipped. Tall, well-muscled with high cheekbones and a ready smile, if this was Gopal Acharya, Curran could see the appeal to the women he hunted.

Jayant had described him as the cousin of the local baker who had charmed his way into the Kumar family home, sharing meals and bringing presents. Then one morning he was gone, Samrita and Lakshmi with him.

Gopal spread his arms wide, smiling as he said, "Welcome Mr. Bullock-Steele, you have brought a new guest?"

"This is Mr. Sutton, Gopal. He's just visiting KL and I trust you to ensure he has an enjoyable evening. Sutton, this is our host, Gopal Acharya."

Gopal inclined his head. "Everyone calls me Gopal."

Curran could think of several less flattering names including the one Jayant had called him: 'Gopal the Procurer'.

"You are most welcome, Mr. Sutton. And how did you learn of our humble establishment?" Gopal's smile was not echoed in his eyes.

"A man I met in Colombo gave me your card," Curran brandished the little business card. "Said if I ever was in Kuala Lumpur, I would be assured of a warm welcome."

"We pride ourselves on the exclusivity of our clients," Gopal said, "but if Mr. Bullock-Steel can vouch for you, then you are welcome."

George clapped Curran on the shoulder. "Oh yes, I've known Sutton since university days."

Gopal stood aside and gestured to the open front door. "Then you are indeed most welcome. We ask only that you sign our guest register."

He indicated a large leather-bound folio on a table and turned to a blank page.

Unsurprisingly, it required the guest to enter his name and address. Curran completed his entry, inventing a fictional address that in England may have carried overtones of aristocracy. When he turned back, he was alone with Gopal.

The man coughed discreetly. "Did Mr. Bullock-Steele tell you we also ask for an initial donation of twenty pounds?"

Curran suppressed a gasp. An astronomical sum.

"No, he must have forgotten," Curran said.

"It covers the cost of food, drink ... and whatever is your pleasure for the evening," Gopal continued with a smile.

Luckily, Curran had come prepared, thanks to the largesse of the allowance provided by his employer, and he handed over the notes, which Gopal stowed inside his jacket.

"I will show you around and then you can choose your preferred activity."

In the largest of the downstairs rooms, a gramophone played while several couples danced or reclined on the sofas. There were at least half a dozen women fanning themselves while a *punkah* stirred the warm air above them. It could have been a tea dance anywhere. The women were Chinese, Indian, and European, all dressed in elegant Western evening wear, and all were beautiful.

None of them were Samrita.

He thought of Lakshmi and her pink evening dress. That garment would have been *de rigeur* for an evening at the Topaz Club.

In another room were the gaming tables. More women hung over the shoulders of the gamblers.

Gopal gestured for a blonde woman, and she sashayed across to them.

"This is a new friend," Gopal said. "Mr. Sutton."

The woman smiled, flashing neat white teeth, but her eyes remained dead and cold. "I am Pansy," she said in heavily accented English.

"Fetch a whisky," Gopal ordered. "I am correct in assuming you are a whisky man, Mr. Sutton?"

Curran nodded. It better be good, he thought, thinking of the notes he had handed over.

"My contact recommended a girl called Lily," he said.

Gopal's smile remained fixed as he spread his hands in apology. "Sadly, Lily is no longer with us," he said.

"That is disappointing," Curran said.

Gopal effected a shrug. "That is the way these things are," he said. "If girls like Lily are to your taste, I can introduce you to Hyacinth." He indicated a pretty Indian girl on the far side of the room, apparently engaged in assisting a man with laying bets on a roulette wheel. "Here is your whisky. Enjoy your evening, Mr. Sutton."

Curran took the drink, grateful for the smooth, high-quality whisky. It was indeed top-shelf Scotch.

"What is your pleasure?" Pansy asked. "Roulette, cocaine—opium?" The look on his face must have given her the answer to that question. She laughed and tucked her hand around his arm. "Or would you rather have someone to ease your loneliness?"

The words were so well rehearsed, so mechanical, it was all Curran could do not to run for the door. He drained his drink and handed the glass to the girl, asking for another.

Tonight was about reconnaissance, he reminded himself.

"I just want to talk," he said when Pansy returned with his refilled glass.

She smiled. "Then talk we shall. Come with me, sir." She slid her hand into his elbow and led him toward the stairs. She smelled of an expensive rose-scented perfume. Alcohol and perfume were a heady mix.

Upstairs, in an elegant bedroom, with large double doors leading onto a verandah, she excused herself for a moment.

He threw open the doors and stepped onto the verandah, grateful to be out in the fresh air. Music and light from the downstairs rooms spilled out, illuminating a broad expanse of lawn leading up to the high wall. No trees or shrubs to afford cover and, moving in the shadows, he could detect the unmistakable shapes of at least three large dogs.

"Come back inside and shut the window," the girl's soft accented voice came from behind him.

He turned.

She had discarded her elegant evening dress for a frothy robe of silk and lace over her corset and chemise.

He raised his eyes to meet hers.

"I do just want to talk," he said.

Pansy walked over to a cabinet, opening it to reveal a row of crystal decanters. She poured him another whisky and one for herself and sat on the edge of the bed, glass in hand.

She patted the bed beside her, but Curran chose the chair on the far side of the room.

"You do not strike me as the shy sort," Pansy said. "You are thinking of your wife? Your children?"

He shook his head and then remembered he was supposed to have a fiancée in England. "Maybe," he said. "Missing my girl back home."

"Well, then we sit here, and we talk. It is of no matter to me."

"Where are you from?" he asked.

"Poland," she said.

"And what brought you all the way out here?"

The humor faded from her eyes. "A violent man," she said. "I left him behind, along with my old life."

He wanted to ask if she had come to the Club of her own free will but refrained. Maybe not all the girls at the Topaz Club had been coerced, as Samrita and Lakshmi had been.

As if she read his mind, she said. "A woman can crave adventure too, Mr. Sutton."

"When did Lily leave?" he asked.

"You are very curious about Lily," Pansy said.

Curran shrugged. "Just the chap I spoke to seemed keen on her."

Pansy laughed, but there was no humor in the bitter sound. "A few months ago," she said.

"Did she leave of her own accord?"

Something flickered in Pansy's eyes. Fear? he wondered.

"Of course," she said too hurriedly. "We are all free to leave if we choose."

The words were too pat, too well rehearsed. "With armed guards at the gate and guard dogs in the garden?" Curran said.

Her eyes widened. "Who are you?"

He held up his hands. "I'm just curious. I've never come across a place quite like this before."

They eyed each other across the distance of a large oriental rug, like two cats circling each other, waiting for the other to move first.

"What will you tell your masters?" Curran asked.

"I will tell Gopal that you and I had an enjoyable evening," she replied. "What will you say?"

"That I had an enjoyable evening."

"Will you come again?"

"I don't know. What is your real name?"

She hesitated. "Maria Vlasek. And is Sutton your real name?"

"It is."

She considered him for a long moment. "You are a policeman?"

"What makes you say that?"

She shrugged. "There is a look ... either police or military. It is unmistakable."

"I was a soldier," Curran replied, truthfully.

"There are police who visit."

Despite himself, he asked. "Who?"

She put her finger to her lips. "I do not ask questions."

He smiled. "You do ask questions. Plenty of them."

She laughed and, for the first time, he sensed her amusement was genuine. "I ask questions because I have not entertained a gentleman who has resisted my charms before and that has made me curious."

"And that is what I am, just curious," Curran said.

Maria stood up and made a dismissive gesture with her hand. "As pleasant as this is, if you do not wish my company, Mr. Sutton, you can return to your friend at the gaming tables. I have others who are more willing."

Curran set a couple of pound notes down on the table beside him and rose to his feet.

Maria Vlasek deftly pocketed the notes and as Curran passed her, she sidestepped, winding her arms around his neck as she kissed him. Her heavy perfume surrounded him in a sickly miasma, but his body responded to her proximity and the sudden intimacy.

"They watch us," she whispered. "It would be good to at least pretend."

And he did, kissing her fulsomely but revolted by the thought of an unseen eye watching the sport in the elegant room.

"You could have told me this before," he whispered back. "Were we overheard?"

"Probably," she replied. "But it does not matter. It was a conversation of no importance."

Curran disengaged the woman and outside the room, took a moment to adjust his jacket and compose himself as he replayed the conversation with Maria. What did it matter if they had been spied on? He'd merely been enquiring about a girl who used to work at the club. Nothing suspicious about that.

Curran returned to the gaming room. George, red-faced and sweating, stood beside the roulette wheel. He turned his head and, on seeing Curran, his eyes widened.

"Just the man. Can you lend me some pounds, Curran—" He stopped, fear registering on his face. "Sutton."

But the damage was done. Curran braced, ready for whatever came next. He would fight his way out of the Topaz Club if he had to.

Nothing happened. Maybe no one had noticed George's slip.

He crossed to George and took his arm. "Time to go," he said into his cousin's ear.

"Sorry, old chap," George mumbled.

With a companionable arm across George's shoulders, Curran steered him toward the front door.

"Our carriage," he told the man at the door.

They stepped out onto the front porch to wait.

Interminable minutes ticked by without the carriage appearing. Every nerve in Curran's back prickled, expecting trouble to burst through the door at any moment. But the carriage arrived, and as it drew to a halt, Gopal stepped through the door.

"Goodnight, gentlemen," he said. "I trust you had a pleasant evening?"

George blustered a response. Curran summoned a smile and thanked the man.

Gopal inclined his head. "I hope you will return tomorrow night," he said. "I assure you of a welcome."

What did that mean, Curran wondered as he settled back in the coach.

When he got back to his room at the Empire Hotel, he remembered the note from Harriet. He went through every pocket, but the envelope had gone. He ran his hands through his hair and walked across to the window, looking out at the dark, silent town beyond.

Maria Vlasek must have picked his pockets when she kissed him. He cursed himself for a fool to fall for that old trick. What had the note said? It was too late to go to Harriet's room and ask her.

It would have to wait till morning.

THIRTY-FOUR

WEDNESDAY, 7 DECEMBER

When Harriet came down for breakfast, she found Curran waiting for her at the bottom of the stairs. From the dark circles under his eyes, she wondered how much sleep he had managed.

"May I speak with you, Mrs. Gordon?"

Almost before she could reply, he took her arm and steered her into the garden.

"How was—" she began.

"That note you left me ... what did it say?"

"Didn't you read it?"

"No, and now I've lost it."

"That is unusually careless of you, Curran," Harriet said.

A muscle twitched in his jaw. "I lost the note at the Topaz Club last night."

Harriet stared at him. "How?"

Two spots of color appeared on his cheekbones. "It doesn't matter. How specific was the note?"

"I tried not to be specific. No names. Hopefully, it will be meaningless to anyone else."

"Tell me exactly what you wrote."

"It said ... it implied ... I had found Samrita," Harriet said, hurriedly adding, "I didn't say it in so many words, Curran. I tried to keep it ambiguous."

He stared at her. "Samrita? What do you mean, you have found Samrita?"

"I did as you asked. I went to the Blake house. The woman Simon met, Jameela, is your Samrita."

"How do you know it is her?"

"I had the photograph. Of course, she is older, but unmistakable."She touched his arm, searching his face for his reaction. "She has been hiding in plain sight, Curran."

Curran threaded his fingers through his hair. "It is good news, Harriet. Jayant will be pleased. He never lost hope."

Harriet let her hand drop at the mention of Jayant. "You should know that she wants nothing to do with you or Jayant. She said as far as the two of you should be concerned, she is dead."

Curran frowned. "Why? Is she afraid of us? Our reaction to her?"

Harriet shook her head. "She is afraid, but not of you. At the moment, I think she is under Ashton Blake's protection, but if you try to interfere—" She looked away. "She has a baby, Curran, and a mother will do whatever it takes to protect her child. I just have a feeling we have already put her in danger."

"I'll go back this morning," he said.

"Shall I come with you?"

He didn't answer immediately. A hundred conflicting emotions crossed his face. "Harriet, this is nothing to do with you. I should never have involved you."

"But I am involved, Curran, and have been from the first moment I encountered Jayant."

He looked away and nodded. "Yes. Come with me. Your presence may help."

Harriet laid a hand on his arm again. Beneath her fingers, his muscles tensed but instead of pulling away, he laid his hand over hers, his fingers tightening on her hand, his gaze never leaving her face. She had the strange sensation that she was looking into the eyes of a drowning man.

Abruptly, he pulled away, straightening his jacket and flicking back the disordered hair from his face.

"There you are!" Griff Maddocks came striding across the terrace toward them. Beside him, the tall, solid figure of Sergeant Gursharan Singh, dressed impeccably in civilian clothes and looking every inch a prosperous businessman.

"I found this gentleman in the foyer asking after you, Sutton," Maddocks said.

"It is good to see you, Singh," Curran said, clasping hands with his sergeant.

"And I am heartily glad to be relieved of traffic duties. My wife's cousin lives in Kuala Lumpur and it is an excellent opportunity to see him and his family. He is a most excellent goldsmith—"

"This isn't a social visit," Curran said.

Singh grinned. "No, but if I do not return with new earrings for my Sumeet, I will be in deepest trouble. What is it you wish me to do?"

"Whatever it is you are up to, I'm here, Curran," Maddocks said. "I am completely bored. I can't get near the Robertson woman." He cast a reproachful glance at Harriet. "So, I am just kicking dirt on the Padang, hoping for a story. I will be forced to visit the museum today if I don't find something useful to do."

Curran looked from one to the other and a smile tugged at the corner of his mouth.

"Thank you for the offer, Maddocks. See what you can find out about a man called Gopal Acharya. He is the face of the Topaz

Club, but I don't think it is his venture. For now, I need to pay another visit to the house of Ashton Blake and his wife. Harriet? Singh?"

Harriet and Singh exchanged a quick glance and both nodded.

THIRTY-FIVE

An unnatural silence hung over the Blake's home in the quiet residential street. Curran exchanged a quick glance with Singh and his fingers closed over the butt of the Webley that he now carried, loaded, in the capacious pocket of his jacket.

"Something is not right," he said as they opened the gate. He turned to Harriet. "Wait here."

Her eyes widened. "Why?"

"Harriet!" It was not an argument he wanted to have. He should never have agreed to let her come.

She nodded. "Very well."

"Singh, with me?"

The two men approached the front door, which stood slightly ajar. Curran stopped in his tracks, his nerves jangling at the sight of a handprint on the white plaster beside the door ... a handprint dyed in the reddish brown of dried blood.

It was no accident. Could it have been intentionally placed there ... as a warning?

Using his elbow, he pushed the door open and, holding his weapon in both hands, moved into the house. The long corridor beyond the living room was dark and silent. No servants' chatter or sound of the baby.

"Curran," Singh said in a low voice. "Over here."

Curran turned to look at what had attracted Singh's attention.

Partially concealed by a table, Ashton Blake lay face up and spreadeagled on the oriental rug. The white of his nightshirt was stained dark brown with drying blood, and his eyes were open. Insects buzzed in the warm air and the smell of death had already overwhelmed the room.

Curran hunkered down and touched the man's neck. No warmth in the cold, dead flesh. By Curran's rough estimate, Blake had been dead since the previous night.

"What's happening?" Harriet's voice came from the doorway.

Gursharan Singh turned and moved to the front door. "Do not come in, Mrs. Gordon."

"Curran?" Harriet sounded agitated.

Curran joined his sergeant. "Ashton Blake is dead."

Harriet stared at him, her eyes wide with shock, and he once again regretted bringing her. She had seen enough dead bodies for one trip to Kuala Lumpur.

"And Samrita?" Her voice sounded tight with suppressed emotion.

"I don't know. We need to search the rest of the house." He reached out and took her by the forearms. "Go back to the hotel, Harriet. You don't want to find yourself tied up in another death."

As he spoke, the thin wail of a baby broke the silence. Curran let his hands drop and whipped around, looking toward the back of the house. Singh moved faster stopping outside a door in the corridor.

Harriet had still not moved. "Samrita said she was in danger.

She would never have left her baby by choice. This is our fault, Curran."

My fault, he thought, turning back to her.

They stood looking at each other and Curran saw the pain in Harriet's eyes, the rigid set of her shoulders as she sought reassurance that all would be well.

He had nothing to offer her.

"Harriet, I should never have involved you. None of this is your fault. Take the *gharry* and go back to the hotel." He tried to sound gruff and professional.

"The baby—"

"Go. There is nothing for you to do here. Singh and I will deal with it. I want ... I need you to be somewhere safe."

Finally, she nodded. "Very well, I'm going. Be careful, Curran."

He managed a smile. "I'm always careful."

She held his gaze. "No, you're not," she replied and turned on her heel, hurrying down the path to where the *gharry* waited.

"Curran," Singh called him.

With his Webley in hand, Curran crept down the silent corridor, opening the doors onto a dining room and the Blakes' bedroom where the bedding had been dragged to the ground, leaving the mosquito net torn and barely hanging from its hook.

Singh stood beside the last door. From within that room came the wail of a small, angry baby that increased in volume as Curran joined him.

"It's locked. No key," Singh said.

"You know what to do."

Singh threw his shoulder at the solid wooden door, but it refused to budge. It took him several attempts before the wood cracked and yielded.

As the door swung open, a woman screamed.

Curran flinched from the hysterical high-pitched wailing

from the woman and child as he stood back and held out his free hand.

"Friend," he said.

The room appeared to be a nursery with a baby's crib, a table and chair, and a low, narrow bed, the only furnishings. A woman crouched in the corner, a veil drawn over her head, and the howling baby hugged close to her. Seeing the weapon in his hand, the woman's ululations grew more frantic.

A wave of disappointment flooded over Curran.

Not Samrita.

This woman was older, her dark hair threaded with grey.

"Policeman," he said.

Singh spoke to the woman in Tamil, and the woman's cries subsided. She hunched down, trying to hush the child, but it would not be comforted, its screams growing louder and more desperate, setting Curran's teeth on edge.

Singh held out his arms, and the woman rose to her feet and, to Curran's surprise, handed the child to the man. The large policeman jiggled and crooned with all the experience of a well-practiced father and incredibly the child fell quiet, uttering nothing more than a noise that sounded like a gurgle or a giggle as it reached for Singh's beard.

"Ask her what she knows about what happened here," Curran suggested to his sergeant.

Singh obliged, and words and tears, accompanied by extravagant hand gestures, tumbled from her. Singh nodded and handed the child back to the woman, patting her on the shoulder as he did so.

"She is the child's nursemaid," he said and frowned. "What is the word? Wet nurse? She was asleep in here with the baby when she was woken by the sound of knocking on the front door. She heard Blake go to the door and much shouting. Before she could open the door to see what was happening, the key turned in the lock and she was locked in. She heard Jameela scream and two shots and then silence. She has been locked in here all this time. When she heard us arrive, she was afraid the wicked men had returned. I have told her we are police and can be trusted."

For the first time, Curran looked at the baby. Not that he could make much of it except a shock of dark hair.

"Is it a boy or a girl?" he asked.

"A girl. Her name is Kamini"

"You stay with her. I'll search the rest of the property."

Afraid of what he might find, Curran went back through the house and then turned to the servant's quarters, finding them deserted. The servants had either fled on hearing gunshots or been frightened off by the intruders. It seemed evident that the men who had come in the night had only been interested in Blake and Samrita, and now Samrita was missing again.

Curran's heart clenched. He had been so close and now his clumsy interference had probably resulted in this new tragedy.

He returned to the baby's room and found Singh seated on the chair, playing games with the baby. The amah stood in the corner, her arms wrapped around herself, watching the interaction between man and child.

"You've done this before," Curran said.

Singh smiled. "Three times, Curran, and each one a delight. If the child's mother is your sister, then little Kamini here is your niece."

Curran stared at the baby. His niece? He was already wrestling with the concept of family responsibilities over Jayant and Samrita and now this helpless child?

"How old is she?" he asked.

Singh directed the question to the nurse.

"This woman, Padmi, says she has been with the baby since shortly after she was born. She says the child is just over four months old."

"What are we going to do with her?" Curran asked.

Singh exchanged another conversation with the nurse. "Padmi

says she is happy to take the child back to the safety of her own family until other arrangements can be made."

"Can we trust her?"

"I do not see a choice," Singh said. "The baby's mother is missing, and you are in no position to care for a child, particularly one as young as this. I will go with her and see that all is in order."

Outside in the corridor, Curran pulled out his wallet and handed Singh a couple of decent banknotes. "Please. Give this to her and tell her there will be more when we have resolved what has to happen with the child."

Singh pocketed the money and returned to the woman. Padmi hurriedly selected what was needed for the care of the baby and when Singh indicated to her it was time to leave, she nodded, pulling her sari around her face, and settling the child in her arms. She picked up the bundle of clothes and they left by the back door, leaving Curran alone in the house.

He stood looking at the empty crib. Harriet had said that no mother would willingly leave a child. He could only hope that if Samrita had been taken by whoever had killed Blake, she was still alive ... somewhere..

He turned back into the house and with a handkerchief over his hand, he turned the scene into one of chaos ... upending furniture, pulling out drawers and tearing cushions. He had to make the scene look like a robbery gone wrong.

The discovery of a small pistol kicked under the sofa made him wonder if Blake had tried to defend his little family. He picked the weapon up and cracked it open. One shot had been fired. He wiped the weapon and arranged the pistol, closing the dead man's fingers around the butt, so that it looked like Blake had been holding it when he was shot.

He went through Ashton Blake's desk, looking for the connection between Blake and the Topaz Club. The search revealed nothing except household accounts and correspondence relating to Blake's employment, including a glowing reference from the manager of the Laidlaw branch in Colombo. Oddly, he found no family correspondence or photographs or anything to give a clue as to Ashton Blake's antecedents.

Finally, he went through Blake's wallet, removing any money he found there and, after wiping it of fingerprints, threw it on the ground beside the man's head.

When he finished staging the crime scene, he stood back and gave Ashton Blake one last regretful look.

As he walked away, Curran thought Wheeler would most likely see it as a robbery. Wheeler was a decent man, but lacked the imagination to envisage any other scenario. The house had been ransacked, the owner dead. Would he go in search of the missing servants? Would witnesses come forward who had seen three people at the house that morning? Maybe, but it was clear Blake had died last night. Wheeler was under-manned and already swamped by the Robertson case. Ashton Blake's death may well remain unsolved.

Only Curran would know that the responsibility for the man's death and Samrita's disappearance rested with him.

That thought settled on his shoulder like a dark shadow. He had asked too many questions. He had sent Harriet to Samrita. Had the note stolen from his pocket the night before compounded the concern that Ashton Blake and Samrita were about to betray the Topaz Club?

In short, he had left a trail illuminated with flares and now an innocent man was dead, and his sister was ... who knew where?

He whipped off his hat and swiped at his leg. Self-castigation was all very well, but now the search to find Samrita had become urgent and he still had the matter of the Topaz Club to resolve.

This is what happened when the professional and the personal clashed. He should have concentrated on the task he had been given by his masters, from which the solution to Samrita's plight may have resolved itself, instead of fancying himself a white knight intent on slaying every dragon at the same time.

THIRTY-SIX

On her return to the hotel, Harriet found a note from Esme Prynne.

I have the afternoon off. If you have no other pressing engagements, please join me at the Club for mahjong this afternoon.

Harriet let the note fall to the table as she gathered her thoughts. How could she go to the Selangor Club and pretend everything was normal? She had left Curran with a dead body and a missing girl.

Guilt clawed at her.

If she hadn't visited Samrita yesterday morning, would Blake still be alive? Would Samrita still be at home with her baby?

Kicking off her shoes, Harriet fell onto her bed, wrapping her arms around herself as she let the tears fall. It had taken all her self-control not to cry in front of Curran. His world was crumbling around him and the last thing he needed was another hysterical woman, but if he had reached out to her, then neither of them would have to face what lay ahead alone. There was power in two that did not exist in just one person.

But he had stood there, the wall between them as high and insurmountable as it had ever been.

She gave a last shuddering sob and rolled over, staring up at the ceiling. She wiped her eyes, blew her nose, and rose from the bed. Nothing would be gained from sulking in her room. She washed and changed into her freshly laundered blue muslin gown. Fortunately, the laundry at the hotel had proved to be efficient and she could eke out her limited wardrobe.

As she fixed her hair, she looked at her reflection in the mirror. Her eyes were still puffy and red-rimmed and her face blotchy.

She straightened her shoulders and took a deep breath. She would spend the afternoon playing mahjong as if everything in a world preoccupied with Edith Robertson was normal. It was time to find out a little more about society in Kuala Lumpur in general and, for her own curiosity more than anything else, where Edith fitted in.

A club steward admitted Harriet to the pleasant room where the mahjong tables had been set out, four women sitting at each one, the neat ivory tiles in front of them. Esme signaled Harriet over to her table, where one chair remained. The three women sitting at the table had already dealt their tiles but hadn't begun the game.

The woman in the chair opposite Harriet was deep in conversation with a woman at another table and had her back to Harriet as Esme said cheerfully, "Deal yourself in from the wall, and then we can start."

The other woman's head snapped around. "You can't do that," she said, her accent straight from the streets of Manchester or some other northern town. From her hennaed hair to her tight mouth, she bristled in disapproval.

Harriet froze.

"And you're late," the red-headed harridan continued. "Don't you know the etiquette of mahjong requires you to be on time or you wait out the game?"

"I ... I'm sorry," Harriet began, her already fragile self-control beginning to crumble.

"I said she could, Mavis," Esme said. "Mrs. Gordon is a guest at the club, it would behoove us to show her some hospitality."

Clearly, Mavis was not to be mollified. "Aye, that's as good as maybe," she said. "Very well. Go on then, Mrs. Gordon, finish drawing your tiles, and let's start the game. I just hope you know the rules."

"I have played before," Harriet stuttered.

But the woman's antagonism had shaken her to the core and her hand trembled as she drew her tiles from the wall. She stared blindly at her tiles. Everything she knew about the game vanished from her mind as stupid, galling tears threatened once again.

"We haven't even done proper introductions," Esme said. "Ladies, Mrs. Gordon is visiting from Singapore. Harriet, I'd like to introduce Mrs. Mavis Wheeler, wife of the police inspector. And this is Mrs. Jean Driver, wife of the Inspector of Schools."

Mrs. Driver smiled warmly. "Always nice to see a new face," she said.

"I know where I've heard your name," Mrs. Wheeler said. "You're a friend of that little harlot, Edith Robertson."

"She's not a friend," Harriet stuttered. "I've only just met—"

"Pung." Mavis Wheeler laid down her first hand and cast a triumphant look around the table.

"Well played," Mrs. Driver said. She was a small, mousy woman and her voice had a tremor in it. Clearly, Harriet was not the only one intimidated by Mavis Wheeler.

Harriet frowned, the epithet applied to Edith Robertson only just registering with her. "I beg your pardon, Mrs. Wheeler, but that name you just called Mrs. Robertson, is that what you think of her?"

Mavis Wheeler sniffed. "Not just me. We all know she's been

having an affair with poor Mr. Stewart for over a year now. Shameless, she was, shameless."

"It's true," Mrs. Driver ventured. "Back in June, when her husband went to Hong Kong, little Mrs. Robertson was all alone. She invited us to a dinner party at the headmaster's house. It was the strangest affair."

"In what way?" Esme ventured.

"There we all were seated at the table, but we hardly saw our hostess. She spent almost the entire evening in the back seat of Mr. Steward's motor vehicle ... with him."

"Scandalous," Mrs. Wheeler put in. "That girl is no better than she ought to be. My husband was telling me the servants at her house have all sorts of stories of the two of them meeting in her husband's absence. Quite without shame and under the roof of her husband's house."

Harriet studied her tiles without seeing them. "If Mr Stewart had a motor vehicle, why was he using a ricksha on the night he died?"

She looked up to find all three women staring at her. "According to my husband, he had imbibed a great deal over dinner." Mavis Wheeler snorted. "We all know what men are like when they've had too much to drink. Maybe he got a little forward with her, particularly if she was doing her sweet and innocent act."

"She still shouldn't have shot him," Mrs. Driver said.

With all this scurrilous tittle-tattle going on around her, Harriet could hardly concentrate on the game.

"I think I have a set of honor tiles," she said, laying down the tiles with a soft click.

"Don't be ridiculous, that's not a wind, it's a flower," Mrs. Wheeler said. "I thought you said you knew how to play this game."

Harriet retrieved her tiles, her cheeks burning.

Mavis Wheeler waved a hand in her direction. "Hurry up. It's your turn to draw, Mrs. Gordon."

Harriet drew fresh tiles from the wall with shaking fingers, wondering why she had come or indeed, why she stayed.

"Of course," Mrs. Driver reverted to the delicious topic of Edith Robertson. She lowered her voice. "She's not really one of us."

Again, Harriet had heard that expression in the last few days, though the first time it had been Edith who'd used it to describe her husband.

Mrs. Driver's eyes darted around the room, and she lowered her voice as she leaned forward. "The rumor is she is a cuckoo in the nest."

"What do you mean?" Esme Prynne asked.

"No mother listed on the birth certificate," Mrs. Driver continued. "Poor Mary Chapman expected to bring up her husband's by-blow like one of her own."

"Well then, what do you expect?" Mavis Wheeler said. "Those sorts of people are not to be trusted." She gave an unlovely snigger. "Apparently Henry Robertson didn't know. Nobody thought to tell him until after the marriage."

"Well, they deserve each other," Mrs. Driver said. "Him a grammar school boy."

No doubt her own husband was at best a grammar school boy too, but Mrs. Driver would not admit that.

"That is enough," Esme Prynne said. "What must Mrs. Gordon think of us?"

Mavis Wheeler looked Harriet hard in the face. "Mrs. Gordon can form her own judgments about her new friend, but everything said this afternoon is the truth. Worst kept secret in KL."

When they took a break for tea, Harriet stepped onto the terrace. It took a great deal to intimidate her, but somehow the hennaed hellion had hit her mark.

"There you are," Esme said. "We're about to go back inside."

Harriet summoned a watery smile. "If you don't mind, I will plead a headache and leave you to your afternoon, Miss Prynne."

"Esme, please." Esme touched her arm. "Don't take any notice of Mavis Wheeler. She is a known bitch of the first water."

"Miss Prynne, your language." Harriet, who was not above colorful language herself, mustered a smile.

Esme's lips twitched. "Sorry. I had three brothers," she said. "But what they were saying was truly dreadful. Poor Edith."

"Do you mean that?"

"I do, and I'm as guilty as the rest for letting them get away with it." She glanced back at the clubroom. "The English woman abroad is the worst of her species, don't you think?"

"I do."

Esme smiled. "I can't persuade you to stay?"

Harriet shook her head. She really did have a threatening headache. "No. Honestly, I have had a rather trying day and I would like to lie down." She paused. "Why don't you join me for dinner tonight?"

Esme's eyes widened. "I would love that. At seven?"

The two women parted on those terms, and Harriet retired to her room at the Empire. She stripped down to her chemise and lay on the bed staring up at the ceiling.

Her conscience tugged at her, telling her Edith would be expecting her, but the thought of dealing with Edith's self-indulgent and, frankly, rather terrifying delusions was too much. She wished Julian were here to unburden herself, but he was back in Singapore, busy with the day-to-day minutiae of running a school.

She could have sought Griff Maddocks, but he only ever saw a story and was never a trustworthy confidante.

And Curran ...? He had problems of his own.

Harriet rolled on her side and curled up in a ball of lonely misery.

THIRTY-SEVEN

"Y ou just left him?" Sergeant Singh broke the long silence between the two men.

They sat on a bench in the botanical gardens overlooking a pleasant lake, well populated with lilies and waterfowl, but Curran saw none of the beauty of the scene. He was sunk in gloom, failing on all fronts.

"Yes," he said. "I'm not proud of myself, but the last thing I need is to get embroiled in a murder investigation. Blake will be found soon enough. The baby?"

Singh nodded. "She is safe. Padmi has a large family in Brickfields, and she seems genuinely attached to the child. It is the best place for her."

Curran removed his hat and ran his hand through his hair. "So, I found and lost my sister, and I am no closer to resolving the actual assignment given to me," Curran said."

"I think it is time you tell me what this is all about, Curran."

Curran related the briefing from Stephens, concluding with an account of his visit to the Topaz Club the previous night.

Singh shook his head. "That sounds like an impossible task. If they have killed not once but at least twice to protect their secrets, you are walking into danger, Curran. What are you going to do?"

"To hell with anything else. I have to find Samrita," Curran said. Leaving unspoken his biggest fear: Before they kill her too.

"Do you think she is back at the Topaz Club?"

Curran shrugged. "The place is a fortress. Where else would they take her? I have to start there."

"How?" His sergeant could always be relied on for the practicalities.

"I think I can safely assume that those behind the Topaz Club now know exactly who I am, so I can't go back openly as a guest." He cast a sideways glance at Singh. "I am going to have to get in some other way. This must end. Tonight, Singh."

Singh snorted. "And how do you propose to do that? Guards and dogs?"

Curran allowed himself a small smile. "Maybe if there was some way of getting into the compound unseen?"

Even as he spoke, a plan was forming in his mind.

Curran stood up. "I'm going to speak to my cousin and then I'm going to try to get some sleep. I'm going to need my wits about me tonight." He paused. "Can you drive a horse and carriage?"

His sergeant straightened. "I can. Not well."

He arranged a time to rendezvous with Singh that evening and set out on the walk up the hill to Carcosa, the Resident General's residence, a magnificent white mansion that crowned the top of the hill behind the gardens. A tribute to the British colonial rule, it oozed opulence and power.

Curran asked to speak with the Honorable George Bullock-Steele and was shown into a reception room. George entered wearing tennis whites and a wide-brimmed hat.

"What the hell are you doing up here?"

"I need your help again, George."

George glanced at the door. "Topaz Club?" he said *sotto voce*.

Curran nodded. "But not officially. I need you to smuggle me in tonight."

"I say, what are you up to?"

Curran narrowed his eyes. "Were you aware that some of the girls that work at the Topaz Club are victims of kidnap?"

"Rubbish. Lovely girls, all of them." He frowned. "Is this what your secret mission is?"

Curran swallowed his disgust. "We will discuss that later. Can you help me or not?"

George frowned. "I don't know. Am I likely to get into trouble?"

Curran shrugged. "As long as I'm not discovered. At worst, you may find yourself banned from the Club, but I'm sure you can live with that."

"Very well," George said with a resigned sigh. "What do you want me to do?"

"I will bring my man with me, and he can drive the carriage," Curran said.

George tapped his nose. "I see." Although plainly he didn't.

"Georgy... where are you?" A woman's voice with a distinctly American twang came from outside and before Curran could beat a retreat, a woman in tennis whites entered the room.

"There you are." Her gaze fell on Curran. "We haven't met, have we? Sarah Bullock-Steele."

She stuck out her hand in such a way that Curran wasn't sure if he was supposed to kiss it or shake it. He opted for the latter.

George seemed to have lost the power of speech, so Curran smiled and said simply, "Robert Curran. A pleasure to meet you." He would leave it to George to explain the relationship.

"We better get back to the tennis," George said hurriedly, adding, "See you tonight."

Curran sloughed off the marbled halls and overt opulence on his trudge back down the hill. He passed the hospital and spent some time with Jayant, who was asleep. The fact he had survived the night was reason for hope, the doctor told him.

At the hotel he collected his key and hurried up the stairs, his mind full of plans for the evening.

He turned the key in the lock and opened the door, nearly jumping out of his skin as a shadow moved across the window. The Webley was under the mattress, and he was calculating how to reach it as the shadow resolved into the government agent, Archibald Stephens.

Curran allowed his breathing to return to normal. Shock giving way to anger.

He closed the door behind him, leaning against it. "What the hell are you playing at, Stephens? I could have shot you. How did you get into my room?"

Stephens sat down in the one armchair and crossed his legs. "My apologies, Curran. I prefer not to be seen talking to you in public."

"What do you want?"

Stephens produced his pipe and clenched it, unlit, between his teeth. "An update."

"If you wanted updates, you should have asked for them."

"You are correct, but it has come to my attention that you have been a little less than discreet. Summoning your sergeant from Singapore, for example?"

"I needed someone I trusted. It was obvious that this job was bigger than one man."

"And what about the civilians you've dragged in? The woman, Mrs. Gordon and, God forbid, a journalist."

Stung by the telling off, Curran bridled. "They are friends and completely trustworthy and I assure, I have told them nothing about my official assignment. They are helping me with a side matter."

"You don't have permission to go off on side matters."

"It is related to the Topaz Club." Curran sounded defensive

even to his own ears.

Stephens pointed the stem of the pipe at Curran. "Your meddling has resulted in the unfortunate death of Ashton Blake. What did you think you were doing, going openly to him?"

"The girl he lived with had the information I needed to give me insight into the workings of the Topaz Club." Curran narrowed his eyes. "How did you know Ashton Blake is dead?"

Stephens rose to his feet and pocketed his pipe. "A couple of hours ago, one of his employees went to his home to look for him. Found him shot dead on the floor of his living room. The house had been ransacked. Looks like a robbery. Is that what you intended?"

"I didn't kill him," Curran said.

"No, but you were there this morning with your sergeant and the woman. If Blake's woman was your little side matter, it is thanks to you he is dead, and she is missing. Clumsy, Curran, very clumsy. What do you propose doing now?"

"I think," Curran said slowly, "they will have taken the girl to the Topaz Club. She has the answers, Stephens. Find her and I unlock the secrets."

"And how do you propose to get into the Club?"

"That is up to me, Stephens."

"Be careful, Curran. There are always eyes watching."

"I'll bear that in mind," Curran said. "Is that all?"

"I want an update every day from now on," Stephens said.

After he closed the door on the Government agent, Curran swore softly under his breath. The last thing he needed was interference from Stephens. He sat down at the table with a sheet of hotel stationery and drew a rough plan of the Topaz Club from both inside and outside. He sat staring at it for a long time as he formulated a plan for infiltrating its formidable defenses without being caught.

"Samrita," he said aloud as he tossed the pencil onto the table. "Where are you?"

THIRTY-EIGHT

Caught in the maelstrom between Edith Robertson and Robert Curran, Harriet looked forward to an evening of getting to know Esme Prynne better. She had a good feeling about Esme, her instinct that there could be seeds of a genuine friendship between them.

Esme arrived at the Empire punctually at seven in the evening and they took their seats in the dining room.

"I believe the chicken curry is very good," Esme said as she perused the menu.

They both ordered curry and Esme sat back. "I'm so glad I have finally met you. Lavinia has mentioned you so often in her letters."

The familiar misgiving caught at Harriet, and she shifted in her seat, wondering exactly what her friend Lavinia Pemberthey-Smythe had said to this woman.

"How do you know Lavinia?" She tried to keep her voice light and conversational.

"I took a teaching position in Singapore when I first came out East. I found—I still find—the company of the English women on these postings tedious. Just like that dreadful woman at mahjong. All I hear are complaints about the heat, the servants, the children, and their husbands. I'm sure I don't need to tell you that there is nothing worse than a memsahib. I yearned for some intellectual company. When I was working in Singapore, I attended a lecture given by Lavinia."

"The subject was orchids?" Harriet suggested.

Esme smiled. "It was, but when I spoke to her afterward, she invited me to morning coffee and there I discovered a group of women who shared my beliefs in suffrage and provided me with the intellectual company I sought."

"And have you found a like-minded group here in KL?"

Esme shook her head. "If anything, they are worse, but I have to take work where I find it and the school here offered me far better pay and conditions than that in Singapore."

"It was very brave of you to come out East as a single woman," Harriet said.

Esme shrugged. "Not so very unusual. I had nothing to keep me in England. My parents have both passed on and my brothers are busy with their own concerns. Why not seek a little adventure? I would have thought you of all people would understand that, Harriet?"

"I'm not sure I would have quite found the courage to have gone to India if it hadn't been for my husband."

"Do you regret it?"

"Not at all."

Esme fiddled with her table napkin for a moment or two before looking up and saying in something of a rush. "I do know of your involvement with the WSPU and the consequences you faced. I read about your case in Votes for Women and recognized your name in Lavinia's letters." She paused to pour them both a glass of water. "Believe me, she is quite discreet, Harriet, but where do you stand with the WSPU now?"

Harriet took a breath. "You are very direct, Esme."

Esme shrugged. "I have been alone too long to dissemble."

Fortunately, the arrival of their meals interrupted them and they returned to polite conversation while they ate.

After the table had been cleared, Harriet sat back. "You asked where I stood with the WSPU? I support the ideals and aims, but I do not believe that the philosophy of deeds, not words, will win us the support we need. I want no woman to endure what they inflicted on me and from what I read, the force-feeding and harassment of the women is getting worse. It is nothing less than torture, Esme."

Esme nodded. "It is so frustrating. When there is suffrage in countries like Australia and New Zealand, the United States, and Canada, why is Britain so intransigent?"

"The roots of society go too deep, Esme. It will take some major cataclysm to shake that tree."

"It will happen," Esme said with absolute confidence. "It has to." She smiled. "Let's change the subject. What brought you to KL?"

"My brother, Julian, is restless and looking for a new challenge," Harriet said, "and an opportunity at the Prince Alfred School has presented."

Esme straightened. "Really? Do you think he will take it?"

"That is something we are yet to discuss. We have a young ward for whom we need to find a good school and Prince Alfred sounded ideal, were it not for recent events." She looked around the dining room and lowered her voice. "I don't feel comfortable here, Esme. There are undercurrents I don't have the time or patience to understand."

"I couldn't agree more," Esme said. "There are too many Mavis Wheelers who aggrandize themselves in a way they would never get away with back in England."

Harriet changed the subject. "Julian was very taken that you had read his work."

Esme's eyes sparkled in the candlelight. "You told him? I am a classicist at heart and have read many of your brother's papers. Have you read his treatises on Virgil?"

"I have typed some of them," Harriet said, "but personally, that level of intellectual discussion is not my interest. My father believed further education was wasted on girls, so I missed out on the classical education lavished on my brother."

"My dear papa was a clergyman like your brother, so there was no money for me. I am fortunate I had a wealthy aunt who disagreed with archaic views about a woman's education and provided the money to send me to Girton College in Cambridge," Esme said. "I studied classics and literature." She sighed. "And yet here I am, thirty-four, a confirmed spinster, teaching the basics in a Methodist Missions school with little to show for my life."

How do you measure achievement? Harriet wondered. What did she have to show for her life? A dead husband, a dead child, a criminal record, and a qualification in shorthand and typing.

She chided herself for her dour mood and was relieved when Esme glanced at her watch.

"It is time I was home. A full day of teaching tomorrow. Wednesday afternoon is my only reprieve during the week." She held out her hand. "Until next time, Harriet."

Harriet saw her to the door of the hotel and waved Esme off in a ricksha before she turned for the stairs, grateful for her bed after the long and trying day.

THIRTY-NINE

It lacked a few days to the full moon, but the waxing gibbous moon shone clear and bright as the darkened carriage turned in through the gates to the Topaz Club. Secreted under a seat in the carriage, Curran flinched as the carriage hit a bump. Sergeant Singh had many skills but driving carriages was maybe not one of them. They had swapped drivers when George stopped to pick up Curran, mollifying the disgruntled Residence driver with a few shillings.

The downside of the plan was that Singh would have to return to town with George, leaving Curran on his own within the compound. However, they had agreed that it enabled Singh to undertake some discreet investigations of his own among the other drivers and staff.

The carriage came to a halt, presumably under the *porte cochère*. Light shone into the interior as the door opened. George's exit caused the carriage to lurch and sway.

"Your friend, Mr. Sutton is not with you tonight, Mr. Bullock-Steele?" Gopal's voice drifted into the carriage.

"Not my friend, just some chap I met at the Spotted Dog,"

George said. "Are the odds running my way at the tables tonight, Gopal, old chap?"

"I am sure they are. After you."

The carriage moved off again, turning in through the back gates of the premises. The carriage stopped again and Singh spoke in Malay, asking where to leave the carriage and rest the horses.

Rapid fire instructions followed, and the carriage lurched forward again, coming to rest at last. Singh jumped down from the driver's box and Curran rolled out of his cramped and dusty hiding spot. He turned back a corner of the blind on the window. They were in the rear compound with an assortment of motor vehicles and horse-drawn carriages drawn up in a neat row against the wall.

A *syce* was leading the two carriage horses away and Singh leaned against the wheel closest to the door, watching them go. When no one was around, he cracked the door of the carriage open.

"Are you sure about this?" Singh asked, without moving.

Curran was far from confident. "It is the only plan I have, Singh. We have to make it work," he replied.

"Very well. There are men everywhere. Stay where you are for now, Curran. Your cousin will call for the carriage at midnight. I will tell you when it is safe to move."

Curran glanced at his watch, the fluorescent hands bright in the moonlight. It had just gone ten. He unholstered the Webley and sat waiting on the floor of the carriage, every nerve on edge, not daring to move in case some watching eye detected the movement from the highly sprung vehicle.

Singh returned just before midnight.

"Anything useful?" Curran asked through a crack in the door.

"There is one door at the rear of the house. It leads to a passage with a staircase leading up to the private quarters of the man, Acharya. There are three doors off the passage. The room below the stairs is the office. The other," Singh paused. "I am told, is where the girls sleep when they are not required within the Club. The green baize door at the end of the corridor leads to the Club itself. The kitchen and servant quarters are along the back wall to the left of the back gate. To the right, is another walled-off yard. That's where the dogs are. According to the regulars, the dogs are let out to patrol the grounds after the Club closes up, but not this courtyard. There is only a small staff, and there will be a night watchman on duty. There is some sort of guardhouse by the back gate."

"Good work, Singh."

Singh drew in an audible breath.

"Now, I have to leave. I will return with your motor vehicle at six and wait near the turnoff to the main road. I am not certain how you plan to get out of here, Curran. Once those gates are shut, there is no way out, and I do not wish to leave you here alone."

"No choice. I will find a way out," Curran said with considerably more confidence than he felt. There had to be a way over the wall or maybe a Webley pointed at a night watchman might be just as effective.

Singh stepped back and looked around. "You are safe. There is no one around, but I will have to call for the horses shortly."

Singh had positioned the carriage, so it was the last one in the line of carriages and motor vehicles, against a tall wall. Curran slid from the carriage on the wall side. He took a moment to catch his breath as he slung his knapsack over one shoulder. He wore dark clothing and had packed an electric flashlight, purchased that afternoon from John Little, and a few other useful objects such as a rope and knife.

While Singh distracted the attention of the *syces* calling for the carriage horses, Curran made his way along the back wall behind the other vehicles until he reached the buildings that constituted the servant's quarters. Here he found an unlocked door and slipped into the darkened room. A small window above the door let in enough light from the nearly full moon to reveal brooms and buckets. With luck, none of these things would be needed and until the house fell quiet, it made as good a hiding place as any. It was only twelve thirty and he had another long wait ahead.

It was long past two before the compound fell silent, the last of the servants retiring to their cheerless pallets.

Curran lifted the latch and looked outside. The yard was empty and silent. A light burned in the guardhouse and it had begun to rain. That would keep the night watchman in his hut. Circling the wall, Curran made his way to the back door. As he had surmised from his earlier reconnaissance, it was the only entrance to the house from this yard.

With a quick glance toward the guardhouse, he crouched down and tried the latch. To his surprise, it opened without a creak. He supposed that access to the house must be required at all hours and with the gates locked and a guard and dogs patrolling, a lock was unnecessary.

He slipped inside and found himself in the tiled passageway described by Singh. The moonlight coming in through windows over the doorway provided enough light for him to see that directly ahead was a green baize door such as you would find in any grand house in England.

Curran tried the handle of the door to his right and discovered that it was locked. If Singh was correct, beyond the door lay the accommodation for the women when they weren't working. That seemed a logical place to put Samrita.

He knelt to see what he could do about the lock. He carried a lock pick that he'd taken off a thief in London. The same thief had given him lessons in how to pick locks and he had proved an able student.

He had begun to work the lock when he heard a sound. He froze, his ears straining.

A woman weeping.

It came not from the room beyond this door but the second door beyond the stairs, the office. He crept across the floor and held his breath. Like many houses of this design, the wall above the door had an intricate openwork grill to allow the flow of air, and through the grill came the now unmistakable sound of stifled sobs.

He let out his breath and steadied his breathing. He wanted to call out, reassure the woman within that he would have her free within a minute, but he didn't dare make a sound. Even the scratching of the lock pick seemed to reverberate around the silent house.

It took some fiddling to open the lock, and the sweat ran from his forehead before the cylinders fell into place. He stood up, wiping his hands on his trousers before drawing his Webley and turning the handle. The door opened on well-oiled hinges. The room beyond was in darkness, with only the faintest slivers of moonlight creeping in around heavy shutters.

As his eyes adjusted to the light, he had the faintest impression of a woman's silhouette against the farthest window.

He lowered the weapon and held up a hand, hoping she could see him against any light from the hallway.

"Don't scream. I am a friend," he whispered. "Samrita?"

A gasp and a whispered, "Yes."

"We have no time to waste. Come with me."

The woman did not move, and Curran advanced into the room.

Too late, he sensed the movement behind him, and he turned as something heavy crashed into his left shoulder. Stunned, he fell to the floor, the Webley skidding from his hand. An electric light clicked on. He stretched out his hand for the revolver, which lay just out of reach, and a large, booted foot came down on his wrist.

Someone hauled him upright by his collar and twisted his arms painfully behind his back. Through a mist of pain and stars from the blow he tried to focus as the woman by the window stepped into the light, a smile curving her lips. She threw back the dark scarf she had used to cover her blonde hair and pale face.

Maria Vlasek.

As he brought his breath under control, he could see Gopal and two of the burly servants who had been in attendance the night he had come to the club.

Gopal held a short-barreled revolver and his smile held nothing but menace as he said, "Good evening, Mr. Sutton ... or is it Inspector Curran? We've been expecting you."

FORTY

Maria Vlasek sashayed across the room. When she reached Curran, she stooped down and took his face in her hands, kissing him on the lips.

"Good night, Mr Curran," she said. She straightened and looked at Gopal. "Try not to make too much of a mess of his handsome face."

"Go," Gopal said, and she sauntered out of the door, blowing Curran a kiss as she went.

"How did you know I would be here tonight?" Curran struggled to sound in control, but the blow to his right shoulder had jumbled his thoughts. His shoulder hurt like hell and he had only just recovered from a beating back in November. He had a sinking feeling worse was to come.

Gopal snorted. "I have the girl you are looking for. I don't know why you are so anxious to find her, but we knew you would come looking for her. It is in your nature."

"We?"

"Tssk, Mr Curran. I know our colonial overlords have tasked you with the unmasking of the Topaz Club, but we will be gone tomorrow. We have what we need to continue our work with no need for the Club. The men we control within the administration will continue to line our pockets."

Curran shrugged his right shoulder. It didn't feel broken or dislocated, just badly bruised.

"Files," he said. "You have dossiers on these men. What do they contain?"

He tried to sound calm, but his heart was racing. His chances of escaping this encounter alive were not looking good.

Gopal shrugged. "Oh, we found that artistically arranged photographic images were very conducive to cooperation."

Curran momentarily closed his eyes, trying to visualize the sort of image that would secure the loyalty of high-ranked British officials, the sort of image to destroy a career ... a marriage ... a good name.

As if reading his mind, Gopal smiled. "Drugs and alcohol and a pretty woman can make a man amenable to any situation."

"But you no longer have the files," Curran said.

For the first time, Gopal's composure slipped. "Why do you say that?"

"There was a girl, Lakshmi. She took them, intending to hand them over to the British authorities. She died before you could recover them. Did you kill her, Gopal?"

Genuine anger flashed in Gopal's eyes, and he advanced on Curran. The blow, for which Curran had no defense, hit the right side of his face, snapping his head back. Between the stars and the ringing in his ears, the world dissolved for a few heartbeats. He forced himself back to his senses as Gopal seized the front of his shirt, bringing his face down so close to Curran's that he could smell the garlic and onions on the man's breath.

"I did not kill Lakshmi," he said. "I loved her. She was my woman, but she betrayed my trust and I cannot forgive her for that."

Curran swallowed, tasting blood in his mouth.

"Am I going to end up in the Klang?" he managed.

Gopal drew back. "Not tonight."

"And Samrita Kumar?"

Gopal cocked his head to one side. "What is your interest in her?"

"You kidnapped her. Forced her to work here..."

"She was trouble from the first. We thought we had bought her silence but then she had to talk to a journalist and then you and your friend. We do not take well to silly girls who open their mouths. But enough chat. If you are so keen to acquaint yourself with Samrita, you will have plenty of opportunity." Gopal paused and reached in his pocket, tossing a dark cloth to the man not holding Curran. "Blindfold him first."

Curran twisted his head, but any form of resistance was useless as a hood was pulled tightly over his head, plunging the world into the dark.

They hauled him to his feet, and he took advantage of the movement to kick out.

His foot connected with flesh and the man he had hit cursed him roundly in a language Curran did not understand. At least not the words—he got the meaning well enough when a heavy fist thudded into his abdomen and he fell forward, the breath leaving his body as he crumpled heavily onto the tiled floor.

A booted foot caught him in the ribs and a rain of blows from whatever had felled him before rained down on his shoulders and back. His arms were wrenched behind his back again and his wrists secured with rope.

Devoid of breath and unable to defend himself, Curran could do nothing, and the world roared in his ears.

From a long way away, a voice said. "Enough. Our orders are not to kill him. You know where to take him."

Curran was hauled up by his arms with a force that threatened to dislocate his shoulders and half dragged and half carried out into the night, the rain reviving him a little. From somewhere to his right came frantic barking and the snap of teeth. Instinctively he stiffened, causing his guards to laugh.

"You want we set *anjing* loose?" one of them said.

Behind him, Gopal laughed. "That would be fun but, no. Not yet."

Still dazed from the beating, Curran imagined himself being hunted and brought down by dogs. A bullet to the brain would be an easier death.

A door creaked open and a rush of warm air, stinking of bats or worse, rose to greet him. The men relinquished their grip, and they pushed him forward. His feet met air, and he cried out as he fell heavily onto a hard floor of cold stone.

"I don't want his neck broken," Gopal shouted from above him.

Hauled to his feet, they pushed and dragged down an uncertain slope. He stumbled again, falling forward onto cold rock. The warm stickiness of blood from a cut above his eye dripped down behind the hood.

From somewhere nearby, he heard a rustle and a stifled cry of alarm. It sounded like a woman. Someone else shared this hellhole.

"Not a word, you," Gopal said, addressing his fellow prisoner.

Through the fog of pain and darkness, he heard the clink of keys on a ring and a rattle in a metallic lock, and once again, someone hauled him by his arms along the sandy floor and deposited him in a heap. A door clanged shut, and a key turned in a lock, followed by the crunch of heavy feet leading away and up before another door shut.

Curran rolled onto his side with a groan.

"You are hurt?"

The woman's voice cut through the fog of pain and self-deprecatory misery.

He tried to respond but could not find words. He teetered on the edge of unconsciousness, and it took all his energy to fight off the blackness.

"Wait. I shall try to find you," the woman said.

That seemed an odd thing to say but Curran lay still, unable to move even if he had wanted to.

He sensed movement close by and a light touch of a hand on his shoulder made him start.

"I've found you. Wait."

Questing hands found his face and pulled the hood from his head. Curran blinked, trying to bring the world back into focus. It remained resolutely black.

He found his voice. "Where am I?"

"You are in a cave," the woman replied. "They say it is part of the Batu Cave system. There is no light and no one to hear you scream." Her voice wavered.

"Can you undo my wrists?" Curran asked.

The woman turned to his bound hands. She cursed in a language he did not recognize, her fingers scrabbling with the complex knots. Slowly, the pitiless ties loosened, and he suppressed a groan as the blood rushed back into his fingers.

Was there any part of him that didn't hurt? He touched his head, his questing fingers finding a lump on his forehead and the cloying stickiness of drying blood. After a further quick inventory, he concluded he was bruised and battered and maybe had a cracked rib, but was otherwise in one piece.

The woman's fingers found his face again, almost poking out his eye. He took her hand and held it.

"Thank you," he said.

In the dark, her fingers tightened on his. "Who are you?" she asked.

"My name is Robert Curran. I am a police officer with the Straits Settlements Police. Who are you?"

She didn't reply, and he asked again, although he thought he knew the answer.

It came in a voice tinged with tears.

"I am Samrita," she said. "You have been looking for me."

FORTY-ONE

THURSDAY, 8 DECEMBER

As Harriet left the breakfast room, she found Griff Maddocks and Gursharan Singh waiting for her. Neither had a welcoming smile of greeting, and Singh looked like he hadn't slept.

"Is everything all right?" An icy hand caught at her heart. "Curran...?"

"Missing," Maddocks said.

"He went to the Topaz Club to look for Samrita last night and I was to meet him at a rendezvous point this morning, but he was not there. I waited two hours and still he did not come." Singh's mustache twitched. "I fear he has been taken."

"Or worse," Maddocks said. "What do we do?"

"We can't assume the worst," Harriet said, although she may have just been trying to convince herself. "He may just be stuck somewhere, unable to get away until the opportunity presents or darkness, or..." Her words faded away along with her hopes.

The three of them stood in glum silence.

"Should we alert Cuscaden or the Commissioner of the local police?" Maddocks asked. "What's his name?"

"Talbot," Singh replied with a shake of his head. "I do not wish to alarm anyone unduly until we are sure Curran remains unaccounted for. I will return to the Topaz Club and keep watch. We will meet here this evening at five and decide."

"If there's nothing more we can do, I still have a story to write," Maddocks said. "Harriet, would you care to accompany me to Walter Stewart's home at Salak South? I want to interview the man's mistress."

The alternative was a morning with Edith Robertson, and Harriet didn't have the stomach to deal with Edith. She had told herself that her father, the Crown Prosecutor, would not approve of her fraternizing with the defendant when she was a Crown witness.

Harriet and Maddocks hired a carriage for the drive to Salak South. The plain but neat wooden house that had been Walter Stewart's home was easy enough to find. Beyond it lay the now idle mine workings.

After telling the driver to wait, Maddocks knocked on the front door. It opened a crack and a woman peered around it.

"You police?" she asked.

"No," Maddocks replied. "Mrs. Gordon and I have come to see how you are."

The shocking effrontery gave Harriet a momentary qualm, but the door opened a little wider.

"What are your names?"

"I am Mr. Maddocks, and this is Mrs. Gordon. What do we call you?"

"Su Wei," the woman replied.

"Can we come in?" Maddocks asked.

The woman opened the door, admitting them into the living room of the house. It followed the rough design of every house of its type: a large airy living area with bedrooms off it and a corridor leading to the back door with the kitchen and servants' quarters separated from the house.

Su Wei wore a plain *sam fu* of faded blue cotton, her hair in a long plait down her back. Even in the dim light, her eyes were red-rimmed, as if she had been crying.

"Were you friends of Walter?" she asked.

"Yes." Maddocks's ability to lie without a twitch astounded Harriet.

"They buried him on Monday," Su Wei said. "I never saw him. Never said goodbye."

Her grief was real, and Harriet thought of the man who had left her behind. The body she had seen on the carriageway had once been a man who had laughed with and made love to this woman.

In all the drama, the person who had been Walter Stewart had been lost.

"The police came and searched the house. I thought they would have asked me if Mem Robertson ever visited?"

"Did she visit?" Harriet asked.

Su Wei's mouth trembled, and she nodded. "Before I came to live with Walter. Whenever her husband was away, she would visit here, sometimes with her child. She had no shame. But after Walter brought me here, he told her he didn't want her to come anymore. He said he loved only me."

Maddocks and Harriet exchanged glances.

"How long have you been living here?" Maddocks asked.

"Since the festival of the moon," Su Wei said.

Three months at the most.

"And the Mem?" Harriet asked gently. "When did she last come here?"

"She came one day a few weeks ago. Banging on the door, crying, demanding to see Walter, but he was away visiting one of the mines. Since the mine shut, he has been away often. She scared me. I hid. I didn't want her to hurt me."

"You think she would have done?"

Su Wei nodded. "Oh yes, she was very, very angry and she had a gun with her." She held out her hands to indicate a weapon about the size of the Webley.

Harriet's blood ran cold.

"Did you tell the police this?"

Su Wei shook her head. "They didn't ask me. No one asked me anything. No one told me anything."

The tears started and Harriet put an arm around the woman's shoulder.

"I'm so sorry, Su Wei," she said. "What will you do now?"

The woman sniffed, wiping her nose on the sleeve of her jacket. "I cannot stay here and I cannot go home. I have brought shame to my family. I will go to the town and find a job as a servant."

"Can I have a look around?" Maddocks asked.

Su Wei waved a hand which Maddocks took as consent and as Harriet comforted the distraught girl, he wandered around the living room. He entered the bedroom and came out carrying a photograph of two English women. An older woman and her daughter posed in a studio, their smiles stiff and formal.

"Who are these ladies?" he asked.

"That is Walter's mother and sister," Su Wei said. "He sent them money. I do not know what they will do now."

Harriet followed Maddocks back into the bedroom. There was no evidence of a female influence in the plain room. It contained a narrow iron framed bed, the mosquito net coiled above it, a wooden chair, and a battered chest of drawers.

Maddocks set the photograph back on the chest of drawers beside a man's tortoiseshell backed hairbrush and clothes brush. With a quick glance at the door, he opened the top drawer and rummaged through the contents. He turned to look at Harriet and held up a business card ... a black card with a gold circle imprinted on it. Harriet took it and turned it over. It had no writing.

"What is it?" she asked Maddocks.

"It's the card for the Topaz Club," Maddocks said. "Curran showed me the one he had."

Maddocks retrieved the card from her and returned to the living room. He held it out to Su Wei. The woman put her hands behind her back and took a step back, her eyes widening.

"What do you know about the Topaz Club, Su Wei?" Harriet asked.

Su Wei shook her head. "Now Walter is dead, they will come for me and take me back." She ran to Harriet and threw herself on her knees, wrapping her arms around Harriet's legs. "Do not let them take me."

Harriet stooped and pried the woman off, directing her to a chair. She hunched down and took the woman's hands in hers.

"We are your friends, Su Wei. Who are you afraid of?"

Su Wei wiped her eyes. "Gopal and his men."

"You worked at the Topaz Club?"

Su Wei nodded. "I had been there a year before Walter took me away. He was a good man."

"Did you know Samrita Kumar and her friend, Lakshmi?"

"Of course. I was at the Club when they were brought there not long after me." She looked for Harriet to Maddocks. "Where are they? Are they all right?"

Harriet shook her head. "I don't know," she lied.

The woman was frightened enough without knowing Lakshmi was dead and Samrita was missing.

"But how did you come to be with Walter Stewart?" Harriet returned to the reason for their visit.

"He came to the Club, not long after I arrived. He was kind

and gentle. Sometimes Gopal would allow the girls to leave – for the right price. Samrita was one. We were the lucky ones."

And now both Walter Stewart and Ashton Blake were dead.

"And Lakshmi?"

Su Wei frowned. "The man, Gopal, claimed her," she said. "It was good for her. She lived with him in his rooms and no longer had to—" Su Wei shuddered. "When I left, she was with child."

"Lakshmi had a child?" Harriet stared at Su Wei. "Was the father Gopal?"

Su Wei nodded. "He was boasting about what a fine son he would have."

"When would the baby have been born?"

"I came here at the time of the autumn festival. The baby would have been born soon after."

Harriet did a quick calculation. September. The child would be nearly three months old.

"Lakshmi's dead." Harriet said. "What happened to the child?"

Even as she spoke, a suspicion crept into her mind.

Su Wei sank into the nearest chair and buried her face in her hands. "I do not know. I live out here, away from the city. I do not read English newspapers and Walter, he told me nothing."

"When did Samrita leave the Topaz Club?"

Sue Wei frowned. "It was before me. She was so happy."

"Was she with child?"

Su Wei shook her head. Harriet glanced at Maddocks, and he shrugged. Clearly, he had missed the significance of dates. She would explain later.

Su Wei's gaze lifted back to Harriet, her eyes wide. "They will come for me now that Walter is dead. Can you help me?"

"Where do you come from?" Maddocks asked.

"Hong Kong."

Harriet had heard Hong Kong mentioned only recently. *Who had been in Hong Kong?*

"How did you get to the Topaz Club?" Harriet prompted.

Su Wei sniffed. "My father had died and my mother told me I had to leave home and find work. My friend who could read gave me an advertisement from a newspaper. An Englishman was looking for a good, respectable girl to keep house. He was only in Hong Kong a short time and applicants were to go to an address."

"And who did you meet?"

"A *gweilou*."

Her lip curled and Harriet glanced at Maddocks.

"Cantonese for foreigner," Maddocks supplied. "Not particularly flattering."

"What was his name?"

Su Wei shrugged. "I don't think he ever told me."

"Can you describe him? Young? Old?"

Su Wei looked at Maddocks. "Older than you." She touched her hair. "Like Walter... not much hair. Thin and glasses."

Harriet took a deep breath. She remembered now who had business in Hong Kong and Su Wei had just described Henry Robertson.

"He told me to pack my bags and return. When I did it was Gopal who met me." Su Wei straightened in her chair. "I have said enough. I have nothing more to tell you."

"Are you familiar with the property on the Batu Caves road?" Maddocks asked.

Su Wei shook her head. "No. I left before they moved out there and for that I am glad." She looked around the little home she had made for herself and Walter Stewart. "Walter was good to me but the mem, she wouldn't let him go and now she has taken him away from me forever."

"Do you really think they will come for you?" Harriet asked.

"It was a condition of our purchase. If anything were to befall our protectors, we were once again the property of the Topaz Club. I cannot go back there."

Su Wei let her hands fall limply between her knees, her shoulders slumped, a picture of abject misery. Harriet looked up at Maddocks, silently imploring him to do something, anything.

Maddocks fumbled in his wallet and set a few notes down on the table. "I am sorry, Su Wei," he said. "This should be enough to get you on a boat back to Hong Kong ... or wherever you want to go. I hope you can find a new life."

On the ride back into town, they were silent for a long time.

Maddocks said at last. "She genuinely loved him, didn't she?"

Harriet nodded.

"That makes two former clients of the Topaz Club who have died," Maddocks said.

"Yes, but Stewart was killed by his jilted lover. It differed from Ashton Blake. That was an execution." Harriet leaned her elbow on the sill of the carriage and stared out at the rubber trees they were passing, where teams of coolies could be glimpsed in the shadows, hard at work tapping the trees.

She looked back at Maddocks. "I think it is unlikely that the child at the Blake house was Samrita's. The dates don't fit. Even if Samrita got pregnant with Blake, she wasn't with him long enough to have a child that is several months old."

She could almost see the cogs in Maddocks' mind working before he said slowly. "You think the child might be Lakshmi's?"

Harriet nodded and Maddocks let out a low whistle. "This gets murkier and murkier."

"And there's something else," Harriet said. "The man Su Wei described fits Henry Robertson."

Maddocks stared at her. "What? A respectable schoolmaster? What was he doing in Hong Kong on business for the Topaz Club? Should we ask him?"

"No. We need Curran," Harriet said. "This is bigger than us, Griff, and it scares me."

Griff nodded. "This is a wasp's nest and I am afraid Curran has angered the wasps."

"I have a bad feeling about Curran."

Maddocks leaned forward and put his hand over hers. "Curran has been in worse scrapes, Harriet. He'll be fine."

"I hope you are right."

But in her heart, she feared the worst.

FORTY-TWO

In the pitiless dark of their prison, Curran and Samrita sat side by side with their backs to something cold and hard—it could have been a rock or a wall, they had no way of knowing—but its solidity was reassuring. The dark was so profound they could not see each other, but he could sense her presence in the warmth of her body and her soft breathing. The pain from his beating gave him something to focus on other than the claustrophobia of the black hole in which they found themselves.

"When I was eight," Curran began. "My cousin George and his horrible sisters locked me in a cupboard in the attic of Deerbourne Hall. They left me there, shut in the dark, for hours, battering on the door in the hope someone would hear, but no one came. Not until long after dark, when a servant in his room below came to investigate the noise I was making and let me out. I have hated dark confined spaces ever since."

A slender hand found his, and he grasped it thankfully.

"I too hate the dark," Samrita said. "I am glad you are here with me."

"I'm pretty useless."

"But you have been looking for me and that makes me glad. My father never spoke to me about his other family back in England, and I never asked."

"What name did he use?"

"Anand Kumar. Kumar is my mother's name. She saved his life after he escaped from his torturers. We loved him as any child loves their father, but because he was English and yet not English, we were never quite accepted. We would never make good marriages. Jayant would have spent his life in the offices of the railways and if I was lucky, some fat old man who wanted a son may have married me."

He heard the bitterness in her tone and tightened his grip on her hand. "I'm sorry, Samrita." He paused. Her story did not match with what Jayant had told him. "But wasn't Jayant betrothed to Lakshmi?"

"Is that what he told you?"

"Yes."

"For a time they were in love but her family did not permit the match," Samrita said.

Curran could not reconcile what Samrita was telling him with the story Jayant had shared. He shifted his weight and groaned as shafts of pain ran through his body.

"What do I call you?" Samrita asked.

"My name is Robert, but everyone calls me Curran."

"Robert Curran," she mused. "May I call you Robert?"

"I'd like that."

"How is it you were looking for me?"

"Jayant came to me. He has been searching for you since you were taken."

She drew in her breath with an audible hiss. "Has he? I do not think I can return to Laxmangarh but I would like to see my mother again."

Curran tensed. How did he tell her that her mother had died only a few months ago? It seemed to heap one grief upon another, but she needed to know.

"Samrita, your mother is dead. She passed away a few months ago."

Samrita gave a strangled sob. "Dead? I should have been with her. She should not have died alone."

"Jayant was with her."

After a long silence, she said, "Where is Jayant?"

"In hospital. He has dengue fever. We nearly lost him."

She jerked away, the movement exaggerated in the dark. He reached for her again, as much seeking the reassurance of her presence as to provide comfort to her.

After a little while, she said, "Ashton is dead, isn't he?"

"Yes. I'm sorry, Samrita. I blame myself."

"No. I am to blame When I read of Lakshmi's death, I wanted revenge. That is why we spoke with the journalist. I should have realized how much danger that put us in." She took an audible breath. "Kamini? They didn't hurt her?"

"No. She's safe with her nurse. I am just getting used to the idea of having a brother and sister and now I find I am an uncle."

Samrita gave an audible gasp. "Kamini is not my child," she said. "She is Lakshmi's daughter. Lakshmi and Gopal's child. Gopal wanted a son but when the baby was born, he said he would not keep a daughter. I never spoke with Lakshmi, but she must have been distraught to be separated from her child. Gopal agreed to let me have the child to raise. He brought Kamini to us when she was only a few weeks old. We had to find a wet nurse for her but Ashton was happy. He loved her." Samrita's voice broke at last, and Curran held her as she wept.

They must have slept, a reprieve from the stuffy dark of their prison. Curran woke with a start, stiff and sore from his beating and desperately thirsty. Samrita lay with her head in his lap, and he gently disengaged her, forcing himself to stand and stretch his aching limbs.

"Robert, where are you?" Samrita's voice held a note of desperation.

"I'm here."

He found her in the dark, took her in his arms and held her until her panicked breathing returned to normal and they slid back to the floor, sitting side by side in silence.

"They will kill us, Robert," she said at last. "They keep asking me if I know where Lakshmi hid the papers. I have not spoken to Lakshmi since I left the Topaz Club. I know nothing about papers."

Curran stiffened and said, "How much did Gopal trust Lakshmi?"

"She lived in his quarters, but she could not leave. She was still as much a prisoner as the rest of us. Do you know what she took?"

"Documents, photographs. They used it for blackmail," Curran said. "I think she wanted to hand the documents over to the authorities, but our friends at the Club stopped her."

Samrita fell silent. "I received a postcard in the mail from Lakshmi. Maybe it is a clue to where she hid the paper? I have given it to your friend, the woman you sent to talk to me. After you and then she came to the house, I knew they would come for me, so I gave her the card. I didn't want them to find it."

Harriet had said nothing about receiving a postcard from Samrita, but then, he reflected, there had been little time for a proper conversation.

"What was on the postcard?"

"It was an image of the Batu Caves and she had drawn a picture on the back. That is all. It meant nothing to me."

But it may mean something to Gopal and his master.

"Say nothing about the card, Samrita."

"What does it matter if I tell them or not? They have no reason to keep me alive. It will not be long before I join Lakshmi—an unidentified body in the Klang."

"No," Curran said fiercely. "That will not happen. We will get out of this, Samrita. My friends will be looking for me."

Her fingers tightened on his. "I wish I had your faith," she said. "But your friends will never find us here."

"Samrita, who is behind the Topaz Club?"

She did not answer.

He asked again and this time she said, "You will find out soon enough, Robert. I think you have stirred enough trouble for them. You should never have come!"

"But I did and I want this to end ... for you and for all the girls."

"No. You can say you were looking for me, but you are here because your masters want you to end it for them. We are just an inconvenience."

"That is unfair," Curran said.

Samrita stood up and distanced herself from him.

"You are correct," she said at last. "That was unfair. I don't know you. I should not pass judgment on you just because your skin is white."

"Regardless of what official task I may be on, we share the same blood, Samrita, and I will do whatever it takes to give you back your life."

She snorted. "Don't make me promises, Curran." She sighed. "I am very tired. I think I will sleep again. You should too."

She hunched down beside him and he laid a hand on her shoulder, grateful to be sharing this hellhole with her. He wondered what time it was, but didn't have the energy to even try to look at his watch. He hadn't eaten or drunk anything for hours and he was in considerable pain from his ribs and the blow to his head and shoulder.

As he leaned his head back against the hard rock, he made a silent vow that he would face whatever lay ahead with one goal in mind—protect this woman. But for now, he needed to sleep. He closed his eyes, letting oblivion wash over him, taking him away from this terrible place where he would probably die.

FORTY-THREE

After a quick lunch with Griff, Harriet gathered her strength to visit Edith Robertson.

She found Edith in a petulant mood. The young woman reclined on a planter's chair on the verandah, wearing a loose, lacy house coat over her petticoats and corset. Such *deshabille* in the middle of the day would have caused Harriet's mother to have a fit of vapors.

Even Harriet found her spine stiffening as Edith did not rise to greet her, but merely waved a languid hand at a chair.

"I'm so glad you are here," she said. "Mr Hughes came this morning, and he was absolutely beastly. You would almost think he didn't believe me."

Harriet knew from working with her father that it was not the lawyer's role to believe his client or not. His role was to take her instructions and present the best possible case based on those instructions. But Edith would try the patience of the most hardened criminal barrister.

"I am quite prostrate," Edith continued. "The court needs to know I am not well. Ever since Dottie was born, I have been afflicted with ill health. I am a virtual invalid, Harriet. There are days I can hardly rise from my bed."

"What sort of ill health?" Harriet enquired, remembering how Edith had bounded up the difficult slope to the entrance to the Batu Caves and her energy at the shooting range.

Edith lowered her eyes. "Women's problems," she said. "I told Mr Hughes that Dr McGregor will tell the court that I have suffered all my life." She turned her head away, her hand going theatrically to her brow. "You have no idea how I suffer."

Invalid my foot, Harriet thought uncharitably. But if that was how Edith wished to play her defense, far be it for Harriet Gordon to voice an opinion.

"Did you play mahjong yesterday?" Edith asked.

"Yes. I met a most unpleasant woman. Mrs. Wheeler."

Edith pulled a face. "The Mahjong Monster, we call her. She thinks because her husband is a police inspector, she can lord it over us. Was Mama or my sisters there?"

"No."

"Do you know they haven't been to see me? Even Papa has stayed away. You are my only friend, Harriet."

Harriet looked around the silent house. "Where's Dorothy?"

"Henry sent her to stay with Papa and Mama. He said I didn't need the bother of a small child at this difficult time."

"And Henry?"

"I think he is avoiding me, Harriet. We had a fearful row about Walter, but he's a hypocrite. He thinks I don't know about the women he sees."

"What women?" Harriet asked through stiff lips.

If her suspicion was correct, Henry Robertson was not only a member of the Topaz Club but actively involved with the recruiting of girls for the club. So much for being a pillar of moral rectitude.

Edith waved a hand. "There's some sort of club for men he visits. Club!" She spat out the word. "It's just a glorified brothel.

All the wives pretend it doesn't exist, but we all know about it and what the men do there."

Harriet couldn't help herself. "You surprise me. Why would Henry go to such a place?"

"He says it's because I ... we ... no longer ... you know... and a man has needs. What about women? Don't women have needs, Harriet?"

Harriet had no answer to that question, so instead, she asked, "Was Walter Stewart an answer to your needs, Edith?" she asked.

Edith gave the smallest of shrugs.

The houseboy arrived with the tea tray, and Harriet busied herself pouring the tea. After settling down with a cup in her hand, she looked at Edith and asked, "Henry mentioned he has business interests in Hong Kong. What are they?"

Edith met her gaze. "He is setting up a school in Hong Kong," she said. "There are meetings he must attend. Why do you ask?"

"It must have been difficult for you to be left alone for such long stretches."

"I hate it," Edith said. "I'm not the fool everyone takes me for, Harriet. I know I don't have any real friends and my family dislikes me. That's why when Walter was kind to me..."

She broke off, her blue eyes brimming with tears, her mouth trembling. For the first time, Harriet had the impression she was seeing the real Edith Robertson.

"I loved him, Harriet." She lowered her head, and the tears fell onto the fine cotton of her housecoat. "But he threw me over for one of those damned whores from the Topaz Club."

There, it had been said aloud—the Topaz Club.

"Edith, is it possible Henry's visits to Hong Kong are also connected to the Topaz Club?" Harriet pushed.

Edith sprang from her chair and faced Harriet, a barefoot tragic heroine in her pretty peignoir, her fair hair falling around her face. She pointed a shaking finger at the steps.

"Go ... leave now and don't bother calling again, Harriet

Gordon. I never want to see you again. I thought you were my friend, but you're just the same as everyone else."

Harriet set down her cup and stood up. "Edith, I want to understand about the Topaz Club. I have a friend in terrible trouble, and I think it is because of the Topaz Club."

But Edith's mouth had set in a hard line. "I can't help you. I have nothing to do with it and I refuse to discuss it. I'm very tired, Harriet. Please go."

Without looking back, Harriet walked away from the headmaster's bungalow toward the road where her ricksha waited. Her mind churned, first with relief that she was now absolved from further obligation to Edith Robertson and second because she had another piece of the puzzle of the Topaz Club. She couldn't wait to share her suspicions about Henry Robertson with Curran ... and hopefully, Curran would be waiting at the hotel.

FORTY-FOUR

"**R**obert! Robert... wake up."

With a supreme effort, Curran brought himself from the deep, bottomless, dark hole of semi-consciousness into which he had fallen, to the dark hole that was now his reality. A band around his chest tightened as the absolute blackness wrapped itself around him again.

Samrita was shaking his arm.

"I can hear them," she said. "Robert, I'm scared."

He found her hand and squeezed it tight. He wished he had some words of comfort and reassurance to offer her, but he had to admit that he had nothing. His own heart beat a rapid tattoo of fear.

He could hear the scrabbling coming from above and a low murmur of voices. A square of light cast the cave into low relief. As his eyes adjusted, he could see that he and Samrita were held in a small alcove about six feet square, with enough room to stand. A stout metal grill set into the rock barred the only exit. The perfect prison cell.

Beyond their cell, the cave stretched into blackness. A table with some rickety chairs had been set up on a level area of the floor. The only way in and out was some twenty feet above the floor of the cave, broken into shorter levels, the steeper parts traversed by wooden ladders. He assumed that these were the parts of his entry where someone had pushed him down. He had been lucky not to break his neck.

The soft yellow glow of a lantern shone in the entrance and he could make out the outlines of three, or was it four, men making their way down the ladders to the cave. One of Gopal's men, the one Curran had kicked the previous night, carried the lantern. He cast Curran a malevolent grin as he set the light on the table. The other visitors remained in the shadows.

Gopal crossed the floor toward the prisoners, standing back from the grill door, just out of arm's reach had Curran felt inclined to make a grab at him. Curran struggled to his feet, helping Samrita to stand. She pressed against him, and he pulled her behind him, a useless gesture in the circumstances but all he had.

"I see you two have become acquainted."

"Let her go, Gopal. She knows nothing that is of any use to you."

Gopal shrugged. "This one was a troublemaker from the beginning. I nearly left her in Calcutta, but her friend pleaded with me to bring her. A decision I regretted. We were glad to be rid of her."

"Then let her go."

"It is not for me to say," Gopal glanced behind him into the gloom beyond the range of the lantern and Samrita shrank further behind Curran.

"What do you wish to do?" Gopal addressed the dark space beyond the lantern light.

"I would like a conversation with my friend, Inspector Curran. Bring him out." The voice came from the shadows.

Curran's blood froze. He knew that soft voice, the intonation that came to him in his worst nightmares.

Khoo Zi Qiang, Li An's brother.

Any hope Curran may have entertained about escaping his present predicament alive dissolved.

"Robert Curran," Zi Qiang said, coming forward into the light.

"Khoo Zi Qiang," Curran kept his voice level. "Have you been keeping well?"

"Very well, thank you. However, I am tiring of your interference in my business interests." Li An's brother gave a theatrical sigh. "You and my sister were put on this earth to try me." He nodded to his two offsiders. "Bring the good inspector out here so we can have a civilized conversation."

Samrita's grip on Curran's arm tightened as the men approached the cell. Gopal held up a key turning it in the lock. One man held Curran as the other pulled Samrita away, throwing her against the hard wall of their prison. She sank to the ground and pulled her knees up to her chest, wrapping her arms around them and lowering her head.

The man not holding Curran retrieved the hood and rope from the floor of the prison and nodded to his companion, who pushed Curran into the cavern. The grill door slammed shut behind him.

"You are not looking well, Curran," Zi Qiang said, making a show of studying Curran's battered face. He gestured at one of the chairs. "Take a seat."

The man holding him pushed Curran down onto one of the chairs, tying his hands behind him and his ankles to the front legs. Curran tried flexing his wrists against the rope bindings, but the man knew that trick and rewarded him with a well-aimed cuff to the side of his head.

His head ringing, Curran struggled to focus. Zi Qiang leaned his back against the table, his arms and ankles crossed and a Colt revolver on the table beside him, leaving Curran in no doubt that if he made one wrong move, Zi Qiang would have no hesitation in using it.

The silence that stretched between them seemed to last forever.

"What do you want to do with him?" Gopal asked.

"Nothing for the moment. Mr. Curran and I have not seen each other in some time and we have some catching up to do."

Curran said nothing.

Zi Qiang drew up a chair across the table from Curran.

"My sister finally had the good sense to leave you," Zi Qiang said, "although her return to Penang is something of a thorn in my side. Our dear mother left this earth only days after Li An returned. I permitted my sister to pay her last respects."

"That was generous of you."

"It is important to show respect to your elders, Curran. I have our mother to thank for setting her up as a rival to my business. She and our dear cousin, Ah Loong make a formidable partnership." He paused and his lips curved in a smile. "I believe they are to be married. Does that upset you?"

Curran swallowed, his tongue thick and dry, but he knew it was pointless to ask for water. Zi Qiang would use it as a new way to torment him.

"Li An is free to make her own way in this world," Curran said.

In the few moments of silence that followed, someone hidden in the shadows beyond the light of the lantern coughed. Curran turned to peer into the darkness, but could see nothing.

"Who's there?" he demanded.

But the unseen watcher kept his silence.

Gopal laced his fingers in Curran's hair and wrenched his head back to face Zi Qiang.

"This is the only person you need to concern yourself with," Gopal snarled in his ear before releasing his painful grip.

Zi Qiang inspected his fingernails. "I will not ask you why you are here, Curran, because I know our colonial overlords have sent you to discover what we are about."

"You are using the Topaz Club as a means to blackmail senior colonial officials."

"That is correct. We have ... How many, Gopal?"

"Eleven."

"Eleven such men in my ... our pocket."

Curran picked up the word 'we'... did he refer to himself and Gopal or was there another party to this arrangement lurking in the shadows?

"So not every man who comes to the Topaz Club?"

Zi Qiang laughed. "No, only those that are useful to us. Your friend Bullock-Steele, for example, is of no earthly use except for his propensity to lose large amounts of money at the gaming tables. The Club has proved profitable in so many ways. I should have thought of it earlier."

"But your operations are based in Penang. What are you doing in Selangor?"

"There is a market for opium, and I wanted a way around the tedious taxes imposed by the colonial government. That's where it started. Now, thanks to my co-operative friends, I have branched into lucrative mine contracts and land developments."

"But you have a problem ... you've lost the evidence you used to blackmail your clients," Curran said.

Zi Qiang pushed himself out of his chair. He paced away from the table and stood looking down at Samrita who huddled in a corner of her cell, her arms still wrapped tightly around her legs. Curran could see now she wore only a nightdress and was barefoot. They had seized her from her bed just as quickly as they had shot Ashton Blake.

"That little bitch Lakshmi stole them," Zi Qiang said. "And I think this one knows more than she is saying."

Samrita raised her head. "I don't," she said. "You must believe me. I hadn't seen Lakshmi in months and I was free of the Topaz Club. I was even happy, but you have taken that all away."

"Ashton Blake's death was unfortunate. Some misguided English principle about defending you. You were undeserving of his sacrifice," Gopal said.

Samrita gave a choked sob and buried her head in her arms again.

"I am guessing your clients don't know the documents are missing, so where is the problem? You can just pretend to still have the incriminating photographic images or whatever it is you use," Curran said.

Zi Qiang turned back to face him. "You are correct. Photographs mostly. It was not hard to drug the idiots and place them in suggestive positions." He shrugged. "But there are also letters and other documents, equally incriminating. At the end of the day, what does a man possess except his reputation? Men are venal and weak, Curran." He returned to the table and leaned over Curran, so close Curran could smell the tang of expensive French cologne. "You should know that. You, more than anyone, know how easy it is to be charmed by a woman."

"This has nothing to do with Li An," Curran said between gritted teeth.

"Everything has to do with Li An," Zi Qiang said.

"She did not leave me to return to your clutches, Zi Qiang."

"No ... pity. We would make a formidable business partnership, but she has the same streak of honesty our father had. Play by the rules? Not cricket, old chap?" Zi Qiang's lips drew back in a nasty sneer. "That will never make her fortune." He straightened and gestured at Samrita. "I am curious, Curran. What is your interest in this girl?"

"Her brother came to me looking for help to find her. That's all."

"Her brother, Jayant Kumar, the one-eyed man who asks too many questions? How do you know him?"

"A mutual acquaintance," Curran said.

"Where is this brother now?"

Curran said nothing. If Zi Qiang's men had been keeping an eye on him, then Zi Qiang knew Jayant had been hospitalized.

Zi Qiang shrugged. "I was going to say that you can tell your friend he will not find his sister, but unfortunately you will not be in a position to tell him anything."

"You'd be a fool to kill me," Curran said, hoping he sounded more confident than he felt.

"Why is that?"

"People know where I am ... that I came here tonight ... last night."

Zi Qiang spread his hands. "And when they come, they will find the place deserted. Your interference has forced me to move again, but we are used to that. We have other such houses. What I liked about this one is this cave. Part of the Batu Caves, they tell me. It is well-hidden and soundproof. Your friends won't find it. If someone does eventually stumble upon it, they will find nothing but your stinking corpse. The question is whether I leave you to die slowly or ..." He reached into his pocket and drew out a cloth-wrapped object. With infinite care, he unwrapped it to reveal a knife. The green eye of the dragon on the hilt of the beautiful and deadly object winked in the lantern's light—as it had on the Penang Harbor, two years previously.

"You remember this, my friend? I have cut you once, Curran. You and my whore sister carry the mark of this knife."

Curran turned his head away.

Zi Qiang's man grabbed him by the hair again, forcing him to return his gaze to Zi Qiang and that knife ... that wickedly sharp blade that had so nearly taken his life and left both himself and Li An scarred for life.

Zi Qiang stepped forward and ripped the front of Curran's shirt open, sending buttons flying. He held the blade of the knife to his chest.

Curran's skin contracted at the touch of that cold blade.

"Have you heard of *lingchi*, Curran?"

Curran didn't answer. He couldn't. To have spoken would have betrayed his fear.

"The Westerners call it death by a thousand cuts. A particularly nasty way to die. Outlawed in China now, I believe." Zi Qiang drew the point of his knife down Curran's breastbone, producing a thin ribbon of blood.

He moved closer, resting the point of the knife against Curran's throat. With his head immobilized by Zi Qiang's man, Curran could do nothing. If Zi Qiang intended to cut his throat, at least it would be quick.

Zi Qiang snorted and withdrew the knife, returning to lean against the table. A nod of his head and his man released his grip on Curran.

"I don't have the time or patience to practice *lingchi*. I shall leave you here to ponder on our next meeting, if we have one. It is time to leave, gentlemen." He gestured to Samrita. "Bring the girl."

As the two men approached the cell, Samrita curled up. "Please don't take me. Kill me now, but don't take me..."

The men opened the door to the cell and one of them jerked Samrita to her feet. She did not go willingly, struggling and biting down hard on the hand that held her. The man responded by slapping her soundly across the face. Samrita whimpered and stopped struggling.

The man pushed her out, her arm bent behind her back, her face creased in pain as she cast a despairing look at Curran.

"I'm sorry," he said.

She shook her head. "No, do not say that. There is evil here, Robert, and nothing you could say or do will prevent it. If you see Jayant again, tell him I pray for him."

Zi Qiang executed a mock bow. "Goodbye, Curran. We may

meet again in this world ... or the next. I will be sure to remember you fondly to my sister."

He reached into his pocket, drew out Curran's Webley, and laid it on the table. "It has one bullet in it," he said. "If you manage to free yourself from your current predicament, you may wish to take the easy way out and before you think you can shoot your way out of here, the door up there," he indicated the square of light, "is steel and sealed with a bar. One shot will do nothing."

Curran stared at the weapon on the table, fixing its position in his mind, although how he would find it in the dark, even assuming he could free his bonds, was not a thought he wished to entertain.

"Throw him back in the cage," Zi Qiang ordered. "I will also leave the key for you, Curran. Freedom so close and yet so far away."

The man not holding Samrita, pulled the hood over his head and untied him from the chair. Curran had no fight left in him and did not resist as the man dragged him back to the cell and threw him to the ground. A well-aimed boot took the breath from his body and as he gasped for breath, the grill door shut with a click as the key turned in the lock. The faint light beyond the hood moved away, and he heard the creak of the wooden ladders as they ascended. The door above shut with a thump, followed by the shriek of a bolt shot home.

Curran wrenched the hood from his head and pulled himself up to sit with his back to the unforgiving rock wall, his hands between his knees and his head lowered. The dank, stuffy darkness folded around him. Even the word 'darkness' did not adequately describe the complete absence of light. If it wasn't for the floor beneath him and the hard rock in his back, he would have no sense of what plane he now existed in.

His last shred of courage deserted him. It had taken his last reserves of strength not to cry out, to plead with Zi Qiang not to leave him, but he knew such a plea for mercy would be exactly what the man sought.

He closed his eyes and steadied his breath. His other senses heightened in the absence of sight, and he detected the faint scent of Zi Qiang's cologne lingering in the air, along with another, previously unnoticed but not unpleasant odor.

It meant nothing. The Webley and the key were well out of reach, swallowed up in the dark and no one knew where to find him. In all his professional life, he had never been so completely and utterly trapped and for once, he could see no way out.

He closed his eyes and let despair wash over him.

FORTY-FIVE

As arranged, Harriet met Sergeant Singh and Griff Maddocks on the terrace of the Empire Hotel late that afternoon. Their grim faces told her everything she needed to know. She sat down heavily and signaled the waiter to bring tea, although she would have preferred something stronger.

"I watched the house for most of the day," Singh said. "They have spent the day packing up. Bullock wagons arrived this afternoon and started taking away the furnishings."

"And the girls?"

"They went with the wagons."

"Where did they go?" Maddocks asked.

Singh shook his head. "There is only one of me. My priority was Curran, and I saw no sign of him. By four this afternoon, they had gone. I considered taking the risk and going into the property, but they may have left people to watch, so I came here to report and decide what we should do next."

Maddocks ran a hand through his hair. "We've lost Curran, we've lost Samrita—"

"No!" Harriet said with such vehemence that several other

couples on the verandah turned to look at them. "No," she modified her tone. "We have not lost Curran."

Singh regarded her. "You must prepare yourself, Mrs. Gordon. These people are ruthless and I fear he may already be dead."

Harriet shook her head, refusing to believe for even a second that Curran had left her life. "We need someone who knows these people, knows their secrets," she said.

"And who in their right mind would talk to us? Stewart is dead, Blake is dead—who else is there we can trust?" Maddocks said.

"Robertson—Henry Robertson is still alive," Harriet said.

Singh stared at her. "The headmaster of the school?"

"The same."

She recounted the morning's visit to Walter Stewart's house and Su Wei's story of being recruited in Hong Kong.

"When I visited Edith this afternoon. She told me her husband frequents the Topaz Club, but when I pushed her about what he does in Hong Kong on his business trips, she asked me to leave."

"Why would he talk to us?" Maddocks said.

"We won't know unless we ask him," Harriet said.

Maddocks jumped to his feet. "I'm not wasting any more time. Let's speak to him."

———

Henry Robertson rose from the table where he had been working and came down the stairs to meet them as they dismounted from Curran's motor vehicle at the headmaster's house.

"Mrs. Gordon, what on earth are you doing here? And who are these gentlemen?"

Harriet introduced Singh and Maddocks as her friends and apologized for their unseemly, unannounced arrival.

"Edith is lying down," Robertson said. "She seemed very out of sorts when I got in this evening. Said you and she had some sort of row."

"I asked her about the Topaz Club," Harriet said without preamble. "She said you frequented it occasionally."

"The what ...? I've never heard of it," Robertson blustered, but the fear in his eyes and the sheen on his brow told its own story.

"Mr. Robertson," Singh interposed. "Mrs. Gordon is a little remiss in her introductions. I am Sergeant Singh of the Straits Settlements Police and my friend Maddocks here works for the Straits Times."

"A journalist?" Robertson looked more concerned by the presence of a gentleman of the press than the policeman.

"We are not here in any official capacity," Singh continued, "although Maddocks always has an eye for a story, and if it comes out that a respectable man, such as yourself, was involved in the kidnapping and trade of women to work in a brothel—"

He left the rest unsaid.

Robertson glanced at the door to the house. "Please keep your voice down. Edith is sleeping." He mopped his face with a handkerchief. "What is your interest in the Topaz Club?"

"It began with a search for one of the young women," Harriet said. "Now two people are dead. The girl is still missing and so is the man who was looking for her. We know these people are dangerous and there will be more deaths if someone doesn't help us."

Robertson swallowed. "Who is dead?"

"A girl called Lakshmi and Ashton Blake. Do you know him?"

Robertson nodded. "I heard he had been killed in a robbery." He looked from one to the other and sighed. "How did you make the connection to me?"

"We talked to Walter Stewart's girl, Su Wei. I am sure she would have no trouble identifying you as the man who recruited her to work in the Topaz Club and I use the word 'work' advisedly. You sold her, and who knows how many other girls into slavery," Maddocks said.

Robertson's mouth tightened. "Ah yes, Stewart's little friend, Su Wei. They should have dealt with her as soon as they could after Stewart died."

"Dealt with her the same way as they dealt with Lakshmi?" Maddocks said.

Robertson stared at Maddocks, genuine shock in his eyes. "I didn't mean *kill* her. I meant give her the money to leave KL. I would never hurt any of the girls."

"But you engaged in the vile trade. Is that not hurting them?" Gursharan Singh said.

"You have to understand, I had no choice," Robertson said.

"Of course you did. You had the choice not to go to the Topaz Club," Maddocks said. "How did they snare you?"

Robertson licked his lips. "Things with Edith have not been easy," he said. "Not since the birth of the child. Not long after the Club began, must be nearly two years ago, my brother-in-law took me to the Club. I was beguiled ... the girls made me feel alive again." His bravado was brief. His shoulders slumped. "Then they must have found out about my connection to a school in Hong Kong and my visits there. The next thing I know, an envelope containing photographic images arrived." He looked from one to the other. "It was me in ... in compromising positions with young ladies. I had no memory of them being taken. I think I must have been drugged or drunk ... but if they ever got into the hands of the school trustees, I would have been destroyed professionally and privately. It would be the end of my career, and my marriage ... so, yes, I agreed to their requests. The girls I met came willingly. I never forced any of them."

"You were the one who sent them to Gopal. You are as guilty as he is," Harriet said. "Where are Samrita Kumar and Robert Curran?"

Robertson blinked behind his glasses. "Who? I know nothing about those two people. Believe me."

"Robert Curran is an Inspector in the Straits Settlements Police," Singh said. "You will be in more trouble if you do not help us."

"The Straits Settlements Police have no jurisdiction here." Robertson tried for bravado, but his courage failed as Singh straightened to his considerable height, leaned in, and grasped Robertson by the lapels of his shirt, lifting him from the ground.

Singh dropped Robertson and the man subsided on the steps to the verandah, burying his head in his hands. "This is a nightmare," he said. "I'm just a schoolteacher. I never meant for it all to end up like this."

"Please don't expect us to feel sorry for you," Harriet said.

"Whatever reputation you may have enjoyed, your wife already destroyed on Sunday night," Maddocks said.

Robertson took a deep shuddering breath and looked up at them. "What do you want to know?"

"Our friend entered the Topaz Club last night, but we don't believe he left. Is there somewhere in that building they could have imprisoned him?"

Robertson shook his head. "There was talk ... I overheard that man, Gopal, say that the house was built over the cave system that extended from the Batu Caves and they had adapted one of the caves as a useful place to hide their contraband."

"What contraband?" Maddocks asked.

"Opium? Spirits? Weapons even? I don't know. I saw nothing, and I never asked questions."

"Do you know where on the property this cave was?"

"No ... well ... maybe it was accessed from one of the outbuildings."

The three friends looked at each other. "It's possible," Singh said. "There are many outbuildings."

Robertson stood up, puffing out his thin chest. "Look, I'm

not proud of my part in the Topaz Club but does it need to get out?"

Maddocks looked at him. "Face it, your career is over, Robertson. Your wife is going to be standing trial for murder ... a murder that has nothing to do with the Topaz Club." He narrowed his eyes. "Or does it?"

Robertson shook his head. "No."

His shoulders sagged, and he slumped back to his chair, his face crumpling with the tremendous sadness of his life unraveling before his eyes.

"One last question," Singh said. "Who is behind the Topaz Club?"

Robertson looked up, his gaze going around the circle of faces. "I don't know. Believe me, I really don't know. The only man I had any dealings with was Gopal, but I think he was just there to provide the face ... the face of evil."

"If you are looking for sympathy, you need to look elsewhere," Maddocks said, his usual congeniality gone to be replaced by a man Harriet had never seen before. He looked at Harriet and Singh. "We're wasting time here."

"Mrs. Gordon—"

Harriet met Robertson's red-rimmed eyes with a steely glare. "Yes?"

"I'm sorry," he said.

"Sorry for getting involved with the vile trade or sorry you got caught?" Harriet said and turned away.

FORTY-SIX

I wonder how long it will take me to die.

This had been Curran's only thought for some time, although exactly how long he had no way of knowing. He had spent a fruitless amount of time and energy trying to work the latch securing the grill free of the rock that anchored it. All he had succeeded in doing was tearing his fingernails to the quick.

Now he sat slumped against the wall, every bone, nerve, and muscle in his body reminding him of the beating Gopal's men had given him. The pain was probably the only thing telling him he was still alive.

The story of his imprisonment in the cupboard at Deerbourne Hall had not been told just to give Samrita comfort. He had never liked being alone in the dark since that incident and always slept with the curtains open to let in some light.

Compounding his memory of that incident was the injustice. There had been no punishment for his cousins. Instead, he had been the one punished for 'playing silly tricks.' His aunt had ordered the tutor to beat him with the birch stick for his impudence while George and the girls looked on and giggled.

Now he was going to die in the unforgiving dark. Die slowly

and painfully of thirst and hunger. No one knew where he was, and even if someone came knocking on the door of the Topaz Club, there would be no trace of him. They may even search the premises, but a cursory inspection would not reveal the secrets of whatever concealed the entrance to this cave.

Little wonder he had begun to consider death a good friend.

Would his colleagues and loved ones spend the rest of their lives wondering what had become of him, blaming themselves? One face, more than all the others, came to his mind.

Harriet Gordon.

Why was it Harriet and not Li An that he thought about? Two very different women. Where Li An had been the fire to his passion, what had grown between himself and Harriet since that first day when he had met her at the scene of a murder, was a deep and abiding friendship. The word *companion* came to his mind, and he amused himself by dredging long-forgotten Latin for the origin of the word. It meant literally *with bread*... but what did that mean? Bread ... the staff of life. A companion who nourishes and sustains. His Latin master would have been proud.

"Harriet," he said aloud into the suffocating darkness. "I would like to see you again."

That seemed like a forlorn hope. Khoo Zi Qiang should have finished the task he had begun on the harbor in Penang. At least bleeding to death would have been swifter. This would be so much worse.

He realized he was trembling, his heart racing so fast he thought it would burst out of his chest and he closed his eyes, trying to steady his breathing. When he dared to open them, he was not alone.

"How long will it take me to die?" he asked the tall dark-haired man in the scarlet jacket with the green facings of the South Sussex Regiment who stood watching him, visible even in the dark.

His father shook his head. "The human spirit is remarkably

resilient. I prayed for death in the months I was held prisoner by Ahab Khan, but God is perverse. If I survived, you can too."

"But that was different."

"Not so very different. They tortured me, they starved me, they beat me, they broke every bone in my right hand, but I survived."

"Did you think of me?"

"Every day."

"Why didn't you tell me you were alive?"

Edward Curran shook his head. "Better for you to think me dead, Robbie."

"But you're dead now. It's too late ..."

Even as he said the words, the image faded.

He swore, the words bouncing off the cavern walls, swallowed up in the muffling darkness.

FORTY-SEVEN

After leaving Robertson, Harriet, Singh, and Maddocks returned to the hotel to organize themselves. This provoked a heated argument when Sergeant Singh insisted Harriet remain at the hotel.

She had refused.

Although now, as she looked at the padlocked gates to the Topaz Club, she wondered what earthly use she could be. Both men were armed, Singh with a service issue Webley and Maddocks with a smaller pistol. She had nothing useful.

"Could we smash the motor into the gates?" Maddocks suggested.

"Absolutely not," Harriet said. "We need the vehicle in one piece."

Singh tugged the padlock. "I will shoot it," he said.

"Will it not alert someone to our presence?" Maddocks said.

"If it does, I will shoot them too," Singh replied, his lips compressed in a tight line. "Stand clear."

The crack of the revolver sounded like cannon fire. Singh pushed the gate and the chain rattled off, but as it swung open there was a shout from inside.

"Stay out of sight, Mrs. Gordon," Singh ordered. "Follow me, Maddocks."

Singh kicked open the gate and, with his revolver firmly grasped in both hands, disappeared from Harriet's sight. Concealed behind the heavy gate post, Harriet crouched down as she heard more shouting. Another shot was fired. More shouting and then silence.

Maddocks reappeared and gestured for Harriet to join them.

"It's safe, Harriet," he shouted, but his voice sounded shaky and the hand holding his own weapon shook.

Harriet sidled around the gate onto the well-kept carriageway leading up to an elegant two-story house. Singh stood over a man lying face down on the ground, his Webley pointed at the back of the man's head.

"Is he alone?" Harriet asked.

"It would appear so," Maddocks said. "Left on as a caretaker. Singh just had to fire one shot in his general direction, and he gave up. Not prepared to give his life for his master, it would seem."

Maddocks walked across to the man and picked up the man's fallen weapon, a revolver of some antiquity. He cracked it open.

"Fully loaded," he said. "Harriet?"

He handed it to Harriet, and she took the weapon without hesitation.

"Bring me the rope from the car and we will tie this wretch," Singh said.

While Maddocks went to fetch the rope Singh had brought with them in case they had to scale the walls, Harriet asked, "Does he know where Curran is?"

Singh pulled the man's head up by the hair and fired the question in Malay. The caretaker shook his head and gabbled a reply.

"He says not. They gave him a few dollars to watch over the place. He knows nothing about who owns it or what it was used for."

Maddocks returned with a length of rope and Singh secured the man to a hitching post after relieving him of a set of keys.

"Where do we start?" Harriet asked.

"The house?" Maddocks suggested.

The doors were locked, and the windows barred, but after a few tries, they found the key that opened the front door. The electric lights did not work, but Maddocks had brought torches for each of them. Weapons in one hand and torches in the other, they started a thorough search.

Some furniture looked to have been removed and the downstairs rooms already had a dusty, deserted feel to them.

"So, this is what a bordello looks like?" Harriet mused.

"I wouldn't know," Maddocks responded, his teeth flashing white in the dark.

They checked cupboards and tested floorboards, looking for a cellar before pushing open a green baize door and entering the private part of the property. A narrow back stair led up from the black and white tiled floor. To one side was a large office. Singh directed Maddocks and Harriet to look over it. It contained a heavy desk and an empty safe. Not a shred of paper had been left in any drawers or cupboards.

However, they found a knapsack containing rope, a knife, and a set of curious metal objects tied up in a leather roll, thrown in one corner.

When they rejoined Singh, they found him standing at the other doorway. He stood aside, his face grim. Beyond the door was a large room that resembled the dormitory of Harriet's boarding school with narrow iron bedsteads down two sides and an open area in the middle with sofas and comfortable chairs, and off it, a large bathroom. The windows were shuttered from the outside and barred from the inside. The hurried departure of the inhabitants had left enough evidence to support that theory—wardrobe doors stood open and ribbons, magazines, and hair pins littered the floors.

Harriet shuddered. "The poor girls. They really were prisoners."

Maddocks showed Singh the knapsack and its contents. Singh looked down at the objects in the leather roll and shook his head.

"This was Curran's lock pick set," he said. "He was here."

"We should check upstairs," Maddocks said.

The rooms upstairs were chilling. The half-a-dozen bedrooms, still furnished with large gilt beds and decorated with luxurious wallpaper and drapery, gave some indication of both opulence and intention. They all opened out onto the wide verandah that ran around three sides of the house. Between each room was a narrow corridor with hidden doors into the bedrooms and holes, which would allow someone standing in the corridor to spy on what was happening within.

"I feel quite ill," Harriet said after Maddocks had explained the purpose of these secret passages to her. "This is a vile, evil place."

They searched the private apartments behind the upstairs green baize door but found it cleared out. Maddocks even checked the roof space.

"Nothing," he said as they all reassembled in the front hall.

"That leaves the outbuildings," Singh said.

They scanned the servants' quarters, workshops, and stables but found nothing unusual. Singh pushed open the gate that led into another courtyard and empty dog pens and beyond that, yet another gate that led into a garden.

At first, they didn't notice the structure built against a rock outcrop in a far corner. It had been well disguised behind a riot of bougainvillea. On closer inspection, it proved to be a concrete building set into the ground with steps leading down to a low door below ground level, the door secured with a large padlock of the same type as Singh had shot off the front gate.

"What is this place?" Maddocks asked. "A garden shed? If so, that's a sturdy lock for a few gardening tools."

"It looks a little like the cold rooms you find in country houses in England," Harriet said.

Singh wasted no time shooting the lock away and kicking the metal door open. The inside of the structure held nothing but a shelf of lanterns. The back wall of the room had a door, like the one they had entered, secured by a long metal bar and another padlock.

"I am wasting bullets," Singh muttered, dealing with the padlock as he had the previous locks.

The door swung open, revealing a dark maw. They all recoiled from the blast of warm, fetid air that escaped.

"A cave," Harriet said, her voice tight with apprehension. "This has to be it."

Singh stepped into the entrance, training the fading light of his electric torch down into the hole. His shoulders stiffened, and he leaned forward, peering into the gloom.

"Curran, is that you?"

If anyone responded, Harriet heard nothing.

Singh turned to her with a grin.

"We've found him," he said.

FORTY-EIGHT

Curran raised his aching head, shielding his eyes from the sudden, blinding light that flashed down from the entrance to the cave. If this was Saint Peter coming to fetch him to his eternal rest, then Saint Peter came with the unmistakable form and bulk of Sergeant Gursharan Singh.

"Curran, is that you?"

He could have wept at the sound of the familiar voice.

"Here," he croaked.

The light from the electric torch wavered and danced as Singh picked his way down into the cavern. Another figure followed, obscured by the light of a second torch. Curran blinked and tried to focus. A woman? Surely not Harriet?

He would have words with her, but for now, he just wanted to throw his arms around both of them.

"I think the key is on the table," he said as Singh reached him.

"Good, I really don't want to waste another bullet shooting off a lock, particularly down here. It could start a rock fall," Singh said.

"Hurry, sergeant!" Harriet Gordon herself.

Curran closed his eyes and smiled. The key rattled in the padlock, and the grill squeaked open.

Harriet reached him first. She went down on her knees and took his face in her hands, her eyes angry and concerned.

"What have they done to you?"

"It probably looks worse than it is," Curran mumbled, his tongue thick. "Do you have any water with you?"

"Maddocks has a flask. Let's get you out of here."

"Maddocks is here too?" Curran croaked.

"We left him up there to keep watch," Harriet said. "Didn't think to bring the flask with us."

"Can you stand?" Singh asked.

Singh's voice came from a long way away and Curran considered the question but couldn't find the strength to answer.

Now he was safe, it was as if every resource he had summoned to keep himself going for the past twenty-four hours abandoned him. He managed to pull himself to his feet, but his legs would not support him and he fell sideways into Singh's arms.

"Sorry," he mumbled.

Singh steadied him with one arm around his waist. "No matter. You are a bit of a mess, Curran. Take the torches, Mrs. Gordon, and lead the way."

"My Webley..." Curran muttered.

"I have it," Harriet said. "Hurry, Sergeant."

"You want to carry him?" Singh grumbled. "I am sorry, Curran, but you are going to have to climb these ladders."

With Singh steadying him from below and Harriet from above, Curran managed the ladders, but when they reached the top, he could go no further. Singh was saying something, but his sergeant's voice had faded to a distant whisper and Curran let the darkness close in.

———

Outside the fetid cave, Harriet took a deep breath, the air redolent with damp humus and the scent of night flowers. Monkeys crashed in the trees surrounding the compound and insects buzzed. The jungle was never quiet and never had she been so pleased to take in the sounds.

She looked up at the moon, still bright in the clear sky, grateful to be out of the cave. She didn't want to think about what Curran had endured in the suffocating darkness.

Singh laid Curran on the grass and straightened, shaking out his shoulders.

"They've cleared out. The place is deserted." Maddocks bent over the semi-conscious man, shining his torch on Curran's bruised and battered face. He swore softly. "They did a good job," he said.

Harriet went down on her knees beside Curran.

"Maddocks, your flask."

Maddocks handed her the flask, and she took the scarf from around her neck, dampened it, and wiped blood and dirt from Curran's face.

His eyes flickered open. "Harriet. What the hell are you doing here?" he muttered.

"Rescuing you. A little gratitude please, Curran. I have water. Can you prop him up, Sergeant?"

She held the flask to Curran's mouth, and he drank greedily, one shaking hand steadying the canteen.

"Slow down," she said, but sheer relief softened her tone.

Curran pulled himself into a seated position and ran a hand through his hair.

"What time is it?"

Maddocks shone a torch on his watch. "Just on midnight," he said.

"That was the longest twenty-four hours of my life," Curran said.

Harriet sat back on her heels, a rage of emotions from relief to fury stormed within her. "They left you there to die," she managed at last.

Curran nodded. "They did indeed." He looked around at the three anxious faces. "I don't know how to thank you. How did you know where to look?"

"That's a story for tomorrow," Harriet said. "Who did this to you?"

Curran's mouth curved in a humorless smile. "An old friend. Khoo Zi Qiang."

Maddocks let out a low whistle. "Li An's brother?"

"The same, with a bit of help from Gopal and his thugs." Curran frowned. "There was someone else in the shadows. There was something about him ... I am sure ..." He shook his head and winced. "Ouch ... that was a mistake."

Harriet gently probed the bump on his forehead. Curran snatched at her wrist, removing her hand. "That hurts like hell," he said.

"We need to get you to the hospital," Harriet said.

His fingers tightened on her arm. "No. I don't need a hospital. They gave me a pretty good beating and I've got a splitting headache and possibly a cracked rib, but right now all I want is a bath and a bed."

"Don't ignore a head wound," Harriet protested, her husband's medical training resurfacing in her mind.

His grip relaxed, and his eyes held hers for a long moment. "I appreciate your concern, but I have a tough head and it's just a knock. Nothing some rest won't fix."

She thought of arguing with him, but she knew him well enough and the argument would be futile. He let his hand drop and his eyes closed.

"If someone can help me to my feet, I would dearly love to get away from this place," he said.

Singh obliged, taking Curran's weight with an arm around his waist. Maddocks paused long enough to release the desperate caretaker, who jumped up and ran from them as if they were the hounds of hell.

In the motor vehicle, Curran slumped against the back seat, his eyes closed.

Harriet slid in beside him. The few inches between them seemed like a vast tract of desert, but Harriet slid her hand across the leather until her fingers touched his. He didn't look at her, but his fingers curled around hers so tightly she thought the bones in her hand would crack.

Harriet looked across at Curran, wondering how close she had come to losing him. A world without Curran was unimaginable.

FORTY-NINE

FRIDAY, 9 DECEMBER

C urran woke with a start, his heart racing. In his
nightmares, he was still in the stifling dark of the cavern,
but as his eyes adjusted, he realized he lay in a bed,
between clean sheets. Curtains drawn across open windows
moved in a slight breeze, admitting shafts of daylight. He rolled
onto his back with a groan and lay still doing an inventory of his
injuries.

The pain in his head had subsided to a dull ache. He was stiff
and sore, but he was alive and that was all that mattered.

A shadow moved across the window, pulling back the curtains
and letting in the bright light of day.

Harriet Gordon bent over him. "Good morning," she said
with a smile.

He tried to speak, to ask for water, but it came out as a strangled croak. She guessed his question and expertly assisted him to
take a long drink of tepid water from a glass beside his bed.

"What day is it?" he asked, falling back on the pillows.

"Friday morning. More like lunchtime, really. You've been

asleep for a good ten hours."

"How did I get here?"

"What do you remember?"

Rather more than he would like to recall.

He closed his eyes. "Motor vehicle," he said. "Maddocks ... terrible driver."

"We brought you in through the back entrance. Singh had to intimidate the night clerk into giving him the key to your room, and we brought you up the back stairs." She smiled. "Maddocks and Singh shooed me from the room, and I think they rolled you into the bed. The housekeeper will not be terribly impressed with the state of the sheets. You really are a terrible mess, Curran," she said.

He tried to smile at her scolding tone, but even that hurt.

"You always seem to be the one to pick up the pieces," he said.

She smiled. "I am just glad you are still relatively whole." The humor went from her face. "I really feared the worst."

"So did I," he admitted.

Curran held out his hand. Like the rest of him, it was bruised and bloodied, the fingernails torn from his unsuccessful attempts to free himself. He looked up at Harriet, seeing the dark circles under her eyes and the lines of exhaustion around her nose and mouth. She drew a little closer, and her fingers touched his. He curled his hand around hers, grateful for the warmth of human connection.

"Have you been here all night?" he asked.

She shrugged. "James always said that head wounds, no matter how innocent, could not be trusted and the patient should not be left alone. I dozed in the chair," she added.

"Thank you," he said.

Her lips parted as if she was about to speak. Instead, she squeezed his hand and released him, stepping away from the bed and smoothing down her crumpled skirt.

"You must be ravenous," she said. "I will send for some food."

"I need to get up," Curran said. "Mrs. Gordon, if you would be so good as to pass my dressing gown and turn your back. It would appear that," he cleared his throat, "I am somewhat under-dressed for company."

"Curran, you are blushing," she said with a laugh.

"I don't know how you can tell," he said, running a hand over his bruised face.

She handed him the black silk Chinese gown that Li An had given him for a birthday, embroidered on the back with a red and gold dragon, and left him alone to contemplate the physical effort required to get out of bed.

Every muscle in his body seemed to have atrophied, and in the bathroom, he conducted a quick inspection of the damage in the floor mirror that occupied a corner of the room. He concluded Gopal's men had done a comprehensive job on him.

Someone—Harriet?—had washed the worst of the blood off his face and chest, but as he traced the line of the Zi Qiang's dragon-handled knife down his chest with a shaking finger, he shuddered. Zi Qiang knew his weakness and he had seen his death in that man's eyes twice now.

There wouldn't be a third time.

He ran a bath and lingered for a long time, letting the warmth soak into the bruises. As he stood in front of the mirror, shaving off the hated beard, he heard voices in the room next door and the smell of a rich chicken curry.

He had eaten nothing since Wednesday night, and he was famished. He pulled on the loose linen trousers and shirt he had selected and padded barefoot into the bedroom. A hotel servant was setting out a meal on the table, supervised by Harriet. Singh stood with his back to the window and Maddocks lounged on one of the chairs. He jumped to his feet as Curran entered.

"Good to see you up," Maddocks said. He narrowed his eyes. "They really worked you over, didn't they? That's an absolute shiner you have."Harriet shut the door behind the servant and turned to face him.

"That's better," she said.

Curran touched his left eye, conscious that one blow to his face had contributed to a stupendous black eye.

"I'll mend."

His friends threw questions at him, and he held up a hand. "For God's sake, save your questions. I must eat."

The others sat around the table and went through the events of the previous night and Curran let them talk. They needed to share what they had been through. He, on the other hand, didn't think he would ever talk about what he had endured.

When a man has walked to the brink of his own sanity, let alone his life, it takes a lot of strength to come back from that, and he needed every ounce of strength he could muster to get through what needed to be done next.

Only when he had finished his meal and pushed the empty plates away did he give an abbreviated account of his capture and imprisonment. When he reached the encounter with Samrita, Harriet interrupted.

"Do you think she's still alive?"

"I hope so. As long as they think she might know where the documents are hidden, they wouldn't have a reason to kill her. Harriet, she said she gave you a postcard. Do you still have it?"

Her eyes widened. "I'd forgotten about that. Do you want me to fetch it?"

"Please."

She left the room, returning within a few minutes with a book in her hand. She turned back the pages and pulled out an envelope, which she handed to Curran.

Curran studied the image, a standard tourist postcard of the interior of the Batu Caves, the sepia image rendering the shadows and alcoves dark and the soaring ceiling, a place of mystery.

He turned it over. A drawing of four elephants was not helpful. It had been too much to hope that Lakshmi might have written something useful like "The documents are hidden at..."

"I think it is time you told us exactly what you are up to, Curran," Maddocks said.

He looked around at his friend's concerned faces. They deserved to know. They had risked their own lives to rescue him and he owed them honesty and he laid the story out for them.

When he finished, they sat in silence, looking at him.

"I thought Khoo Zi Qiang operated from Penang?" Maddocks said at last.

"He is ambitious. I am guessing he wanted to expand his market for the illegal importation of opium and a perfect opportunity presented here in Selangor. Opium, spirits, girls, favorable contracts, tin mining ... I am betting Zi Qiang now has a finger on every money-making venture in Selangor State and all because he controls the men who control the decisions." He paused, recalling the shadowy figure who had witnessed his interrogation by Zi Qiang. "But he must have someone here protecting him. He couldn't have done it all alone."

"And Samrita?" Harriet asked.

The icy hand of dread clutched Curran's heart. He had failed his sister on at least two occasions. Thanks to his heavy-handed interference, he had plunged her into danger and then failed to protect her. He had to make it right.

It wouldn't be long before Khoo Zi Qiang knew he had escaped from the Topaz Club. In which case, he needed to be careful. With their carefully constructed web dissolving around them, the conspirators were cornered and dangerous, and they had Samrita. The matter had to be brought to a head.

"Whether Samrita lives or dies now is tied to the recovery of their files," Curran said. "I don't think she realized the significance of the postcard, but her captors might if she describes it to them."

Harriet took the card from Curran. "When I was at the caves

with Edith, I saw a carving of an elephant family, but there are other carvings. Could she have secreted the documents in the caves?"

She returned the card to Curran, and he tapped it thoughtfully.

"Could you find the carving again?" he asked.

"I think so."

Curran nodded. "Then if you tell me where to look, I'll go out to the caves this evening." He glanced at his watch, annoyed by the new scratches on the glass casing. "We've wasted too much time already. Singh, I need you to pay a call on Inspector Wheeler of the FMP and take him this note."

He scrawled a lengthy note and handed it to Singh, who excused himself, leaving Harriet and Maddocks.

"What can I do?" Maddocks asked.

Curran looked from Maddocks to Harriet. "Both of you look dead on your feet. Grab some sleep and Singh and I can take it from here. I don't need your assistance any further."

Harriet and Maddocks exchanged mutinous glances, and he felt a momentary stab of guilt. They had come so far, but they'd both put themselves in enough danger already. He couldn't risk them getting hurt.

When he was alone, Curran pulled out his pipe and stepped out onto the verandah. He sat down heavily in one of the comfortable rattan chairs and began the methodical process of filling and lighting his pipe. He always found it helped him think.

He put a match to the tobacco and gave it a puff to get it going. As the first smoke curled upward into the heavy air, he started and pulled the pipe from his mouth, looking down at the glowing embers in the bowl.

Scent was a powerful stimulant for the memory. He knew, without any doubt, who had been with Zi Qiang in the cave.

FIFTY

Curran had given Wheeler all the information he needed to know in the note he had sent with Singh. He just hoped Wheeler didn't take umbrage at being ordered around and turn up on his doorstep, demanding to know what Curran was up to. Perhaps the mention of Commissioner Talbot's name might be enough to mollify him.

In the meantime, he needed to see Jayant.

On his way out of the hotel, he left two envelopes at the front desk. One with a task for Maddocks and the other for Stephens requesting the government agent to come to his room at four.

He had the ill luck to encounter the bird-watching desk clerk.

"Mr. Sutton," the man exclaimed. "What happened to you?"

"I was on the hunt for a speckled horn bill," Curran replied without missing a beat, "and I tripped over a tree root."

"A speckled horn bill?"

But Curran turned away before the man could engage him in conversation. He was certain he heard the man mutter, "I've never heard of a speckled horn bill. I must look it up."

At the hospital, the doctor waylaid him on his way to the ward. "Mr. Sutton, a moment of your time."

"Is it bad news?" Curran asked.

The doctor shook his head with a smile. "Mr. Kumar has turned the corner and should be well enough to leave in a day or two," the doctor said. "Is there somewhere he can go to rest and recuperate?"

"I will make some arrangements," Curran said.

The doctor frowned. "Forgive me, Mr. Sutton," he said. "But would you like me to take a look at you? You look like you've been in the wars."

Curran affected a laugh and touched his black eye. "Oh this, just a stupid accident. I was birdwatching in the jungle and tripped over a tree root. It looks worse than it is."

"If you're sure," the doctor said with a frown. "You will find me in my office."

Curran managed a reassuring smile and excused himself. He found Jayant sitting up in bed, reading the *Malay Tribune*. His brother set the paper down, the welcoming smile fading from his face as he scanned Curran's injuries.

"Robert! What happened?"

"It's a long story, and one I wish people would stop asking me about," Curran replied, as he sat down on the chair beside his brother's bed. "Suffice it to say, I crossed the Topaz Club, and they roughed me up a little. The good news is, I found Samrita."

Jayant's eyes widened. "Alive?" The word came out in a breathless rush.

"Yes. She was calling herself Jameela."

Jayant frowned. "The woman your journalist friend spoke to?"

"The same. But—"

"But?"

"She is back in the hands of the Topaz Club."

Jayant threw his head back against the pillows and covered his face with his hands. "No! How could this happen?"

"God willing, she's alive for now and that is what matters. But

they think she has some information that they want." Curran
pulled himself painfully to his feet. "Jayant, I'm sorry. I feel I have
failed you. I seem to have failed everyone lately."

Jayant shook his head. "No. It is I who has failed Samrita. I
have faith in you, Curran. You found her once, you will find her
again."

Curran laid a hand on his brother's shoulder. "Thank you.
Now I have work to do. You rest and continue to improve, Jay. I
will have news tomorrow."

Before returning to the hotel, he went in search of the doctor
and had his injuries assessed. There was nothing broken but the
doctor suggested he should rest and recuperate for the next few
days. Curran had to stop himself from laughing. Rest and recuperation would have to wait.

———————

Archibald Stephens arrived at the appointed hour, looking as neat
and as cool as he had the first time they'd met in the Batu Caves.
Curran breathed in the lingering scent of the tobacco that clung
to Stephens' clothing and knew he had been correct. Stephens had
been the hidden man in the cave, but he needed more than his
sense of smell to make the connection.

"Good God," Stephens said. "What happened to you? Have
you seen a doctor? That eye looks terrible."

"Thank you for your medical advice. It just looks worse than
it is. I will be frightening small children and timid women for a
few days. To answer your question, I fell afoul of the Topaz Club.
I'm lucky to have got out alive."

Stephens frowned. "Is that why you didn't report in
yesterday?"

"Unavoidably detained."

"What did you discover?"

"Nothing that you don't know already. The blackmail documents are missing and the man behind the club's activities is Khoo Zi Qiang. Unfortunately, my blundering in on them has had the effect of uprooting the club once more."

Stephens stood up and paced the room several times. At the window, he stopped his pacing and stood with his back to Curran.

"Any idea where he is?" Stephens asked.

"Khoo? None. He has at least twelve girls with him. This is a small town. This is now a job for the police to find him."

Stephens hefted a heavy theatrical sigh. "You are right, of course, but we still need those documents."

"Your contact at the club, Lakshmi. She took them, but she died before she could divulge where she hid them."

Stephens turned back to face Curran. "And you have no idea where the girl hid the documents?"

"For all I know, she could have burned them," Curran said. "We can look for them but if they don't exist, we won't find them."

Stephens frowned. "I don't believe she destroyed them. She probably wanted to use the documents for leverage of her own. To secure the freedom of the girls at the Topaz Club."

Curran quirked an eyebrow. "And how do you know that?"

"I don't," Stephens said. "It is supposition. Just because Khoo Zi Qiang doesn't have the documents doesn't mean the crisis is averted. The men he was blackmailing don't know that the material is missing and the absence of the proof doesn't make them any less vulnerable. We need to know the names of those men Zi Qiang had on his list and stop him before he leaves Selangor."

"What do you want me to do?"

"Nothing," Stephens said. "You have made a complete hash of the whole assignment. I suggest you get on the next train back to Singapore and leave me to clear up the mess."

"Give me another chance, Stephens. I have one possible lead to follow up."

Stephens frowned. "What is it?"

Curran shook his head. "I would prefer to keep it to myself. If I am wrong, as you said yourself, you can just add it to the list of failures."

Stephens snorted and turned for the door. "My report on your conduct of this investigation will not be favorable, Curran."

"Rightly so," Curran said. "It was doomed to failure from the start."

Stephens turned back.

"What do you mean?"

"I mean, you were right when you said it was impossible to know who to trust."

FIFTY-ONE

O n her way to Curran's room, Harriet passed a well-dressed Englishman in the hallway. He pushed past her without apology and a face that would curdle milk. Harriet watched him until he turned down the stairs, before knocking on Curran's door.

Curran stood by the window looking out on to the street, his hands behind his back. He glanced around as she entered.

"Harriet, have you managed to get some rest?"

"Thank you," she said. "Who was that man who just came out of your room?"

"His name is Stephens, Archibald Stephens. He has been my principal contact in this case."

"Is he police?"

Curran shook his head as he turned back to contemplation of the outside world. "No. Commissioner Talbot didn't want the police involved until it came to actual arrests. Stephens is a functionary in the department of Accounts and Auditing."

"Odd choice to run an operation of this sort?"

"I suspect the administration is more concerned with excise

duties and questionable contracts than it is with the trafficking of women." Curran's tone was bitter.

"He did not look pleased," Harriet said, coming to stand beside him at the window.

"He's not. I have singularly failed the mission he gave me, and he would like me on the next train to Singapore." He paused. "Maybe."

"What do you mean?"

"I mean this is not done." He gave a humorless laugh. "I like being right, Harriet. The hotel is being watched."

All Harriet could see from the window was the gaggle of ricksha wallahs waiting at the stand across the road. Archibald Stephens had just climbed into one, his arms crossed as the man pulled out into the street.

"See the coconut seller?"

"Yes. He's been there every day. How do you know he is watching you?"

"Because my friend Archibald Stephens has just had a conversation of several minutes with the man without buying a coconut."

Harriet looked at him. "Archibald Stephens?"

"Is Khoo Zi Qiang's partner. I just can't prove it."

A firm knock at the door admitted Singh and a damp and flushed Maddocks. The journalist mopped his face with a handkerchief and accepted the whisky Curran handed to him.

"How did you go?" Curran asked.

Maddocks glared at him. "You didn't give me much time. I don't have the contacts here that I have in Singapore. However, I managed to catch one of the chaps from the *Malay Tribune* and he gave me some sketchy details about your man."

"And?"

Maddocks pulled out his notebook. "Archibald Stephens was born in Penang. Father English, mother not in the picture. May have been local, but no one would admit to that. Went to school at..." He squinted at his scrawl. "St. Xavier's Institution—"

"That's it!" Curran said. "Li An's father sent her to the convent school in Penang. There is every possibility he sent his son to St. Xavier's. There's the connection between Stephens and Zi Qiang. It won't be hard to verify. What else?"

"He spent some time in England, which gave him a qualification in accounting and auditing. He applied for the colonial civil service and returned to Penang."

"He said he was there when I was," Curran said. "I don't think we ever met."

"My contact says he keeps himself apart. The sniff of illegitimacy and dubious parentage makes him not quite *pukka*. You wouldn't see him at any of the sporting clubs or social events, although he is a member of the volunteer fire brigade."

"For that matter, so are Henry Robertson and Edith's father," Harriet said.

"And we know Robertson was involved in the Selangor venture," Maddocks said.

"Is that what you are calling it?" Harriet put in.

Maddocks shrugged. "It makes a good headline." His eyes brightened. "Or how about Terror at the Topaz Club?"

"When you have quite finished," Curran said. "Anything else on Stephens?"

Maddocks scanned his notebook again. "Lives by himself. No ostentatious shows of wealth ... nothing that would not be expected of his rank in the colonial civil service."

"Why do you suspect this man?" Harriet asked.

"I am certain he was in the cave when Zi Qiang and I had a conversation. I recognized the scent of his tobacco. Habitual smokers carry it with them."

"That is hardly evidence," Singh put in. "You smoke a pipe too."

"I know, but he smokes a particular twist I've never come across before."

"But he is the one who gave you your orders?" Singh frowned.

"And as good as set me up to fail," Curran said. "I told him I was going to the Club that night. They were waiting for me."

Maddocks let out a long breath. "Curran, I don't understand why they didn't just kill you while they had the chance. Leaving you alive seems a misstep."

That question had also been bothering Curran. A quick bullet to the head would have solved all their problems. "Perhaps it was Zi Qiang's hubris," he speculated. "He wanted me to die a slow, painful death."

Singh snorted. "Who is to say Zi Qiang hasn't already left Selangor?"

Curran shook his head. "They still want the documents Lakshmi took."

"But what if she destroyed them?" Singh said.

"She may well have done, but if she wanted to use them to buy freedom for herself and the others, why would she destroy them?" Harriet said, echoing Curran's thoughts.

"If that's the case, why did they kill her?" Maddocks said.

"Perhaps they didn't intend to kill her. Maybe her death was an accident?" Singh put in.

"They certainly killed poor Blake," Maddocks said.

"That too may have been self-defense if he fired first. One shot had been fired from his weapon," Curran said.

"So, they are kidnappers, blackmailers, and frauds, but not murderers?" Maddocks scoffed.

"At least two people are dead and there is no doubt that it suited their purposes for me to die, so I don't think they escape that charge," Curran said.

"This is all very well, but it doesn't get us any closer to

bringing these men to justice," Singh said. "What do you propose?"

"The only thing we have is this." Curran produced the post-card of the Batu Caves from his pocket. "I think it's saying that she has hidden the documents somewhere in this cave."

Maddocks rolled his eyes. "It's enormous. It could be anywhere."

Curran shook his head. "I don't think I have to search the entire complex, Maddocks. Harriet says she has seen this carving. If she can tell me where it is, I still have daylight to look for it. Singh, is Wheeler briefed?"

Singh nodded. "He is not happy, but the Commissioner had a word with him. I just need to confirm the details."

"You go then. I need you with Wheeler."

"And you?"

Curran winced. "I was going to say that I will drive up to the Batu Caves, but I don't think I can manage the vehicle with a bad shoulder."

"And you can't go by yourself," Singh protested. "Look what happened last time?"

"I can drive you," Maddocks said.

"And I just need to fetch my hat," Harriet said.

The three men stared at her. "You're not coming," Maddocks said.

She looked from one to the other. "I'm not sitting here with my knitting while you three go in search of Lakshmi's documents. You seem to forget I'm the only one who knows exactly where the elephant carving is."

Curran ran a hand through his hair. "Harriet—"

"You have no choice. I must come with you."

"On one condition. You stay out of any trouble. Fetch what-ever you need. We leave here at six."

"You will be followed," Singh said.

"That is the intention," Curran said.

FIFTY-TWO

They reached the Batu Caves with little daylight to spare. The evening rainstorm had chased away the last of the sightseers and the vendors of tourist tat, and they had the place to themselves as they clambered up the well-worn path, made slippery by the rain, to the mouth of the cave.

Hampered by her skirts, Harriet trailed after the men. Once within the shelter of the cave, she stopped to catch her breath. Rain rarely had a cooling effect in the tropics, serving only to heighten the humidity, and all three were damp with that odd combination of rain and perspiration. Curran bent over, his face creased with pain, his hand to his side. Harriet kept her peace. He wouldn't thank her for fussing.

She sat on a rock and mopped her face with a damp handkerchief and looked around. The gloomy evening had already plunged much of the cavern into darkness, and she could imagine ghosts and ghouls lurking behind the ancient rocks and broken stalagmites.

They had two electric torches between them, and flicked them on, the lights making little impact on the shadows

"Where's the carving, Harriet?" Curran said.

She led them to the place she had been sitting when she'd noticed the carving, playing the torchlight across the walls and rocks, startling bats and other hidden creatures who scurried away out of the light. She had been so sure she knew the location of the carving, but now the rocks merged and pooled in the dark and she saw only lichen and mold adhering to the rock face. It had only been the sunlight slanting at an angle that had illuminated the little elephants.

"Hopeless," Harriet said. "I'm sorry. I've brought you here on a wild goose chase."

"We can't give up, Harriet," Maddocks said and shone his torchlight into a hidden recess. "Wait. Here ... what is that?"

Two feet from the ground and obscured by an overhang was the carving of the four little elephants, blurred by time and the elements.

The three of them knelt on the ground, looking at it for a long moment. Harriet didn't remember it being so tucked away from view. She traced the images with her finger. If she was wrong, then where would it leave them?

Curran took the postcard out of his pocket and studied it. "It looks to be the same image," he said. "Now where would she put a folio of documents?"

The ground at the foot of the rock was packed hard and clearly untouched by recent digging, so they played their torches across the face of the rock, looking for niches and crevices. It was Curran who found a crevice large enough to conceal a slender package well hidden beneath the overhang.

Maddocks trained his light on the opening. "I think I can see something," he said.

"Hold the light," Curran ordered. He had to lie on the ground to get a purchase on whatever was secreted there. His face creased. Whether from pain or exertion, Harriet couldn't tell.

"I can feel something, but I can't reach it."

"Let me. My hand may fit better than yours," Harriet said.

It took an effort to close her fingers on the edge of a packet and she lost her grip a couple of times before it came loose, and she could pull a canvas-wrapped package from the cleft.

She handed the packet to Curran, and he crouched down beside her, turning the packet over in his hands. The packet was the size of a conventional cardboard folder or large envelope, and someone had wrapped it well and tied it with string. Curran tugged at the first knot, but only succeeded in tightening it. Maddocks produced a penknife and cut the string, letting it fall to the ground.

They all held their breaths as Curran peeled back the canvas to reveal the package contained large envelopes.

He took out the first one. It had not been sealed, and Maddocks shone the torch on it as he withdrew the contents.

"Good God, that's—" Maddocks began.

Curran laughed. "Inspector Jack Keogh in all his glory."

Harriet put her hand to her mouth to stifle her shock and her amusement.

"The sanctimonious hypocrite," she said, trying to make some sense of the image of naked limbs. At least Keogh's face was clearly visible, the mustache unmistakable, his eyes half closed either in ecstasy or drugs.

Curran returned the images to the envelope and stood up. "I can only imagine the damage that has been done, the crimes overlooked because of this," he said.

He stiffened and turned on his heel.

"Switch off the torches," he said, his voice low and urgent. "Keep down."

Harriet and Maddocks complied and the three of them crouched in the dark, ears straining and nerves jangling as low voices drifted in on the still humid air.

FIFTY-THREE

Even though he had been expecting company, Curran's heart hammered, and he cursed the fact he had been forced to bring Maddocks and Harriet with him. He just hoped Wheeler was not too far behind.

He held up his hand, stilling his companions, as he drew the Webley from its holster.

"Don't move and stay as low as you can," he whispered.

"Curran! I know you are there. Have you found my missing property?" A voice echoed around the cavern.

"Khoo Zi Qiang," Curran said in a low voice, and heard Harriet's swift intake of breath.

A crack rang out and something hit the rock above their heads, sending splinters raining down on them. The sound echoed and reverberated in the space, causing the monkeys in the adjoining cave to disperse screaming up the tendrils of tree roots, while bats fluttered in a dark, panicked cloud.

"Curran! I have run out of patience with you."

Another bullet hit the rock behind which they were sheltering.

Curran crawled into a position where he could see the cave

entrance. It had gone dark now, and he only had the faintest impression of shadows moving across the mouth of the cave. He just hoped he hadn't misjudged the situation. Surely Zi Qiang would have come if only for the satisfaction of facing him again. Would Stephens trust Zi Qiang or was there something more at play here? The Selangor venture, as Maddocks had named it, was unraveling.

Stephens had done a good job of convincing his superiors that he was to be trusted with the assignment. But with Curran's appointment, Stephens would have felt the walls beginning to close in and recognized it was time to take his profits and run. His profits and those of his partner. He had set Zi Qiang up to take the responsibility for the whole affair and what better way to remove Zi Qiang and distract Curran than to pit them against each other?

Even as this revelation worked its way into his mind, a third shot rang out and he slithered back to rejoin his friends.

"Are we going to stay here all night?" Zi Qiang sounded querulous. "Answer me."

Curran remained silent.

"I don't have time for this," Zi Qiang said. "You have something I want, and I have something you want. Shall we do an exchange?"

"Robert!" It was Samrita, her voice high and desperate. "Do what he says! You know he will kill me."

As if to illustrate her words, she cried out in pain. Curran clenched his fist in impotent fury. Behind him, he heard Maddocks ask Harriet about the identity of the woman.

"It's Curran's sister, Samrita," Harriet said.

A light flashed on, and two figures rose out of the shadows. A man had his arm around Samrita's slender shoulders, the muzzle of a gun resting against her neck. From the man's build, Curran guessed it was Gopal. The second man, a revolver in his hand, Zi Qiang.

"Robert!" Samrita whimpered. "Please."

"My patience is running out, Curran," Zi Qiang said. "Bring me my package."

"I'm not a fool, Zi Qiang. The moment I get within a few feet, you will shoot both me and the girl."

"You don't trust me, Curran?"

"No. Who wants these documents, you or Stephens? You are there, Stephens?"

"How did you know, Curran?" Stephens' voice came from a dark corner of the cave.

"Your tobacco," Curran answered.

A silence lay between them that seemed to stretch an eternity before Stephens spoke again.

"Very well, as a mark of good faith, send out the woman you have with you—Mrs. Gordon isn't it—and we will do an exchange."

"Absolutely not," Maddocks said. "I'll go."

"No," Curran said. "Neither of you are going."

Before either man could move, Harriet snatched up the package and stood up. She was beyond Curran's reach and while Maddocks lunged for her skirt, he was too slow. Holding the package above her head, she walked forward.

Zi Qiang stepped out of the shadows, his weapon leveled at Harriet.

"Give the papers to me and you can have the girl."

"You don't get the papers until Samrita is released," Harriet said.

Zi Qiang fell silent. "Very well. Gopal, take the girl to her."

Curran steadied himself, ready to do whatever it took to save the women. The documents didn't matter. Zi Qiang and Stephens would not get away, not with half the Federated Malay Police force between them and freedom.

Gopal pushed Samrita closer toward Harriet, but to take hold of the documents, he either had to release Samrita or his revolver.

In a swift movement, Gopal shoved Samrita away from him. Samrita stumbled and fell to the ground.

Harriet held out the envelope, but as Gopal reached for it with his spare hand, Samrita reared up and flew at him. Gopal's weapon fired. Harriet gave a sharp cry and crumpled to the ground.

Curran rose to his feet, took aim, and fired. The back of Gopal's head exploded, and the man toppled backward, sending up a cloud of dust as he fell.

Curran ran toward the women as Stephens let out a roar and raced forward, seizing Gopal's fallen weapon. He stood, his eyes blazing, one hand around Samrita's wrist, the weapon trained on Curran.

Curran stopped. He stood in the open, a clear target for both Stephens and Zi Qiang. He didn't dare look at Harriet, who lay unmoving at Stephens' feet.

Stephens backed away and swung his weapon between Curran and Zi Qiang.

"Both of you, drop the weapons."

"What do you mean?" Zi Qiang sounded genuinely confused.

"You heard me, Khoo."

Curran let the Webley fall and Stephens swung his weapon onto Zi Qiang, who had not dropped his weapon but held out his hand at arm's length, the revolver hanging from his fingers.

"You're a liability, Khoo. I knew as soon as I heard they were sending Curran that it was all over so I have taken the precaution of gathering in the proceeds of our little venture. It will all be coming with me. As for this little troublemaker." Stephens shook Samrita. "I should have dealt with her when I disposed of her friend."

"You killed Lakshmi?" Samrita shrieked and kicked out at him.

"She fell and hit her head," Stephens said. "You don't think I would have killed her without first finding out where she hid the bloody documents?"

"And Blake?" Curran asked.

"He shot first. It was self-defense." Stephens pushed Samrita away and he scooped up the documents. "Thank you, Curran. It's been a pleasure making your acquaintance."

He turned, running toward the entrance to the cave. A single shot rang out and Stephens stumbled, took a few more steps, and fell face down, the package flying from his hand.

Lights and the shadows of men flickered at the cave entrance. Curran raced forward to where Samrita stood, frozen. He wrapped his arms around her and held her close.

Maddocks was at his side. "Curran. There will be time for reunions later. Khoo shot him and he's getting away."

FIFTY-FOUR

Curran looked around. Zi Qiang was nowhere to be seen but there could be no escape. The one known entrance to the cave was now controlled by Wheeler and his men.

"Curran, he went that way." Maddocks pointed toward the second cavern.

Curran made a snap decision. Zi Qiang could wait. First, he had to see to Harriet.

He released Samrita and hunched down beside Harriet. Please, dear God, don't let her be dead, he prayed as he clumsily felt for a pulse in her neck.

He released a breath as he felt the strong, rhythmic pulse under his fingertips. From the dark stain spreading across her skirt, she had taken a shot to her leg. If it had hit an artery...

He pulled her into his arms and held her close. "Don't you dare die on me," he whispered.

"Curran!" Maddocks again. "I think I can see him."

Maddocks fired off a shot that was answered by another shot.

Curran looked at Samrita, who knelt beside him. "I think it's her leg. Look after her. See if you can stop the bleeding."

With a shuddering breath, Curran released her, laying her gently on the ground. Palming his Webley he rose to his feet, straining his eyes into the darkness.

Where was Khoo Zi Qiang?

He ran toward the second cavern. As he passed Maddocks, the journalist handed him the electric torch and pointed to a pile of rocks. He crested the rise at the mouth of the second cavern and paused, conscious he made an excellent target. The risk paid off. A shot rang out, coming so close that he could feel its path as it went past his head, but it told him where to find Zi Qiang.

He crouched down and swung the light around, catching Zi Qiang in its beam, slithering behind rocks. There was no way out, but plenty of places a man could hide.

Zi Qiang fired again, the bullet going wide of its mark as he ran.

White hot fury drove Curran on, ignoring the rocks that tripped him, and he caught Zi Qiang hard against a rock fall in a rugby tackle that would have made his sports master proud. Zi Qiang's revolver flew from his hand, skittering out of reach as they crashed to the ground with a force that made them both gasp as the breath was knocked from their bodies.

While he had a good grip on Zi Qiang's left leg, Zi Qiang's other leg was free, and he kicked at Curran's head and hands. With a primeval cry, Curran momentarily released his hold on the man's leg and lurched forward, pinning Zi Qiang to the ground with his knee to the man's chest. Taller and stronger than his lithe opponent, he had him at last.

He glimpsed steel as Zi Qiang, undeterred, slashed at Curran with his knife, catching his left arm. Curran seized his wrist and bent it, hearing a crack and a cry of pain, and the knife dropped to the ground. Curran snatched up the dragon-handled knife, driving the point into the man's throat just far enough to draw blood.

Zi Qiang fell still. His dark eyes, unnervingly like his sister's, fixed Curran with an unblinking gaze.

"So? Kill me, Curran."

Curran had wanted nothing more in his life. One thrust of the knife could avenge all the pain and humiliation that this man had caused him and not only him but his sister, the girls at the Topaz Club, and his countless other victims.

"Curran!" Singh's voice came from behind him.

"You are a coward, Curran," Zi Qiang taunted, and Curran forced himself to look into the man's handsome face.

"If I were a coward, I would kill you," he said, "but you are not worth the effort. This is for Li An."

With the same deliberate care he had witnessed Zi Qiang employ, Curran drew the tip of the blade down the right side of Zi Qiang's face from the temple to the corner of his mouth.

Zi Qiang screamed, his hand going to his face in a vain attempt to staunch the blood.

With a grunt, Curran stood up, wiping the blade of the knife on Zi Qiang's shirt. He handed the knife to Singh.

Inspector Wheeler, red-faced and panting, joined them.

"Who is this?" he asked, looking down at the man, huddled, bleeding on the ground.

"Khoo Zi Qiang," Curran said. "One of the men behind the Topaz Club. The other, Stephens, is dead."

Wheeler signaled one of his constables. "Deal with him."

The constable hauled Zi Qiang to his feet, securing his hands behind his back with handcuffs.

Dripping blood from the wound to his face, Zi Qiang did not look at Curran as he was led away.

"What happened to his face?" Wheeler asked.

"Cut himself on a rock," Curran replied.

Wheeler regarded him with narrowed eyes. "You've left us a hell of a mess to clear up, Curran, but all in a good night's work. Who took Stephens and Acharya down?"

"I will put it in my report," Curran said.

FIFTY-FIVE

"If you only knew how much I wanted to kill him," Curran said to Singh.

"But you didn't, and that makes you the better man," Singh said.

Suddenly weary and aching in every fiber of his being, Curran picked his way back into the main cavern. Gopal lay on his back, his unseeing eyes open and staring up at the bats, which had returned to the ceiling of the cave now the gun firing had ceased. Stephens had been turned onto his back, his chest shattered by the force of Zi Qiang's bullet.

Samrita knelt beside Harriet, pressing a wad of fabric against Harriet's leg. Harriet still lay unmoving, only the slightest movement of her chest reassuring Curran that she was still alive. Maddocks stood over the two women using the second torch to provide light.

Curran hunched down beside Harriet, and her eyes fluttered open as he picked up her right hand.

"Curran. I think I've been shot." She sounded surprised.

Relief flooded Curran. She was conscious. That had to be a good sign.

Samrita nodded. "You were correct. She was hit in her left leg. She needs to go to the hospital."

Harriet stared up at him with wide, frightened eyes, her hand tightening on his. "Is it bad?"

"I am not a doctor," Curran said, "But if it had hit anything important, you would be dead by now."

She managed a watery smile. "Thank you. That is very reassuring."

He pushed back a stray lock of hair from her clammy forehead. "Harriet, what were you thinking? I had no intention of letting you go out there alone."

"I knew he would kill you and I didn't want you dead, Curran."

He picked up her hand and pressed it to his lips. "I will have strong words with you later, Mrs. Gordon," he said.

She closed her eyes. "I'm sure you will."

He rose to his feet as two burly constables arrived with a stretcher and a satchel.

Curran rummaged in the satchel and found a wound dressing and bandage. He turned back the edge of Harriet's skirt to expose the ruined petticoat Samrita had used to staunch the blood.

Samrita stared at him. "Robert, you cannot. It is not proper!"

"Do you know how to dress a bullet wound?" Curran countered.

"No."

"Then you can help me by removing your dressing. I need to get to the wound."

"Curran..." Harriet protested.

"Lie still. This is going to hurt," he said.

Putting aside the thousand conflicting emotions that suddenly crowded his mind, Curran was back on the battlefields of South Africa. But this was not an anonymous soldier on a battlefield. He glanced at Harriet's pale, damp face ... this was a woman ... a woman he loved.

Samrita held Harriet's hand while he applied the rough dressing. It would hold until a doctor could see her. He stood up and nodded to the constables.

"Get her to the hospital as quickly as you can."

She groaned as they lifted her onto the stretcher and he caught her hand. "You'll be fine, Harriet. A few stitches and you'll be back playing tennis in the new year."

Her bloodless lips parted, and her fingers tightened on his. "Thank you," she said.

Thank me for what? All I've done is nearly get you killed!

"I'll go with her, Curran," Maddocks said.

Curran nodded in agreement with Maddocks' suggestion and turned to Samrita. She stood, shivering in the filthy and torn remnants of her nightdress, her bare feet cut and bleeding. He put an arm around her shoulder and pulled her into his embrace.

"Are you hurt? Do you need to see a doctor?"

She shook her head. "Is it over, Robert?"

"It's over," he said. "You are safe now."

"I hate to interrupt," Wheeler's voice, officious and commanding, cut across them. "I need to talk to this woman."

"This is Samrita Kumar," Curran said. "And you can talk to her in the morning. Now she needs food and rest."

"That's all very well, but you have no—"

"She is my sister, Wheeler."

The policeman blinked. "Your sister?"

"It's a long story I don't intend to go into, but you have my word you can speak with her in the morning. Right now she is coming with me."

Wheeler grunted his reluctant consent. "I think I'm owed a full explanation."

Curran stooped to pick up the canvas-wrapped package Stephens had dropped as he fell.

Wheeler held out his hand. "I'll take that."

Curran should, by rights, have handed it over to Wheeler, but he could no longer be sure of anyone's loyalty.

He shook his head. "I will give it over to Talbot tomorrow," he said.

Wheeler scowled but didn't protest. "I think you should see a doctor too, Curran. Looks like that bastard managed to slice you as well," Wheeler said.

Curran looked at his left arm. Singh had put a rough dressing on it and it wasn't bleeding but now the adrenalin was fading, it burned.

"It's only shallow," he said.

Another scar to add to the tally.

"Inspector Wheeler." Singh's calm, measured voice came from behind them. "If you have no further need for Inspector Curran and Miss Kumar, I will convey them to the hotel."

Wheeler gave a dismissive wave of his hand. "Go on. You've done enough for one night. I'll speak with you both in the morning."

Someone inside the cave called Wheeler's name, and he strode off.

Singh looked at Samrita. "Miss Kumar. You cannot walk to the vehicle with no shoes. Allow me to carry you."

Before Samrita could object, Singh swept her up. She wrapped her arms around his neck and buried her head in his shoulder. Curran limped behind them, suddenly so tired he could scarcely put one foot in front of the other.

FIFTY-SIX

Singh left them at the hotel and took the motor vehicle to fetch a respectable matron, a relation of his wife, who lived in Kuala Lumpur. Curran, with an arm around his sister's shoulders, led her into the hotel lobby. The reception clerk looked aghast at Curran's request for a room for Samrita, looking her up and down as if she were a verminous street puppy he had brought in.

"Mr. Sutton," he said. "We cannot have people like this in here."

"I am too tired to argue," Curran said. "And my name is Inspector Robert Curran of the Straits Settlements Police. This lady requires a room, and I will thank you not to judge people by how they may appear."

The clerk furrowed his brow in a mutinous gesture of capitulation. "Very well, if you are prepared to take responsibility for her, but she is not to appear in the public areas of the hotel again."

Samrita laid a hand on Curran's arm. "I just want a bath and bed," she said.

The room assigned to Samrita was small, at the back of the hotel, and on the top-most floor, but it had a bathroom and a narrow single bed. Samrita spread her arms wide and fell face down onto the bed.

Curran collapsed into the one chair and closed his eyes, trying to ignore the exhaustion and pain that wracked his body.

Samrita sat up and pushed the hair from her eyes.

"I am glad they are dead. Is that wrong?" She lowered her head. "That man—he killed Lakshmi and Ashton. He was evil. Who was he?"

"His name was Archibald Stephens."

Her mouth drooped. "I loved Ashton Blake," she said. "He was good to me and took Lakshmi's baby in without any argument." Her eyes widened. "What do I do about Kamini?"

"She is fine where she is for now, Samrita. We will leave her as a problem for tomorrow. Now you should run a bath and get some sleep."

Samrita climbed off the bed and crossed to him. She cupped his face in her hands. "And you," she said.

He shook his head. "I'll clean up and change and go to the hospital," he said. "I need to make sure Harriet is all right."

Samrita nodded and smiled. "She did a brave thing tonight."

"She did a foolish thing," Curran said.

"She saved your life. The moment he had those documents, he would have killed you and with you dead, he would have killed me. I had no value to him once you were gone."

She was correct. As Curran dissected the confrontation with Zi Qiang, he realized that if not for Harriet's foolhardy action, they would all have died. A knock on the door made them both start. He drew his Webley and crossed to it.

"It is I, Singh."

Singh had brought with him a small, elderly woman in a green sari, whom he introduced as Balvinder Kaur. She set the bundle she carried down on the bed and made shooing gestures with her hand.

"Men out. Leave this little one with me. I will take care of her."

Samrita opened and shut her mouth, but Balvinder Kaur was not to be argued with. "You, my girl, need a long bath and my salve for those cuts and bruises."

Now the danger had passed, Curran thought he could have done with some of Balvinder Kaur's salve for his own cuts and bruises. He leaned against the wall and ran a hand across his eyes.

"My wife's aunt will stay with her tonight and keep her safe," Singh said.

Curran nodded, overcome with relief at having Samrita safe and cared for. "Can you take me to the hospital?"

"Of course. You should have that wound on your arm looked at."

Curran nodded, aware that cuts of any sort were not to be ignored in this climate. He looked down at his filthy, torn, and bloodstained shirt and trousers. "I will have a wash and put on some clean clothes."

"I will meet you downstairs."

In his own room, Curran closed the door and leaned against it. His bed, pristinely made up with clean, white sheets, beckoned him, but no matter how tired he was, he would not sleep until he knew Harriet was out of danger.

FIFTY-SEVEN

At the hospital, Curran was told he would have to wait to see Mrs. Gordon. She was in the operating theatre.

Curran consented to have the wound to his arm stitched and bound and, ignoring the prohibition on visiting hours, paid a visit to Jayant. He found his brother in a state of agitation. He almost leaped from his bed on seeing Curran.

"Robert, what is the news? I have been lying here all day, waiting and waiting, but no one came. Where have you been? Why is your arm in a sling?"

Curran laid his good hand on Jayant's shoulder. "I came to tell you, it is over, Jay. Samrita is safe. The Topaz Club is no more."

Jayant fell back on his pillows. "I must see her. When can I see her?"

"She has been through a hell of an ordeal and we still have the police to deal with tomorrow, but I'll bring her to you as soon as possible."

Jayant grasped his wrist. "How can I ever thank you?"

Curran cleared his throat. "By getting over this bout of dengue, Jay. That will be a start. We will talk tomorrow."

He left Jayant and found Maddocks sitting in a small waiting area in the hospital, his head in his hands, his shoulders slumped. For a moment he feared the worst, but Maddocks looked up and smiled.

"Curran. Good to see you. How's the arm?"

"It's fine. Any news of Harriet?"

Maddocks shrugged. "Still in theatre."

Curran gestured at an external door that stood ajar. "I need a smoke."

"I'll join you."

They stepped out onto the covered walkway. Curran lit a cigarette, an effort that took several attempts as his fingers shook. He passed Maddocks the cigarette case and matches.

"You knew Zi Qiang and Stephens would follow us, didn't you?" Maddocks said.

"Yes. I deliberately put you all in danger and now Harriet is hurt," Curran replied.

Maddocks said nothing for a long moment. "I don't think Harriet will blame you, but I don't think I can forgive you. Not for me, you understand ..."

And Curran did. He had long suspected Maddocks held a torch for Harriet.

"Sorry, Maddocks. I know you care for her."

Maddocks sighed. "But it's you she loves."

Love was a four-letter word so fraught with meaning.

"I hate seeing her hurt—and I don't mean physically, although that is bloody annoying too," Maddocks said.

Curran leaned against the wall. "Maddocks, I don't know what to say."

"Don't say anything. Just don't leave her hanging, Curran. Get out of her life if you don't intend to reciprocate her feelings."

"No," Curran said.

"No?"

"No. I'm not getting out of her life, Maddocks."

The cigarette in Maddocks's hand burned to his fingers as they stood in silence.

"I see," Maddocks said, and Curran hoped he did. He was not given to sharing his private thoughts with anyone, particularly not another man.

"I'm sorry," he said at last.

Maddocks gave a snort of laughter. "So am I, but all's fair in love and war. Isn't that what they say, Curran?" He sniffed and straightened. "Is this Selangor Venture over now?"

"I hope so. The police still have to find the girls from the Topaz Club," Curran said.

"Where does this Stephens fit in?"

"He was Zi Qiang's local partner. I suspect it is a partnership that goes back to their school days," Curran said. "Stephens is ambitious but tainted by an illegitimate birth and possibly mixed blood, and his friend Zi Qiang needed a contact high enough in the administration to influence without drawing attention. Stephens convinced his superiors that he was a suitable man for the job of undoing the Topaz Club. I think the police will find that he had every intention of absconding tonight with the entire profits of the enterprise in his accounts."

"So he was double-crossing Khoo. That is a dangerous enemy to make. Quite the alliance."

"No honor among thieves, Maddocks."

Maddocks rose to his feet and glanced at his watch. "I should go," he said. "I have copy to write. This story will be the making of my career."

Curran flinched inwardly. He hated having to inflict another blow on his friend.

"You can't ever write about it, Maddocks," he said.

"Why not? It's the best story of my career—"

"And if word gets out that the incorruptible British adminis-tration is corruptible, then we are all finished," Curran said. "It's a damnable piece of work, but it can never be made public."

Maddocks ran a hand through his hair and swore.

"The story of my lifetime and I can't report it?" He glared at Curran. "Another thing I'll never forgive you for."

Curran laid a hand on his friend's shoulder. "We'll talk about it later and you can take it up with the Resident General if you wish, but the answer will be the same. For now, go back to the hotel, Maddocks. There's nothing more you can do here."

Maddocks shoved his hands into his pockets. "I'll leave you to it, Curran. I'm done in."

Curran watched his friend walk away, his shoulders slumped either with exhaustion or disappointment or both.

Leaving aside the death of Maddocks's future career, it had been a hard conversation, but maybe one that needed to be had.

What if Maddocks was wrong in his summation of Harriet's feelings?

Curran lit another cigarette.

What if he was correct?

"Can you spare a cigarette, Curran?"

A solid figure in khaki loomed out of the darkness.

"Wheeler, what are you doing here?"

"Just checking that one of my principal witnesses is going to live," Wheeler said.

He took the proffered cigarette case and lit a cigarette, handing the silver case back to Curran. "Nice case."

Curran glanced at the object. A Christmas present from his cousin Ellie many years ago. The silver case was battered now. A little like myself, he reflected as he restored it to his pocket.

"Have you found the girls?"

Wheeler shook his head. "Not yet. We did, however, find a girl in Stephens' bungalow. Calls herself Maria Vlasek. They had suitcases packed, one with enough money in it for me to buy the Isle of Wight. They were all set to catch the next boat sailing from Port Swettenham." He regarded the glowing tip of his cigarette. "I must say your note advising me to arrest Stephens floored me. Of all the men, I would never have looked at him. He was..."

"Invisible?" Curran suggested. "A career civil servant with a spotless record? Those are the ones you have to be careful of."

Wheeler nodded. "We're questioning the Vlasek woman about the girls. It's in her interests to cooperate." He ground the butt of his cigarette under the heel of his boot. "Damnable business. I knew about the Topaz Club of course, but had no reason to suspect it was ... what it was. It's a pity that Stephens and Acharya are dead. I would have loved to see them hang."

"I think Stephens was the killer. He as good as confessed to killing Lakshmi, and Ashton Blake," Curran said.

Wheeler sighed. "And the other girl ... the one that was there tonight. Your sister, you said. What was her name?"

"Samrita Kumar. She's at the Empire Hotel in good hands."

"I will need to speak to her."

Curran nodded. "In the morning. I promise, Wheeler."

"And what news of Mrs. Gordon?"

Curran glanced back at the waiting room. A nurse had just entered and was looking around. The men stepped into the room.

"Well?" Curran demanded.

"If you are here to enquire after Mrs. Gordon, I am pleased to say she has lost a good deal of blood of course, but the wound was clean, and she is resting comfortably."

Curran nodded. "I would like to see her."

"I don't think we can permit that," the nurse bridled.

Curran straightened. "My name is Inspector Curran of the Straits Settlements Police, and she is an important witness."

The nurse glanced at Wheeler. "Inspector Wheeler? You permit this?"

Wheeler nodded. "I can vouch for him."

"I will check with the doctor. Wait here."

Her straight back bristling with disapproval, the nurse swept out.

Wheeler straightened his shoulders. "I have a long night ahead, so I will bid you good night."

The doctor was the same young man who attended Jayant.

"Mr. Sutton, this is a surprise. The nurse gave me another name, said you were a policeman."

"I am. I would like to see Mrs. Gordon."

Clearly, the doctor had more questions, none of which Curran was prepared to answer.

He led Curran to a small, private room. A light burned in the corner, casting a warm glow across the still figure in the bed. In typical hospital fashion, the sheet covering her had been tucked in so tightly she probably could not move even if she had wanted to. Someone had tidied her hair into two plaits over her shoulders, and her hands were folded over her chest. She lay so still that she could have been a marble effigy in a church.

Curran bent over her, alarmed by her pale face and the dark circles under her eyes. He brushed the hair from her forehead, tucking the stray locks behind her ears, and pulled the chair across to her bed. He laid a hand over hers and her eyes flickered open.

Harriet turned her head on the starched pillow and a slow smile caught at the corners of her mouth. "Curran."

A lump formed in Curran's throat.

"Don't do that to me again, Mrs.Gordon," he said.

She frowned. "Do what?"

He took a deep breath and closed his eyes, then lifted her hand, pressing it between both of his.

"Try to save the day," he said, his voice cracking. "You could have died."

Harriet frowned, as if trying to remember the exact sequence of events.

"I... I saved the day, didn't I?"

Curran smiled. "You did."

She looked around the room. "Where am I?"

"Kuala Lumpur General Hospital. They gave you an anesthetic while they patched you up. The bullet went through without hitting anything important, but you'll be sore for a little while."

"I'm very tired," she murmured.

He straightened and released her hand. "I will leave you to sleep."

She caught his sleeve. "Curran, don't go."

He smiled. "I must. I am under strict orders from the sister in charge not to stay and, frankly, she scares me more than Khoo Zi Qiang."

He leaned his hands on the bed and bent toward her. She reached up and touched his cheek. "You have to get some sleep, too."

"Oh, trust me, my bed is calling me."

Harriet let her hand fall, her eyelids closing. "I love you, Curran."

"Harriet," he whispered, but she made no response.

He bent down and kissed her forehead. "Thank you for saving me."

FIFTY-EIGHT

SATURDAY, 10 DECEMBER

Harriet lay quite still, her eyes shut tight. She was sure that heaven did not smell of carbolic and antiseptic. Experimentally, she moved her fingers, grateful to find they seemed to work. It was only when she tried to shift her weight that a sharp pain in her left leg evoked a groan.

She dared to open her eyes to find herself looking up at a whitewashed ceiling, light streaming in through double doors that opened on to a wide verandah. These were open, setting the plain curtains fluttering in the breeze.

"Harri, thank God you are awake."

A male voice, deep and familiar and dear to her.

"Julian, what are you doing here?"

She held out her hand to her brother with what she hoped was a reassuring smile. Julian's dear, beloved face wore the strain of exhaustion and worry in the dark circles and heavy lines.

"I came up on the night train to spend the next couple of days with you before court, only to encounter Maddocks at the hotel.

He told me you had been shot and were in hospital." His fingers tightened on hers. "SHOT, Harriet! I leave you in Kuala Lumpur for a few days and this happens. How did you manage to get yourself shot?"

"It's not serious, Julian. A bit sore now, but they tell me I'll be playing tennis again in a few weeks."

"Not serious? If that bullet had been an inch to the left, it would have hit your femoral artery. Honestly, Harriet, I give up! You better tell me everything."

Harriet gathered her scattered thoughts together, recounting the events of the past few days which had culminated in the confrontation in the Batu Caves. Julian sat, holding her hand without interrupting her.

"I don't remember much after I realized I'd been hit," Harriet concluded.

There were things she remembered, but they were private, and she did not wish to share them with anyone, let alone her brother.

Had she really told Robert Curran she loved him? Had he kissed her...?

Julian blew out a breath. "I will be having words with Robert Curran when I see him. Fancy putting you in so much danger."

Harriet choked back a sob. "Curran nearly died."

Julian laid a hand on her arm. "And so did you, but you didn't and for that, I can only thank the providence of our good Lord."

"You do that," Harriet said.

A nurse in an apron so stiffly starched that it crackled, bustled into the room. "Oh good, you are awake. I am sorry, Reverend, but it is not visiting hours. I must ask you to leave. You may return at the proper time."

Julian stood up and fingered his dog collar. "They gave me special dispensation to sit with you, Harriet," he said.

The nurse sniffed. "Policemen and men of God all think they

have special dispensation," she said. "Good morning to you, Reverend."

Julian squeezed Harriet's hand. "I will see you this afternoon," he said.

FIFTY-NINE

Curran turned the key he had borrowed from Wheeler and pushed open the door to the little bungalow Samrita had shared with Ashton Blake. It had only been a few days but already an air of musty neglect hung over the once-happy home.

Samrita held back, and he turned to her.

"Don't look," he said, conscious of the bloody stain that still marred the wooden floor in the living room. Someone had rolled up the carpet, but Ashton Blake's blood had seeped through, and the stain would be hard to remove. An unpleasant odor lingered in the air.

Samrita looked up at him. She wore a borrowed *kurta* and *pajamas* of dark blue that were far too big for her and kept slipping off her shoulder. The color only served to emphasize her pallor and the dark circles under her eyes. She straightened her shoulders, hitching up the *kurta,* and stepped into the house, her gaze going at once to that hideous stain. She stood for a long moment, looking down at it.

"I loved him," she said, her eyes filling with tears. "Is he buried, Robert?"

"The funeral was yesterday," Curran said.

She nodded. "Then, before I leave this town, I must say my farewell. He died trying to protect me. It is my fault he is dead."

"It is not your fault. You are the victim of heinous crimes, Samrita."

She straightened her shoulders and shook her head. "No. I refuse to think of myself as a victim, Curran. I must look forward, not back."

He had nothing to say to that.

She turned on her heel and Curran waited on the verandah as she packed the remnants of her life with Ashton Blake into a bag. When she came out, she wore a western-style skirt of grey cotton with a matching waistcoat over a high-necked white blouse. She had wound her long plait into a chignon at the base of her neck and topped it with a straw hat.

All traces of the vagabond girl in the oversized *kurta* had gone. Samrita Kumar was the picture of respectability.

"Now, I feel ready to face the world," she said.

And face the world she must. Inspector Wheeler was waiting for their return and the long, tedious business of sitting in a hot police station giving statements. Statements that Curran knew would never be used in a public forum. They would disappear into a filing cabinet and the unfortunate affair of the Topaz Club or the Selangor Venture, as he had increasingly come to think of it, would be conveniently forgotten.

The British administration had no intention of airing its dirty laundry in public.

SIXTY

Police Commissioner Henry Talbot looked up from his desk across which were scattered the contents of Lakshmi's package. He straightened as Curran entered and ran a hand through his thinning hair.

"Has your girl made her statement?"

"Yes. I sent her back to the hotel to rest. She's been through enough."

Talbot frowned. "Not sure I understand the relationship, Curran. Friend of yours?"

Curran braced his shoulders. "My sister ... half-sister."

Talbot stared at him. "Good God. I'd never have asked for you to go on this case if I'd known you had a personal interest."

Curran had no answer for that except that he would probably have got in the way of anyone else tasked with unraveling the Topaz Club.

Talbot waved at the papers and photographic images on his desk.

"What a damnable mess," he said. "I don't know how to even begin untangling this ..." He waved a hand across the vile images and scribbled notes.

"We both know that it will be swept away into a cupboard to be forgotten?" Curran said, unable to mask the bitterness in his tone.

Talbot glared at him. "You are a cynic, Curran. Not quite. None of these men will ever see a promotion or good postings again."

Curran picked up one of the images, squinting to make sense of what he was looking at. "Henry Robertson," he said.

"The school has already got his resignation. Even without his wife putting a bullet into Walter Stewart, his career was over."

"And Keogh? What will become of him?"

Talbot snorted. "I know what I'd like to do with him. However, first things first. I've spoken with Cuscaden. You are to be restored to your position, Curran. He would like you back in Singapore on Monday if you can manage it. There'll probably be a commendation in it for you."

Curran thought of Samrita, Jayant, and Harriet. "I've a few loose ends to tie up here first, sir but I'll be on the night train tomorrow."

Talbot nodded.

"One last thing, sir?"

Talbot raised an eyebrow.

"I would like to see Khoo Zi Qiang," Curran said.

"You're welcome. He is in the cells."

"What's going to be done about him?"

Talbot glowered. "Pity of it all is we can't put him on trial without the whole disaster being made public. The Resident and the Resident-General intend to consult with the Sultan and authorities in Penang. If it is agreed, then he is to be banished. Sent to China probably. Never to return to the Crown colonies or the Federated Malay States. Sorry. I'm sure you'd like to see him hang."

Curran shrugged. "Not my decision, Talbot."

Talbot scribbled a quick note and handed it to Curran. "With my compliments."

The holding cells of the Federated Malay Police Force were no better than those in Curran's own headquarters on South Bridge Road in Singapore. His nose twitched as he approached, the smell of urine and boiled cabbage mingling with bad drains, all too familiar.

Khoo Zi Qiang had a cell to himself. He lounged, with his hands behind his head, on the concrete block that served as bed and table, the hardness only slightly relieved by a thin mattress.

"Come to gloat?" Zi Qiang said without moving.

Curran tried to muster some small shred of guilt for the state of the man's swollen face, the long cut Curran had inflicted, only partially concealed behind a large sticking plaster and padding.

"The knife slipped. A terrible accident. I am so sorry," Curran said without a trace of remorse in his voice.

Zi Qiang's mouth jerked, but if he had been trying to smile, the injury to his face stymied the effort.

"What do they intend to do with me?"

"You will probably be exiled to China."

To his surprise, Zi Qiang laughed. "China? That will please my sister."

Ever since that fateful night in Penang, Curran had imagined a thousand different conversations he would have with this man. Now, he realized, he had nothing to say.

He banged on the door and the turnkey opened it to let him out. He paused in the doorway and turned back.

"Our paths will not cross again, Khoo Zi Qiang."

Zi Qiang said nothing, but his dark eyes remained fixed on Curran's face as Curran closed the door behind him.

SIXTY-ONE

Curran and Samrita stood at the door to Jayant's ward in the hospital. Now she was here, Samrita hung back, her hand tucked into his elbow, gripping so tightly the knuckles showed white.

The nursing sister looked him up and down, taking in the crisp, starched policeman's uniform that contrasted with his black eye, bruised face, and arm in a sling. Her eyes burned with curiosity as her gaze flicked from Curran to Samrita, but Curran had no intention of enlightening her.

"Your friend is on the verandah," she said.

Jayant lay on a daybed on the wide verandah, a light blanket over his knees, his eyes closed. His face still had an unnatural pallor, and he had lost a good deal of weight over the last week, but his breathing was even.

Curran shook his brother's shoulder and Jayant started awake.

"Robert—"

His gaze went past Curran to the woman standing behind him and he half rose from the daybed, his face alight. "Samrita!"

Samrita walked up to him and, without glancing at Curran, slapped her brother across the face with a force that echoed down the length of the verandah. Curran stared at her, too shocked to say anything, while Jayant subsided on the bed, his mouth open and his hand on a cheek that flamed red.

"I would do worse," Samrita said, balling her fists at her sides.

Curran grasped her arm, pulling her back before she did any more damage to her brother.

She turned to Curran. "It was his doing that I fell into the clutches of Gopal."

Curran looked from sister to brother, but Jayant averted his gaze, his fingers pleating the blanket.

"Jayant?" he prompted.

"She is telling the truth. It will be to my eternal shame," Jayant said.

Samrita turned to go, but Curran caught her arm. "Sit," he ordered.

Samrita subsided onto a nearby chair, glowering at her brother.

"You." Curran glared at Jayant. "You told me that Gopal wormed his way into your family home, and showered Samrita with presents before making off with her. Then you tell me it was Lakshmi who you introduced to Gopal. Lakshmi who broke off your betrothal, and Lakshmi who went willingly with Gopal, taking Samrita with her."

Samrita jumped to her feet. "Liar! Filthy liar."

"Samrita, please sit down." He addressed his sister. "Now you tell me that Jayant was never betrothed to Lakshmi. Is that correct, Jayant?"

Jayant nodded.

Curran looked from one to the other. "Where is the truth?"

Jayant did not meet his eyes. "I loved Lakshmi, but we could never be married. Her family would never have approved the match even if Lakshmi wanted it—"

"Which she didn't," Samrita put in. She addressed Curran, "Have you asked him how he lost the sight in his eye?"

"Not a childhood accident?" Curran said.

Samrita snorted. "An argument with Lakshmi. She threw a handful of builder's mortar at him, and some got in his eye. The doctors said it was quick lime and nothing could be done."

Anger flashed in Jayant's good eye. "She blinded me."

"And you wanted revenge?"

Jayant's silence gave him the answer.

"After the accident, my precious brother frequented the opium dens. Gopal came to Laxmangarh for the wedding of his cousin. Maybe that is where they met, where Jayant plotted his revenge." Samrita looked at Jayant but he said nothing. Her lip curled.

"And your parents?" Curran asked.

Jayant looked up as Samrita continued. "Papa had died. Mama was too deep in mourning to know or care what was going on under her nose. Jayant contrived for Gopal to meet Lakshmi. Gopal could be very charming and he offered her the life she craved, a life away from Laxmangarh and marriage—a respectable job in Calcutta, parties, gaiety."

Jayant lowered his head into his hands. "It is all true. Gopal made no secret of the fact he was looking for pretty girls. I was angry with Lakshmi and I wanted her to suffer."

"Gopal arranged to meet Lakshmi to discuss how they would run away together." Samrita continued, her voice low and bitter. "Lakshmi asked me to come with her to meet him. He drugged our drinks and when I woke, I was on a train. He kept us drugged, and we had no sense of where we were being taken."

Curran turned to Jayant. "If you knew who Gopal was and

what his intentions were, surely it would not have taken you so long to find him."

Jayant raised his head. "I didn't know. I didn't ask questions, Curran. I just wanted Lakshmi gone from my life. She had taken my eyesight and my pride, humiliated me. How was I to know she would take Samrita to that meeting? When I knew she was gone and I could see the distress in her parents and my mother, I realized what I had done. I thought maybe his business was in Calcutta and I searched that city, but found no trace. It was only after I received that letter from Samrita that I had any clue that he had brought the girls to Malaya." Tears now streamed down his face. "And Lakshmi is dead and you, sister, I can never, never make recompense for all that you have suffered."

Samrita rose slowly to her feet. She swallowed, but tears were forming in her eyes as she said, "No, you cannot. I was fortunate in the end that I had a man who cared for me and took me away from the hell that was the Topaz Club but he, too, is dead and now, what am I...?" She looked at Curran. "Spoiled goods, is that what you English would call me?"

"I wouldn't—" Curran began.

"Of course you wouldn't. You are a decent, honorable man. Not like this spineless, worthless piece of dirt." She addressed the last to Jayant, following it up with a stream of invective. Curran's limited knowledge of the language did not permit interpretation, but he got the meaning from Jayant's increasing color.

A nurse appeared at the door. "What is going on out here? Please behave yourselves!"

Jayant wept into his hands. Samrita took a step back and Curran put an arm around her shoulders.

"I never want to see this man again," Samrita said at last, all anger gone from her voice. "Let him return to his shame in Laxmangarh. Let him tell the parents of Lakshmi how their daughter died." She looked up at Curran. "I will wait for you outside."

She shook off Curran's arm, turned on her heel, and walked away. Curran glanced back at his brother who raised his head to look at him. Tears stained Jayant's cheeks.

"It is true, Robert. Everything she said and there is not a day that has passed that I have not wished I could take back my foolish, prideful actions."

"Everything you have done over the last year... The lies you have told me..." Curran began but could not finish, his own anger barely contained.

Jayant looked up at him. "It is your right to despise me," he said. "But believe me, everything I have done has been an act of contrition."

"No, everything you have done has just put Lakshmi and Samrita in more danger. Do you have any idea what they suffered?"

He nodded. "And now Lakshmi is dead. My sister is right, I must go to her parents and tell them I found her, but was too late to save her. Will you promise me one thing?"

"What?"

"Will you take care of Samrita? As soon as the hospital will release me, I shall take a ship to India. We need never meet again."

"Jayant—"

Jayant smiled. "No. Do not pretend something you do not feel in your heart, Robert. You can never forgive or forget. I am pleased that we have met. Honored to call you my brother, but I am not your responsibility."

Curran shook his head.

Jayant looked away. "Please go, Robert Curran. Go to my sister. Give her back the life I took from her."

Curran had no words to describe the profound sadness and grief that threatened to overwhelm him. He turned on his heel and walked away.

In the corridor outside the ward, he leaned against the wall and took a deep, steadying breath. How had he got it so wrong? He had found his brother only to lose him again. As Jayant himself had said, he could never forgive or forget the horror of what Jayant had done in condemning two innocent girls to the Topaz Club.

Jayant would forever have to live with his own conscience. All he, Robert Curran, could do was be the brother Samrita deserved.

―――――――

He found Samrita sitting on a bench under the covered walkway, dry-eyed and straight-backed, her hands folded in her lap. He sat down beside her, and they sat in silence for several minutes.

Samrita took a deep breath. "Every day I have wondered what I would say to my brother when we met again ... if we met again. Now the words are said and cannot be unsaid."

"If it makes any difference, I believe Jayant is truly contrite. He has literally traversed the world looking for you. Given up everything he had at home."

"Then why didn't he find me?"

Curran spread his hands. "We found the house where you had been, but it was deserted."

She shot him a sharp glance. "You don't need to defend him."

"I know, but I have lived over thirty years believing my father dead, never dreaming that he had not only survived but had a second family. You and Jayant are both my family, but what Jayant did to you—"

The initial shock and horror of the morning's revelations were giving way to anger now and the policeman in Curran—his need for justice, to see Jayant properly punished for what he had done, undo the lies he had been told, circled his chest in a tight band.

"What do you want me to do?" he asked Samrita.

She shook her head. "It is a Christian notion to forgive, is it not?"

"Not an easy path to follow."

"I can never forgive him."

"No. I understand that. It is not something I can do either."

He thought of Lakshmi's battered body and Ashton Blake lying dead on the floor of his bungalow. Of the life that Samrita had been forced into. Direct consequences of Jayant's selfish pride. However, he had seen enough remorse from people he had arrested to believe Jayant was truly remorseful, but it was not enough. His half-brother had to make his own way in the world and live with his own conscience.

He took his sister's hand. "I can't right the wrongs of the last eighteen months, but I can, I hope, offer you a brighter future. What do you want to do now?"

She shrugged. "I have not dared to dream or to hope. The only reason I would return to India would have been to see my mother—" She looked away. "She will never know my shame and for that, I must be grateful."

He gave her hand a squeeze. "If you want to talk about your time at the Topaz Club—"

This time, her laugh was bitter. "You do not want to hear what I have endured since that day Gopal took me from my."

"I am a policeman, Samrita—"

"And you have heard it all before? Gopal is dead, the Topaz Club is finished. I am free."

As he cast around for something to say, something to fill the silence, Samrita said,

"Lakshmi always dreamed of a life beyond Laxmangarh. I would have been content being a teacher, a wife, and a mother, but she craved excitement, and that was what Gopal offered her. I told her she was a fool, but I foolishly agreed to go with her to meet with him."

She stopped, and Curran knew the telling of the next part of the story was too painful. "Gopal told us we were not slaves. We were free to go when we had paid our debt to him."

"Debt?"

"The cost of passage, clothes, a bed, food ... the bill was beyond any of us to satisfy from the few shillings we received as payment for services rendered. I was fortunate that Ashton wanted me enough to pay my debts. That is how I escaped. Lakshmi chose a different path. She became Gopal's woman."

"There are some things I don't understand. Why, if you were in so much danger, did you talk to the journalist?"

"That was Ashton's idea. He wanted an end to the Topaz Club, for the wicked men behind it to be exposed. He met the journalist at the Selangor Club and brought him to meet me. The journalist ... he made it easy to talk, but I knew if Gopal and the others found out, then Ashton and I were in trouble, so I made Ashton promise me that the journalist would never print his story."

"He kept his promise," Curran said.

"But then you came looking for me. They knew who you were ... but they did not know why you were looking for me. Ashton and I did not know either, but they didn't believe us."

"Is that why they killed him?"

"He was trying to protect me. Me and Kamini ..."

Curran shook his head. "Whatever decision you make about your life from now on has nothing to do with anyone but yourself but know this, whatever is in my power I will do to help you."

And for the first time, Samrita smiled, a genuine smile that went to her tired, world-weary eyes—the eyes of a woman who has seen and known too much of the evil of men.

She patted his arm. "You are a good man, Curran. A good brother. I think what I need is time ... and distance."

"Come back to Singapore with me. I have a friend who can give you whatever you need in wise counsel and motherly advice."

He was thinking of Lavinia Pemberthey-Smythe, the army

widow who was perhaps the only person in the world who knew Curran better than he knew himself. She was also the only person who had known his father. He had a feeling that Samrita and Lavinia would get on very well, despite their age difference.

Samrita nodded. "I think that is good counsel, Curran. Now I have faced Jayant and said the things that needed saying, my heart is lighter, and time will heal." She took a deep breath. "I have been Samrita Kumar, I have been Lily and Jameela, now I will be who I truly am."

They stood up and Curran put out a hand to hail one of the ricksha wallahs from the stand outside the hospital.

"Let's walk," Samrita said. "It's not far, and it's not raining." She tucked her hand into the crook of his arm.

"Do you know what it is like to be free to walk the streets again?" she said. "Even when I was with Ashton, I dared not go far from our home. They were watching ... always watching. I would like to see Kamini. She has been in my care for most of her life but she has a family in India—Lakshmi's family."

"Would they accept her?"

"They are kind people. I would hope that Kamini might be some comfort to them when they hear of their daughter's death."

"I will see what can be done."

Samrita stopped and turned to face him, laying her hand on his chest, and searching his face. "Do you feel this urge to save everyone whose path you cross?"

"No," he said. "But I know what it is to be abandoned by your parents."

Samrita nodded. "You are like our father," she said. "Stray dogs, kittens ... any beggar at the door ... none went away empty-handed. There are worse things in this world than to have a good heart."

The words *like our father* stabbed him. The very parent who had abandoned him. Who could, at any time in the last thirty years, have put pen to paper. His face must have shown the pain because she took both his hands in hers.

"What have I said?"

And he told her, this wise, young woman who had suffered so much. Told her how he wished he had known his father and how he envied what she and Jayant had had. She listened without comment.

"None of us can bring back those lost years, Curran. You are the man you are today because you had to fight for your place in the world. Sometimes love is not enough."

She tucked her arm into his again and they walked on in silence. As they passed the Selangor Club, a chauffeured motor vehicle pulled up. Three men alighted from it. Curran stopped in his tracks, prepared to pull into the shadows, but it was too late. He had been seen.

George Bullock-Steele gave him a hearty wave. "Cur... sorry, Sutton... where have you been?" He stopped short at the sight of Curran's battered face. "Good God, man, have you been in the wars?"

"It's Curran, George, and yes, I have been in the wars."

George leaned in. "Did you hear the gossip? The Topaz Club has shut up for good."

"I am aware of that," Curran said, conscious of Samrita's fingers digging into his bruised arm.

"Your doing?" George narrowed his eyes.

When Curran didn't reply, George turned his gaze on Samrita. "I say, who's this?"

Curran recognized the lascivious gleam in George's eye and took a breath. "May I present my sister, Samrita Kumar. Samrita, my cousin the Honorable George Bullock-Steele."

Samrita held out her hand, forcing George to take it. "Samrita Curran."

George looked from Samrita to Curran and back again. His mouth opened and closed.

"It's a long story, George, and one I do not have time for now. Good day to you," Curran said.

And they continued on their way, leaving George staring after them.

SIXTY-TWO

Harriet refused to stay in the hospital another day and she left the hospital on Sunday morning with a pair of crutches and admonitions about staying off her leg.

She returned to the Empire Hotel, escorted by Julian and driven in Curran's motor vehicle by Griff Maddocks. Installed back in her comfortable hotel room, she reclined on the daybed with a pile of magazines and penny dreadful novels supplied by Esme Prynne, who had taken it on herself to be Harriet's guardian angel.

However, even guardian angels and reverend gentlemen need a break from sick room duty and Harriet had sent Julian and Esme out for a walk, leaving her alone to flick through an old copy of *The Lady*.

Expecting no visitors, the rap on her door made her start.

"Come in. The door is unlocked."

Robert Curran stood in the doorway, his arm in a sling. His impeccable uniform did not hide his bruised face or the dark circles under his eyes, but he was smiling and if she had been able to, it would have taken all her strength not to jump up and run to him.

"I feel I should be bearing chocolates or flowers," he said, setting aside his uniform pith helmet, "but neither commodity is easily procured in Kuala Lumpur on a Sunday afternoon."

"I was thinking you had forgotten me," she said.

He shook his head. "I apologize. I have been rather busy, but you have been on my mind."

Harriet gestured at the chair beside her day bed.

"Your company is enough," she said. "Tell me what has been happening?"

He perched on the edge of the chair as if he would spring into action at any moment. "I can't stay long," he said. "I am heading back to Singapore this evening and I will have the singular pleasure of relieving Inspector Jack Keogh of his duties with the Straits Settlements Police and giving him orders to return to KL."

"Will you tell him you've seen the file?" Harriet said.

Curran grinned. "I would dearly love to do that, but no, that pleasure is for his superior." The humor drained from his face. "I don't know what else he has done, but he is the reason Lakshmi's death was never properly investigated. I suspect he will find himself posted to some obscure island in the South Atlantic for the rest of his career." He leaned forward. "That's the damnable thing, Harriet. None of this will ever come to public attention. All the men Zi Qiang was blackmailing will quietly resign their posts over the next few weeks and return to England or accept lesser postings to unpleasant corners of the empire. Maddocks has been ordered to print nothing about it."

"I bet he's furious."

"Livid. He may never speak to me again," Curran said.

Harriet smiled. "He'll forgive you. There is always the possibility of a better, more interesting, and printable story next week."

Curran snorted. "I hope not. I've had enough excitement over the last week for a lifetime of policing."

"Have the girls been found?"

"Yes. Wheeler has taken statements from them and they are free to return home or wherever they wish to go."

"That's good news."

"And Khoo Zi Qiang? Where does that leave him?"

"There won't be a public trial. There can't be, not without any of this coming out."

Harriet swore. "But the kidnappings ... the brothel ... the deaths ..."

"I don't believe he is guilty of the deaths of Lakshmi or Blake. That was Stephen's work. Running a brothel is not illegal," Curran said. "Kidnapping is, but Samrita and the other girls won't go to court. Even if it did, he was careful to keep himself at arm's length from the dirty business. He left that to Gopal. He did, however, shoot Stephens ..." He shrugged.

"So Zi Qiang walks free?"

"Not quite. He will be exiled from the colonies."

"To wreak trouble elsewhere in the world?"

Curran shrugged. "It is proposed that he be banished to China."

Harriet stared at him. "China?"

Curran did not reply, and she knew the answer. It didn't matter that the man had no connection to China, it was enough that he was not English.

"Has Samrita seen Jayant?"

Harriet had been imagining a happy reunion of brother and sister, but Curran's face told her everything.

He coughed. "The reunion with Jayant was not quite what I expected."

He recounted the meeting between the siblings and when he had finished, Harriet stared at him for a long moment before she found her voice. "Jayant sold the women?"

"Yes. Strictly speaking, he was wreaking revenge on Lakshmi, but Samrita got caught in the net."

"But that's..." Harriet cast around for the words, "... horrible."

"It's beyond horrible," Curran said. "I went back to see him this afternoon and I will pay his passage back to India." He sighed and grimaced as he struggled to find the words. "I am ... Harriet, there are no words for what I feel ... Appalled? Horrified? Sickened? I feel I gained and lost a friend, if not just a brother, in the space of a few short weeks."

"He has to live with the consequences of his actions," Harriet said. "How is Samrita?"

"Samrita is coming to Singapore with me. I sent a telegram to Lavinia this morning to ask if she will take her in. Samrita needs time and a solid shoulder to lean on."

"Lavinia is an excellent choice, Curran. I would trust her implicitly to know what Samrita needs."

Curran leaned back and ran his hand through his hair. "Harriet, I can't even begin to imagine what the girl has been through or how any person overcomes those memories."

"Curran, women are stronger than you think. From what you have told me, she is a survivor. She will not let herself be brought down by what evil men have wrought on her."

She held out her hand, and he took it, his fingers tightening on hers. "Are you speaking of Samrita or yourself, Harriet?"

"I survived Holloway," she said. "I have the love of my friends and family to sustain me."

"Harriet ..." His voice had an odd crack, and she held her breath, willing him to repeat back to her those foolish words she had uttered in her morphine-induced haze, but he released her hand and straightened in his chair.

"And that's it," Curran said. "Now you know everything. My first task in Singapore will be to restore all my staff who were seen off by Keogh. That includes you if you want your job back."

She wanted to scream at him, but instead, she smiled. "I'll see," she said.

He stood up. "Are you attending court on the Robertson matter tomorrow?"

Harriet shook her head. "Not unless I am absolutely required. Julian will give my apologies."

"Then I will see you back in Singapore," he said and left, shutting the door with a soft click.

Harriet hurled the magazine she had been reading at the unmoving cedar with an accompanied growl of frustration.

After the last week's tumultuous events, she felt bereft, as if she were being parted from the one steady rock in her life. She had a foolish wish to cling to him, hold him to her, tell him she could not imagine life without him, but instead, all she could do was smile and wave as he walked away from her once more.

SIXTY-THREE

The night train for Singapore stood at the station platform, building up steam as Curran walked onto the platform with Samrita. He had booked sleepers, but the train was not ready for boarding and the platform bustled with passengers of all races together with families and friends who had come to see them off.

As the crowd parted, he recoiled. A slender, dark-haired woman dressed in a dark blue *cheongsam* embroidered with peonies on the shoulder stood looking at him.

Khoo Li An.

She smiled and as their eyes met, he found himself holding his breath. He had forgotten how beautiful she was, despite her scarred face—her brother's legacy.

Telling Samrita to wait, he crossed the infinite yards that stood between him and the woman he had loved.

But the woman who waited for him was not the Li An he had known. That Li An had hidden from view, her life with him the curtain beyond which she had not dared move until she was ready. This woman stood straight and tall, her hair no longer concealing her scarred face but swept back in a loose chignon at the back of her neck. She held a blue and gold handbag on a golden chain in front of her and she made no move as he came to her.

"Good evening, Curran," she said.

He found he had been holding his breath. "Good evening, Miss Khoo. Why are you here?"

"I arrived this morning. News reached me yesterday that my brother had been taken into police custody and I felt compelled out of familial duty to see for myself."

"And how did you find him?"

"He is angry, and you have made rather a mess of his face, Curran. Such a shame his good looks are now gone forever." Her lips tightened. "He was even angrier by the time I left." This time, she smiled. "He has signed over to me all his interests in my father's business and ... everything else. I have made it clear that if he ever sets foot in Penang again, I cannot guarantee his good health. So many ways to die in the tropics, do you not agree?"

Curran shook his head. "He will be put on a boat to China, Li An. God willing, neither of us will see him again."

She nodded. "I now must undo the evil that he has wrought and regain the honor of my family's name." She looked up at him from under her eyelashes. "Within the bounds of proper business practice, of course." All humor vanished from her face. "I will begin by paying every one of the girls who were his prey in the Topaz Club one hundred pounds to start a new life." Her gaze went past his shoulder to Samrita who stood watching the people start to board the train. "Is she your sister?"

"Yes."

She nodded. "I am pleased you found her, Curran."

"So am I, Li An."

"What of your brother?"

"Ah, that is a little more complicated. He is returning to India."

Li An nodded. "Family is a complex construction, Curran." She hesitated before saying, "Ah Loong wishes to marry me."

"Will you?"

She studied his face for a long moment. "Probably. We are stronger together and it is lonely by myself." She paused and brought her hand up to his cheek, her mouth curling in a smile. "I consider myself blessed to have known the love of a good man and that is enough."

"You talk about me as if I were dead," Curran said.

She smiled. "I can see in your eyes, Curran, that what we had is faded. In your heart, you love another. Love her as you did me."

"What do you mean?"

Li An rolled her eyes. "It is time for you to board your train. Look after your sister. If you and Harriet are ever in Penang, you are very welcome to come and take tea on the verandah of my father's house."

Before Curran could answer, Li An leaned forward and kissed him on the cheek and then she was gone, swallowed up in the departing crowd.

Samrita tugged at his sleeve. "It is time to board, Robert. Who was that lady?"

Curran looked down at his sister. "That lady is Miss Khoo Li An," he said. "Sister of Khoo Zi Qiang."

Samrita's eyes widened. "But—" she began, but he raised a finger.

"It is a long story. I will tell you when we are on the train."

SIXTY-FOUR

MONDAY, 12 DECEMBER

All anyone in Kuala Lumpur could talk about was the committal hearing for Edith Robertson. The paper was full of it and Julian reported that the speculation in the breakfast room had been whether the charges would be dismissed or if she would go to trial.

Esme Prynne had taken a day off work to keep Harriet company and the women were playing two-handed patience when Julian arrived back at the hotel from the day in court looking hot and disgruntled.

"I can't believe it. I come all this way only to be told I was not required as a witness," he grumbled. "They had enough evidence without our testimony, apparently."

Harriet set down her cards and gave her brother her full attention.

"Tell me about it."

"Not unexpected," Julian said. "Edith Robertson has been committed for trial, probably February. No bail this time. Wheeler took her off to Pudu Prison pending the trial."

"Oh," Harriet said. "She won't like that."

"No. Poor Robertson is beside himself, protesting his wife's innocence to anyone who will listen. The problem is no one is listening. They've all decided she's guilty."

"She is," Harriet said. "We were there."

"I'm not denying she shot him," Julian said, "but there may have been extenuating circumstances."

"Do you really believe Walter Stewart tried to ... have his way with her?" Esme put in, a slight color rising to her cheek as she wrestled with the word she was trying to avoid.

Julian shrugged. "I don't know what to believe. What I do know is that something in this tropical heat affects men."

"Don't excuse the behavior," Harriet said. "It hasn't affected you."

"I'm not talking about me," Julian protested. "But this entire society changes people and they behave in ways they never would back in England. We've met them, the lonely men on plantations and mines who take to the bottle. Alcohol and loneliness are a lethal combination."

"From what I know of Walter Stewart, he was none of those things. He lived close to town and he may have had a taste for a drink, but he had a woman in his home who loved him. Edith is an attractive woman, I grant you, but she is married with a child. Stewart had no reason to have his evil way with her," Harriet said.

"How do you know about his other woman?" Julian asked.

"Griff and I visited her. She was bereft," Harriet said.

Julian shrugged. "That is for the court to decide, not us." He paused. "By the way, Henry Robertson has resigned from the school."

Harriet glanced at Esme in whom she had confided much of the story of the Topaz Club.

"I had heard a rumor," Esme said.

"His position was untenable. Aside from the troubles with his wife, there is something you should know about Henry Robertson, Julian," Harriet said. "He was an active part of the Topaz Club conspiracy."

And she told her brother about Robertson's trips to Hong Kong and the recruiting of Su Wei.

Julian stared at her. "I'm speechless," he said.

Harriet took a breath. "I think it was Walter Stewart's relationship with Su Wei that prompted the jealous rage in Edith. The more I have thought about it, the more convinced I am that Edith planned the rendezvous on Sunday night. She left a loaded revolver where she could reach it. She may have only intended to frighten him but by the time he had told her for, no doubt, the hundredth time that he didn't love her and wanted to be with Su Wei, she flew into a murderous rage and shot him ... and went on shooting him."

"That was the part I never understood," Esme said. "It is one thing to shoot a man but to continue firing as he is running away and then to empty the weapon into his fallen body. That is murder, isn't it?"

Julian nodded. "I think our father would agree with you."

Esme rose to her feet and glanced at her wristwatch. "I really must go. I promised Miss Marsh I would be back in time to supervise the boarders' dinner." She leaned forward and pecked Harriet on the cheek. "Safe travel back home, dear Harriet, and I will see you soon."

She straightened to face Julian, holding out her hand. "Goodbye for now, Reverend Edwards. I so look forward to having time to discuss Virgil again with you in the not-too-distant future."

A flush rose to Julian's cheeks and he had to push his glasses back up his nose as he stuttered. "The pleasure will be all mine, Miss Prynne."

As the door closed behind her, Julian sat down in the chair vacated by Esme and mopped his face with a handkerchief. "I have to say, I find Kuala Lumpur much warmer than Singapore."

Harriet reclined back on the daybed. "I hope you don't mind me saying this, Julian, but if Prince Alfred's should offer you a job, I will not be accompanying you. I never want to see the place again."

"Can't say I blame you." Julian sat forward and looked down at his hands, clasped together in front of him. "They did offer me the job. In fact, they have offered me the acting principal role until the return of the headmaster next term and then senior classics master. I turned it down."

"Oh ... Julian, ignore what I just said. That would have meant a place for Will."

Julian shrugged. "I like St Tom's and as for Will, a letter came during the week. He has won a scholarship to the Royal College in Colombo."

Harriet stared at him. Royal College was one of the most prestigious schools in Ceylon ... in the whole of the Far East.

"How did that happen?"

"I know the principal and they have a program of support for boys with Will's background. I wrote to him more out of hope than expectation. However, that, and his own academic results, have secured Will a full scholarship."

Harriet's initial excitement tempered as she realized what the news meant.

"Colombo is so far away."

"Not as far as England. It means he can come home for the holidays," Julian said.

Tears welled in Harriet's eyes, pride and devastation mingling together. She groped for her handkerchief.

"Silly old thing," Julian said.

"I know," Harriet said with a final sniff. "It's all changing, isn't it?"

Julian nodded and glanced at the door. "In more ways than one."

"What do you mean by that?" Realization dawned and

Harriet gave a cry of delight. "Oh ... you like Esme! I knew you did."

Julian turned bright red. "I've no idea what you mean."

Harriet cocked her head and fixed her brother with a hard, knowing glare. If it was possible, he went an even brighter shade of pink.

Julian tried changing the subject. "How's the leg?"

"Sore, but I can take some weight on it," Harriet said. "I just want to go home. Do you think you can organize tickets for tomorrow night's train?"

"Of course. The school isn't expecting me back for a few days and Will is staying in the boarding house, so there is no hurry if you need longer."

"No, tomorrow night, please Julian."

Julian stood up. "I better wash, and I'll order dinner to be delivered."

He paused by the door and looked back at her. "It is all changing, Harri. For the better, I hope."

SIXTY-FIVE

TUESDAY, 13 DECEMBER

Leaning heavily on her borrowed crutches, Harriet limped through the main gate of Pudu Prison. Like so much of the architecture of KL, the entrance was topped with Moorish towers, an oddly fanciful embellishment for such a grim place. Once inside, the smell of unwashed bodies mingled with the cloying smell of rancid cooking oil.

A grim-faced English officer signed her in and escorted her through the series of locked gates to the women's section of the jail, which stood to the left of the main gate. The women's block huddled in the shadow of the men's prison that loomed above her.

She ignored the jibes of the men who gathered at the gate to the men's section, curious about the visitor, and looked up at the grim walls soaring above her. Somewhere within these walls, Khoo Zi Qiang nursed his wounds and his grievances.

She shuddered at that thought. He should hang for his crimes, and it galled her that he wouldn't see justice in that sense. But maybe exile would be enough.

As she followed the stiff, khaki-clad back of the officer, memories of Holloway tugged at the corners of Harriet's mind, triggering a desire to turn and run while she could. But as she was physically incapable of running anywhere, her sensible self reassured her that this was not Holloway and she was not a prisoner.

The officer showed her into a small visitor's room furnished with a scuffed and scratched table and two chairs. A female guard inspected the parcel Harriet had brought and left her, returning ten minutes later with Edith Robertson.

Any resemblance to the pretty, vivacious woman Harriet had first met had gone. Edith wore a prison uniform of a grey smock with a white apron pinned to it. No longer did she affect a bouffant hairstyle. Her fair hair hung down her back in one long braid.

Edith burst into tears as soon as the door closed. Harriet passed over her handkerchief and ineffectually patted her shoulder until the sobs subsided. Edith wiped her eyes on her apron, and they sat on either side of the table.

Harriet handed her a parcel containing clean linen and some culinary treats from John Little. Edith gave these no more than a passing glance.

"Why are you limping?" Edith asked at last.

"I was shot," Harriet said.

Edith blinked. "Is that why you weren't in court yesterday?"

"Yes."

To her surprise, Edith asked no more questions about how Harriet came to be shot, instead turning the conversation to herself and her own misery.

"I shouldn't be here," she pouted. "I told the magistrate that I wouldn't run away."

"Edith, the charge against you is too serious," Harriet said. "You were fortunate to have been allowed out on a surety the first time. Now they have decided you have a case to answer and that is why you are here."

Edith looked away and when she returned her gaze to Harriet. Harriet saw something in the woman's eyes she had never seen before. A glittering hardness.

"He should never have taken up with that ... that ... native woman."

Harriet held up a hand. "Please, Edith, I don't want to know."

But Edith ignored her. She seemed oblivious to the fact Harriet was in the room. She stood up and paced the room, twisting her hands in her apron. "He told me at the Batu Caves it was over, but I had to see him one more time. I thought, maybe, one last chance ... he would see what he was missing—"

Harriet thought of the perfume, the pretty evening dress— the lack of underwear—and knew her summation to Julian had been correct.

Edith stopped her pacing and brought her gaze back to Harriet, but she was not seeing Harriet. Her gaze was fixed on the man in front of her, the man who had just told her he no longer loved her ...

"I just meant to scare him," she said, "but he made me so mad, telling me how he loved her and not me. I had to make him stop—"

Harriet pushed her chair back and stood up. "Please, Edith, say no more."

The blank look went from Edith's eyes. "What did I say? Do you have to go?"

"I am leaving Kuala Lumpur tonight, Edith."

"Will I see you again?"

"The lawyer doesn't think Julian and I will be needed at the trial."

Edith nodded. "When I am free, Henry and I will come and visit you in Singapore."

Harriet managed a smile. "That would be nice."

She doubted Edith Robertson would ever be free. Unless

some miracle occurred at the trial, she would only be freed by the gallows.

Edith's face clouded again. "Except Henry has resigned from the school. He won't tell me why. I suppose it's because of me. I don't know where we will go, but I don't want to go to England. I hate it there."

The litany of complaints she had heard from Edith before began again, mercifully cut short by the guard, returning to tell Harriet that visiting time was up.

The heavy gate of Pudu Prison clanged shut behind her and Harriet took a deep breath, thankful to be walking free of the taint of prison.

Julian had been waiting with a carriage and, as he helped her back into it, he asked how the interview had gone.

Harriet shook her head. "She really believes she will be given a slap on the wrist and allowed to go back to her life as if nothing had happened. I'm glad I'm not required to give evidence, Julian."

She turned to look out of the window at the curving roofs of the Malay homes that comprised the Pudu village.

If I had to give evidence, she thought, I might have to testify that Edith Robertson just confessed that she planned the evening. It may not have ended as she intended, but if she couldn't have Walter Stewart, no other woman could.

Sixty-Six

Singapore

Saturday, 20 January 1911

Curran sat on the verandah of his friend Lavinia Pemberthey-Smythe's house in Scotts Road sipping tea and watching Samrita throw a small red ball for Pansy, Lavinia's dog, taken in by Lavinia after Pansy's mistress had been brutally murdered back in August.

Samrita picked up the disreputable object at her feet and, with a laugh, threw it again. The little dog set off after it, yapping happily.

"Dogs ... girls ... the sad and the broken all find their way to your door, Lavinia," Curran said at last.

"What on earth do you mean?" Lavinia set her chipped and faded cup down on the table.

"I include myself in that list," Curran said.

"Do you indeed?" Lavinia said. "I think the person responsible for bringing you back to life is not me."

Curran looked away.

"I am talking about Harriet Gordon," Lavinia said.

Curran shifted and coughed. "I know," he said.

"She's been away for nearly six weeks. Have you written to her?"

"I ... no ..."

He had started letters. Every evening, he had sat down with pen and paper with news of his commendation and the return of his staff, but the recounting of day-to-day minutiae felt wrong. There had been so much he wanted to say to Harriet, but it would have to wait.

Julian, acting on advice from Dr. Mackenzie, had almost immediately on return to Singapore, taken Harriet and Will to Ceylon, partly to visit Will's new school in Colombo but mostly so Harriet could recuperate from her injury in the cool of the highlands. Busy as he had been, with winding up the affair of the Topaz Club and restoring the Detective Branch, there had been no opportunity for any sort of private conversation with Harriet before her departure. He had stood on the quayside with Harriet's friends watching as the ship pulled away, the pain of parting and the sense of unfinished business, a physical ache.

"In fairness, all I've had from her was a postcard of some clock tower in Colombo wishing me happy Christmas," he said.

Lavinia rolled her eyes. "You are as bad as each other. Just so I am sure, you are not still hankering after Li An, Curran?"

He cast her a sharp glance. "What Li An and I shared was wild and desperate and could never have lasted." He sighed. "I would be lying if I said there isn't a part of me that will always remember that passion." He drew in a breath. "What I feel for Harriet is different ... deeper ... a meeting of souls. I just haven't found the words to tell her how I feel. I'm a policeman, Lavinia, not a poet."

"Maybe it doesn't need words, Robert. Her ship docks this evening. Will you be there to meet her?"

Curran shook his head.

"Why not?"

He shrugged. "I don't know what to say to her."

Lavinia leaned over and tapped him on the knee. "Yes, you do. Be at the dock tonight, Robert."

Samrita abandoned the game with Pansy and subsided into a chair, fanning herself with her hand. Pansy collapsed at her feet.

Lavinia poured Samrita a cup of tea.

"Samrita has a great interest in orchids," Lavinia said.

"Samrita is being polite," Curran responded.

"I am not. I think orchids ... all plants ... are fascinating. Lavinia has loaned me books on botany. Perhaps I can learn to be a botanist?" Samrita cast her brother a querying glance.

Lavinia smiled at the girl. "She has a genuine talent for botanical drawing. Fetch the drawings you did this morning, Rita."

A flush rose to Samrita's face but faced with Lavinia Pemberthey-Smythe's order, she had no choice but to leave them and return with a drawing pad. She handed it to Curran.

"They are not very good," she said.

Curran was no judge of botanical art, but the simple lines and delicate colours of the orchids Samrita had drawn could only be described as beautiful. He said as much and her color deepened.

"Do you really think so?"

He set the portfolio down on the table beside her. "I do."

"I intend to introduce her to Mad Ridley," Lavinia said, referring to the director of the botanical gardens. "He is always looking for good botanical artists. With some proper tuition, she could have quite a career."

Samrita bit her lip and glanced at Curran. "I would like that," she said. "Is it possible, Robert?"

"Of course it is. I will gladly pay for lessons ... whatever you need."

"And before you raise the question of lodging, I would like Samrita to stay as long as she wants. I am old and I need a companion to fetch my knitting and read bible verses to me," Lavinia said.

"You don't knit," Curran retorted. "And as for bible verses—"

Samrita laughed, and Curran and Lavinia exchanged a quick glance. For those first long weeks after he had brought Samrita to Lavinia, she had withdrawn into herself and he and Lavinia had despaired of her but in the last few weeks, he had begun to see the happy, loving girl Jayant had described, beginning to re-emerge.

Lavinia glanced at her watch. "You have time, Robert. Go. Now."

SIXTY-SEVEN

It's been a year since I first arrived in Singapore. So much has happened in that year.

Harriet leaned on the rail of the *Nore* watching the activity on the quayside as the ship docked. She breathed in the familiar scents of sea, tar and oil mingled with the underlying fragrances, good and bad, that were essentially Singapore and knew this was where she belonged.

They had spent Christmas in Ceylon. It had not been the Christmas Harriet had planned for Will, but the *Kurengala* Rest House had put on a fine Christmas lunch, and Julian and Harriet had packed presents for their ward. Despite the absence of other children, Will was used to solitary pursuits and had found plenty to amuse himself while enjoying the new books and Harriet and Julian's undivided attention for the playing of card games.

Harriet's leg had mended and after the headlong events of the previous year, all three of them had healed in the cool air and heady scents of Ceylon.

Now they were returning to their everyday lives—Julian to his responsibilities at St Tom's and Will to finish his preparatory schooling and Harriet to ... who knew what? Typing school reports and demands for school fees?

The crowd gathering to meet the *Nore* parted, and for a moment Harriet hardly dared to breathe.

A tall man in a khaki uniform and gleaming Sam Browne stood on the dock, his hands in his pockets. He looked up and their eyes met. She held her breath for a few heartbeats, hardly daring to hope.

He didn't move, made no gesture that he had seen her, but even from the distance, she could see the slow smile that spread across his face.

"Ready to go, Harri?" Julian said from behind her. "They are running out the gangway—"

But Harriet hardly heard him. She pushed through the crowd gathering to disembark, chafing at the slowness in which crew and passengers moved.

The moment her feet touched the dock, she threw propriety to the wind. One hand on her hat and the other lifting her skirt, she ran, weaving through porters and dock workers, hackney drivers, and respectable families, toward the man in the khaki uniform.

The man she had thought about every day since she had left Kuala Lumpur.

Curran swept her into his arms, lifting her off her feet as her arms went around his neck and she buried her face in his shoulder, breathing in the scent of cedar soap and starch and ... Curran. Her hat fell to the ground as she turned up her face, losing herself in his cool, grey eyes and the curl of his lips as one hand curved around the back of her neck, the calloused thumb of the other hand, caressing the line of her jaw.

He lowered his head until their foreheads touched, and he whispered: "Harriet Gordon. I've missed you."

With the first touch of his lips on hers, she let the moment take her. Shards of liquid gold ran through her body as, heedless of the curious stares from the onlookers, their bodies melded together as if they could never be parted again.

"Curran," she whispered some moments later. "Am I a fool?"

"For what?"

"Letting myself fall in love with you?"

She tensed, half expecting him to laugh ... or push her away ... or something.

Instead, he shook his head. "I think," he said with a crack in his voice, "I think that makes us both fools."

She laughed. "Say it, Curran."

His arm tightened around her and they were both laughing, like two small children caught in a secret joke.

"I love you, you infuriating, maddening, wonderful woman. Would you...?"

"Curran, put my sister down!" Julian's voice cut across them.

Suddenly conscious that they were standing on a crowded dock, Curran released his hold on Harriet and she took a step back, covering her discomposure by stooping to retrieve her hat. As she straightened, her eyes met Curran's, and a smile curved his lips.

Julian stood with his hands on his hips, grinning at them. "This will be the talk of town tomorrow," he said, without rancor.

"Inspector Curran, Inspector Curran—" Will had come running up to them. He looked up at Curran with bright eyes. "I have taken very good care of your cricket bat. When do you want it back?"

Curran laid a hand on the boy's shoulder. "Thank you, Will." His gaze met Harriet's again, his fingers brushing hers as he said. "It's important to take good care of the things you love."

AUTHOR NOTES

Thank you for reading TERROR IN TOPAZ.

Moving the action in this story to Kuala Lumpur was a challenge, particularly as I could not visit, as I had intended, owing to the travel restrictions over the last few years. I had to rely on my own memory of previous visits as well as the usual fabulous resources available on the internet and through primary sources of the day.

The genesis of this story is an actual murder that took place in Kuala Lumpur in April 1911 when Edith Proudlock, the young wife of the acting headmaster of the Victoria Institute, shot dead her lover William Steward on the steps of the headmaster's house.

Does this story sound familiar? It should. A young writer, Somerset Maugham, on his visit to Malaya in the 1920s found himself in a bar in conversation with a lawyer, E A Wagner, who had represented Edith Proudlock at her trial. Wagner shared his recollections of that time and as all good writers do, Somerset Maugham saw the germ of a story that became THE LETTER ... which became a movie, an opera and more.

The Proudlock murder fitted so well into Harriet's world that I originally intended for the Proudlock case to become the focus of the book, but realized I needed to tie Harriet and Curran's story arcs together so I fictionalized it. William Proudlock became Henry Robertson etc. That said, my fictional account of the "Robertson" murder is taken directly from the newspaper reports of the Proudlock proceedings (as well as secondary accounts). Of course there was no Harriet Gordon or Julian Edwards present as witnesses.

Edith Proudlock was convicted of the murder and sentenced to hang, but the intervention of the Sultan of Selangor saved her from death. She and her husband and child returned to England. The marriage did not survive and she later remarried, dying in the United States, while her former husband went on to teach in schools in South America.

I (or should I say, Harriet) have tried to convey my own theory regarding Edith Proudlock and her motive for killing Stewart (or William Steward as he was in real life). If you are interested or intrigued by this case, I highly recommend you find a copy of DEATH ON THE VERANDAH by Eric Lawlor, in which he examines the Proudlock case in the context of British Malaya at the time. It is a fascinating read.

Of course, apart from the characters of the Resident-General, the Resident and the Police Commissioner of the Federated Malay Police and the Vicar of St. Mary's, the rest of the story is entirely fictional. There was no Topaz Club or large-scale corruption of the colonial administration that I am aware of.

At this time prostitution was not illegal, nor was it illegal to run a brothel. However, in 1904 and 1910 the first international treaties aimed at preventing the trafficking of human beings, particularly women, to work in brothels was signed. So, it was recognized as a problem that had to be addressed. Sadly, it is still all too prevalent today.

If you are ever in Kuala Lumpur, the Batu Caves are a 'must see'. These days they have become a Hindu shrine devoted to *Lord Murugan*. It is some years since I visited them, but I remember being overwhelmed by the sheer number of devotees and I believe they have only grown in size and popularity.

According to my guidebook of the time, however, in 1910 they were not in use as shrines—or at least not as we would recognize it today. Other reports say that there may have been shrines withing the caves but they don't appear in in any of the contemporary images, including the sort of postcard sent by Lakshmi, I have posted to my Pinterest board.

Just a quick note on currency. The Straits dollar was the currency used across the Malay Peninsula (Until it was replaced in 1939 by the Malay dollar). Some of my characters do occasionally speak about British pounds but their day-to-day dealings would have been the dollars and cents.

As with all these books, I am writing as a modern woman with one eye on the past and I am conscious that I am portraying a time and characters with views and attitudes repugnant to our modern sensibilities. The past is indeed a foreign country; they did things differently there.

ACKNOWLEDGMENTS

First and foremost I have to acknowledge with thanks my amazing writing group, The Saturday Ladies Bridge Club, for being there with virtual cups of tea and sympathy, necessary brainstorming and tissues as required.

And my darling husband who is happy to brainstorm, take me traveling for research and has been known to provide actual cups of tea and glasses of wine as required.

Then there is the team required to get a book to publication. I had to 'go it alone' with this book and I could not have done it without my fabulous cover designer, Fiona Jayde of Fiona Jayde Media Services, my structural editor, Shannon Valaquez of SJV Editorial and my copy editor, Cathleen Ross.

Alison Stuart

ABOUT THE AUTHOR

Australian author, A.M Stuart, creator of the popular Harriet Gordon Mystery series, lives in Melbourne, Australia but over her life she has travelled extensively and lived in Africa and Singapore, experiences which she brings to her writing. Before becoming a full-time writer, she worked as a lawyer across a variety of disciplines including the military and emergency services.

As well as the Harriet Gordon series, writing as Alison Stuart, she is multi published in historical romance and short stories with settings in England and Australia and spanning different periods of history.

If you enjoyed this story, please leave a review or a rating on your favourite review site or bookstore.

AND YOU ARE INVITED TO SIGN UP TO ALISON'S NEWSLETTER for news, updates, exclusive content and contests.
www.amstuartbooks.com

BOOKS

BY A.M. STUART/ ALISON STUART

(Writing as A.M. Stuart)

The Harriet Gordon Mysteries

SINGAPORE SAPPHIRE (Book 1)

REVENGE IN RUBIES (Book 2)

EVIL IN EMERALD (Book 3)

TERROR IN TOPAZ (Book 4)

(Writing as Alison Stuart)

Australian Historical Romance

THE POSTMISTRESS (also in audio)

THE GOLDMINER'S SISTER (also in audio)

THE HOMECOMING (also in audio)

The Guardians of the Crown Series

BY THE SWORD

THE KING'S MAN

EXILE'S RETURN

GUARDIANS OF THE CROWN (BOX SET)

The Feathers in the Wind Collection

AND THEN MINE ENEMY

HER REBEL HEART

SECRETS IN TIME (also in audio)

FEATHERS IN THE WIND (BOX SET)

Regency/World War One

GATHER THE BONES (also in audio)

LORD SOMERTON'S HEIR

A CHRISTMAS LOVE REDEEMED (Novella)

Printed in the USA
CPSIA information can be obtained
at www.ICGtesting.com
CBHW010825090324
5168CB00018B/1483

9 780645 237900